A TREASURE DEEP

ALTON GANSKY

INCALCULABLE WEALTH AWAITS. . .
BUT IS IT WORTH THE COST?

PROMISE PRESS
An Imprint of Barbour Publishing

ISBN 1-58660-673-5

Acquisitions & Editorial Director: Mike Nappa
Editorial Consultant: Liz Duckworth
Art Director: Robyn Martins

Published by Promise Press, an imprint of Barbour Publishing, Inc., P.O. Box 719, Uhrichsville, Ohio 44683, www.promisepress.com

 Member of the
Evangelical Christian
Publishers Association

Printed in the United States of America
5 4 3 2 1

PROLOGUE

His legs were on fire, the muscles mere kindling in a blast furnace of exertion.

He stumbled ahead, forcing one foot to follow the other. Each step splashed through inky puddles on the asphalt. The cold rain that fell, feeding the coursing gutter rivers and the asphalt ponds, did nothing to cool the electric heat charging through his body. His chest tightened again, squeezing as if he were in the hand of a malevolent giant intent on slowly crushing him until his eyes popped and his ribs shattered like late summer twigs.

Another step; another stride; he couldn't—must not—stop. Pain was irrelevant; escape mandatory. Weary legs protested and sent the fire in them burning to his lungs. He was no longer inhaling; he was gulping for air like a fish tossed on a cold, dark shore.

Water from the storm poured through his hair and into his eyes. Would the case be secure enough? Would the rain get in? That would be disastrous; a loss of historical significance. He clutched the leather satchel to his aching chest and swallowed more air.

He moved more slowly now, not by choice, but because his old body could offer no more. Too many decades had passed; too many years had piled upon his stooped shoulders.

Still he ran. He had run from the car when the attacker pushed him from the road. He had run along the vacant downtown Seattle street, and now he ran down a narrow alley. Light from street lamps pushed back the predawn darkness with a jaundiced glow.

Dr. Jamison Henri played no games with himself, held no foolish hope of escape. This alley was the gullet of the monster that would bring his death. He knew that this was the last day of his life, that his existence could now be numbered in moments. The face of his wife flashed into his mind with the intensity of a strobe light. He could see her gray-black hair and crooked smile. "You be careful, old man," she'd said this morning as he walked from the house.

"I want you back." He'd assured her that he would be home in time for dinner.

He'd been wrong.

Now he needed to hide. The wet footfalls of his pursuer echoed down the alley. To his ear they sounded like the beat of a kettledrum. The man was coming. Unlike Dr. Henri, the attacker merely walked. Henri had seen that each time he had cast a fearful glance over his shoulder. Walking was all that was necessary. Henri couldn't run far, and he couldn't run fast.

"Hide it," Henri mumbled to himself. "Let God protect it. Please, God, don't let that man have it."

A sharp pain dug deep below his sternum as if someone had driven a spike there with a hard blow from a mallet. A deep groan spewed from Henri's lips, and he doubled over. Only the strength that came from fear kept him standing.

Heart attack. Again. He'd had such an episode two years before and knew the symptoms well: tightness in the chest, difficulty breathing, pain spreading from his chest to his left arm. Open-heart surgery had saved his life then, but there would be no saving him this time.

Another step, then another. His feet felt weighted with lead, and his knees threatened to buckle. Tears came to his eyes, not from the pain in his chest, not from the fear of death, but from the realization that this act of violence would crush his dear wife. "Dear, gentle Claire," he whispered. Thirty-five years she'd been by his side. They'd traveled the uncertain paths of life in unison, reared a special child together, and fallen more in love with each passing day. His death, he knew, would wound her with a grief that would never heal. His attacker was killing two people.

"Where ya goin', Pops?" The attacker's first words. His voice was cold and hard as ice. "Ain't no place to run, old man."

"Leave me alone!" Henri called back. *What a stupid thing to say,* he thought. No words would appease the animal behind him—there was more demon in him than human. Henri stumbled to the side, his shoulder slamming into something hard. The large object gave off a hollow sound. He clawed the metal dumpster, using it to steady himself before trying to run again.

"I'm younger than you by thirty years, old man. You really think you can outrun me?"

Henri clutched the satchel even tighter to his heaving chest, as much to protect it as to ease the pain of his heart. His body was betraying him when he needed it the most. He started forward again.

There was an ear-popping crack, and Henri was spun around. A half second later a new pain flooded his body, and he immediately knew what had happened. The pursuer had shot him. Instinctively, Henri dropped a hand, grabbed the back of his left thigh, and found it sticky wet. He turned around and tried to take another step, but only his right leg was working. Henri thought the bullet had shattered the bone in his left leg.

There would be no more running.

He hopped once in a brave effort to distance himself from the criminal behind him and to protect the precious bundle in his arms. It was one hop too many. Dr. Jamison Henri fell to the wet, trash-littered alley. The asphalt met him with unforgiving resistance, his head bouncing off the hard surface and his shoulder driven from its joint. The new pain didn't matter; his brain could embrace no more anguish. "I've failed," he said. "I've failed the world. I've failed God."

He began to weep.

"Crying don't move me none, Pops."

Henri rolled onto his back and looked up into the dimly lit face of his attacker. He was smiling in the yellow light. It was a smirk of pleasure.

"I've failed," Henri mumbled between sobs. "God forgive me, I've failed so badly."

"That you did, old man. That you did." It was too dark to make out details, but the attacker's voice and manner made Henri think that he was facing a young man. What had he shouted? Something about being "thirty years younger."

Through tear-washed eyes, Henri watched the attacker raise his hand. Despite the dim light, Henri could make out the outline of a gun. "The bag goes with me, Pops."

"No," Henri protested. His heart seized for a moment, then returned to its irregular, ineffectual beating.

"No?" The attacker laughed. "I don't think you can do anything about it."

Henri's eyes focused on the muted outline of the man's finger. He could see it begin to tighten.

"Whatcha think? Head shot? Or maybe the throat? Hmm. Decisions, decisions. I know, how about—"

The attacker was gone.

Henri blinked, and in that time, he heard a hollow crash. Something had hit the dumpster. There was a cry of pain. There was another crash; then Henri caught a glimpse of a body staggering backward across the alley. There was another sound, one of metal skipping along the asphalt. The assailant had lost his gun.

"Stay out of this," the attacker shouted. "This ain't no concern of—"

There was another sound, much softer. The attacker backpedaled into the alley wall, closely followed by another form. A man. Henri rolled on his side to better see what was happening. The man was taller than the attacker, and he was giving no quarter. Before the gunman could regain his footing, the stranger threw a punch that landed squarely on the jaw. Dr. Henri's attacker went weak in the knees and stumbled forward, only to be driven back with an uppercut that nearly lifted him from his feet.

The gunman dropped face first to the wet pavement. The stranger stood over the still form for a moment, then approached.

"No," Henri said. "You can't have it. It's too important."

"Settle down," a smooth, strong voice said.

Henri watched as the stranger reached to his side. *A gun!* Henri thought. A second later he saw, not a gun, but another small device appear in the man's hand. He raised it to his head and spoke: "Nine-one-one."

Perry Sachs held the phone to his ear with his left hand while the voice-activated dialing feature of the cell phone placed the emergency call. He exercised his right hand, extending his fingers and clinching them into a fist, gritting his teeth as he did so. No broken fingers, but he was sure he'd damaged something. He didn't know the unconscious man lying on the damp pavement, but he did know that he had a very hard head.

Perry Sachs had rounded the corner in his BMW after a late night session reviewing drawings for an industrial project in Canada. Tomorrow he'd scheduled a meeting with project engineers, so he had stayed late at the office to prepare. The last thing he expected to see at two in the morning was an elderly man running from the scene of a fender bender. At least, Perry had assumed it was a fender bender. The man who walked quickly after the elderly gent caught Perry's attention. There was something about his manner—something that couldn't be explained but that made the hair on Perry's neck stand on end. Pulling to the side of the deserted downtown street, Perry exited the car and followed at a discreet distance. He watched as the old man turned down an alley. *Not wise,* Perry thought. He picked up his pace.

"Ain't no place to run, old man." Perry heard the words. They were hot with threat. A second later, he heard the crack of a gun. His first urge was to turn the other way and run for the safety of his car, but Perry was not one to surrender to urges. He peeked around the corner of the alley and saw the second man standing over the first. He watched as the standing man raised his arm. Perry knew what was coming.

Words were exchanged between the downed victim and the gunman. Perry chose to ignore the conversation, grateful that they gave him the two things he needed most: time and surprise.

"Whatcha think?" the gunman asked. "Head shot? Or maybe the throat? Hmm. Decisions, decisions. I know, how about—"

Perry stepped within arm's reach and seized the attacker by

the shoulders from behind, grabbing the material of his coat in tight-wadded fists. With all his strength, he pulled back and spun around, dragging the attacker with him. The man stumbled back, losing his balance, exactly what Perry had hoped for. Perry continued his spin, releasing the attacker at the last possible moment. Momentum sent the man cascading backwards into the side of a large dumpster next to the alley wall. He hit the metal container hard and dropped to a sitting position. The gun he held had come loose from his grasp and bounced down the alley. Perry was on the offensive before the startled thug could shake loose the surprise that stunned him. Clutching the front of the man's shirt, Perry pulled with all his might, yanking the man from the ground. The gunman said something, but Perry wasn't listening. He did, however, hear a thick thud as the man's body slammed into the alley's other wall.

That should have been enough to take the wind out of anyone's sails, but the man straightened himself and shouted, "Stay out of this. This ain't no concern of—"

Perry finished the conversation with a right fist to the attacker's jaw and a sharp uppercut. Pain ripped up Perry's arm as his knuckles made contact. The gunman dropped like a board. Moments ticked by, and Perry waited for the man's next move. There was no next move, just the paralysis of unconsciousness.

Turning his attention to the victim on the ground, he approached slowly.

"No," Henri said. "You can't have it. It's too important."

"Settle down," Perry said softly. Pulling his cell phone from its belt clip, he had called 911. His words were firm, calm, and to the point. He gave his name, location, then added, "There's been an assault. Shots fired. We need an ambulance and police." The operator asked a few questions, which he answered quickly before hanging up.

Now he looked down at the man before him. Even in the little light that was available, he could see that the gentleman was in bad shape. His face was screwed into a scowl of pain and fear. "Did he hurt you?"

"My chest. My heart. My leg."

The man wore a suit and tie. Perry quickly loosened the tie and unbuttoned the collar. "Help's on the way."

"They can't have it," the old man said. "It's too important. Secret. . .until the right. . .time." He was struggling to breathe.

"The police will be here in a minute, sir. I'm sure they can sort things out."

"No. . .you don't understand. They won't know. . .wrong hands. . .disaster." He convulsed, and Perry reached down to support his head. He saw the man clutching what looked like an old leather attaché case.

"Why don't you set that down?" Perry suggested. "You'll be more comfortable."

"No. Can't."

"I can put it under your head. You can use it as pillow, and you'll know right where it is."

The man began to sob. "I've failed. I've failed the world. I've failed God."

"Take it easy, friend," Perry said. The man was working himself into a frenzy—the last thing he needed if he was having a heart attack.

The seizure eased. "I'm too weak. The strain. . .too much."

"Just take a few deep breaths," Perry said softly, wishing that he had hit the attacker harder than he had. To do this to an elderly man was beyond reason, even for a street thug. *Distract him,* Perry thought. *Get him to think about something else.*

"My name is Perry. What's yours?"

"Henri. Dr. Jamison. . .Henri."

"You're a medical doctor?"

Henri shook his head. "Teacher. North Pacific Seminary. New Testament. . . " He seized again. A moment later he took a deep breath and said, "Take it. I have to trust you." He released his arms

11

from around the leather case. "Let no one have it. Trust no one. Learn from it. Promise me. Learn from it. Protect it."

"Everything's going to be fine—"

"More important than. . .everything. Belongs to world. . .but wait for the right time. More to be done. Joseph. . ." He convulsed again then went limp in Perry's arms. A wet gurgle rose from his throat.

"Stay with me, partner," Perry said. "Dr. Henri?" Nothing. Perry lowered the professor's head to the cold ground and placed two fingers on the man's throat. There was no pulse. Quickly, Perry set aside the leather case, tilted the professor's head back, placed his mouth over the old man's gape, and blew into his lungs. No response. With the urgency fueled by desperation, Perry tore the man's shirt open, ran a finger down his sternum, noted the aged scar from a previous surgery, found the end of the sternum, placed his hand a few inches farther up, and began compressions.

"One, two, three, four," he counted to himself. "Come on, buddy, stay with me. You made it his far—don't quit now. One, two, three, four." A cracking sound, like the breaking of pencils, erupted into the darkness as the man's ribs gave way. In the distance, the sharp call of sirens saturated the wet Seattle night.

"One, two, three. . ."

CHAPTER 1

The ground twelve hundred feet below Perry Sachs's feet scrolled by in a 110-mile-an-hour blur. He knew it was he who was moving and not the ground, but the plush interior of the Augusta A109 Power helicopter and the finely honed skill of the pilot made it feel otherwise.

The craft, aided by a spring sun directly overhead, cast a shadow that ran along the supple, green hills like a child on a bicycle trying to outrace his father's car. Unlike many mountainous places he had visited, Perry saw that these hills lacked sharp angles, deep gouges, and jutting rock faces. Here the hills looked like ocean swells frozen in place. Where mound met knoll there was a smooth, sinuous valley. An abnormally wet Southern California winter had left the towering hills decked in a deep carpet of green punctuated by the thick trunks and outstretched limbs of ancient oak trees. The dark leaves of the trees contrasted with the lighter bottle-green of the wild grass. To him, the trees looked like monks stretching prayerful hands to the sky.

Perry was tired, his neck hurt like a bad tooth, and his eyes burned. He'd slept only a handful of hours over the last few days. Two nights ago he had "hopped the pond" from Edinburgh, Scotland, to New York after a weeklong consultation with the European branch of Sachs Engineering. Travel was one of the perks of being vice president of the firm and the founder's son, but it was also one of the curses. Losing sleep had never been a problem for him, but now at the age of thirty-eight, it was more difficult to do and much less fun.

The hopping continued from the Big Apple to Atlanta then on to San Diego where he arrived at one that afternoon. He then made his way through the Lindbergh Field terminals until he found the company's bright yellow helicopter warming up on one of the heli-pads. SACHS ENGINEERING was painted along the craft's body in maroon letters. Still dressed in the dark blue suit he'd worn at his last meeting in Scotland, he boarded the aircraft and found he was not alone. Five minutes later, everyone aboard the A109 was airborne and headed north.

"Thinking of jumping?"

Perry turned to look at the only other person in the six-passenger cabin. John Dyson—Jack to everyone who knew him—was staring back, his ebony face creased with a subtle smile. Jack was big, the size of an NFL linebacker, yet there was more to him than met the eye. Many, to their embarrassment, had made the mistake of assuming that a large man couldn't be quick in mind and wit. Perry knew differently. Both he and Jack had attended MIT, Perry taking a degree in architecture and Jack graduating at the top of his class in civil engineering. It was there they'd met and there where their friendship had been cemented. Jack joined Perry at his father's firm immediately after graduation. In five years his skill and creative approaches earned him the title of project manager.

Over the years, Henry Sachs, the firm's founder, had offered Jack many promotions, but all were declined. His degrees might be prestigious, but his love was rooted in hard work. He was his happiest when surrounded by big, noisy equipment, and it was there he planned on staying.

"I wouldn't mind taking a little nap under one of those trees down there. I don't suppose you thought to bring a hammock?"

"How can you think of sleep?" Jack said. "This is what you've been looking for since college. Don't you remember all those late night lectures you gave me? 'Building is great,' you said, 'but finding the hidden, that's where the real excitement is.'"

"I remember. I also remember you falling asleep in the middle of my stories. It's a good thing I've got thick skin."

"How did things go in Scotland?" Jack asked, shifting his bulk in a seat made for men two-thirds his size.

"They went. The British government is excited. The project's a go. I'm looking forward to it."

"More underground work?" Jack asked.

"Yup. Military communications complex. Guess who is going to oversee the project?"

"Let's see," Jack said as if contemplating a math problem. He raised a finger to his chin. "Military in nature, secret, underground, engineering intensive, why, it can only be a resident genius and your trusted buddy. . .me."

"Good thing there are only two of us back here. Otherwise your ego wouldn't have enough room to fit in this cabin."

"You wound me. I'm not an egotist. Simply confident."

"A rose by any other name. . ." Perry began.

"Ooh, Shakespeare. Not bad for a sleep-deprived mind."

"Wait until you see how sharp I am after a meal and a nap."

"Maybe I should sell tickets," Jack offered with a laugh.

"We may have to," Perry said. "This is costing the company a pretty penny, and while my father loves his darling boy, he does want to see some return. I assume the equipment is on the way?"

"Of course," Jack replied. He looked out his window. "In fact, there they are now." He motioned with his thumb.

Perry released his lap belt and slid across the seat to Jack's side of the passenger compartment. Jack's long legs filled the space between the opposing benches so Perry had to lean over the last seat to see. Below was the black asphalt river of State Highway 58. On the road was a caravan of two semitrailers, three flatbed rigs loaded with yellow heavy equipment tractors, a drilling rig, and a bus.

"I assume the rest of the equipment is coming later?" Perry asked.

"You'd assume wrong," Jack answered. "Most of it's already there. The porta-potties got there early this morning. I have the heavier equipment staged in Bakersfield and can have it on-site in less than two hours if we need it."

"Gleason is on-site?"

Jack laughed loudly. "Try to get him to leave. He has his toys, a challenge, and an open-ended budget. He's not going home anytime soon."

"Good, we'll need him." Perry slid back to his spot and refastened his lap belt. Gleason Lane was Sachs Engineering's "head techie." An MIT graduate in computer science, he turned his back on the keyboard-in-cubical environment for outdoor tech.

"He's been busy for the last two weeks. Just about worn out the ground penetrating radar and fried every earthworm and squirrel in the area."

"The results remain consistent?"

"Absolutely. Gleason found something. That much is for sure."

Perry settled back in his seat, his fatigue evaporating under the heat of excitement. He'd built buildings in Africa and South America; he'd constructed secret military sites and large industrial complexes in Europe as well as the U.S.A., and he enjoyed every challenge. By comparison, this was a small project. But this went beyond all he'd ever done before.

He ran a hand through anthracite-colored hair. Gray had yet to touch his black mane, but he knew it was just around the corner. A few more trips like the one he'd just taken would see to that.

Doubts surfaced like a whale breaching and spouting. The odds that he was right were astronomical, the evidence he followed was thin, and the experts who agreed with him were zero. Still, he thought he was right, and more importantly, he *felt* he was right. And if he was, the world would never be the same.

"We should beat the caravan by twenty minutes," Jack said. "Those rigs don't move up long winding grades very fast."

Perry nodded, then slipped on a headset that would allow him to talk to the two pilots forward of the soundproof cabin. He asked how long before they would reach the site and was told five minutes.

"Take us around the area a couple of times," Perry said into the microphone. "I want to get the lay of the land."

The pilot confirmed the request and started a gentle turn to the right. Perry removed the headset and placed it back on the rack. Below him, he saw the terrain change slightly. Flying from the south, they'd cruised over the cities between San Diego and the Tehachapi Mountains. The larger urban areas of Riverside and San Bernardino had given way to the sparse, flat California high desert. Joshua trees—their conical, viciously pointed leaves spread out like daggers—punctuated the tan, sandy ground. The path the pilots took was nearly twice as long, as if they had flown in a straight line, but Edwards Air Force Base, not many miles east, was particular about what aircraft passed through its air space. The pilots had flown farther north before banking west and were flying over the desert communities of Boron, California City, and Mojave.

Rising out of the stark dirt of the twenty-thousand square miles of Mojave Desert grew the round hills of the Tehachapi Mountains, an oasis of beauty between the desert and the fertile farm land of California's central valley.

The helicopter bounced and slid to one side. Perry and Jack exchanged glances. "Wind," Jack said. "The region is known for its wind."

"Which explains those." Perry pointed out the window near Jack's head. Tall, white towers with gigantic three-bladed propellers stood in long rows like soldiers on a parade ground, the blades turning in lazy circles. "Wind-generated electricity. I read that it's one of the largest wind farms in the world."

"Impressive," Jack replied. "Think we can install a few of those in Seattle?"

"Maybe we can just take a few home with us," Perry joked.

The twisted oak trees that dotted the hillsides thinned, revealing clear, sloping grassland. Angus cows chewed the turf, confined by long stretches of barbed wire fences. "Looks idyllic," Perry mused. "Rolling hills, grassland, trees, small communities. Maybe I'll retire here."

"Retire? You?" Jack laughed. "You'll be buried with a shovel in one hand and a drafting pencil in the other."

"You don't know me as well as you think you do."

"You'd be surprised," Jack retorted.

Perry wouldn't be surprised. There were precious few things that these two men didn't know about one another. Perry knew he was fortunate. Most men made many acquaintances but few friends, at least close friends. Jack was family. In fact, Perry had been best man at Jack's wedding.

"Tehachapi," Jack said, gazing out the window. "Quaint little town of about six thousand."

Perry waited until the helicopter turned enough for him to see. "I see you studied for this project. Of course, we'll be closer to Tejon, just outside their city limits."

"Two miles outside," Jack added. "So we can run in for pizza when the mood strikes."

"A man your age should watch the cholesterol."

"A man my age. How about a man your age?"

"I'm younger than you, remember?" Perry joked.

"By four months, that's it. Besides, it's not the age; it's the mileage. And you've definitely got more of that."

The power-producing windmills disappeared behind them, replaced by more open grazing land. They'd flown over the highest part of the mountain range and were now on the northwest side. The terrain was sloping downward; the highway changed from a sinuous course and became arrow straight. Again, Perry picked up the headset, this time directing the pilot to "Take us in." The helicopter changed course and headed back toward the mountains. A few minutes later the pilot directed the craft in a lazy circle over a grove of oaks. Perry could see several large trucks nearby as well as a few Ford Explorers painted the same yellow as the helicopter.

"We'll have to land uphill where it's clear," Jack said. "The site is near that stand of trees. I hope you're not too tired to take a little walk."

"I'll manage," Perry replied. His weariness was all but forgotten. The excitement of arriving on-site had given him a jolt of adrenaline. "I want to see the images Gleason made from the GPR. I assume he did an EM survey, too?"

"Just as you requested. The electromagnetic conductivity survey was done first, then the GPR. If I know Gleason, he may have tried a few new things too."

"No doubt."

The helicopter descended in a slow, fluid motion, but Perry noticed a slight tilt and sideward shift. Apparently the wind was not intimidated by the multimillion-dollar craft. Despite the stiff breeze, the pilot set her down as light as a feather. Perry exited the moment he felt the skids touch earth. Jack was on his heels. The men pulled their well-worn travel bags from the storage compartment, waved to the pilots, then started down the gentle slope to the grove they had seen from the air.

It was less than a quarter of a mile from the makeshift landing site, but the descent was made slippery by the shin-high grass that blanketed the soil. From the air, it had looked short, like green shag carpet. Perry was surprised to find it so tall. No cows had been grazing here. The wild grass, which had matured with heads that looked like grains of wheat, stuck to Perry's pants. He wished he'd changed before leaving San Diego. Traveling in a suit was uncomfortable to begin with, but hiking through uneven ground with a tote bag of clothing and personal supplies thrown over his shoulder made it worse.

Five minutes later they exchanged the blue sky for a green canopy of leaves. Wind rustled through the branches, carrying the

perfume of sweet grass and fecund hillsides. The verdant pano-
rama, framed by the trees and augmented by the quiet countryside,
made Perry feel as if he had walked into Eden itself.

"Well, look who's here," came a tenor's voice. "It's *the man*
himself."

"Dr. Gleason Lane, I presume," Perry said.

"In the flesh," Gleason answered. Gleason was taller than Perry's
six-foot height by at least two inches. He had kind blue eyes, a strong
chin, and was known for his good humor. A devoted family man, he
was fond of showing off pictures of his wife and two kids—photos
he kept electronically filed in his hand-held computer. Gleason's
wheat-colored hair was cropped close to the skull, but not so close
as to be confused with a Marine in boot camp. He turned and
shouted to a young man hovering over some equipment. "Hey,
newbie, come here for a minute."

The young man looked up. He was thin and sported brown hair
that hung to his shoulders. He pushed the hair from his eyes. "Yeah,
okay." He sauntered over, and Gleason made introductions. "This is
Brent Hapgood. He's a senior at Caltech and helping us as part of
his senior project."

"Pleased to meet you," Perry said, extending his hand.

"Hey," Brent replied with a nonchalant head nod.

Gleason chuckled. "He's not much on conversation, but he's
good with electronic equipment. A friend of mine who teaches at
Caltech recommended him. He checks out and understands the. . .
nature of what we're doing."

Perry nodded and studied the young man for a moment. He
struck Perry as a cross between surfer and geek. He seemed fit
beneath his T-shirt and jeans, and his handshake had been firm.
Still, Perry would have preferred that only men he knew be on the
team, but that was impossible. Laborers had to be hired from
Tejon and even Bakersfield. Not ideal, but necessary.

"What's your major?" Jack asked.

Perry watched as Brent turned his attention to Jack. His eyes

20

widened for a moment. Perry had seen this reaction many times. Jack's size could intimidate anyone.

"Um. . .electrical engineering."

"Pity, you could have gone into civil engineering. . .a real science," Jack said.

"I tried," Brent retorted, "but my grades were too high."

"Oh, a comedian," Jack shot back sternly. The boy's eyes widened even more. "You'll fit in nicely." Jack stepped forward and gave him a slap on the right shoulder. It wasn't brutal, just a gesture between men—albeit one that made Brent take an unplanned side step.

"If you don't mind me saying so, Perry," Gleason said. "You look liked warmed-over death."

"Who signs your paycheck?" Perry asked.

Gleason said, "Like I said. You look great. Better than ever. Even though you obviously don't need it, do you want to ride into town with Brent and freshen up? We've taken over the Oak Glen Lodge. It has a pretty good restaurant."

"Let's hold off on that for awhile. I want to see what you've found, and then I want to take a quick tour of the camp. Maybe after the caravan arrives."

"You sure? You look—"

"I'm sure. I can sleep later. Show me your findings."

Gleason shrugged and led Perry and Jack to a tiny trailer that had been towed to the site. Perry noticed that it was already leveled and blocked in place. "It's cramped," Gleason said, "but it works. I decided against the larger trailer since we're only going to be here a few days."

"You hope," Jack interjected.

"Not hope," Gleason retorted. "Experience and planning. I think we can do what needs to be done in a week to ten days. Two weeks tops, at least for the initial work. If you're right, detail men will be here for months." He opened the door, stepping up on a large block of wood that served as the only step. Jack followed, and

Perry started in when he noticed Brent on his heels.

"Brent," Perry said. "I have to make this a closed-door meeting. I hope you understand."

The student seemed shocked but quickly regained his composure. "Um, sure, I understand. Let me know if you need anything."

Perry said he would and pulled the thin door closed behind him.

"Let me guess. You want a take-home box."

Anne Fitzgerald looked up from her plate and met eyes with the waitress standing next to her table. "Just because I ask for a doggy bag every time I eat here doesn't mean I want one now," she chided with a smile. The waitress was named Sara, and she had worked at the Tejon Table and Grille since her high school days two decades before. Anne knew her well and liked her. The friendly give-and-take had been their pattern of relating through the years.

"So you don't want one."

"Of course I do. Don't be silly. I'm not going to throw half a tuna melt away. I'll eat it for lunch tomorrow." It was a habit. At the age of thirty-six, Anne had gained barely five pounds over her weight in college, but it was only because of her disciplined eating. For her, weight was a struggle against more than carelessness; it was against genetics and middle age. So far she had won, but victories came one meal at a time. Years ago, a doctor had told her to eat whatever she wanted—within reason—but to eat only half of it. So when she ate out, which was most days, she would dutifully cut the food in half, eating one portion and taking the other portion home for the next day's lunch.

The waitress disappeared and returned a moment later with a Styrofoam container. "There you go, Mayor. By now you should have enough of those to fill a room."

"Or a landfill, Sara." Anne picked up her plate and slid the remaining fries and open-faced sandwich into the container. "How's the family?"

"Pretty good. Living with a middle-aged truck driver and two teenage boys is making me old."

Anne started to remind her that Sara's husband was living with a middle-aged woman, but thought better of it. "Well, living alone isn't all it's cracked up to be. I can tell you that." Anne had lived alone for five years. *Five years since John's. . .* She refused to finish the thought.

"Maybe not, but there are times when I envy you. More iced tea?"

"No. I need to get back to the office." The thought of her dead husband blew a dark cloud over Anne's mind. She needed to move on to other things and to do so quickly.

"Which office today?" Sara asked as she picked up the empty plate and used silverware.

"Business, but I'll be in the city building most of tomorrow. The mail is starting to pile up."

"How you keep both jobs going, I'll never know. Waiting tables taxes what little brain I have."

"Don't sell yourself short, Sara. There's nothing wrong with being a waitress. And you're a good one, even if you do give me a bad time every time I come through the door."

"That's part of the charm of this place; mediocre food but stellar service."

"Stellar, eh? Is that the word? Stellar?"

"What word would you use?" Sara asked.

"I'd tell you, but you might poison my food."

"What makes you think I haven't already done that? I've been thinking about running for mayor myself."

"Good luck," Anne said. "There are days when I'd give it to you. That way you could hold down two jobs."

"Well, selling real estate has to be easier on the feet than running between tables."

"I'm sure it is, but it has its. . .challenges too."

A low rumble vibrated the floor, window, and booth in which Anne was sitting. She turned and looked out the widow. Just beyond the restaurant's parking lot ran Tejon's main road: Oak Glen Avenue. It was a four-lane strip of macadam the State of California had given the ignoble designation "Business 52." A large and loud eighteen-wheeler rumbled past, immediately followed by another. Behind it came a flatbed toting a backhoe. A second later another flatbed rumbled past carrying a piece of equipment Anne didn't recognize.

"Wow," Sara said. "It looks like someone is getting ready to do some building."

"Sachs Engineering," Anne muttered.

"What?"

"Sachs Engineering," Anne repeated. "The trucks had Sachs Engineering painted on the doors."

"Who are they?"

"I have no idea. I'm not aware of any large construction going on in the area. No permits were filed."

"They're building without permission?" Sara asked. "Don't they need permits to do that kind of work?"

"They do if they're building in the city," Anne replied. "Outside city limits they'd have to go through the county—"

"Look, there's more." Sara pointed out the window. Another flatbed went by with a large yellow tractor in tow. Immediately after came a bus. "I wonder who's on the bus."

"Don't know. The windows were tinted. I couldn't see in."

Sara picked up Anne's empty tea glass. "I guess we'll know sooner or later. I just hope the bus isn't filled with hungry people. The boss would like it, but then he doesn't have to juggle all those plates of food."

Anne reached into her handbag, removed her wallet, and placed several dollar bills on the table. "The rest is for you," she said as she slipped from the booth.

"Back to the office?" Sara said.

"Yes, but I'm going to take a little detour first."

CHAPTER 2

The private meeting in the trailer was brief but long enough for Gleason and Jack to bring Perry up to speed on the more sensitive and secret details of the work. Once that was done, they traded the cramped confines for outdoor elbowroom.

Standing at a folding table situated under a green plastic sunscreen, Perry felt out of place, like a prune in a basket of oranges. Gleason had dubbed the outdoor area next to the trailer "the office." Around him were Jack, Gleason, and the intern Brent, all dressed for the work and terrain. Perry, however, was beginning to sweat in his suit. The sunscreen was held in place by nylon cords strung between oak trees. The trees provided the necessary shade but had an annoying tendency to drop leaves on papers and equipment. The birds that flittered through the thick limbs were another and more distasteful concern.

On the table under the sunshade were a laptop computer, color ink-jet printer, and several pages.

"This is the magnetic survey," Gleason remarked. "We're repeating everything just to be sure. That's what they're doing over there." He nodded in the direction of a young woman in a white T-shirt and shorts with a metal pole in her hand. Near the base of the pole was a black cylinder. Perry watched as she took a step, placed the end of the pole to the ground, waited, raised it, took another step, and repeated the process. A cable ran from the pole in her hand to a computer that rested before a young man. After each stop, he would say, "Good. Next." The woman took another step.

"That generated this?" Perry asked. He held a piece of paper that was marked with curving black lines. It reminded him of a contour map. While he was familiar with the process, he liked to review all the details.

"Yes," Gleason said. "First we did a general survey by eye, but, as expected, found nothing. No news there. We then did the electromagnetic scan and covered about five acres' worth of ground. We found anomalies right off the bat. We then narrowed the area of search, taking readings every meter to get a more detailed picture. That's what you're holding. As you can see, to the left of center, the lines of magnetic force have changed."

"Indicating what?" Perry asked.

"A shaft or maybe a chamber," Brent piped in.

"Brent helped with the initial survey and analysis," Gleason said, then added, "That survey alone would be enough to convince me that something is down there."

"Could it be something natural?" Jack asked, always the pragmatist.

Gleason answered quickly. "Could it be natural? Yes. Is it likely that it's natural? No. But to be sure, we're repeating the survey. This time, we're taking readings every half meter."

"Of course," Brent added, "there's this." He handed Perry a color image. "That's the GPR image of yesterday's survey. GPR stands for—"

"Ground penetrating radar," Perry interjected. "I'm familiar with it."

Brent cleared his throat. "Of course. I was only. . .I mean. . ."

"It corroborates the EM survey," Perry remarked, letting Brent off the hook. "Odd."

"I wondered if you'd notice that," Gleason said with a knowing smile.

"Notice what?" Jack asked. He moved closer to Perry and peered over his shoulder.

"This." Perry pointed to a gray-white blob at the bottom of the printout. The rest of the image was a mottled blend of reds, purples, and blacks. "Looks like a chamber or something buried. I expected that. It's this that strikes me as odd." He ran his finger along a fuzzy streak on the page.

Jack huffed. "You mean the blue-gray smudge that goes from the blob to the surface?"

"That's what I like about you engineer types," Gleason said, "all that fancy technical language."

Perry ignored the remark. "I was expecting a vertical shaft, but this looks to be angled at, what, thirty degrees?"

"Twenty-five degrees on average," Gleason said. "I say 'on average' because it's not consistent, which could mean many things."

"Such as?" Jack asked.

"Such as it was dug by amateurs or people with poor equipment, or that the ground has shifted over the years."

"Which is the most likely cause," Brent said. "This is California, home to shifting ground and earthquakes."

"We can run the GPR over the area again," Gleason said.

Perry shook his head. "No need. This is more than enough evidence to take the next step."

"Next step?" Brent asked.

Perry shifted his gaze to the two field workers taking EM readings. "When they're done," he said, "let's set up to take some cores." He turned to Jack. "Where's the equipment? The trucks should be here by now. Let's get them on the cell phone—"

"No need, buddy," Jack said. "I hear them coming."

Perry tilted his head and strained his ears. The sound of diesel motors rolled faintly up the hills, carried by a scented wind.

"It's not going to be easy setting up the drilling rig," Jack said, "not on a slope like that."

"We have permission from the land owner to grade the hill

as necessary," Perry said. "Let's work quickly but not foolishly. Safety first."

"You don't have to tell me twice," Jack said. "I've had enough close calls in my life. I don't need any more."

Perry nodded. He too had faced his share of disasters. It came with the job. Cranes, concrete, and steel were unforgiving if taken for granted. And of course, there were always the people who made life difficult and sometimes deadly. Perry's life had rarely been dull.

"Any special place you want us to drill?" Gleason asked.

Picking up the printouts from the EM and GPR surveys, Perry marched from beneath the canopy of oaks and into the sun-washed clearing. He stepped off the distance until he found himself standing just north of the field's middle. He removed a fountain pen from his pocket, drew an X on one of the printouts, and then returned the pen. Reaching into the pocket of his trousers, he removed a small penknife, opened it, squatted down, and plunged the knife through the paper and into the soft ground.

"X marks the spot. Can't dig for treasure without that." He stood and looked around. "Let's begin five meters up and along the area where the GPR shows where the ditch used to be. Take a coring a meter on each side of that and work your way here. Of course, I just paced this off. You'll be able to determine a more precise location once your crew finishes the last survey."

"We won't be able to finish by nightfall," Gleason said. "You want us to set up the lights for night work?"

Perry nodded. "Yes. The men are here; let's put them to work."

"I may be crossing the line here," Brent said. "But what are we looking for? I mean, if that's not too much to ask."

Perry studied the young man for a moment then said, "Sorry, newbie. You're asking too much—at least for now."

"I was just curious," Brent remarked. "I feel like we're working in the dark."

"Only four people know what we're looking for, and three of them are standing in front of you. I can tell you it's not oil."

"You said 'treasure,' " Brent said. "I've got an image of a pirate's chest filled with booty."

"Trust, kid," Perry said. "Learn to trust. It makes a big difference in life." He turned to Gleason and asked, "Who has the keys to the Ford Explorer over there?"

"I'll get them for you," Gleason answered. "You ready to head to the motel?"

"No. I have another stop to make first; then I'll go into town."

"Where're you going?" Jack asked.

"While you are enjoying a casual day in the sunshine, I'm going to go talk to the man who made all this possible."

Jack chuckled. "Day in the sunshine. Sounds great. Birds singing, diesels belching. . .who could ask for more?"

"I thought you'd enjoy it," Perry said, and he knew Jack would. Three minutes later, Perry pulled away from the work site and headed up a dirt road. He'd already seen and done more than most engineers did in a lifetime. This, however, was beyond even what he could fathom. And that sent the electricity of enthusiasm through him.

Before him lay an open dirt road that wound through the hills; around him was country as beautiful as any he had ever seen; above him was a bright sky of ocean blue. As he glanced up, he saw a small white airplane cruising through the crystalline air and mused, "A perfect day to go flying."

"Can't you smooth this out any?" The man's question carried a harsh tone of voice with it.

The pilot laughed. "I told you it'd be rough. You can't fly through the kind of winds we get here and not expect some bounces. Besides, I don't usually let clients fly with me."

"I paid you enough for it," the man snapped. He was thickly built, broad in the shoulders, and broader around the waist. His size was a cramped fit in the twin engine Cessna 320 aircraft.

29

Shoulder rubbed against shoulder. Behind them, Jim Willis, the pilot's brother and partner, snapped photos with a Leica RC-30 aerial camera.

"That you did, Mr. Dawes," the pilot said. "That you did."

The plane bounced again, and Dawes released a little groan.

"You're not getting sick, are you?" the pilot asked. The thought of his customer losing his lunch in the cockpit made him shudder.

"Of course not," Dawes shot back. He raised a hand to his mustache-crowned mouth and belched loudly. "Just fly the plane, and let's get this over with." Dawes raised a pair of Tasco binoculars to his hooded brown eyes and peered out the window.

"How's it going, Jim?" the pilot asked his brother in the back.

"Just peachy. Hold course, and I'll snap a few more shots, then one more pass ought to do it."

"How long before I have my photos?" Dawes asked, the binoculars still glued to his eyes.

"You got a computer?"

"Yeah, what's that got to do with anything?"

"This is the digital age, my friend. I'll send you home with a CD full of photos. I can print them out if you want, but there's an extra charge for that. And if you want a larger print. . ."

"The CD will be fine."

Ron Willis, founder and pilot for Willis Aerial Photography, looked at his impatient customer and thought he detected a slight green hue about the face. He wondered if the man could control his stomach for one more pass.

The plane bounced again. Dawes swore.

"Sorry, Mr. Dawes, but there's nothing I can do about the CAT."

"Cat? What cat? What are you talking about?" He lowered the binoculars and took a couple of deep breaths.

"Clear air turbulence," Willis explained. "You fly over the mountains; you get bounced. Especially on a warm day like this."

"Whatever." Dawes raised the binoculars to his eyes.

"You know," Willis added, "if you're feeling a little sick, then it would be best if you looked ahead, toward the horizon. Looking down through binoculars will only make you feel worse. Motion sickness is bad. I know—"

"Just fly the plane."

"You're the boss," Willis shrugged.

Dawes had come to the Bakersfield airport just before lunch, insisting on hiring a plane for an aerial survey. Willis had tried to schedule a day for the following week, but Dawes had been too impatient for that. "It has to be today, and it has to be soon. I'm. . . I'm here on business, and I have to leave this afternoon."

"I can send you the photos over the Internet," Willis had offered. Again Dawes had shot the idea down. "I have to give a report to my boss when I get back, so I need the pictures today."

"I'm afraid I'm already booked."

Willis recalled how the man's hooded eyes narrowed and his voice lowered. "I'll pay double. You can keep the extra for yourself or use it to pacify the other customer. Frankly, I don't care. Just get me in the air, and let's take some pictures."

Double was a lot of money, and the other customer was a friend. He would—and did—understand. The company stood to make a little extra and not lose anything in the process. But now Willis was starting to regret the decision. Several times he'd tried to learn more about the man who sat next to him, asking where he lived, if he was looking to buy property in the Tehachapi Mountains, and so on. But the man was slippery. Willis talked it over with his brother and partner Jim, and the best thing to do, they decided, was do the job as quickly as possible, take the money, and hope the guy never came back.

"That's it," Jim said. "Swing us around. I'll shoot one more pass, then we can go home."

"With pleasure," Willis said under his breath. One more glance at his passenger found him gazing down at the ground below. "They sure have a lot of equipment to do it," he muttered.

"What's that?" Willis asked.

"Nothing. Did you get a picture of those trucks down there?"

Jim heard the question. "Yup. We're going to take shots of the area just south of that now."

"Forget it," Dawes said. "I have what I need. Let's head back."

"Are you sure?" Jim said. "One more pass and we'll have a complete set—"

Willis cut his brother off with a raised hand. If Dawes wanted to call it a day, that was more than fine with him.

Anne was torn. Her first impulse was to follow the caravan of trucks she'd seen roar by the Tejon Table, but that seemed a little too impulsive even for her. It was possible that they were just passing through town headed for one of the larger ranches. It wasn't unusual to see trucks and flatbeds carting heavy equipment around. Ranchers needed everything from septic tanks to large structures for their work. The local vineyards that populated the lower hills had their fair share of big equipment needs too. What bothered her was the caravan style and the name Sachs Engineering painted on the sides of the trucks.

Squelching the impulse to pursue, she turned her Toyota Camry onto Central Avenue and aimed for City Hall instead. With less than seven thousand residents within its borders, the City of Tejon was definitely a smaller town. Known as a "general law" city in California, it had the various departments common to cities of all sizes. It also had a city council composed of five elected representatives, one of whom was selected to serve as mayor. This year that privilege fell to Anne, beginning her third term on the council.

City Hall itself was a single-story building composed of slump stone topped with a red Spanish tile roof. Built in 1980, it had weathered well but was starting to show wear. Two council members were proposing renovations—refurbishments the city couldn't really afford.

Anne parked her car and entered the building through the double glass doors of the lobby. Turning right, she followed the corridor to her office at the southwest corner. June, her part-time secretary, was absent. It was Tuesday, and since Anne only came to the office Wednesday through Friday, there was no need for her to be there. The full-time receptionist who sat in the information booth near the lobby took messages for Anne.

The office was a twelve-by-fifteen affair and simple in décor. A large color photo of snow-dressed hills hung prominently on one wall. On the other was a photo of Oak Glen Avenue, the locale's main street in 1922, the year the city was chartered.

In the center of the small office was an oak desk, scarred with age. It had once belonged to her father. Several pink message slips were laid out on her desk awaiting her attention. She stacked them and put them aside. Lowering herself into the leather executive chair behind the desk, she snatched up the phone and dialed a two-digit number.

"Bob Vincent," the voice on the other end said.

"Bob, it's Anne. Are you aware of a large construction project going on in town?"

"No. Should I be?"

"I just saw a caravan of trucks go by, and some of them were transporting large equipment."

The director of the planning department asked, "What kind of equipment?"

"I saw a backhoe and dozer and something I didn't recognize. There were also a couple of semis and a bus."

"A bus? You're kidding."

"Straight-up truth, Bob. I assume that they're bringing their own workers in."

"That's possible. Makes me curious."

"Me too," Anne agreed. "Have you ever heard of Sachs Engineering?" She spelled the name.

"Can't say that I have, but that doesn't mean much. Engineering can mean anything. It's like companies with 'Communication' in their name. That covers speechwriters to telephone companies. Have you tried the Internet?"

"Not yet; I wanted to see what you knew."

"Sorry I can't be more help. You want me to call the county and see if they know anything?"

"That'd be great. I'll see what else I can find."

Anne was on her computer within seconds of returning the phone to its cradle. Keys clicked and clacked until she was on the Internet searching for "Sachs Engineering." A list of over 150 hits appeared on her screen. Most were dead ends. She wanted the business site and found it near the top of the list. A mouse-click later she was looking at a professionally designed, brightly colored web site. Across the top of the page were photos of skyscrapers, industrial centers, and airport terminals.

"Wow," Anne said to herself. She studied the web page and found a button titled ABOUT US. She clicked it and watched as the screen dissolved to yellow then reassembled itself into a grouping of text and photos. She read quickly, mumbling the words aloud.

"Sachs Engineering. . .founded in 1975 by Henry Sachs. . .specializing in major construction projects around the world. . .Hong Kong. . .Bombay. . .London. . .Dublin. . .Rio de Janeiro. . ." She stopped short. A quick count revealed fifteen projects in South America, twenty-eight in Europe, eight in Africa, and sixteen in Asian countries. She didn't bother counting the long list of projects in the U.S. "What are you doing in our little neck of the woods?" she asked the monitor.

She spent the next twenty minutes perusing the site. It was a professional and impressive presentation but still simple. There were no flashing images or sounds. Just straight-to-the-point information.

Anne's phone rang, and she jerked at the sound of it. It was Bob Vincent.

"Ready for what I found?" the planning department head asked.

"That didn't take long," Anne said.

"It didn't take long because I struck out," Bob explained. "I called the county, and they don't show anything going on in the areas just beyond our city limits. I also checked with the utility companies, and they said they had no projects in our area. I made other calls and struck out everywhere. No one knows anything."

"I saw the trucks and equipment go through town," Anne said.

"I don't doubt you," Bob interjected. "Maybe they were just passing through."

"Did you check with San Bernardino County?"

"Yeah. I also had my aide call Bakersfield and Mojave. Nothing doing."

Anne's mind processed the information. "I wonder if they're planning on doing something sneaky. They're a huge firm," she said, then told him what she had learned.

"Firms like that don't sneak around," Bob said. "If they want to do something in a small town like ours, then they would just bowl us over with high dollar attorneys."

"Something's not right," Anne said. Her curiosity began to churn. "You want to take a drive?"

"Where?"

"To wherever they are. I don't think they were just pulling through town, Bob. We're a little off the beaten path. They are either completely lost or are headed here. And they had enough equipment to make me think that some big project is in the works—a project that no one knows anything about."

"Maybe it's a government thing," Bob suggested. "You know those guys. They think they're exempt from every law, especially those in jerkwater towns like ours."

"Tejon is not a jerkwater town, Bob. People live here because the air is clean, they can see the stars at night, and it's a great place to raise kids."

"I know that, Anne," Bob said defensively. "But to big city clowns that come through here on occasion, we're just a little hamlet in the hills."

"You want to go with me or not?" Anne demanded.

"Yeah, I'll go. Someone needs to keep an eye on you. You sound like you're in the mood for a fight."

"Not really," Anne replied. "I just don't like someone taking advantage of our city or our county."

"I'll drive," Bob said. "We'll take a city vehicle. That way we'll look official. Any idea where they went?"

"No, not really. I know they were headed west through town. That was half an hour ago. They can't have gone far."

"Moving big rigs on these roads is a slow process. Still, we better get going."

"Okay," Anne said. "I'll meet you out front. I'm going to make a quick call first." She hung up, pulled a city directory from her desk, searched for a number, then placed a call. Three minutes later she was in the front seat of a white Dodge pickup. Bob, a tall man in his fifties, sat behind the wheel. He smiled through gray eyes. "Ready for Anne's big adventure?"

"Just drive, Bob," Anne said as she slipped her seat belt on.

"Who'd you call?"

"Sergeant Montulli. I thought extra eyes might be useful, so I asked him to alert his deputies. If they see the caravan, he'll call me on my cell phone, assuming we're not in a cell phone dead zone. Connections are iffy in these hills."

"Pretty smart. I guess that's why you're mayor and I'm just a city employee."

"Let's see, who gets the full-time salary? Wait, don't tell me. That would be you."

"Ah, small town life." Bob dropped the truck into gear and drove it out of the parking lot.

CHAPTER 3

Perry knocked lightly on the wood jamb and waited. The front door was open, and he could see through the aged screen door into the simple living room. The house was a white ranch style that he judged to be less than fifteen hundred square feet. When he pulled his vehicle up the dirt drive and into the gently sloping front yard, he noticed that the home was in need of repairs. The roof was a blanket of weathered composition shingles, many of which were askew or missing. The walls were covered in shiplap siding that had been exposed to years of California sun and roughly abused by decades of persistent wind.

To the south side of the house stood a simple vegetable garden, bordered by a three-foot-high fence of chicken wire to keep out rabbits and squirrels. Now he stood on a creaky wooden porch waiting for someone to answer his knock. Gentle music wafted out the door.

Perry knocked again. The music died, and he heard the sound of a sliding glass door opening, followed by muted footsteps. A woman with a wrinkled brown face approached.

"Yes?" she said softly. She stayed a few steps back from the door. Perry could see her apprehension.

"Good afternoon, I'm Perry Sachs. I'm here to see Hector and Rose Trujillo."

"Oh, Señor Sachs," the woman said with a broad smile. "I am

Rose. Please come in, come in." She approached, pushed the screen door open, and Perry entered. The room was filled with the lush smells of food, and his stomach came to attention. "I didn't know you were going to stop by," she said. Her voice was spiced with a Mexican accent but not as strongly as he had expected. He had spoken to her previously, but only on the phone and only for a few moments before being handed off to her husband. "Hector is in the back." She led the way.

"I hope I'm not interrupting," he said.

"Oh, no. We don't get much company out here," she said.

"Out here" is right, Perry thought. The nearest neighbor was several miles away. Nestled in the hills as the home was, no other house could be seen.

Rose led Perry through the small living room, past the dining area, and back outside through a sliding glass door. "Hector, it's Señor Sachs."

Perry descended a three-step set of creaky stairs and found himself standing on a cracked concrete patio covered with a worn, whitewashed latticework that checkered the floor in squares of shade. The patio was furnished with two cushioned lounge chairs and two plastic chairs. A small, round redwood table separated the lounge chairs. On the table were plates and two half-filled glasses of tea. One plate held only a few crumbs; the other had a half-eaten portion of casserole.

A thin, brown man who looked to be in his early seventies was seated on one of the lounge chairs. Perry knew the man was only fifty-eight. He was dressed in jeans, a tan work shirt, and one tennis shoe. Only one shoe was necessary since his left leg was missing. Next to the chair was a pair of crutches. The man reached for them.

"Don't get up," Perry said quickly. "I didn't mean to disrupt your lunch. I assume you're Hector." Perry extended his hand and approached.

The man settled back in the chair and shook hands. "Yes, I'm Hector. It's good to have a face with the name," he said. He smiled, showing straight, white teeth. Perry wondered why he had expected a gap-toothed grin. "Please sit down. Can Rose get you some tea?"

"No, thank you," Perry said. "I won't keep you long. I'm just back in the country, and I'm a little worn out from the trip. I'm looking forward to a nap in my motel room."

"I didn't expect a personal visit," Hector said. His voice was strong, but his eyes revealed an inner weakness. Perry knew he was sick, but seeing it firsthand filled him with a deep pathos.

"How are you feeling, sir?" Perry asked, pulling up one of the plastic chairs. Rose returned to her lounge.

"Some days are better than others. The cancer continues to spread, or so the doctors tell me."

"You're undergoing chemotherapy?"

He nodded. "It leaves me tired. My house grows old with me, and there's nothing I can do about it."

It was Perry's turn to nod. "I came by to say thank you for letting us investigate your property and to give you this." Reaching into his suit coat pocket, Perry pulled out a slip of paper. "It's another check."

Hector took the check and looked at it. "Ten thousand dollars," he said with surprise. "This is very generous. You've already paid ten thousand. That was our agreement."

"I know," Perry said. "But I was able to get more. You have been very gracious to us. I appreciate that."

"Most businessmen don't pay more than they have to," Hector said. "This I've learned from years of life."

"True, but Sachs Engineering isn't like other businesses. I also wanted you to know that we're on the site now. When we're done, we'll return the ground to its original condition just as promised in the contract. We'll also be as speedy as possible."

Hector passed the check to Rose. "Take your time," Hector said. "I can do nothing with the land now. I can no longer ranch. The cancer has stolen my livelihood." He shifted his gaze to the green hills beyond. "It has been two years since I sold my livestock.

That was during my first fight with. . .with this." He motioned to his body. "They took my leg back then. I suppose I could have adjusted, but the cancer continued to spread. All I have now is the land—the land and my wife."

"We have our children," Rose said.

"I suppose, but they are not here, are they?" Hector turned back to Perry. "We have two children; both have moved out of state. One teaches; the other is a nurse."

"Noble professions," Perry said.

"Yes, but what of the land? I suppose I can sell it, but it's been in the family for many generations. My grandfather made a ranch of this place and gave it to my father, and he gave it to me. I will pass it to my children, but they will sell it. Do you have any children, Señor Sachs?"

"No, I've never married. Been a little too busy, I guess."

"Children make you old," Hector said.

"You stop that," Rose demanded. "Children are a blessing from the Lord."

Hector smiled then winked at Perry. "I can't run from her anymore, but I can still find ways to irritate her. It's good entertainment for a man in my condition."

Perry chuckled politely.

"What are you looking for?" Rose asked.

The question caught Perry off guard.

"Rose," Hector said quickly. "I told you that they want to keep that secret."

"I know it sounds strange," Perry interjected, "but I can't tell you."

"It's not oil," Rose said. "You have to go down into the valley for that, and all those sites were bought up two generations ago."

"No, it's not oil," Perry replied.

"Gold?" Rose prompted. "There's no gold here."

Hector frowned. "Rose, leave the man alone. We agreed to let them have their secret."

"Why can't we know?" Rose persisted. "It's our land. We may

be cash poor, but we still have the land, and it's valuable. We own whatever there is in it."

"Mrs. Trujillo," Perry said. "Your land remains yours, including all mineral rights. We're not prospecting or mining. We should only be here a few weeks at most and probably much less than that. Right now I have to keep certain things under wraps, but when the time comes, I promise to tell you."

"But—"

"Leave it alone, Rose," Hector commanded. "We decided to trust Mr. Perry. We've made the right choice. Look, he even brought us more money than we agreed to. Who does that these days? No one, that's who. Let him alone."

Perry could see that Rose was not satisfied, but there was nothing he could do about that. Secrecy was part of the deal. They had a right to be curious and he regretted that he couldn't bring them into the picture, but sometimes situations dictated actions.

"Well," Perry said, rising from the chair. "I've taken enough of your time. I do thank you for your trust."

"And I thank you for the check," Hector said.

"I can see myself out," Perry offered. "When we pack up everything, I'll come to say good-bye."

"Gracias," Hector said, slipping back into Spanish.

Perry looked at the man in the chair who had given them the go-ahead to search and dig on his property and wondered if he would live to see the end of the project. *"Via con Dios, amigo."*

The room was dark, made so by thick plastic blinds that hung like vault doors against the window wall of the nineteenth floor of the Straight Building, home and headquarters of RS BioDynamics. The brilliant late-afternoon sunlight pressed against the glass and blinds, attempting to fulfill its purpose of dissolving all darkness. It failed. The room was a sepulcher, and its lone inhabitant preferred it that way. The darkness's only enemy was the soft glow of four computer monitors that did little more than tint the gloom with muted illumination.

The room was large, a man-made cavern of extreme expense. The floor was hand-laid teak; the walls were dressed in thick purple drapes. No pictures hung anywhere. Despite enough room to hold a houseful of furniture, only a single glass-topped desk broke the monotonous expanse. There were no chairs, no sofas, no place for anyone to sit. Such things just encouraged people to stay longer than the owner cared to entertain them. It was from this large desk that the computer monitors trickled forth their anemic light.

Dr. Rutherford Straight was behind the desk in the only chair he'd sat in for more than six years. His body leaned forward, swayed from side to side, then bobbed up and down. His eyes were closed, completing the darkness he craved, but he was not asleep. His mind was awash with thoughts, ideas flying through the gray matter like angry hornets around a threatened nest. Music as dark and thick as the shadowed room bounced from the hard floor and ceiling. Baritones, sopranos, deep brass tones from horns, sharp notes from violins and violas filled the space like smoke from a fire. Mozart's classical compositions fit the room and its lone inhabitant as if they'd been hand tailored by the maestro for this purpose.

A bell, gentle as a kitten's mew, added three notes to the concert. Other men would have missed the addition, but not Rutherford Straight. Nothing got by him. Fifteen years ago, just three years out of university with his doctorate, *Newsweek* magazine had declared him the "most brilliant scientist since Pasteur and more significant to the realm of biogenetics than Gregor Mendel." Others had joined in the chorus of praise: *Technology Review, Scientific American,* the *Journal of the American Medical Association,* and twenty other periodicals, scientific and popular, had shown his face on their covers or in their pages.

His mind made him conspicuous, his research made him famous, and his forty-eight patents on biological material and genetically enhanced animals had made him a billionaire. "No man knows more about the processes of life than Dr. Rutherford Straight, nor does anyone know how better to make millions from that knowledge." The words had been inked in the *Wall Street Journal*.

The bell chimed again, but Rutherford ignored it.

How ironic life had become. How viciously, bitterly ironic, that a man who knew more than anyone about the processes of life would have so much of his own existence stripped away. In college, through graduate school, he had been vibrant, healthy, and had moved with the spring of youth. He'd been out of grad school less than a year when he noticed that the sharp edge of his strength had been dulled. He ignored it. There was research to do, a company to found, patents to be obtained and defended. Genetic manipulation of food and animals were the keys to the future. Humans too could be altered, life extended, babies improved, and much more. Time was one thing he couldn't control, and he was therefore committed to not squandering it.

Yet as the days passed, his strength waned. Graceful walking was replaced with a limp. Standing straight gave way to wobbling. Soon, too soon, a wheelchair replaced his legs. That was the way with ALS—Amyotrophic Lateral Sclerosis. His future was darker than the room in which he sat.

The bell chimed again.

"All right!" Rutherford said. He meant to shout it, but his days of shouting were gone. At least he still had a voice, he told himself. He could still speak. He had not had pneumonia, which afflicted every ALS patient sooner or later, nor had the affliction forced him to have a tracheotomy—yet. Those things loomed in his future—unless his plan was successful. Raising a tremulous hand that wore a thin, stiff brace, he muted the music in the room and pressed a large button on a console mounted to his wheelchair. The brace, plastic and leather, provided the strength his wrist could no longer supply.

The automatic door to his office opened with a whirring sound, and a tall man with broad shoulders and narrow waist entered. He was dressed in a dark blue tailored suit. A yellow silk tie hung from his neck with the precision of a plumb bob.

Rutherford knew the man well. And he hated him, hated him for his erect stature and the firm muscles that he knew were hidden away under the suit. He hated him for his freedom of mobility, his clear, precise voice, and for the fact that he didn't drool, a new indignity Rutherford was forced to endure.

He also loved the man. No employee was more loyal or enduring. Alexander Olek crossed the threshold, and the automatic door closed behind him. "I was becoming worried," he said in a smooth baritone.

With a tightly-trimmed gray beard that matched the band of hair that formed a reverse crown on his otherwise bald head, he could easily be confused with a manservant. As Rutherford's constant companion, many had made that assumption. But Alex was much more than he appeared. He'd come on staff as "personal security" for Rutherford when a disgruntled competitor had threatened his life for stealing pharmaceutical trade secrets. The accusation had led to a bitter lawsuit in the civil courts. The competitor lost the suit, and financially ruined beyond any hope of salvage, committed suicide a month later. Rutherford had sent flowers. It was the least he could do, or so he told himself.

"I'm fine. I was just thinking," Rutherford replied. His words came intermittently and were often slurred. "Have we heard?"

"An early report," Alex answered. "The flyover went well, and our man is back in Bakersfield. He's waiting for the pictures which should be ready within the half hour."

"He's sending the images by E-mail?" Rutherford asked. He struggled to keep his head up and his eyes fixed on his aide.

"Yes. As attachments."

"He knows to encrypt everything?"

"Yes, he's a professional," Alex offered. "The E-mail account cannot be traced to us."

"But he's not one of us. He's outside the office, a hired hand."

"That's right. A private detective. I personally checked his references. He's tenacious."

"Just so long as he's not stupid. Does he know why we want the pictures?"

"No. I allowed him to believe that it was a business survey. He was happy with that and asked no questions."

"Except what he'd be paid."

Alex nodded. "He did ask about that, but he was happy with what I offered."

"Can he be bought off? Can someone else get to him?"

"Perhaps in regard to his other cases, but not this one. I made it clear that I wouldn't tolerate such a breach of trust. He understood the danger to his health."

"I assume that he doesn't know that he's working for RS BioDynamics."

"I buried the paperwork in a fictitious business. He can't trace anything back to us."

"Were they there?" Rutherford asked. He closed his mouth and concentrated on swallowing the saliva that had accumulated. Swallowing was becoming more difficult each week. He wondered how long he had before all his nutrients would come to him through a tube in his stomach.

"Sachs Engineering? Yes, and our man said he saw a fair amount of equipment. It appears they came to dig, not just hunt."

Rutherford worked his jaw up and down. "They must be confident of the location." He swore quietly. He wanted to scream the words, but just making them audible was difficult enough. "This accelerates things."

"We still have time," Alex said.

"Only the healthy have time, Alex. Every minute that ticks by, I move closer to the grave."

"I suppose that's true for all of us."

"It's not," Rutherford snapped in a whisper. "True, we all die, but I'm slipping away faster. Velocity and acceleration. Velocity and acceleration. I'm falling into the open maw of death quickly and picking up speed. My seconds are your hours; my minutes your days. I have more money than time and without the latter, the former means nothing."

"Of course," Alex conceded.

"How did they get there before us? How did we let them take the lead?"

"I guess it all goes back to the alley, sir. If Perry Sachs hadn't interfered, our man would have had the document sooner. Then we would have had all that was needed. Of course, there were the translation problems."

"But he did interfere," Rutherford said. "He showed up on his white horse and made a fool of the man you hired."

"Yes, sir, he did," Alex agreed. "It was unfortunate."

"It was more than that! It was disastrous. My life is tied up in this. That's not hyperbole, Alex. I mean it literally. This is my last hope, and it's a flimsy hope at best. Thin as it is, I have no intention of letting it pass. I want that material. It's the only treasure that matters to me. Is that clear?"

"It is, Mr. Straight."

"This isn't going to be easy. There's something about this Sachs Engineering. I assume you've done the same research I have."

"I have. They have money, equipment, and expertise in building. They may prove formidable."

"This same Perry Sachs leads the team?"

"Yes. He has the authority to move equipment and personnel. If our research is right, he always takes the lead on the bigger projects. Compared to what they've built around the world, this project is small potatoes as far as construction goes, but if he knows what's below the ground—and I think we have to assume that he does—then this will far exceed anything else he is likely to do."

"We can't let word get out, Alex. We simply can't. Nor can we let them head off into the sunset with our prize."

"Agreed."

"I want you to oversee the actual operation, Alex. No more outside hirelings. Understood? Get the pictures, pay off the private eye, and make sure he doesn't connect the dig with us. Do what you have to."

"It will be handled. We do have one advantage," Alex added. "Apparently the site is isolated. The closest town is two miles away."

"We need all the breaks we can get. I want you to send everything you've learned to my computer. Send the pictures too when they come in. I'm going to be involved from beginning to end on this. I have to be."

"I understand," Alex said. As usual, he showed no emotion. It was one of the things Rutherford appreciated about Alex. He never coddled him, never patronized him.

Rutherford pressed the large button on his wheelchair console, and the door to his office swung open again. "There is no time to waste."

The moment Alex crossed the threshold, Rutherford returned his attention to the four monitors before him. Two displayed video pictures of the eight laboratories that filled three of the lower floors. The images changed as the surveillance program cycled through various cameras. At any time, Rutherford could touch a button with his hand that was still responsive and cause the system to focus on just one location. He could then zoom in or out to see the various projects being conducted under his name. From his desk he could speak to the scientists and direct their research without leaving his office. There were over forty different cameras in the building, and he had immediate access to any of them.

The other two monitors were program displays. On one was a spreadsheet of a transgenic experiment whose results would be published next month. He was pleased with what he saw. Officially, over three billion dollars was spent worldwide in developing genetically enhanced plants. A comparable amount was spent on genetically altering animals. The real numbers were much higher. RS Bio-Dynamics alone spent that much, and they were just one of the fish in the sea—albeit the largest one. The other monitor was a written report regarding another successful experiment. But unlike the previous experiment, which would be published in a major scientific journal, this one would never see the light of day. The world, Rutherford had decided, was too backwards to appreciate what he and his team had done.

The world had changed, and most people didn't even know it. While the media discussed the ramifications and ethics of animal and human cloning, almost no one mentioned the "blending" milestones that had happened in the last five years. In 2002, Japanese scientists successfully combined vegetable matter with an animal by inserting a spinach gene known as FAD2 into a fertilized pig embryo which was implanted in a sow's womb. The end result was the birth of pigs designed to give healthier pork.

A Canadian company had, about the same time, announced that it had achieved the unbelievable pairing of spiders and goats. Spider genes were crossed with genetic material in goats so that the much sought-after spider silk could be produced in the goat's milk. It was heralded as a source for everything from artificial tendons, to lightweight body armor, to biodegradable fishing line. The world barely blinked.

As early as 2000, China's Office of Genetic Engineering Safety Administration approved over 250 biotech plants, microorganisms, and animals. And Rutherford knew they were at least three years behind the curve.

The industrial wave had crashed to shore three hundred years ago; the information age less than seventy-five. Each changed the world remarkably and with unexpected suddenness. The biotech wave was no wave at all. Instead of crashing to shore with tsunami-like intensity, it rolled in like an unusually high tide. People remarked about some of the "Hollywood" issues like cloning, but were blissfully unaware of other developments. The waters of change would be over their heads before people knew their feet were wet. That was just the way Rutherford Straight liked it.

He refocused his attention on one of the screens. Money was being made by the truckload. The era of scientists seeking knowledge for its own sake was gone. Words like "insight," "discovery," "world knowledge" were replaced by other terms: "patents," "IPOs," and "secrecy." Where once scientists freely shared information, they now hoarded it until they could realize the full financial benefit. Despite science journalists and ethicists who decried the practice as selfish, it made perfect sense to Rutherford.

The image on the monitor showed a shaggy, blond-haired man in the traditional lab coat seated at a metal desk next to a wall. His hair hung to his shoulders. Before him was a computer terminal, and he was hunched over the keyboard. Dr. Benton Carmack, M.D., Ph.D.

He was a rail thin man who seldom spoke. Rutherford had never known him to initiate a conversation other than when the scientist talked to himself, which he did frequently. The man was a poster boy geek with no life outside the lab. Rutherford understood and admired that. Few things mattered more than what went on inside these walls. Marriage, family, entertainment—they were all things that got in the way of work and slowed progress. Carmack went home only to sleep, and Rutherford had seen him work two or three days with only an occasional nap. Carmack's focus and genius came close to that of his own. Rutherford had assigned him several assistants, each one trained to do more than science; they made sure the scientist ate and rested. It was a difficult task.

Rutherford pressed another button on his portable console. The action was carried to the computer by an infrared beam. A slight sound came from the computer's speakers, letting Rutherford know that the communication link was open.

"Good afternoon, Dr. Carmack," Rutherford said.

There was no response, but he knew the system was working. He could hear the keys clacking and clicking as Carmack typed on the keyboard.

He tried again. "Hello, Dr. Carmack."

"Go away, I'm working," Carmack snapped with a wave of his hand. His eyes never left the computer monitor.

"It's Dr. Straight; I'm sorry to interrupt."

"I said. . .who? Dr. Straight?" His voice was thin and sharp. Rutherford watched as his employee raised his head and looked around. He had never adjusted to talking to an empty room.

"Press F12 on the keyboard, Doctor."

"What. . .? Oh, of course."

Carmack did. Rutherford zoomed the camera in for a tighter shot and had the odd experience of seeing his own face on Carmack's computer. "I'm sorry to disturb your work, Doctor, but I wanted to make you aware that our little project may be moving ahead soon."

"Project?" Carmack said to the computer. "Oh, yes. Yes, I remember. Soon, you say?"

Rutherford let slip a crooked smile. He seldom smiled now, but when he did it was always crooked. One more thing he could no longer do well. He smiled because Carmack spoke like an elderly man although he was only thirty-two. It was the result of too great a focus and too little time in social environments. None of that mattered to Rutherford. "Yes, perhaps in the next few days. Will you be ready?"

"Of course. I've been ready. I'm ready now."

"Very good, Doctor. I'll let you know more soon."

"I'm ready. The equipment is ready. The lab is ready."

"I will have a new assistant to aid you. The others should not be told of this."

"I can do it myself. I don't need help. I don't need an assistant."

"Nonetheless, Doctor, I prefer to do it this way. It will help me feel more involved. You can understand that, can't you?"

Carmack nodded repeatedly. "Involved. Yes, of course. You should be involved."

"You know, only the two of us can make this a success, don't you?"

"Yes. I know. I know. I'll make it work."

"I trust you will, Dr. Carmack. I trust you will."

CHAPTER 4

Perry took the drive from the Trujillo residence slowly. The narrow dirt road had taken a downhill turn. That was no problem for the Explorer, which was designed for much more challenging terrain. The road, however, was serpentine with several blind turns. Perry was more worried about an unexpected meeting with another car than losing traction.

He was also tired. The fatigue of travel with little rest over two days weighed upon him like lead clothing. His eyes were burning from weariness, and his stomach was a churning cauldron of acid, the result of too much coffee and too little food.

His plan was simple. Drive straight to the motel, surrender to a few hours of much needed nap time.

He'd already checked in with Jack using the truck's CB radio and received a report of the last hour's activity. The various surveys were being reviewed again and a few small surveys done. "Measure twice, drill once," Jack had said.

Jack had then told Perry to get some rest, threatening to kick his fanny all the way down the hill if he showed up anytime in the next few hours. Perry needed no coaxing.

Staying awake long enough to find the motel was his most pressing challenge. Steering the big SUV around another turn, Perry tried to bridle his excitement, but it was a wrestling match he was doomed to lose. He just hoped that he'd be able—

There was a loud and sustained horn blast.

Perry hit the brakes and turned the steering wheel sharply to the right, running the big vehicle up a small embankment. He felt the front fender dig into the soft soil. Next to him a white Dodge pickup shot past, missing the Explorer by inches. Perry stopped the car and looked at his side mirror just in time to see the driver offer an apologetic wave as he drove off.

"No, really, I'm fine," Perry said sarcastically as he eased the Ford back on the road and started downhill again. "And they say city folk are crazy drivers."

The near collision removed the shroud of sleepiness that had been descending upon him. Adrenaline laced his blood, and his heart was running a few beats faster. He shook his head and continued toward town. The time slogged by, but Perry finally arrived at the two-story building. An oval green sign read: OAK GLEN LODGE. The structure looked to be twenty years old but well taken care of. Air-conditioning units hung from the beige wall just below each window.

Perry had hoped for better, but he knew Jack had worked to arrange rooms for the entire crew in the same building. Communication was more efficient when everyone was nearby.

Jack had told him that the place was clean and had two conference rooms. A restaurant shared a parking lot with the motel. Just as important, it had a recently updated phone and Internet system. *That'll make things easier,* Perry thought.

The manager greeted Perry as if he were a long lost uncle, something Perry attributed to his firm having filled three-quarters of the total rooms—and paying in advance. After a handshake and short conversation, Perry walked into room 110.

He was pleasantly surprised. He'd assumed that the building would have displayed its age in old furniture and scarred walls. Instead, he found a queen-size bed, a large table/desk, and a fully refurbished bathroom. *This'll do,* he thought.

Closing the door behind him, Perry finished his survey. A fireplace was tucked away in a corner. His practiced eye could see that it was a recent addition. His luggage was situated on his bed. As usual, Jack had arranged for everything. On the table was his Hewlett-Packard laptop computer, already plugged into the wall, as was the modem cable. Jack had seen to everything.

Ten minutes later, Perry had stripped off his suit, washed his face, unpacked his clothing, and settled down on the bed.

"I'm driving us back," Anne Fitzgerald said sharply. "Assuming we arrive at our destination safely."

"Come on, Mayor," Bob replied with a wide grin. "It wasn't that close. Consider it just another little adventure in your life."

"Some adventure. Do you know how much work it is to keep the gray out of my hair? You set the process back at least a year."

"You know what driving these back roads is like. They're narrow and winding. That's why we drive slowly. Do you know who that was?" Bob steered around the next corner, and Anne held her breath.

"No, but I think it was one of the workmen from Sachs Engineering. The truck was the same yellow as the ones I saw in the caravan."

"Too bad we didn't bump fenders. It would have saved us the drive to the site. Assuming we can find the site in the first place."

"I don't want to talk to some employee. I want a face-to-face with the head honcho." Anne shifted in her seat.

"Curiosity killed the cat," Bob said.

"Especially if the cat was in the car with you."

Bob replied with a laugh. "Has anyone ever told you that you have a tendency to make mountains out of molehills?"

"A few people."

"Like who?"

"Like every one of my friends and family. It's what endears me to them—Wait! Stop!"

Bob brought the pickup to a halt. "What? What is it?"

"Back up, Bob. I think I saw something down that side road we just passed."

Putting the truck in reverse, Bob backed up slowly until he was at the narrow intersection of dirt roads. Another dirt path veered east from the road they were on.

"There," Anne said, pointing at a black puff rising from beyond a hill. "Is that diesel smoke?"

Bob nodded. "It sure looks like it. There are tracks on the path, big tracks. They look fresh too."

Anne strained against her seat belt and peered out Bob's window. "Tire tracks and they're close together, like those big trucks with two tires on the back."

"Maybe you should be a detective, Mayor. That's a pretty keen insight."

"That's the road we want. Drive on, Jeeves."

"Jeeves? Great, I've been demoted to chauffeur."

"Not yet," Anne said, "but the day's not over."

Anne kept her eyes fixed forward as the truck pulled up the rise. Oak trees dotted the hills, rising from the gentle green slope of the mountains. Warmth swelled in her, and she almost felt guilty for living in such a beautiful place. She felt as if they were driving through a post card. It was this unspoiled beauty she wished to maintain from wanton development. It was bad enough to have hundreds of giant windmills spinning their propellers in the ever-present wind. She lost more battles than she won when it came to preserving the paradise of the Tehachapi Mountains. But she did win enough to keep fighting.

The crest of the hill gave way to a slope sharper than the one they'd just ascended. At the bottom and just to the south of the road were a string of parked vehicles, the same ones she'd seen pass through town.

"Bingo," Bob said. "You got a nose for this kind of thing."

"Pull behind the bus. We found the caravan; now let's see if we can find the people who go with it."

Anne was out of the truck before Bob had set the parking brake. She walked along the line of parked vehicles. Some were painted yellow and had the words SACHS ENGINEERING printed on the side. The sound of a diesel engine rolled down the hill. Anne turned and saw truck tracks leading up the hill to a grove of oaks a quarter mile up the grade.

"Walk or drive?" Bob asked. He had come up behind her.

"Drive," Anne decided. "I'm not wearing my hiking boots. Besides, the city paid for a four-wheel-drive truck; it's time we got our money's worth out of that investment."

Once back in the truck, Bob dropped it into gear and pointed it up the hill. From a distance, the surface looked smooth and even. In the cab of a truck with stiff suspension, Anne learned that there were more bumps than she could have imagined. Her small frame was bounced against the door, and at times her head hit the ceiling.

"Could you make this a little rougher?" she snipped. "I'm starting to doze off."

"That sounds like sarcasm," Bob replied.

"You *are* perceptive."

The hill gave way to an open expanse of pasture outlined by several groves of trees. To Anne's right and ahead about a quarter mile was a large truck with thick metal tubing swaying in the back. The truck was headed to the oak grove. "What is that?" Anne asked.

"It's a drilling rig," Bob said.

"You mean like for oil?"

"More like water," he explained. "I've seen them before. Farmers and ranchers often hire companies to come out and drill wells. All that metal you see at the back of the truck is the drilling rig. The truck backs up to the right spot, erects the rig, and starts drilling right from the back of the truck. Pretty neat really."

"There's too much equipment back at the road for them to

be looking for water."

"I suppose they could be drilling for something else."

Their truck took another bounce, and Anne swore and rubbed the side of her head where it hit the doorframe. "You're trying to kill me, aren't you?"

"I've always wanted to be mayor."

"You're not in the line of succession, Bob. Just try to avoid the holes and gullies."

"Sorry, but the grass obscures everything, and I left my X-ray vision back at the office." Bob turned the wheel right and directed the truck toward the grove. He slowed as he approached.

Anne was looking around like a child in an amusement park. The drilling rig was not the only vehicle present, nor was it the only piece of equipment. Two yellow SUVs were parked to one side of the grove and another truck at the south end. That truck had a large machine attached to the bed. Bob nodded at it and said, "Generator."

Bob pulled his pickup under one of the trees. He and Anne exited and took in the situation. There were about twenty men working in different areas of the meadow. They were assembling what looked to Anne to be aluminum towers. "Any idea what they're doing?" she asked Bob, directing his attention with a pointed finger.

He studied the work for a moment then replied, "Lights. I used them in my construction days. These guys are planning on working around the clock."

"There're a lot of them."

"Lights or people?"

"Both, but I meant the lights." Anne noticed a pattern. "It looks like they're setting them up in rows."

"That's how I see it. Three banks of lights in two rows." Bob pointed to the ground where the different teams were working. "See those markers? The sticks with the colored ribbon on them? Those are surveyor marks. Whatever they plan to do, they plan on doing it between those rows of markers."

"Let's see if we can find someone to talk to." Anne started off with determined strides, marching to the cluster of oaks. Twenty steps later she found herself standing beneath a plastic canopy. Several plastic tables were standing with legs propped against the downhill slope. On the tables were computers and various pieces of electronics she didn't recognize. All the tables faced out toward the open field. In the center of "camp" was a larger table covered with sheets of paper held in place against the stiffening breeze with rocks and various travel-mugs. Several paces beyond that was another table upon which were large plastic containers.

Anne watched as one of the workmen came in from the meadow, picked up a paper cup, and filled it from a spout in one of the containers. He took a long drink then threw the cup in a dark green trashcan. *At least they're tidy,* Anne thought. A small trailer was parked to one side.

Redirecting her attention to the table with the papers, she saw three men huddled over some document and conversing quietly.

"They look like a good place to start," Bob said.

Anne agreed and walked to the table. "Excuse me," she said. The three men turned their attention to her. One was young, fresh-faced, and couldn't be older than a college student. The next man was tall, trim, and wore wire-rimmed glasses. It was the third man that caught her attention. Unlike the other two, he was ebony-skinned and massive. Thickly muscled and intimidating in appearance, Anne thought he could have a stellar career as a bar-room bouncer. "Excuse me," she repeated, using her best professional tone. "I'm looking for the person in charge."

The three men looked at each other for a moment then back to Anne. "In charge of what?" the man in the glasses asked.

"In charge of all this." Anne motioned to the trucks and equipment.

"He's not here, Ms. . ." the big black man said.

"Fitzgerald. Anne Fitzgerald. I'm the mayor of the City of Tejon. You passed through it on your way here." She introduced Bob.

"It's a pleasure to meet you, Mayor. I'm Jack Dyson, assistant project manager." He motioned to the others. "This is Gleason Lane, one of our engineers, and this is Brent Hapgood, a college intern with Sachs Engineering. How can I help you?"

"I would like to know what you're doing here," Anne asked. She directed the comment to the man who identified himself as Jack Dyson.

"Why?" Jack asked.

"What do you mean, why?"

"It's a simple interrogative," Jack said. "I don't mean to be impolite, but I'm not obligated to answer a question simply because it's been asked."

Interrogative? Anne thought. *Boy, did I underestimate this guy.* "I think I have a right to know what you're doing."

"Why?"

"As I said, I'm mayor of Tejon, and I'm interested in everything that may impact my city."

"This will have no impact on your city, ma'am," Jack said. "I don't believe we're in city limits."

"Events outside of our borders can affect the city," Anne protested. She felt her ire heating up. This man was being evasive. She told him so.

"I'm not being evasive, ma'am. I'm simply stating the facts. We're not in city limits; we're on private property in the country, and we are here with the permission and blessing of the landowner. Again, nothing we do here will impact your lovely town."

"I have a right to know," Anne protested but knew it was futile. It was clear Jack Dyson was as resolute as he was big.

"I'm sorry, but you don't have that right."

"So this is a secret project?"

"I suppose you can call it that. We have a confidence to keep, ma'am. We plan to keep it."

Bob chimed in. "I could find no county record for a building permit."

58

"We're not building," Jack said perfunctorily.

Anne decided to take another approach. "You said you were the assistant project manager. Who is the project manager you assist?"

"His name is Perry Sachs, and as I said, he's not here."

"Sachs?" Anne responded "As in Sachs Engineering?"

"Perry is a senior vice president and senior project manager."

"Where is he now?" Anne pressed.

"Resting."

"Resting while you work. Nice job." Anne was getting irritated. "Precisely where is he resting?"

"In his motel room, and no, I won't tell you where that is. He's had only a few hours' sleep over the last few days. He doesn't need to be disturbed."

Anne sighed loudly. She had run up against a brick wall in a man the size of a brick wall. "I could have a sheriff's deputy up here in no time."

Jack nodded and reached into the breast pocket of his work shirt. "Here's my card. It has my name on it so the deputy will know who to ask for." He handed the card to Anne. She took it reluctantly, and before she could retract it, another hand appeared with another card. It was from the man with the odd name: Gleason Lane.

"You can have mine too," he said.

Anne caught sight of the college kid patting his pockets. He shrugged, smiled, and said, "I'm just an intern. I don't get cards, but I could write my name down if you want."

Her anger had been brought to a boil, but expressing it would be futile. She had no authority to demand answers, and it galled her. Then she had another idea. "So you're telling me this Perry Sachs is not on location. He's resting."

"That's right," Jack answered.

Anne spun and snapped, "Let's go, Bob." Several steps later she turned to look at the men who stonewalled her. They had returned to their computer and papers. Back at the truck, Anne asked, "You're the local building specialist; what do you think they're doing?"

He dropped the truck into gear and pulled away, descending the slope slowly. "I'd only be guessing."

"Guess. It's more than what I've got."

"They're excavating."

"Excavating what?"

"Could be anything. If I were a betting man, I'd say they're about to drill test holes. Once they learn what they want, then they're going to bring up that backhoe we saw on the truck parked by the road and start pulling up dirt. Whatever they're after, it's underground."

"How do you know that?"

"Those papers on the table. While you were trying to be the irresistible force that moved the immovable object called Jack Dyson, I was getting an eyeful of those papers."

"And?"

"They were printouts of underground surveys. I recognized one set of images as being what you get from a GPR survey. They're definitely searching for something."

"GPR?"

"Ground penetrating radar. It's a way of seeing what lies below grade. The technology has gotten pretty sophisticated, and I bet these guys don't use anything that isn't top of the line."

"What could be underground that is so important?"

"Who knows? Maybe they found someone's treasure. Maybe they're doing something for the government. If it's a federal project of some kind, then that would explain why they're so tight-lipped."

"And why they could care less about me bringing the sheriff's department up."

"True. What now, coach? Back to the office?"

"No." Anne found her cell phone in the small purse she carried. "As soon as I get a cell signal, I'm going to make a few calls."

"To whom?"

"We have only three motels in Tejon, Bob, and we know this Sachs guy is in one of them. They have to put those workers up somewhere. I'm betting they've taken a block of rooms somewhere. We're the closest town, so it would make sense that they stay there."

"You're going to hunt this guy down?" Bob asked as he directed the truck back down the road. "You're that curious?"

"It has nothing to do with curiosity, Bob. It's the principle of the thing."

Twenty-four-year-old Joseph Henri sat at the dining room table rocking like a metronome. Back and forth, back and forth, then side to side. His eyes were open and staring blankly at the tabletop that was covered in open books. The tomes were unrelated. One was a Latin grammar; another, an atlas of the United States; still another, the phone directory for San Francisco.

Joseph grunted. He always grunted when he rocked, but he did so with clock-like precision. Every thirteenth movement came with an "uhh." Thirteen beats later, "uhh." He could do this for hours and often did, never missing count, never varying. Thirteen rocking motions. . .grunt. . .thirteen. . .grunt.

As he repeated his little choreography, body firmly planted in the dining room chair, he stuck his tongue out and licked his lips. This he did every seventeen cycles. Rock. . . "uhh". . .rock. . .lick. . . rock. He could do calculations "normal" humans couldn't. But Joseph couldn't read. He could, however, absorb books and even memorize entire volumes word for word. Words, numbers, sounds, pictures, songs were all stored in his mind. He never forgot anything. He understood almost nothing.

Rocking. . .swaying.

Joseph's tongue fired out again and ran across his thick, chapped lips. An image was on his mind and he was examining it. This picture was not from a book but from a person, although he had trouble distinguishing an image from an object. The image was a face. *A deep voice face like his father's. A smile fun word face like his mother's.* "Uhh. . .Perry. . .uhh. . .Perry."

Joseph stopped suddenly and began to cry.

CHAPTER 5

Perry's mind, despite the thick shroud of sleepiness that covered him, still ran in high gear. It had always been that way for him. Even as a child he didn't simply "have" ideas; he was infected with them. Once a thought wormed its way forward in his brain, he couldn't expel it. Many thoughts bounced around in his mind like ping-pong balls in a cement mixer.

It had begun. What was originally an effort to save a man's life had become a project more important than anything he'd ever done, and probably more than anything he would do. As he lay back on the motel bed, he took a deep breath and let it out slowly, hoping to calm his thoughts.

This was more than a project, he reminded himself. He'd built buildings above and below ground. He had traveled to every industrialized country in the world and many third-world lands. He'd spoken to heads-of-state and military leaders; the wealthy were impressed by him and sought his counsel. But all of that was dross to the gold for which he now hunted. In a few hours, he would return to the spot that very well might change the world. It would be dark by then, but that didn't matter. This was an around-the-clock operation. Things had to be done quickly, accurately, and without mistake. They would push on at the best speed possible but not so fast as to make mistakes.

Controversy lay around every corner, but that couldn't be avoided. For now it was a secret, but soon it would be world news. This was no mere project, Perry reminded himself; this was a mission for God, and he planned on treating it as such. The best research had been done, the best equipment requisitioned, and the best workers brought to bear. Each key man had in the past proven himself to be trustworthy and loyal. Each worker on the site had signed a detailed nondisclosure agreement—not that it was needed for his regulars. Perry would trust his life, and had in the past, to these men, Jack and Gleason in particular.

Again, Perry took a deep breath and released it. His mind wound backward, becoming a mental time machine that took him back to Seattle, back to the night when a young gunman attempted to kill Professor Jamison Henri. . . .

The police arrived in the dark alley as Perry administered CPR to Henri. Perry prayed with each compression and with each breath he blew into the elderly man's lungs. CPR was hard work. Perry was soaked from the inside with sweat and from the outside by the chilling Washington rain.

Paramedics relieved him of his efforts, doing the work with more practiced hands. Perry watched them load Dr. Henri into the back of a wide, modular ambulance. The ambulance might as well have been a tomb.

The police were full of questions, and Perry obliged them for nearly forty-five minutes before they let him go with a pat on the back and the words, "It's a shame more citizens aren't like you."

"A lot of good it did," Perry muttered to himself. He then asked to what hospital the ambulance had gone. He thought about leaving it alone. He'd done all that he could do, and it was late. The next day was packed from early morning until late in the evening. He needed the rest. The victim was in the best hands possible for now, if he was alive. Going home was the wisest thing to do.

Perry pulled the car from the curb, made a U-turn, and drove to the hospital. Beside him was the leather satchel that had mattered so much to the old man. He'd picked it up from the damp ground when the paramedics had arrived. At first he was just moving it out of the way, but then noticed that he held it tightly to his side. The police made no inquiries about it, and Perry offered no explanations. One thing of which he was certain was that whatever was in the case was more important to Henri than his own life.

With the case resting on the front passenger seat, Perry drove into a night that seemed far darker than it had a few minutes before.

They had taken Henri to the closest hospital, St. John's Regional. The drive through the near-empty early morning streets took only fifteen minutes. A quarter of an hour after he'd left the crime scene, Perry was standing in the waiting area of the hospital's busy emergency room. Surrounding him were mothers with sick children, a homeless man with gauze wrapped around a dirty hand, and a host of others with ailments Perry couldn't fathom. He found the environment unsettling.

He approached a nurse who sat at a small desk behind security glass. After identifying himself, he asked to be informed of the patient's condition. The nurse nodded and said, "They're working on him now. Are you family?"

"Friend." He had endangered his life and performed lifesaving techniques on the man. He also held a package the old gent was willing to die to protect. As far as Perry was concerned, that made them friends. He found an open corner of the waiting room and settled into it. A television mounted to a sturdy black wall bracket played quietly. On the screen was a well-dressed young woman touting the millionaire potential of real estate purchased with no money down. Perry tuned out the infomercial.

In his hand was the satchel. It was made of leather that had seen a great many years. Initials had been carved onto the wide flap that covered the opening. As yet, Perry had not peered inside and wondered if he should. For all he knew, he could be holding a package of heroin or counterfeit money. But he doubted it. The man he had tried to save in the alley didn't seem the type. Still, he had to wonder. For what would a man sacrifice his life? If it were mere money, he would have handed it over to the thief. No, there was something else in there, something very important.

Perry studied the bag some more. It weighed maybe two pounds. The flap was held in place by a brass buckle. At one time it must have been an expensive item. Perhaps it still was. Perry certainly hadn't seen anything like it. The style and workmanship suggested that it had been made a lifetime before. Perhaps it had been handed down from father to son.

He squeezed the case gently, and it gave easily. There was nothing hard inside. Trying to appear subtle, he gave it a little jiggle. Something inside moved but made no noise. Perry guessed it held paper. That would make sense. A professor with a bag of papers. Perhaps tests and homework from students? What didn't make sense was why he was so agitated when Perry touched it. And why the attacker wanted it so badly.

All the questions could be answered by simply opening the case, but Perry couldn't bring himself to do it. The man had entrusted him with it, and Perry would honor that. Of course, it might be a moot point if the paramedics and doctors hadn't been able to get the old man's heart kick-started again, and if they couldn't, what would he do then? He would be forced to turn it over to the police or family, if he could find them.

The sliding glass door that led from the hospital parking lot swooshed open, and a woman with tousled gray hair hurried in. Her clothing was loose-fitting and disheveled. Behind her followed another person, a young man Perry judged to be in his early twenties. He moved with an odd gait: hands motionless at his side, torso hunched over, head down. He shuffled more than walked, and he followed no more than two feet behind the woman. He wore a jogging suit and bedroom slippers.

Perry watched as they approached the nurse at her glass barricaded station. The young man stopped behind her and leaned his head on her right shoulder.

Her voice carried as she spoke. "Yes, I'm. . .I'm Mrs. Henri. . . Claire Henri. Someone called and said my husband was here."

The nurse said something Perry couldn't hear.

Yes," the woman said. "It's spelled like Henry but an *i* at the end instead of a *y*."

Perry started forward.

"May I see him? How is he?"

He stepped next to the distraught woman.

"Just a moment," the nurse said. "I'll check." She rose from her chair and disappeared into the back.

"Mrs. Henri?" Perry said softly.

She turned at looked at him. "Yes?" There was anticipation and fear in her voice. She looked him in the eye then let her eyes drift down.

"My name is Perry Sachs," he began. "I'm the one. . ." How did he describe what happened? *I'm the one who rescued your husband? I'm the one who beat up the attacker?* Some rescue if the man was dead. "I'm the one who called the ambulance."

"What happen—" Her eyes fell to the satchel. "Where did you get that?" she asked, eyes wide.

"It was with your husband," Perry answered. His tone was quiet and smooth. "I didn't think it should be left in the alley."

"Have you opened it?"

Perry shook his head. "It didn't seem appropriate—"

"Mrs. Henri." The nurse had returned. "The doctor said you can come back. Your friend can come with you."

"My friend?"

The nurse cut her eyes to Perry. "It might be good if he came along."

Perry didn't like the sound of that.

"Through those doors," the nurse said, pointing to her right.

Reaching for the metal handle, Perry pulled the door open and stepped to the side to allow Claire Henri and the tailgating young man to pass. Perry followed a few steps behind.

The inside of the ER was unnaturally bright, belying the fact that it was now well after three in the morning. The overhead fluorescents could expel the dark of night but not the abysmal gloom of fear. That gloom seemed to hover over the woman before him, and she seemed to age a decade with each step.

The room was large, with a ring of beds lining the wall, and was separated from the neighbors by a curtain that seemed all too thin. At least half of the beds were filled. Sounds and smells assaulted the senses. This was as foreign a world to Perry as it must have been to any other except doctors and nurses. Here a special language was spoken, medical shorthand that took years to fully understand. Here, people came with everything from cuts to gunshots. Beleaguered and weary looking physicians moved from the beds to a U-shaped set of counters behind which sat several nurses doing paperwork and fiddling with computers.

Claire stopped, clearly uncertain where to look. She raised a tremulous hand to her mouth. Perry placed a gentle hand on her arm. "This way," he said and led her to the nurse's station.

Several eternal moments passed before one of the nurses looked up. She looked as tired as Perry felt. Perry initiated the conversation. "This is Mrs. Henri. Her husband is here. We were told to come back. May we see the doctor who—"

"I've got it, nurse," a man said. The nurse said nothing and quickly went back to writing something on a clipboard. "I'm Dr. Reddy," he said. His skin was dark, and he peered back through large eyes. He spoke with an accent that Perry recognized as Indian. In his hand was a metal clipboard, and a stethoscope hung around his neck. Both looked well-used. "I've been treating your husband. Let's step over here."

"Can I see him?"

"In a moment," the doctor said. He led them to one of the empty beds. "Can I get you anything?" he asked.

"Just tell me about my husband."

"Of course," Dr. Reddy said. "Your husband was brought in

about an hour ago suffering from a severe coronary event and a gunshot wound to the leg."

"Gunshot?" Claire gasped.

"Yes. The wound has been cleaned and treated. It missed the bone and passed through the muscle cleanly. It should present no problems. It's his heart that concerns me most. The attack was critical."

"But he's alive?"

"Yes, but he's not conscious. I understand that someone gave him CPR at the scene. That kept him alive. The paramedics kept up the efforts from the scene here. We were able to get his heart going again, and it seems fairly stable for now. However, I'm sure there has been serious damage—how serious I can't say until further tests are run. Those will be run by a cardiologist."

"What is the prog–prognosis?" asked Claire. Perry could tell she was fighting back tears, and he couldn't blame her. She had just heard horrible news.

"Unknown right now, Mrs. Henri. There are many things to consider, and many enemies to overcome."

"Enemies?"

"Blood clots, renal failure, another heart attack."

"I want to see him."

"Of course, but I need to tell you one more thing first. Your husband is not breathing on his own. We've had to put him on a breathing machine. When you see him, there will be a tube down his throat."

"So he won't be able to talk," Claire said.

"That's true, but for now he won't even recognize you. We have sedated him. It's often called twilight sleep. He's not fully out, but he can't respond. Feel free to speak to him. Let him know you're there, but don't expect him to respond in any way." The doctor paused and looked at the young man standing inches from Claire's right shoulder. "Is this your son?"

"Yes," Claire said.

"Developmentally disabled?" Reddy inquired.

Claire nodded. "He'll be all right. He shows very little emotion."

"Okay, this way, please." Reddy turned and led them to the back corner of the ER and pulled back the curtain. He entered first, followed by Claire and her son. Perry entered last, the satchel still in his hands.

When Perry had first seen Henri, he had been lying on the wet pavement, looking up through terrified eyes at a gunman. With the attacker gone, Perry had approached and found a man in vicious pain. He'd looked as bad as anyone Perry had ever seen.

Here in the hospital, Dr. Jamison Henri looked worse.

Machines surrounded the bed, beeping and whooshing. A chrome metal stand held several plastic IV bags. A clear tube, held in place by a thin piece of white medical tape, ran from a high-tech looking machine into Henri's throat. A catheter, used to empty the bladder, ran from beneath the covers to a bag that was hanging at the bottom of the bed. A heart monitor kept track of the heart rhythms. Taken as a whole, it reminded Perry of some absurd scene from an old science fiction movie.

Claire inhaled deeply and took a step forward to hold her husband's hand. He remained motionless.

"I'll let you have some time with him. We'll be moving him to ICU in about fifteen minutes. You can visit up there as well." Dr. Reddy left, closing the curtain behind him.

Claire turned to Perry. "You're the one who did CPR?"

"Yes," Perry said. "I happened along at the right time."

"I see," Claire said. She moved closer to Henri's head, leaned over, and kissed his forehead. It moved Perry to his core.

She said to her husband, "The satchel is here."

There was a pounding. Perry tried to ignore it, but it repeated itself, worming its way through his sleep. It took a moment, but he realized that someone was knocking on his door and knocking hard. He sat up, turned, and set his bare feet on the thin carpet, then attempted to shake the cobwebs loose.

The banging returned.

"Who is it?"

The only answer was more knocking. He rose on wobbly legs and peered through eyes still bleary from sleep. The clock said he had been napping for only forty minutes. Before lying down, he'd laid out the work clothes he planned to wear when he returned to the site. Certain that no one wanted to see him in his underwear, he slipped on his jeans and donned a brown long-sleeved work shirt. The shirt he left unbuttoned.

More knocking.

Perry gritted his teeth, took two long strides to the motel room door, and snapped it open. "What?"

Not a gracious greeting, but the incessant pounding coupled with his groggy mind drowned his normal genteel attitude. Before him stood a pleasant looking woman with short, blond hair and a determined look on her face. The determination gave way to surprise as the door sprang open, and she took a step back, treading on the toes of a brown-haired man. Both looked to be in their late thirties. The man released a yelp of pain and backed up a step too.

"Um," the woman began. Perry could see she was trying to regain the intensity she had had moments before. "Are you Mr. Sachs?"

"One of two," Perry replied.

The woman dropped her eyes and looked at his bare chest, then raised them again. Her face flushed slightly.

"I wonder if I might have a moment of your time," she said. This time her words were more certain.

She recovers quickly, Perry thought. "I was napping, and I have to work tonight. I'm not really in a mood for questions."

"I'm Mayor Anne Fitzgerald, and this is Bob Vincent. He's the head of our planning department." Perry gave a short and simple nod, which Bob returned. "We were just out at your work site."

71

"Mayor?" Perry said.

"Yes, mayor. I noticed your caravan of equipment go through town, and since we had no record of permits for construction, we thought we would take a look."

"We're not building, and we're not in city limits," Perry said. "I don't understand your interest." He was being short with her, and a twinge of remorse nagged at him.

"Problems don't stop at borders, Mr. Sachs. I spoke to some of your employees, but they just stonewalled me."

"Who did you speak to?"

"Big guy. . .um. . ." the woman began.

"Jack Dyson," Bob chimed in.

"Ah, Jack. I'll have to give him a bonus." Perry smiled.

The mayor's face turned sour. "We may be a small town, Mr. Sachs, but we are not stupid. We have certain rights and powers, and I intend to use them."

"Really?" Perry asked. "Like what?"

"Listen, Mr. Sachs. I just need a few questions answered."

"No." Perry was blunt. "Every thing we are doing is within the scope of law. Trust me. I had six attorneys working on it. We're breaking no laws, local, county, or state. Our work requires. . ." He paused for a moment, searching for the right phrase. ". . .a certain measure of discretion."

"Secrets, you mean," the woman snapped.

"That's one way of putting it, Mayor. Now if you'll excuse me, I have only a short time to catch a few winks, and I'd like to catch every one." He started to close the door.

"I have only a few questions. It won't take too long."

"With all due respect, this has already taken too long." Perry closed the door, peeled his shirt from his back, and crawled back on the bed, not bothering to remove his jeans. He listened carefully. The knocking didn't return. He heard several indistinguishable words. The tone, however, was clear. "Temper, temper, Mayor," he said softly, then closed his eyes. He heard the sound of a car motor starting.

❖❖❖

Anne stormed back to the pickup, cursing under her breath. Bob followed quietly and took his place behind the steering wheel. He fastened his seat belt and avoided eye contact.

"Who does he think he is?" Anne snapped. "He can't treat us this way."

"I think he just did," Bob replied.

"This goes beyond the pale. I'm tired of city people thinking we're nothing but backwoods idiots. He probably thinks we drink moonshine at barn dances. This is Southern California, and our citizens are every bit as erudite as the people he hobnobs with."

"You may be overreacting, Anne," Bob said softly. "He has a point. He's outside our sphere of influence, and if he wants to keep secrets, he can. He sure seems good at it."

"But why? What are they doing that requires such mystery? It makes no sense."

"Who knows? Maybe they've found a treasure."

"Whatever it is, I'm going to find out."

Bob sighed. "Don't you think you may be pushing this too far? You've already grilled the supervisor at the site, called every motel in town until you found where Mr. Sachs was, then banged on his door until you awakened him from his nap, and immediately barraged him with questions."

"It wasn't a barrage, just my attempt to open communications and find out what is going on under our noses."

"We're lucky he didn't come out swinging."

"You would have protected me, Bob. It's your duty."

"Sachs looked like he could take care of himself. We might be safer banging on the muzzle of a sleeping bear." Bob backed the car out of the parking slot and started for the street.

"He wouldn't have hurt us. He has kind eyes."

"Kind eyes, eh?" Bob laughed. "They looked like sleepy eyes turned angry." Bob stopped the truck where the parking lot met the street. "Back to the office?"

"No," Anne said without hesitation. "Sheriff's substation."

"Tell me you're joking," Bob shot back.

"No joke. These guys have crossed the wrong girl. The only people that keep secrets that tightly held to their chest are government types and crooks."

"You can't be serious," Bob protested. "They didn't sneak into town; they drove right through in broad daylight. They've taken rooms in a motel and not just one room, but a whole wing of them. Doesn't sound like a Mafia project to me."

"Then why the big brush-off? Why stonewall us at every question? They've got something up their sleeve, and I want to have a peek."

Bob cranked the wheel and pulled onto the main street. "I've got a bad feeling about this," he admitted.

"Have I ever led you astray?" Anne asked.

Bob cut a glance her way then returned his gaze forward. He said nothing.

(CHAPTER) 6

I 'm not sure I like this."

Gleason Lane gazed down at the printout of the latest GPR. He was seated on a canvas camping chair. Brent was seated next to him.

"What's not to like?" Jack Dyson asked. He carried a bottle of mineral water with him. It was a passion for which he endured a thousand jokes. "The ground changing on you?"

"No," Gleason said, with a subtle shake of his head. He ran a hand through his hair then adjusted his glasses. "Brent and I have run the program we designed, and it's confusing."

"The one that blends the surveys into a single composite?" Jack asked.

"Yeah. Look." Jack joined Gleason at the table and gazed over his shoulder. What he saw was a mass of lines and colors. Gleason ran his finger along the printout. "We can see this on the computer, but the printout lets us see more at one time than can be viewed on a computer monitor." He tapped a blank area on the left side of the page. "This is an enhanced image based on the surveys. It's the virtual X on the treasure map. As you can see, it lacks density, implying that it's—"

"Hollow," interjected Jack. "We expected that."

"We did expect that, and as we saw with our earlier, preliminary surveys, there appears to be a change in the density of materials running from twenty-five meters southeast of the hollow area to our target area. I still think that it represents an ancient trench."

Jack could see the multicolored lines converge into a tight pattern that looked like a road. "What are those?" Jack leaned over Gleason's shoulder and pointed at several dark objects that lined the path of the ancient trench.

Brent answered, "That's the puzzle. We don't know what they are. They're not large and seem to be made of a dense material or maybe filled with something."

"Like what?"

"Again, that's the mystery," Gleason answered.

"Could they be hoards of something?" Jack wanted to know.

"I suppose," Gleason said, "but we won't be able to tell until we dig one up."

"I count six of them," Jack said. "Why do they show up darker the farther from the site they are?"

Gleason shrugged. "My guess is that the farther away they are, the closer to the surface they are."

"That makes sense," Brent added. "The readings show that the trench descends toward here." He pointed at the blank area of the page. "Whoever built this started twenty-five meters over there and kept digging until they had a sloping trench."

Jack thought for a moment. "Not trench, gentlemen, a ramp."

"Why a ramp?" Brent asked. "If you're going to bury a treasure, why not dig a hole in the ground like the pirates did?"

"It all depends on the kind of treasure," Jack said. "There may be other factors too. How deep is the target?"

Gleason answered. "Deeper than our equipment can read. The image we have is just the top of whatever is down there. We may need to bring in more powerful ground survey equipment. We hadn't anticipated this kind of depth."

"So we know where it is but not how deep."

"We know the top of it is fifteen meters below grade," Gleason said. "That's the equivalent of fifty feet. . .over four stories below ground."

"Pretty deep hole for an ancient people to dig," Jack said. "I know I wouldn't want to be on the shovel team that digs out the last few feet of dirt. If the ground gives way, you'd be killed and buried all at the same time. But not necessarily in that order."

"There's a cheerful thought," Gleason said. "So you think they dug out a sloping ditch and used it as a ramp?"

"Exactly."

"Wait a minute," Brent said. "A deep ditch can collapse as easily as a deep hole. The situation could be just as deadly."

"Right you are, my young friend, but you're overlooking the obvious."

"Which is?"

"Shall I tell him?" Jack said to Gleason.

"How else is he going to learn?"

"You're assuming a ditch with vertical sides," Jack explained. "A ditch with sloping sides would be much safer for the workers and wouldn't require as much shoring."

"But it would require much more time and manpower."

"Perhaps," Jack said. "What's your survey show?"

Jack watched as the young intern studied the wide paper resting on the folding table. "A ditch. A wide ditch."

"That's what I see. I also think we'll find those dark objects are the remains of the shoring, stacked and neatly buried. The years have compressed them under the weight of the dirt."

"So when do we start digging?" Brent asked. "I'm dying to see what's down there."

"We all are, kid, but we do it by the book." Jack finished off his water and tossed the bottle in a nearby plastic trashcan. "Let's flag those dark objects. Once you have that done, I want a crew to chalk the ground indicating the center line of the ancient trench, its width, and each object we know about. The drilling rig is ready to take core samples. Once we've done the preliminary work, then we'll get our hands dirty."

"Can't we just dig a hole?" Brent asked.

"In due time," Jack said. "And due time will be soon. Now let's get to it. I want the flags in place and chalking done before Perry gets back."

"Are you telling me 'no,' Greg?" Anne made no effort to conceal her frustration. "I won't accept that."

Sergeant Greg Montulli leaned back in his desk chair. It protested with a loud squeak. As ranking deputy sheriff, Montulli was in charge of the Tejon substation of the Kern County Sheriff's Department. While larger cities provided their own police force, Tejon contracted with the county for police protection. Greg Montulli had been a deputy for twenty-six years, and now at the age of forty-seven, he was showing the results of middle age and too many hours behind a desk. "What do you want from me, Mayor?"

"I want you to go up there and find out what Sachs Engineering is planning."

"Has any law been broken?" Greg asked. He stroked his thick, graying mustache. "Unless there has, I won't get any farther than you."

"Since I don't know what they're doing, I don't know if any laws have been broken." Anne saw Greg cut a look at Bob, who was sitting in one of the side chairs near Greg's broad metal desk. She followed his gaze in time to see Bob shrug. "Knock it off," Anne snapped.

"What?" Bob said with feigned shock.

"That thing men do, looking at each other in a way that says, 'The woman's lost her marbles.' "

"I'm just sitting here being an obedient employee of the city," Bob said.

"Mayor," Greg began, "I can go out there and ask questions. But they can stonewall me too."

"But you're a cop. You show up in your uniform and ask pointed questions, and they're bound to tell you what's going on."

Greg shook his head. "This isn't the Old West, Mayor. It's improper of me to misuse police authority. I can ask questions, but unless I have reason to believe that they're there against the property owner's wishes, or that they're involved in an illegal activity, my hands are tied. I suppose I could call the land owners—"

"I already did that," Anne admitted. "I called them from the car. They said they knew all about it and that Sachs was there with their blessing."

"You don't let any grass grow under you feet, do you? There's nothing I can do."

"So you won't even try?" Anne said the words like a mother shaming a child. "You can't be bothered enough to go ask a few questions?"

"Mayor, if you tell me to go, I'll go, but I don't want you to think that I'm going to drive into the hills, flash my badge around, and come back with signed confessions."

"Doesn't it strike you as odd that they're keeping everything secret?"

"A little, but not much. We'll know in time. From what you've said about the equipment, they plan on doing some significant work. It's an open area, so we should be able to see something."

"What if the owner puts up a 'no trespassing sign'?" Anne inquired.

"Then we don't trespass without being aware of a crime or obtaining a warrant."

"This is unbelievable," Anne said with frustration.

"Look, Mayor," Greg began. "I've got a couple of things to do here, then I'll take a drive up there and introduce myself. Maybe a softer approach might work."

"What do you mean, softer?"

Neither man said anything. Anne looked at Bob, who raised his hands. "I'm just sitting here, Mayor."

She turned back to Deputy Montulli. "What do you mean, softer?"

"I don't mean any offense, Mayor, but for some reason, you have quite a head of steam up over this."

"I take my job seriously, Deputy; you'd be wise to do the same."

Greg sighed then said, "Yes, ma'am."

Dawes had clicked the "send" button only fifteen minutes before the phone rang. He'd spent the last hour sorting through the digital images taken from the mountain flyover. The pilot and his brother had worked fast, more to get rid of him, he was sure, than to show hustle for a client. He'd waited for the film from the digital camera to be transferred to a CD, but it had happened faster than he had any right to expect. It was a costly business, renting a pilot for an aerial survey and insisting that they put him ahead of others on their schedule. The pictures weren't cheap, either. The expense bill that he'd send would choke most bank accounts, especially after he added his fee and sizeable markup.

It had been an uncomfortable assignment so far. He hated flying, especially in small planes. It didn't seem right, all that metal and fuel winging through the air. Dawes knew that it would take only one little thing to go wrong before he would have been nothing more than a name on the lips of some newscaster.

The phone released another sharp trill, echoing off the walls of his Bakersfield office. He was tempted to ignore it, to let the answering machine take a message. His stomach was still queasy from the flight, and the drive back to the office from the airfield hadn't helped. A semi had overturned, closing all but one lane of the 99. He was stuck in traffic for an hour longer than it normally took to make the drive to his downtown office.

A glance at the caller ID screen on his phone made him change his mind. He snapped up the receiver and tried to sound professional. "Dawes Investigations."

"I was beginning to think you weren't there," a familiar voice said.

"I'm sorry, Mr. Olek," Dawes replied quickly. "For some reason the secretary didn't pick up." There was no secretary. Dawes was what he had always been, a lone player. He liked it that way, and he couldn't afford the cost of it being otherwise.

"The pictures came in a few moments ago. They look pretty good."

"Thank you," Dawes said, relieved that Olek was happy. "It's a good thing I have a high-speed connection. It would have taken all afternoon to send those on dial-up. Sorry I couldn't encrypt them, but I did encrypt the text."

Dawes felt unsettled. There was something about Olek that made him uneasy. Being a private detective required the ability to size up a person quickly. Olek had always been civil and professional, but there was something in his voice, in his choice of words, that unsettled Dawes.

"Did you see anything that is not revealed in the photos?" Olek asked.

"Not really. I used binoculars while I was up there. Made me sick as a dog too. The pictures pretty much caught everything. Well, there was one area that was hard to see. There's a grove of oak trees to the west side of the site. It looks like they may have something hidden under the trees, but I think it's just where their supervisors meet. You know, in the shade of the trees."

"I see no other such place on these photos, but I need to be sure."

"Sounds like more work coming my way," Dawes said.

"I want you to drive up there and see what you can see."

"When?" Dawes asked. "There's only a couple more hours of daylight, and it's going to take me at least an hour to get there."

"Then I won't keep you. Just see what you can and send me an E-mail report as soon as you get back."

"We're starting to get into overtime here, Mr. Olek."

"I understand that. You'll be compensated well. Be careful and discreet. I don't want anyone to know of our interest. That would be. . .unacceptable. Do you understand?"

The last words came over the phone dark and thick with unstated threat. "I'm a professional, Mr. Olek. Discreet is the only way I operate."

"That's good to know," Olek said, then abruptly hung up.

Dawes sat in his office chair with the receiver in his hand. More work was good news. His client base was thin at best and often nonexistent. That's why he answered his own phone in his one-room office. He had no desire to drive back to the area he had just flown over two hours before, but he did want to pay the rent. Setting the phone down, Dawes rose from his chair and started for the door.

Perry's nap had been short but sweet. He felt mildly refreshed, although he would have liked to have had another hour supine on the bed. But his mind wouldn't let him. He was eager to get back to the site to see how things were progressing. Perry knew everything would be going well under Jack's capable leadership, but being on-site was preferable. He took a quick shower and dressed in work clothes. He had one other task to do before leaving the motel room.

He seated himself behind the laptop computer and turned it on. As he waited for it to boot up, he looked at the rest of the setup. A small digital camera was clipped to the top of the computer's monitor next to the built-in microphone. A cable ran from the computer to a port in the wall. "Perfect," he said to himself. He checked his watch. The time was right.

The computer came to life quickly, and Perry typed in his password, brought up the program he wanted, and waited. A moment later a chat screen appeared. It was divided into two "windows." On one side was a white box in which text would appear, and on the other, a box in which an image would come to life. He wouldn't need the text box. The Internet would carry his words

82

and image over the miles. With a few clicks of the mouse buttons, he selected the person he wanted to talk to.

An image appeared, a woman with gray hair and determined eyes. It was the woman he met in the hospital months before, and next to her was Perry's newest buddy.

"Good evening, Claire," Perry said with a wide smile.

"Hello, Perry," Claire replied. "Did you enjoy your trip?"

"I'm glad to be back. Is that the world-famous Joseph Henri behind you?"

Joseph exploded into animated actions. "Perry. . .uhh. . .uhh. . . uhh. . .Perry." He waved then ran in a tight circle.

"Easy, buddy, you're going to make yourself dizzy."

"Perry. . .uhh."

Perry laughed. He'd set up the computer system in the Henri's home for the primary purpose of communicating with Joseph. He also had another reason: He wanted to see what Joseph would do with it.

That night in the hospital when he stood next to the bedside of Dr. Jamison Henri, the man whose life he had tried to save, he'd viewed Joseph as an unfortunate boy, mentally crippled by a fluke of unfortunate genetics. He soon learned that Joseph was something more than that.

Much more, he remembered. . . .

"The satchel is here," Claire Henri said, but her injured husband said nothing back, showed no reaction. He lay upon the bed, a shell of life. His skin was pale and moist, his eyes closed, his breathing made rhythmic by a device that pumped air into his lungs.

Claire stood erect again, and the boy took another half step closer to her, resting his head on her shoulder. He didn't look up, didn't look at the man on the bed.

"I thank you for what you have done," she said to Perry. Her eyes were wet, but no tears flowed. She was controlled, but he could see that a hurricane of emotions raged inside her. He had no doubt the show of strength was for the young man pressed against her side.

"I wish I could have done more," Perry replied.

"Most people would have done nothing," Claire said. "At least he's alive. Where there is life, there is hope."

Perry nodded. "I'm Perry Sachs." He held out a hand.

"I'm Claire Henri. This is Joseph." Joseph did nothing.

There was an uncomfortable pause, then Perry held out the leather case. "Your husband was very concerned about this."

"Yes, yes, he would be." Claire studied the case for a moment then took it, pulling it to her breast. "Did you. . .look inside?"

Perry shook his head. "No, ma'am."

"Most people would have, you know."

"Perhaps," Perry said softly. "It didn't belong to me, so I didn't look."

"Thank you, again."

"Are you and Joseph going to be all right?" Perry asked. "Do you have someone to stay with you tonight?"

"We're going to stay here. I want to be by my husband's side when. . .if things get worse."

She looked up at him, and this time, Perry saw a tear.

"I'm going up to the site in a minute, but I wanted to say hi to the resident genius. How's he doing?"

"Good for the most part," Claire said. Despite the fast connection, her image hesitated, but her voice came across uninterrupted. "But he's been a little agitated. He keeps saying your name."

"Odd," Perry said. Joseph was a savant and largely uncommunicative. He spoke words occasionally, but such times were rare. He had different ways of communicating. Since meeting Joseph, Perry had become a self-educated expert on Savant Syndrome. He knew of the relationship between left-brain damage and the ability of some to perform tasks far beyond what people with "normal" intelligence could do.

Names flooded Perry's mind, names of those incapable of caring for themselves yet who reached a level of accomplishment few could match.

There was the unusual musician Leslie Lemke. At just fourteen years of age, he played Tchaikovsky's Piano Concerto No. 1 without flaw, and he did so after hearing the music only once before while watching television. To make the feat more amazing, he played the piece even though he was blind, developmentally disabled, and afflicted with cerebral palsy. He continued to sing and play concerts in the U.S. and around the world, even though he had never had a piano lesson.

Then there was internationally known artist, Richard Wawro. Margaret Thatcher and Pope John Paul II had collected his work. Praised by art critics, Wawro produced artwork that touched heart and mind. But unlike other artists, Richard Wawro was autistic and unable to communicate with anyone.

To Perry, Kim Peek was the most fascinating savant. Peek had memorized seventy-six hundred books, could state the name of every city in the U.S. and all the highways that connect them, as well as cite their area codes, Zip codes, and television and radio stations. He could recognize most classical music, naming the composer, the composer's birth and death dates, as well as when the music was first published and performed. Developmentally disabled, he depended on his father for his daily needs.

In 1789, Benjamin Rush did research with such remarkable people. He described meeting one young man who, when asked how many seconds a man had lived if he lived seventy years, seventeen days and twelve hours, gave the correct answer ninety seconds later: 2,210,500,800 seconds—and he had taken into account seventeen leap years.

Joseph Henri was such a person. Unable to communicate more than a few words, he could calculate like a computer, remember whatever he had heard or seen and repeat it, draw it, or play it on the piano. Perry never ceased to be amazed by him. It was because of Joseph that Perry was in the motel room.

"Perry. . .uhh. . .uhh."

"He's been saying that all day," Claire said. "You sure must be on his mind. He's never this chatty."

"Maybe he knew I was going to call," Perry said. "How 'bout it, buddy. Did you know I was going to call?"

"Uhh. . .uhh. . .Perry."

"Did you draw any pictures today?"

"Uhh. . .Perry."

"He certainly did. He drew a landscape. That's odd too. He normally draws pictures of animals."

That was true, Perry reflected. Joseph could see an animal once and render it on paper at near photo quality. Claire had told him that he would spend hours on each drawing. He couldn't utter more than a half dozen words, but he could draw a bird with greater detail than John James Audubon.

Joseph disappeared from the camera's eye then returned a moment later with a large piece of paper in his hand. He held it tightly in his fists, crumpling the edges.

Claire chuckled. "I think he wants you to see his newest artwork."

Joseph shook the paper. Even over the video call, Perry could see that Joseph was disturbed.

Taking the picture from her son, Claire held it up to the camera. "Can you see this?" she asked.

"Pull it back just a little," Perry replied. "It's too close to the camera." Claire did as instructed, and the chalk drawing became clear. It was indeed a landscape. Perry had seen all of Joseph's drawings and not one had been a traditional landscape. He could see the vibrant greens, a mixture of several greens from what Perry could tell over the computer monitor. It was perfectly proportioned and balanced with an azure sky over rolling hills. Trees, thick and wide, populated the gentle slopes. They looked like the oaks that Perry had seen when he flew over the site in the helicopter—

A chilling disquiet ran through Perry.

The drawing *was* the site.

He leaned forward, straining his eyes to take in the picture. A cluster of oaks stood to the right, the very place he had stood a few hours before, reviewing the early survey data. Several other trees stood in various places. Dominating the picture was the open, sloped pasture rendered in verdant greens—with one exception. On the lower end of the slope was a spot, not green like the tall grass, but red—red like blood.

"When did he do this?" Perry asked. He had to push the words past lips that didn't want to move.

"This morning," Claire answered, lowering the picture. "He seemed a little sad, so I suggested that he draw. That always makes him feel better. Well, it usually makes him feel better."

"I don't understand," Perry admitted. "I don't know how this can be possible. Did you tell him about where we were going? I mean, did you describe the setting?"

"No. I've never been to Southern California."

Perry took a deep breath then released it slowly. The subject of the picture was unmistakable. Somehow, Joseph had portrayed exactly where he and his crew were working.

"Perry. . .uhh. . .uhh."

"It's a great picture, Joseph," Perry said with a broad smile. "You're the best artist in the world, buddy."

"Claire, has he drawn anything else today?"

"Just this. Why? You seem disturbed."

"Not disturbed, just puzzled." He told her about how the painting mirrored the work site.

"That is a coincidence," she said. "You really think it's that similar?"

"It's hard to tell because I'm viewing it over the computer, but it sure looks like it from here."

"What does the dark red spot mean?" she asked.

"I have no idea, but it seems to be right where we plan to dig."

CHAPTER 7

A lex Olek settled back in the leather chair and checked his seat belt for the third time. He was not a nervous flier, but he was impatient. He also wanted a drink from the onboard bar of the Citation X business jet. A splash of Crown Royal would fit the bill, but he was forced to wait until the aircraft was airborne and above the clouds that were dropping sheets of rain. The craft was perfectly capable of flying through rain. It was, after all, one of the best business jets on the market. It could cruise just below Mach 1, if it ever got off the ground.

Turning his attention to the entertainment center, he watched the stock reports scroll beneath the image of a CNN anchorwoman. The sound was muted. He had little interest in what the pretty brunette had to say. The real news was in the stock numbers.

The craft lurched forward then began a gentle roll as the pilot moved from the concrete apron to the runway. Once on the long, straight path, the pilot brought the jet to a complete stop, powered down the engines for a moment, then brought them up to speed. The jet moved forward, slowly at first, then accelerated with alarming speed. Rain on the wings began to run in rivulets off the metal skin. A few seconds later, Alex felt the craft break free of the ground and smoothly climb skyward. It bounced and shook slightly as it passed through the storm clouds but then settled into an easy glide.

Above the pillowed clouds, the sky was still bright, though dimming quickly as the sun settled toward the horizon. A gentle turn put the plane on course to the south. This would be his first visit to Southern California.

The decision to fly from Seattle to The Site (that was what Rutherford Straight had taken to calling it) was not impromptu. He knew he'd be making the journey the moment he learned that Sachs was onto something. Truth be told, all of this was still an assumption, but an educated one. They'd been unable to get direct information that Sachs Engineering had indeed come up with the right location. Every attempt to hack into their corporate computers had failed. What they did know was that Perry Sachs had rescued Dr. Jamison Henri, and that subsequently he'd had access to the material that Henri had always kept near.

They also knew that Sachs had visited the Henri home many times. Now, the fact that Perry Sachs had brought equipment and workers to a lightly populated area of the Tehachapi Mountains meant that Alex couldn't make the pieces of the puzzle work any other way. Sachs had done what Alex had failed to do.

The jet lowered its nose, decreasing the rate of climb. Alex released his seat belt, made his way to the bar, poured golden scotch into his glass, and dropped in two ice cubes. Although he was alone in the twenty-four-foot, ten-seater cabin, he raised his glass and said, "To fortune."

He hadn't told Dawes he was coming. He preferred to retain the advantage of surprise. Dawes worried Alex. He was the loose end. It was necessary to have a man on the scene, but it also presented problems. The more people who knew, the greater the risk of discovery. That was a fact, and he specialized in facts. Now that Alex was more convinced than ever that Sachs was onto something, he needed to be the one on the scene. The next stage of work couldn't be delegated. He would just have to deal with Dawes, one way or the other.

Perry piloted his Ford Explorer up the dirt road toward the site.

His mind was still saturated with the image that Joseph had drawn. Try as he might, he couldn't convince himself that it was a coincidence. There were too many similarities. Of all the trees that Joseph could have drawn, he drew oak trees—not tall pines or redwoods, not droopy willows, but mature oaks. And not only had he gotten the trees right, but he nailed their location. Where two trees were close on the site, they were close on the drawing, and the clutch of trees that they called "the office" had been perfectly rendered. It wasn't possible. But it was true. And it made no sense.

The Ford bounced and rocked as it moved over the uneven ground. Perry had to interrupt his mental wanderings to focus on the path ahead of him, but the moment the road rills smoothed out, he returned to his wonderings.

Joseph was unique in so many ways, but precognition wasn't one of his talents, at least as far as Perry knew. Had Perry mentioned oak trees? Had he spoken to Joseph of the rolling hills and green grass? No, he was sure he hadn't, and even if he had, he doubted that Joseph would have understood. *Then why,* he asked himself, *did Joseph draw such a picture?*

Something else bothered Perry. The picture included a landmark he'd not seen at the site: a crimson blotch on the ground. Joseph had placed it right where the early surveys placed the target of the dig.

"Doesn't make sense," Perry said to himself. Maybe someone from the site had spoken to Joseph, but he had to dismiss the idea. Of the group, only he had met the prodigy, and only a couple of others—Jack and Gleason—even knew of him.

Pictures? Perhaps Joseph had seen photos of the area, and after hearing that was where Perry was going, copied the image. It was remotely possible, but too difficult to believe. A photo book could contain such an image, but that was an unbelievable stretch. Still, he would ask Claire next time they talked.

Perry steered the big vehicle off the dirt road and onto the narrow path leading to the bottom of the slope that led to the work site. As he crested the small rise to the staging area, he saw the trucks and bus of the caravan. He also saw a white car with a red and blue light-bar on its roof. "This can't be good," he mumbled as he parked behind the patrol car, exited, and marched through the tall grass and up the slope.

He found what he expected. Under the canopy of oak branches stood Jack, Gleason, a sheriff's deputy, and the woman who had come banging on his motel door. Even from a hundred yards, he could recognize her short blond hair. She was standing with her hands on her hips and appeared to be doing all the talking. Several strides later, Perry was in earshot.

"You're being obstinate," the woman groused.

"And you're being. . ." Jack started. He trailed off as Perry approached.

"Annoying?" Perry suggested.

The woman and the officer turned.

"You!" she said.

"Most people call me Perry, but 'you' will work just as well."

"Perry," Jack said. "This is Mayor Anne Fitzgerald. She's concerned about what we're doing here."

"We've met," Perry said.

"You have?"

"She paid me a call at the motel room. I was expecting a basket of fruit but got the third degree instead."

"I didn't tell her where you were staying, Perry," Jack said. "No one here did."

"I know. Madam Mayor is persistent." He looked at the officer. His uniform nametag read GREG MONTULLI, and the three stripes on his sleeve said he was a sergeant. "Officer," he said with a nod.

"You are the man in charge?" Montulli asked.

"Yes. I'm Perry Sachs. How can I help you?"

"Well," the officer began. He seemed uncomfortable, and Perry thought he had reason to, considering the attitude of his mayor.

"You can tell me what you plan to do here."

"Dig a hole," Perry said flatly. "Did anyone offer you a drink? We have water, juice, and soda."

"No thanks," Anne said. "This isn't a social call."

Perry saw Montulli close his eyes then open them slowly. Clearly the man didn't want to be here. "I'm fine, but thanks for the offer. What do you mean, dig a hole?"

"Just that," Perry answered. "We plan on digging a hole."

"You sure have a lot of equipment to just dig a hole." Anne crossed her arms. Her back was now to Jack and Gleason. Both men rolled their eyes.

"Some holes require more equipment than others."

"I know who you are, Mr. Sachs," Anne said. "I know your company builds structures all over the world. Why would a builder dig a hole?"

"Mayor," Perry replied, "we've had this discussion. I'm under no obligation to tell you anything. This is not in the city limits, we have permission of the land owner, and we are doing nothing illegal."

"Why the secrets?"

"Secrets are our choice."

"Perhaps I can have a look at the printouts," Montulli suggested.

"I'm sorry, Officer, but you can't, unless you have a warrant."

"I can get one."

Perry recognized the bluff. "I doubt it, and even if you could, you don't have one now."

The deputy lowered his head. "May I have a word with you, Mr. Sachs?"

"Sure." Perry motioned toward the open field.

"I'm going with you," Anne insisted.

"No, you're not," Montulli snapped. The mayor froze mid-stride. The two walked a few yards away. After they had put some distance between themselves and the others Montulli said, "Listen. You and I both know that I'm on thin ice here. I can't make you tell me anything unless I suspect a crime, but if you could just give me something to quiet the mayor's nerves, then I can go home to my supper, and you can get on with digging your hole."

Perry smiled. "Stuck between the devil and the deep blue sea, eh?"

"You don't know the half of it."

"I can sympathize, Deputy, but I can't be of any help to you. We've done our homework and made certain we are breaking no laws. What we do here will have no impact on the county or the City of Tejon."

"Is it a government project?" Montulli probed.

"I'm not going to play twenty questions, Officer. I'm sorry to be such a stickler about this, but it's the way things must be."

The officer pursed his lips and frowned. "I want to be clear about one thing. If I get wind that anything illegal is going on up here, I'll be back, and I will shut you down."

"No need to worry, we're all good citizens here."

"I hope so," the officer said and started back; Perry followed.

"Let's go, Mayor," he said. "There's nothing that can be done here."

"But we do not know any more than when we came," she shot back.

"That's true, but we still need to call it a day."

"What if I don't want to go?" she asked.

"Suit yourself," Montulli replied. "But you came up here in my car. Unless you have another way of getting home, I suggest you come along."

"And if I choose to stay anyway?"

The officer sighed, turned, and looked her in the eye. "Then they will call and complain that you're being a public nuisance, or the landowner will call and say that you're trespassing, and I'll have to come up here and arrest you, and that may look bad on your résumé."

"You wouldn't dare!"

"I wouldn't have any choice. Now let's go."

Perry watched as the mayor stewed then relented. She strode

off without looking back, leaving the deputy to follow.

"There goes one unhappy woman," Jack said.

"I've got a feeling we're going to be seeing her again."

"No doubt," Jack agreed. "Come over to the table. Gleason and I have something to show you."

Julia Straight walked into Rutherford's office unannounced. Apart from Rutherford himself and the duty nurse, she was the only one on the planet with the identification card that allowed such access. It was a concession reluctantly given when Rutherford's health had reached the point that a simple cold could kill him.

Rutherford looked up from his monitor, his head bobbing slightly as his ever-weakening muscles tried to steady the weight of his skull and brain. His sister paused a few steps past the threshold and folded her arms. She was tall, just under six feet, a trait she never concealed. On dates she wore heels, even if the man was shorter than she. Thick mahogany hair flowed down past her shoulders. Her green eyes revealed a keen intellect nearly matching that of her brother. Science was never her interest, but business was. It was she who guided the fledgling RS BioDynamics from its early "garage" days to the financial force it was today. As president of the company, she answered only to Rutherford and the board, and the board had never had the courage to press her about anything.

"What?" Rutherford snapped.

"The nurse said you refused to eat your lunch."

"I'm not hungry. I'm busy. I have things on my mind." He looked back to the monitor.

"You're the one with multiple Ph.Ds. I'm just a simpleminded businessperson, but I'm pretty sure that eating is necessary for life."

"I know what I need."

"Good, we're in agreement. I'll send the nurse in, and you can have a meal."

"It's way past lunch time," Rutherford protested.

"That's my point. Take some soup, and then we can have dinner later."

"I don't want soup. Leave me to my work."

Julia walked over to her brother and kissed him on the forehead. "Work. It's always work with you."

Rutherford croaked a laugh. "And you're so different?"

"No, but I eat when I should. I need the fuel for brain and body. So do you."

"Neither my brain nor my body is hungry. I don't get much exercise, so I don't need much food."

"There's that sarcasm again." She looked at the computer monitor. "Pretty," she said. "Is that the place?"

"That's it. Alex obtained the photos from an operative he hired."

"Someone outside the company?" Julia didn't like this idea.

"He has it under control. He knows what he's doing. Look here." Rutherford moved his one responsive hand to a small joystick on the panel of his high-tech wheelchair. The infrared beam connected the panel to the computer. The picture grew larger on the screen. "I've digitally enhanced the image. You can see some of the equipment. They're definitely prepared to dig."

"You enhanced the photos? Yourself? Is there anything you can't do?"

"Yeah, get out of this chair. Stop patronizing me."

Julia took a couple of steps away. "You're lucky to have me, you know. I'm indispensable on so many levels."

"You're one of the richest women in the world, Julia. I made you that way."

Julia laughed. "I made me this way. You had the idea, you made the discoveries, you got the patents, but there's more to running RS BioDynamics than just that. Who arranged for the IPO that made you rich overnight? Who put together the staff, the marketing, and the corporate image? There is as much of my blood in this company as yours. I might add that there is as much dirt under my nails too."

"If I eat the soup, will you shut up?"

"Yes." She returned to the computer monitor, this time standing behind her invalid brother. "Do you think it will work?"

"It has to. It's the only hope I have."

"Then we'll make sure it works." Her tone turned icy. "No matter what."

Perry stood in the harsh glare of the lights his crew had erected earlier that day. Four banks of one-thousand-watt halide work lights shone down like artificial suns, casting shadows in four directions. It gave the pasture an otherworldly feel. The deep green of the grass was hued yellow under the artificial light. A stiff breeze blew through, rustling leaves and grass. In various spots, tiny yellow marker flags attached to wire stems fluttered in the wind. A short distance away, the muted, throaty rumble of the Ingersoll-Rand generator used to power the lights echoed off the soft hills.

Other noises filled the early evening, the most noticeable coming from the Diedrich D-50 all-terrain drilling rig. It was one of two that Perry had requested. The D-50 was the smaller one, designed for drilling and coring in areas with limited overhead space. The drill unit was attached to a four-wheel-drive truck with large black tires that were now sunk an inch into the soft soil. Perry watched as the hollow tube of the corer slowly bored into the ground. The shaft was small, only four inches in diameter, but large enough to make the initial coring.

Moving his attention from the D-50, Perry quickly took in the surroundings. Jack had, as always, done a superb job. The longer grass had been cut short; white chalk lines formed a grid on the ground. Yellow chalk lines delineated the width and run of the buried ramp and other artifacts shown by the surveys. Precision, forethought, determination—those were words that every project manager at Sachs Engineering understood. The concepts reached their pinnacle in men like Jack. Perry was satisfied.

Deeper and deeper the shaft went, filling its hollow interior with soil.

"How deep did you say this object was?" Perry asked.

"It's the closest to the surface, just over a meter."

"Over three feet," Perry muttered.

The sound of the four-cylinder diesel that drove the drill changed in pitch. "Sounds like we've encountered a little resistance."

Jack nodded. "It's about the right depth. How much deeper do you want to go?"

"A few more feet. I would rather have too much information than not enough."

Minutes turned into moments as Perry stood by impatiently. What he really wanted to do was bring in the backhoe and rip up whatever was down there. A good night's work and he could have everything dug up by breakfast, but that wasn't an option. Too much was at stake. He'd have to jump through all the hoops and record everything for future study. He glanced to his left and saw Brent with a video camera held to his eye. The lad was going to get quite an education.

The D-50, expertly handled by its operator, had reached two meters when Perry gave the signal to bring the coring up. The core was raised, secured, and detached from the drilling rig. A one-inch slit ran the length of its metal shaft. Perry, Jack, and Gleason laid it on the ground and rolled it until the slit could be seen.

"Looks like typical soil and rock," Jack said.

"This doesn't," Perry said. He was shining a small flashlight on a material darker than the dirt. He leaned over the area and placed his face close to the shaft. He touched the material with a finger. It felt organic. "Anyone have a pocket knife?"

"I do," Gleason said, reaching into his pants pocket. He handed a small penknife to Perry, who snapped it open and returned his attention to the tightly packed shaft. "You getting this, Brent?"

"Yes, sir, every pixel of it." The intern knelt down opposite Perry and to the side so that he had a clear angle on the sample.

The additional light from the camera was welcome help.

Perry touched the dark area with the knife blade, pressing it slightly. "Spongy," he announced, more to himself than anyone else. He then took the point of the knife and dug at the material. A chunk came through the slit easily. Perry picked up the piece and rubbed it between his fingers. It flaked off on his skin. He raised it to his nose and sniffed. Sour.

"Any guesses?" Jack asked.

"Yeah. I think it's wood—old wood."

"Like a tree branch or something?" Gleason inquired.

"Maybe," Perry said. "Whatever it is, it's been there a long time."

"Look at this," Brent said. He had moved the camera along the shaft. "Is that more wood?"

Perry shifted his gaze three feet down the core, which represented three more feet in depth. After repositioning himself, Perry repeated his actions. Gleason hunkered down beside him. "Looks the same."

"That pretty much rules out the tree branch idea."

"Why?" Brent asked.

"We drilled a perfectly vertical hole," Gleason explained. "What are the odds that we would come across two branches aligned one above the other?"

"It could happen," Brent said.

"But not likely," Gleason replied.

"I doubt they're branches," Perry said. "They're not very thick. I'm thinking we just drilled through some planks."

"Stop your smirking, Jack," Gleason said.

"I love being right," Jack replied. "Being a genius is a difficult cross to bear, but somehow I seem to manage."

"What are you guys yammering about?" Perry asked.

Gleason explained. "After the survey discovered the objects, Jack suggested they were the stacks of shoring left over by the people who did all this."

"I hope you didn't put any money on that, Jack." Perry was

staring at the core again.

"Hey, I don't like the sound of that," Jack said. "You're not going to embarrass me in front of my admirers, are you?"

"Yup. The wood is separated by loose soil. If it were stacked wood, I wouldn't expect there to be this kind of distance between the planks. I think what we have here is a box."

"Boxes hold things," Gleason said. "What do you suppose was in this one?"

"Hard to tell from what little information we have. The soil between the planks isn't compressed, so I'm guessing the box held most of its shape. Of course, it could be—" Perry stopped suddenly. He worked the knife through the slit again, this time prying a small brownish object from the core. He put it in the palm of his hand and studied it closely.

"What's that?" Brent asked. "It looks like. . . . It couldn't be."

"Gold?" Jack asked with a chuckle.

"No," Perry said somberly. "It's not gold. It's bone."

"Human?" Brent said. "I mean if it were human, it would mean that we just cored through a grave. Man, that creeps me out."

"We don't know it's human," Gleason said. "There's a lot of wildlife up here and always has been. It could be the jawbone of a muskrat or something."

Perry said nothing; he just gazed at Gleason for a moment. He had known Gleason for years and seldom had he encountered anyone sharper.

"Okay, okay," Gleason conceded. "We found it between what appears to be wood planks. Most people don't bury farm animals in caskets." He rubbed the back of his neck. "This could be bad."

"You got that right," Perry said.

"Wait, I don't get it," Brent admitted.

"If it's human, then we'll have to prove that it's not recent, or that this isn't an Indian burial."

"In other words, the authorities could shut us down." Brent lowered the camera.

"Or slow us down."

"What now?" Gleason asked.

"We have the wood and bone carbon-dated," Perry said. "I assumed we'd find some artifacts, so I made arrangements with a local university to do the work. I just didn't expect to be sending them a bone. If that's what it is. We also continue analyzing the core."

Jack walked to where Perry had been on his knees hovering over the coring. He lowered his great bulk to the ground and studied the long column before him, running his finger along the slit. He stopped. "Let me see that knife." Perry handed it over.

As gentle and methodical as Perry had been, Jack dug in the dirt between the wood layers and extracted a round object. He brushed the dirt away.

"Is that what I think it is?" Perry asked.

"I think so. It's extremely corroded, but I think we can rule out a Native American burial."

"Why is that?" Brent asked.

"Because Indians didn't carry coins."

Across the pasture and behind a stand of oak trees, a pair of eyes peered through binoculars at the brightly lit work area. To the side of one of the trees stood a tripod with a parabolic dish mounted to its top. A line ran from the sensitive microphone to a recording device and from the device to the audio input of the video camera that was mounted on a second aluminum tripod. The equipment's owner listened in through a headset. The wind chopped up the dialog he was recording, but he was getting enough.

Dawes smiled. "Not bad for a nearly broke private eye," he said to himself. "This ought to knock the socks off Olek."

CHAPTER 8

Anne slumped down in her favorite booth in the Coat of Arms restaurant, Tejon's only upscale eatery.

The city had no shortage of eating establishments. McDonald's, Burger King, and other expected fast-food joints dotted the main street that ran through town. A half dozen "sit-down" restaurants filled out the dining needs of the residents, but most were the typical fare found in any Southern California city: Chinese, Mexican, a steak house, and a barbeque joint.

The Coat of Arms was different. It was here that people went for a night out or to celebrate a special occasion. On weekends a live band played in the lounge, and reservations were required. Anne had a standing reservation and frequented the place whenever she entertained on city business. It was also the place she ate when depression came to visit.

She ordered a glass of Merlot and, without looking at the menu, rattled off her meal request: roast beef, red potatoes, and asparagus spears with hollandaise. Comfort food. Normally a light eater, the frustrations of the day had justified the heavy meal.

The restaurant was dimly lit in an effort to create a romantic tone. Candles flickered from cobalt blue tear-shaped jars. Anne moved her glass of wine in front of the dancing flame and stared into its crimson fluid. Light danced through the liquid like carefree nymphs skipping through a pond in a European forest. Anne wasn't feeling carefree.

"I can see the headline now," a voice said from her left. She turned to see David Branson. "Tejon mayor drowns sorrows in a flood of wine worthy of Bacchus himself."

Anne looked at Branson for a moment, trying to understand what he said. "Speak English, David. You're the editor of the town newspaper; you should be able to speak English."

Without an invitation, Branson lowered his lanky frame onto the bench seat of the booth and stared across the table. He was tall, painfully thin, and hair had left his head long ago. He had a keen mind and odd sense of humor. He struck Anne as the kind of person other kids picked on in school because he always tried to sound smarter than he was. "Bacchus. You know, the ancient god of wine and parties."

"I'm not partying. I'm just here having a little dinner. How did you know I was here?"

"I saw your car in the parking lot."

"You just happened to be driving by looking in parking lots for cars you recognized?" Anne took a sip of her drink.

"You want the truth?"

"I have no use for lies," Anne retorted. The comment sounded harsher than she meant.

Branson leaned forward and spoke in a conspiratorial whisper. "I heard about your journey into the hills. Also heard it didn't go well."

"How do you know about that?" Anne asked with surprise.

"Police scanner. I keep one in my office. When a deputy takes a civilian anywhere, it has to be called in. That goes for the cop on the beat and the head deputy sheriff for the substation. He told dispatch that he had you in the car. That made me curious."

Anne thought back and remembered that Deputy Montulli had made such a radio call. "There's nothing secret about that."

"I didn't say there was. I'm just telling you how I knew you went up into the hills. After hearing that, I sat by the scanner and listened with my finely tuned journalist's ear. Nothing, until he radioed that he was back in the car and headed to the station. I let some time pass and went to see the good constable. He didn't have much to say. Just that he drove you to private property to ask some construction workers a few questions."

"There you have it," Anne said.

"There's more. He let on that you were unhappy because they wouldn't tell you what they were doing."

"So?"

"So," Benson went on, "they're keeping secrets, and secrets are news. Skullduggery sells papers."

"What skullduggery?" Anne asked.

"I'm surprised you asked, Mayor." Benson leaned back in his chair. "From what I hear, you think they're doing something on the sly."

"I never said anything like that!"

"Haven't you? I did a little more research. I spoke to Bob Vincent." He quickly raised a hand. "Before you ask, Montulli told me you came to see him and Vincent was with you. Bob said he made a trip up there with you too. Two trips in one day."

"Just trying to do my job," Anne said. She took a deeper swallow of wine.

"Exactly what I'm trying to do, Mayor. I'm on your side. People keep secrets for a reason, and I think the public needs to know the effort you've spent looking out for their interests."

"Don't tell me you wrote an article about this." Anne felt a rush of warmth to her face, and she hoped it was just the alcohol.

"Of course I did." Benson gave a prideful smile. "I had to rework the layout for tomorrow's paper, but I got it above the fold on page one. It will be good press for you."

Anne leaned her head back and looked at the ceiling. "What," she began softly, "could you have written about? I asked a few questions; I learned nothing."

"I wrote about the secret, Mayor. The banner reads: Mayor

Uncovers Treasure Hunt."

The pit of Anne's stomach dropped like a freight elevator in free fall. "What makes you think there's a treasure?"

"Where there's smoke, there's fire; and where there are secrets, there are valuables."

"I can't believe you did that, David. I never said there was a treasure out there."

"What else could it be? We know it's not oil. That issue was settled decades ago. It's not a utility company project like new windmills. And if it was, why would there be such secrecy?"

"It's still a long leap to buried treasure."

"Ah," Branson shot back, "well, I never say what kind of treasure it is."

"You're leaving it up to your readers to make their own leaps in logic?"

"Why not?"

Anne lowered her head and rubbed her eyes. She sat in silence for a moment then drained the wine glass in a single gulp. "David?"

"Yes?"

"Go away. Go away now."

"Why? I've done you a favor. I've shown the voters of this city that they have a hands-on, take-no-guff mayor; someone willing to leave the office and search the hills for truth and to protect the city she loves."

Anne motioned for another glass of wine. The waiter nodded and disappeared into the back of the restaurant. "I'll tell you what the problem is, David. I didn't uncover a treasure hunt. All I know—and that is precious little—is that a group of workers with lots of equipment are up on the hillside doing something they don't want to talk about."

"That's the best part of it all, Mayor. That's the mystery, the MacGuffin. That's what my readers want. Small-town newspaper work is hardly an exciting endeavor. Even the most mundane of men get tired of reporting on petty crimes and farm sales."

"MacGuffin?"

"It's a term mystery writers use," Branson sighed. "It refers to a plot device, something that moves the plot of a book along, taking the reader with it."

"Are you writing mysteries now, David?"

"What's wrong with that? They say everyone has a novel in them."

"Just make sure *your* mysteries don't turn into *my* horror stories."

"I think you're missing the point, Mayor. This will be *good* for you and *great* for the paper. I'm planning a series of articles. I'm writing them all myself. In fact, I plan to go up to the site tomorrow to interview the workers."

"Good luck," Anne said. The words were sarcastic, but they were wasted on Benson.

"Luck is for amateurs, not for the press."

The waiter appeared and adroitly set Anne's plate of food on the table before her. He poured wine into her glass with a flourish. "Will the gentleman be joining you?" the waiter asked formally.

"No," Anne replied.

"Yes," Branson said. And he ordered the rib eye steak to prove it.

Perry rose from a kneeling position and stretched out the kinks in his back. He, Jack, Gleason, and Brent had spent the last hour meticulously studying the core sample. Moving the sample to one of the worktables in the oak grove would have made more sense, but the coin and bone fragment had riveted their attention.

"Okay," Perry said. "Let's get the samples out to the labs. Jack, you choose someone you trust to hand-carry the material out of here. The soil seems pretty straightforward, but I'm especially interested in the Carbon 14. I'll give you the names and numbers of the labs I want to use."

"Got it."

"Also, send the crew home. Keep three workers here. We have

metal detectors, right?"

"Four of them," Jack said.

"Good. Then let's keep four men. I want the whole area searched. Let's see if we can't find more things like this." Perry held up the corroded coin.

"Is that what I think it is?" Gleason asked.

Perry studied the coin for a moment, turning it so the construction lights illuminated its face. The coin was obsidian black and crusted with dirt. Perry rubbed his thumb over the image on one side. He could barely make out the image of a man's head in profile. Letters too worn to read ran close to the irregular rim. "If I were a betting man, I'd put money on it, but it still needs to be confirmed."

"So someone lost their lunch money?" Brent commented.

"It was lost a long time ago," Perry replied. "Here." He held out his hand, pinching the coin between his fingers. "Go take some photos of this. You can rinse it in water, but don't try to rub off the corrosion. We'll leave that to the experts."

Brent took the coin and stared at it for a moment. "It looks, weird. Irregular." He turned his attention back to Perry. "What are you guys going to do?"

"Dig, of course. I want to see what's down there."

"But we found a bone. You'd be digging up a grave."

Perry looked at Gleason. "You're right. He is smart."

"You want me to keep a couple of guys to work the shovels?" Jack asked.

Shaking his head, Perry said, "No. We need the exercise. You're starting to look flabby."

"Is that a fact?" Jack shot back. "Do you think you can remember which end of the shovel to hold?"

"I think I can figure it out."

Gleason, whose only calluses could be found on his fingertips from the hours he spent clicking the keys of a computer keyboard, looked dubious. "We have a backhoe, you know."

"Some things require a gentle touch," Perry said with a broad smile. "You can join the fun as soon as you pack up the samples."

Gleason groaned.

Rain plummeted from the Seattle sky in steady sheets on the large window overlooking the city's skyline. The window was enormous, reaching from floor to ceiling and running the length of the office. Streams of water ran down it in jagged artery and vein patterns. Rutherford stared through the glass and water veil. City lights scattered into starbursts of yellow and white.

The window-wall was a constant temptation for him. When he was first confined to a wheelchair, he'd adjusted the best he could. But when the standard wheelchair gave way to the fully electric device that now served as legs, feet, and spine, he fell into a deep depression. Strapped by a belt to the chair, it had become an extension of his psyche and a constant reminder of his impossible, hopeless affliction. How easy it would be to back the chair up to the opposite wall and then run it full speed into the glass pane.

He had even done the research, calculating the impact speed necessary to explode the tempered glass into "dice." That's what the manufacturer of the glass had called it. Tempered glass was designed not to fragment into shards but to disintegrate into small cubes of glass, hence "dice." He'd done the math and realized it could be done. He would need greater speed than his electric wheelchair could provide, but that could be arranged. No one questioned his requests. If he requested a V-8 engine be strapped under his chair, it would be done.

It was possible, he knew. He had even read about a man who, while showing Japanese businessmen his new office complex, tried to emphasize how safe the glass exterior walls were by throwing his body against the pane. The glass was designed to give, to flex and rebound. It didn't, and the exuberant executive plunged fourteen stories to his death.

The desire to plow through the transparent barrier and pitch himself headfirst to the concrete sidewalk below grew with each passing week. The thought, ironically, comforted him. In a sense, he told himself, he was already dead; at least his body was dead. He was a living mind in a decaying corpse. Each tick of the clock brought him closer to total dysfunction. He wouldn't wait that long. If he didn't find a cure soon, then he would take the "heroic" way out.

Heroic way. How often had he heard suicide referred to as the coward's way? Those who said such things were healthy and vital. They knew nothing of the courage it took for people like him to get out of bed each morning; to endure the condescending conversations of those who spoke and acted like the disease was nothing, that it didn't affect the way they looked at him; but their eyes always betrayed them. Each glance said, "Poor devil, I'm glad I'm not in his situation."

What did they know? He was powerful and respected in the scientific community. He had secured his place in the annals of pure science as well as in the growing scientific entrepreneurship. Only five people in the country had more financial resources than he; and only nine in the world. If all his wealth were known, if all the sequestered, hidden businesses were revealed, those other billionaires would quickly fall behind in the ranking.

But what did that matter? If he owned the world's wealth, he'd still have ALS, he'd still have trouble swallowing his own saliva, and he'd still be welded to the chair he hated so much.

Rutherford heard the door open behind him. "Alex has reported in," a voice said. Since only two people could open that door without his permission, he knew it was either his duty nurse or his sister.

"And?" He didn't bother turning his chair. The voice was enough to identify the visitor.

Julia Rutherford stepped to her brother and joined his gaze into the wet night. She stroked his hair with her long, red-painted fingernails. Rutherford felt some of the tension leave. The gentle gesture always relaxed him, and somehow, Julia always knew when he needed to relax.

"He landed in Barstow and has rented a car."

"Under an assumed name, I assume." It was a rare attempt at humor.

"Ah, word play," Julia said lightly. "He knows what he's doing. No one will be able to trace him to the corporation. He'd cut out his own tongue rather than betray you."

"Why, Julia," Rutherford began. He noticed that there was a slight slur in his words. "Do I hear romantic tones in your voice?" He feared the day when he would be forced to communicate through a speech synthesizer. Others had learned to do so. The famous physicist Steven Hawking seemed to manage with it, but for Rutherford it would be the final insult.

"There's nothing between us. You know that." She paused. "Would you object if there were?"

"A hypothetical question?"

"Of course."

Rutherford unleashed a raspy chuckle. "Let's see, my most trusted employee and my sister walking hand-in-hand through the park. I have trouble picturing it."

"I'm not the hand-in-hand type."

"No, I don't suppose you are," Rutherford said. He changed the subject. "I have something for you to do."

"What is it?"

"It's a bit of unpleasantness, I'm afraid. Does that bother you?"

"Never has before."

"No, it hasn't. Maybe you and Alex *are* a pair."

"Does that have anything to do with the assignment?"

Rutherford turned his wobbly head and looked up at his sister. Any man in the world would want her. She possessed beauty and brains and knew how to use them to her advantage. Before her lay a rich life. Unlike him, she could know companionship, maybe even love. Those opportunities were gone for him, but not for her.

Like him, she was unencumbered with a conscience. It was a family trait. "I want you to pay a visit to someone."

"Social visit? Business? Other?"

"Other," he said flatly. "I prefer you do it alone. We've had trouble in the past with. . .contract help."

Julia continued to stroke Rutherford's hair. "I'm listening."

"Drawing another picture?" Claire asked Joseph, not expecting a reply. Joseph sat at the dining room table, hunched over a large piece of butcher paper. Joseph often spent hours drawing and going through paper at an alarming rate. The solution had been to buy a large roll of white paper used by butchers to wrap meat. The roll lay on a spindle in a wood rack. Jamison had made the rack for the roll, and Claire had carelessly remarked that it looked like a giant toilet paper dispenser. She wished she could take the comment back.

The small house in which they lived suffered from an "open floor" plan. Claire had grown up in an older home in which each room was. . .well, a room. Ever since the sixties, architects and builders had decided that people wanted rooms that were open to others. In her home only a counter separated the kitchen from the dining room, and both were open to the living room. A "great room," they called it. Claire didn't think it was so great, but the house had been in their budget, and it was close to the seminary where Jamison worked. Over time, the house grew on her. Now she couldn't imagine living anywhere else. This house had become home, open floor plan and all.

It was emptier now. It had been six months since that night when the phone call came, when she quickly dressed Joseph and they drove across town to the hospital. After Jamison's death, Claire had come to believe in ghosts. Not disembodied spirits that haunted castles and homes—that was foreign to her Christian doctrine. The Bible spoke of angels, of demons, and other unseen intelligences, but not ghosts as most people understood them.

Still, Jamison "haunted" the house in a thousand little things that reminded her of him each day. His clothing had been moved out, his shoes given away or tossed, but that couldn't remove the impression a man left on a house after living in it for nearly twenty-five years.

Sometimes she'd find something he'd put away, something in the back of a cupboard or on the shelf in a closet. Once she found a bar of shaving soap, the kind that was put in a cup and whipped into lather by a bristled brush. He'd used such soap when they first married, reluctant to yield to shaving cream in a can. He had once said that foam from a can was "unearned." Claire had never been certain what that meant.

Jamison had been an odd man, more comfortable with books and journals than with people. Learning and teaching had been his two great loves, that and his family. Jamison and Joseph had been as close as any father and son. In private, and very seldom did he reveal a hint of the guilt he felt over his savant boy. "Bad genetics," he had said one night while she and he lay in bed. "I gave him bad genes."

She had tried to convince him that it was no fault of his. "Such things just happen." He agreed, but she knew he wasn't convinced. He never spoke of it again, but she was certain that the guilt remained alive, sequestered in some corner of his great intellect.

Claire was fearful of Joseph's response. He'd never seen death before, but her fears had been unnecessary. Joseph had shown no emotion at all. He was a mystery; he'd always been so. He seldom displayed his feelings, but when he did, the display always seemed exaggerated for the event. At times he would cry for no apparent reason, and in those times when sadness seemed appropriate, he was unmoved. There was no understanding a person like Joseph. Intuitively she knew that he processed information, processed life in a way no normal person could fathom.

"Dinner is almost ready," Claire said. Again there was no response; again she expected none. Still she spoke to him as if he could be induced into a conversation. "I made your favorite: macaroni and cheese." Claire didn't know if it was Joseph's favorite or not. He showed no signs of pleasure or disgust when eating. Her only indication was that Joseph ate more macaroni and cheese than anything else she set before him.

Filling two bowls with the pasta and creamy yellow sauce, she added a few shakes of pepper then walked to the table. "How are we going to eat if you have the table covered in crayons and paper—"

Claire dropped the bowls on the carpet.

The earth gave way easily to the assault of shovels. Still, by choice, the digging went slow. Perry and Jack put blade to ground while Gleason poked around looking for any hints of artifacts in the pile of dirt that they had accumulated.

Three feet down, the digging turned delicate. Based on the depth indicated by the coring, Perry knew that he had to be close to the first layer of wood. Instead of plunging the blade of the shovel down into the dirt, he now scraped through it layer by layer.

The texture of the ground changed.

"Hand me your trowel," Perry said to Gleason, who surrendered it gladly. Lying on his stomach, Perry eased over the edge, reaching down into the pit. The trowel extended his reach by nine inches. Gently he scraped away another layer of soil. "It's definitely wood and it's man made. Where's Brent?"

"Still in the grove."

"Have him bring his camera."

Jack let out a shout, and Brent jogged over. Perry pushed himself to his feet. "Get some shots of the pit," he said.

Brent looked down in the hole. "It's pretty dark in there. The work lights are leaving too much shadow. I think the camera's flood will do the job, but just to be sure, let's take a few shots, then let's do a few more with additional light."

"I'll bring over a work lamp," Jack said then trotted off.

Brent started shooting. "Not much to see. The camera is having trouble with its auto focus. It's hard to tell where the dirt leaves off and the wood top begins."

"Wait a second," Perry said. Once again he lowered himself to the ground, reached in, and set the trowel on the wood surface. Rising again, he asked, "Does that help?"

Brent raised the camera back to his eye, aiming its lens at the trowel. "Yeah, that'll do it. The camera can focus on that."

Jack showed up with a metal, yellow stand upon which was mounted a high-intensity work light. "It's plugged into the generator. This should drive away the shadows."

The taller construction lights set up earlier that day bathed the hillside in harsh white light, but the walls of the pit cast deep ebony shadows. A more direct light was needed.

"Hang on a sec," Brent said. He shot another few seconds of video, the camera's electric light shining brightly across the ground. "Okay, fire away."

Jack flipped the switch, and light flooded the open maw. Perry felt like he was looking down the gullet of some great fish. The direct light bathed the pit. Brent started the camera again. "This should work great."

"Okay," Perry said. "I'm going to try and pull back some of the boards. Brent, I want you to videotape the whole thing."

"Will do."

Perry went to his belly again then inched himself forward. He felt a pair of hands grab his ankles. With Jack anchoring him, he knew he wasn't going to fall in headfirst. Placing one glove on the surface of the wood, he picked up the trowel and gently pressed the point of it in the wood. It gave easily.

"It's seen better days," Perry said. "The surface is a little spongy and uneven." With his head down, blood began to rush to his brain. He could feel the pressure build. He had no desire to stay in that position longer than necessary.

He set the trowel down and began brushing dirt aside, searching for what he knew must be there. Probing fingers felt along the coarse surface. Found it—the hole the corer had bored. The digging had filled it with dirt, but Perry cleaned it out easily. The hole was large enough for him to slip in two gloved fingers. A chill ran down his spine as he wondered exactly what he was sticking his fingers into. Driving the discomfort from his mind, he gave a gentle pull. Under the glare of the work light and Brent's video camera light, he saw the board bow slightly.

Before pulling again, he looked around the perimeter of the boards. They had been careful to clean as much dirt away from the edges as possible. He took a deep breath and tugged. The board bowed more but remained intact. Still, it gave more than fresh lumber would have. *This has been buried a long time,* he said to himself.

"Kinda reminds you of an old horror movie," Brent said. "You know, something hidden behind the locked door or in the closet or something."

Perry turned toward the bright light of the video camera and scowled. "Did I just hear young Mr. Hapgood volunteer for a stint in upside down excavation?"

"That's what I heard," Jack said.

"Me too," added Gleason.

"No way," Brent said quickly. "They teach us at Caltech not to get into situations like this."

Perry returned his attention to the task. Positioning his left hand directly under him, he tightened his fingers in the bore hole and pulled. The plank that he used for counterforce bowed down as the board with the core hole bowed up but remained fixed. Perry relaxed for a moment.

"You want me to give it a try?" Jack asked.

Jack could do the job all right, but this was something that Perry wanted to do for himself. "What, and give you something to hold over my head for years to come?"

"Pride goes before a fall," Jack said and loosened his grip on Perry's ankles. For a moment, Perry was certain that he was going to drop face first into the pit.

"Very funny," Perry cried. "Now, if you don't mind, hang on to me. I'm going to apply a little more muscle."

"Oh, so you do want me to do it," Jack jibed.

Perry chose to ignore him. He dug his fingers into the hole a little deeper and curled them to grip the wood. Perry yanked and pulled, grunting with each effort. On the fourth tug a hunk of wood gave way. Perry tossed it up to Gleason. The bore hole was now large enough to admit Perry's whole hand. Able to get a better grip as a result, Perry gave a hard jerk. The lower section gave way, some of the wood crumbling at the edges and in his hand. The piece was too large to toss up the grade, especially from Perry's inverted position. He started to say something, but Gleason had anticipated the need. He reached down with bare hands and took the chunk of lumber.

"Feels slimy," he complained.

"So would you if you had been buried down there," Jack said.

"It's a plank, all right," Gleason said. "About two inches thick, I'd say."

"That's what I like about engineers," Brent said. "The precision of their conversation."

"Hey, Perry," Gleason said. "Brent really wants to come down there."

"Okay, okay," Brent said. "I'll be quiet."

Perry ignored the banter. He recognized it as nerves, something he understood. He switched the position of his hands so that he could grab the remaining half of the central plank. He pulled and the lumber came free easily. "Got it."

"Hang on," Gleason said. "Let me come around." A shadow fell over the opening as Gleason stood in front of the work light, leaving only the weaker light of the video camera.

A second later Perry felt his friend take the board from his hand. He could feel the pounding of his heart in his head as it tried to compensate for his inverted position.

"Got it."

"You're in my light, buddy," Perry said. The exertion and the added blood pressure in his head made Perry feel dizzy. Sweat was running into his eyes and his vision was blurring.

"Sorry."

He could tell that Gleason had stepped aside because the light once again flooded the pit. Perry blinked hard and tried to focus his eyes. At first he saw a glint of metal, then a dark, dirty white tube, like PVC. The synapse in his brain started firing madly as he realized that the tube was not a tube at all, but a long bone. Instinctively, Perry pulled back an inch and turned his head, only to find himself staring into the empty eye sockets of a skull. Where once eyes had been, there were vacant holes.

"Yeow!" Perry shouted. Suddenly he was moving, not by choice but because Jack had pulled him up in a single, fluid motion. One moment he was staring into the face of a dead man, the next, he was face down on the ground. He was instantly thankful.

Quickly, Perry righted himself and came to his feet. His heart rattled in his chest. He leaned over and placed his hands on his knees, forcing his heart to slow and his breathing to ease.

"You okay, pal?" Jack asked. Perry could hear the concern in his voice.

"I was expecting to see that, but. . .I wasn't expecting to see that. If that makes any sense." Perry inhaled deeply then stepped to the edge of the opening, an opening that could now properly be called a grave.

"It makes sense to me," Jack offered. "It's not every day you pop open a coffin."

"Oh, major cool," Brent said.

Perry exchanged glances with his friends then watched as Brent approached the edge of the opening. He squatted down to get the camera a little closer.

"Cool?" Gleason asked.

"More than cool," Brent said. "Beyond cool. No one at school is going to believe this. Do we pull up the rest of the boards?"

"No," Perry said as he returned to the edge of the hole, brushing dirt from his shirt and pants.

"But I can't get a good shot. I can only see part of the skeleton."

"We wait," Perry said firmly. "We have to make sure this is chronicled correctly. It's time to call in our expert."

"Expert?" Brent asked.

"We have a staff archeologist at Sachs Engineering," Perry explained. "You build in enough places and sooner or later you're going to dig something up that may be important."

"This has happened before?"

"Not like this," Perry answered. "Not to me."

"So what are we going to do?" Brent pressed.

"Jack," Perry began. "Let's get a cover on this and set up some stakes and construction tape."

"I have a tarp. I'll stake that to the ground."

"Good. I'll let you take care of that. In the meantime, I'm going back to the motel to place a phone call."

"What's he wearing?" Brent asked. "It looks like metal."

"It's. . ." Perry began. He looked back in the pit. "It's a shield. Now let's call it a day."

"Shield?" Dawes whispered to himself. He adjusted the headset that allowed him to hear the conversation being picked up by the parabolic "spy" microphone. "This is getting weird." He checked the tape deck that he was using to record the conversation. The cassette was running out of tape. He was thinking of changing it when he heard the words, "Let's call it a day."

"It's about time," he mumbled. "This isn't my idea of fun." Through the binoculars, he saw the man he had come to know through his monitoring as Perry walking away. "If he's calling it a day, then so am I."

Dawes shut off the recorder, took off the headset, and rolled onto his back. He had been lying behind a tree for the last four hours, and every muscle in his body ached. *Bed is going to feel good tonight,* he told himself. Dinner and bed. That was the ticket.

Tomorrow he'd give his report to the mighty Mr. Olek and send him a bill—a big one.

CHAPTER 9

J oseph Henri gave no response when Claire dropped the bowls of macaroni and cheese. His attention was fixed on the wide, dull white paper stretched over the dining room table. His head hovered above the drawing by an inch, his nose by a fraction of an inch.

He drew another line. Claire ignored the mess on the carpet and stepped behind her son to study the artwork. There were two drawings, something she hadn't noticed before. Joseph worked diligently on the second, his thin shoulders and large head blocking most of it from view. To his right, there was a drawing that Claire could see clearly. It was unlike anything he had done before. The landscape picture of green hills and oak trees had been a departure from his usual detailed drawings of animals, but this was beyond anything she could imagine him doing.

"What does this mean?" she asked Joseph in a whisper. Joseph gave no indication of hearing her. He pressed the crayon down, moving it slowly along the paper, then he set the crayon down and rubbed the line with his finger, forcing the colored material into the fiber of the paper. He did this anytime he drew, regardless of the medium he was using: pencil, chalk, or markers. The material stained his fingertips. Claire had cleaned those fingers every night for many years.

The picture was dark, ominous, like the foreboding image on the cover of a suspense novel. It chilled her. More frightening than the dark hues was the setting of the image. It was a setting she knew well; she'd been living in it for close to a quarter of a century. She was staring at a startlingly realistic portrayal of the place she and Joseph called home. She could see the windows with the stygian gloom of night pressing in. She recognized the living room furniture, the fireplace, and even the cantilevered brass lamp that bowed on its support over the worn leather sofa.

The front door was also easy to recognize, but what she couldn't identify was the dark figure just inside the opening. Joseph had drawn the image in silhouette black, featureless, like a ghost draped in black satin. Something was in the specter's hand. The object seemed small and lacked sufficient detail to be identified.

A frigid uneasiness swept over Claire. Not wanting to do so, but feeling compelled by a curiosity stronger then her fear, she placed a hand on Joseph's shoulder and gently pulled back. She had to see the next picture.

The doorbell rang. Claire jumped back, gasped, and raised a hand to her mouth. "Oh," she said to Joseph. "That scared me." She lowered her hand to her chest. Her heart was tripping like a machine gun. She took a deep breath.

"Uh. . .uhh. . .uhh." Joseph began to rock in his chair, fingering a green crayon in his hand.

Again the bell rang. The sound of it seemed sharper, louder than it should. Claire walked to the door, placed a hand on the doorknob. She stopped. Joseph's drawing flashed to her mind. She swallowed. "Who. . .who is it?"

"Mrs. Henri?" A woman's voice. "I'm sorry to bother you, Mrs. Henri, but I'm here about your husband."

Husband? She weighed the wisdom of stating that he had died. Claire looked through the peephole in the door. She could make out a figure, but it was too dark to see more than the fact that someone stood on her porch. She flipped a switch next to the door, and the front porch light came on. Again she placed her eye to the peephole. A woman stood outside. The fish-eye lens allowed Claire to see the visitor was well dressed and carried a briefcase.

"My husband is not here right now," Claire said, choosing not to reveal that she and Joseph were alone.

"Yes, ma'am, I know," the woman said. "My name is Veronica, and I'm with the life insurance company. I'm here to straighten things out, to clear up a mistake."

"I'm not aware of any mistakes," Claire said.

"Yes, ma'am. I work with the auditing department. You were underpaid. We owe you money."

Claire took a step back from the door. She had received a small settlement from the life insurance policy Jamison's school provided. It had been enough to cover burial costs, but little more.

"I'm afraid I don't understand," Claire said through the door.

"If I might have a moment of your time, I can explain," the woman said.

Claire looked through the peephole again and saw just the woman. Unlocking the door, she opened it a few inches and peered around the door and past the jamb. The woman smiled, revealing a perfect row of white teeth.

"I'm sorry to bother you at. . ." she stopped and looked at her watch. "Oh, I didn't realize it was after six. I'm going to have to hurry."

"Hurry?" Claire said.

"Yes, I have to catch a plane back to Los Angeles in less than an hour. This evening has been a nightmare. I flew in to give you this check and get your signature. My rental car broke down, and I had to have it towed. The rental agency gave me another car, but the whole thing took much longer than it should. Actually, it shouldn't have happened at all."

"You flew here from L.A. just to give me a check? Couldn't you have mailed it?"

"Normally we would, but it requires a signature first which means we would have to send you the form to sign, wait for you to send it back, then requisition the check, wait for it to be processed, then lose more time mailing it to you. I had to come up here to audit one of our local offices, so I volunteered to bring it myself. Your case is. . .special to me."

"Special?"

The woman looked down; her dark hair fell around her face. She took in a lungful of air then released it. "Like your husband, my husband was killed by an act of violence. It was road rage. Someone didn't like the way my husband was driving, pulled a gun, and killed him. It happens in L.A., but until then it was something I only heard about on the news. So, I thought I'd bring the check myself and see how you're doing."

"I'm so sorry," Claire said as she pulled the door back. "Please come in." As the woman passed, Claire could see that she was dressed in a black, professional-looking pantsuit.

"I promise not to take long. I really need to get to the airport."

Claire closed the door. "I appreciate the extra effort," she said as she twisted the latch on the door, locking it, a habit of many years. "You said your name was Veronica?"

There was no answer. Claire turned and saw the woman standing next to Joseph. He was leaning away from her.

"Uh. . .uhh."

"You must be Joseph," the woman said with a broad smile. She looked down. "It looks likes you had a little accident."

"Yes, I dropped our dinner."

The woman pulled one of the dining room chairs back and set the briefcase on it. Popping the latches, she swung the top open, reached in, and removed a small object. Claire recognized it immediately. The stranger she had let in the house was holding a syringe. With no hesitation, the woman removed the plastic shield from the needle, turned to Joseph, and jammed the needle through his shirt and into the meaty part of his shoulder, then pressed the plunger.

"Owww. . .ahhh. . .uhh. . .uhh."

"No!" Claire shouted, but the attack was over before she could take a step. "What have you done?" She started forward but seized mid-step as the woman raised the hypo to Joseph's neck.

"Don't make me hurt your son." Deftly the attacker pulled the plunger back. "There's nothing but air in the hypo now, but air in the carotid artery would be. . .unpleasant for your son."

"What do you want?" Claire demanded, tears flooding her eyes. Her son was in danger, and there was nothing she could do about it.

"I want you and your boy."

"What did you put in him?"

"I poisoned him, Mrs. Henri. But not to worry, I have an antidote."

"Why would you poison my son?"

"We don't have time for twenty questions," the woman snapped. "The injection will begin working in a few moments, and your son will be dead in thirty minutes if he doesn't receive the counteragent before then."

"I'm calling the police." Claire started for the phone.

"Feel free, but by the time they get Joseph to a hospital, do a blood draw, and identify the toxin, he will be dead. So make your call, Mrs. Henri. Just know that you will be killing your son when you do."

"What. . .I mean. . ."

"Let me fill you in. We're going for a ride in my car. We're going to leave in the next sixty seconds. Any longer and we run the risk of Joseph leaving this world. Once we get to our destination, I will inject him with the antitoxin. Got it?"

Joseph rubbed his shoulder. "Owwww."

"Okay, okay. Let's go."

The woman looked down at the table. "What are these drawings?"

"It's just something Joseph does."

"Really? Interesting. Especially this one of your living room."

Claire saw the woman's eyes track to the other drawing. "This is fascinating too. I'm taking it with me. Get your son. Remember, give me any grief and your son will not see the sunrise tomorrow."

"I won't give you any trouble. But please hurry."

"Good thinking. Now we have only one other concern."

Claire felt sick. "What?"

"Traffic was really bad tonight. You had better pray that we don't get hung up on the freeway. Congestion can be murder."

Claire had already started praying.

Perry made his call to the office and jotted down a few notes in his project diary. He kept the journal on the computer and under three levels of password protection. His laptop came equipped with a biometric security feature that read the fingerprint of his right index finger. Precaution was paramount for many of the projects undertaken by Sachs Engineering. Part of obtaining government contracts around the world was demonstrating a high level of security.

Shutting his computer down, Perry rubbed his eyes. The little nap earlier that day had been too short to do more than take the edge off his weariness, but it was too early to sleep. Even if he did yield to temptation and climb up on the bed, he doubted sleep would come. His mind still raced with what he'd seen in the bottom of the pit. The skeleton haunted his mind. Perry had come to expect the unusual in this project, but finding the remains of a man hidden beneath a bowed rectangular shield had not occurred to him. Still it proved the point. It was undeniable proof that they were in the right spot.

He thought of the other five dark objects revealed by the ground surveys. Were they coffins too? It wouldn't surprise him. A guilty sense of desecration flowed over him. They were digging in a cemetery created long ago, undisturbed for centuries.

Perry rolled his head from side to side, working out the kinks from the day's travel and work. He then gazed around the room and noticed a blinking red light on the phone. It flashed in a rhythmic cadence. Someone had left a message. Placing the receiver to his ear, he punched the button marked "0." The night manager answered.

"This is Perry Sachs, you have a message for me?"

"Yes, sir. Just a moment, I'll connect you."

Perry heard a tone then a recorded message. "Mr. Sachs. This is Mayor Anne Fitzgerald. I was hoping we could meet." Perry sighed. It was the last thing he wanted to do, but that changed a moment later. "I want to. . ." She stopped as if the words were stuck in her throat. "I want to give you a heads-up about something. I'm going to be at O'Tool's Pub a few blocks from where you're staying." She gave directions. "It's close enough to walk if you want. I hope you'll come. It would be to your advantage." The message ended, and Perry hung up.

His inclination was to ignore the call. The first two encounters with the woman had left a bad taste in his mouth, rendering a third conversation far from appealing. But he was intrigued. "I want to give you a heads-up on something," she had said. That was sufficiently cryptic to titillate his interest. The project was too important not to have all the information available. "O'Tool's Pub," he said, shaking his head. "Okay, Madam Mayor. I'll bite."

Perry took a quick shower and donned clean clothes; his others were soiled with dirt and grass stains. Stepping into the warm night, he walked the two-and-a-half blocks to the pub.

The place was as Perry had imagined it: a pseudo-Irish bar in a Southern California village. Dark wood paneling covered the walls, and the only light in the room came from several wrought iron fixtures hanging from a high, open-beamed ceiling. Small square tables, each with four matching chairs, dominated the center of the room. Along the backside was a long, wood bar with a shiny brass foot rail. Bottles of alcohol sat on a counter behind the bar and on the racks that framed an oval mirror. A single television set was tucked away in a corner of the ceiling. A baseball game played there in silence. Around the other three walls were tall-backed booths,

A TREASURE DEEP

intimate in size and decor.

Perry glanced around, feeling out of place and off balance. Bars were foreign territory to him.

"Mr. Sachs." Perry recognized the voice and turned to see Anne Fitzgerald waving to him from the corner booth. He nodded and approached.

"I got your message," Perry said and offered a small smile.

"I figured you did. . .since you're here, I mean. Have a seat." She motioned to the bench seat opposite her.

Perry sat down and leaned over the table. Anne wore the same clothing he had seen her in early in the day. In front of her was a short, wide glass filled with a golden liquid.

A woman appeared next to the table as if by magic. Perry looked up at her. She was rail thin and wore a European barmaid outfit. She looked barely old enough to legally be in a bar. Looking at Perry she smiled, turned to the mayor, and winked. "What can I get ya?"

Perry hadn't considered that. "What kind of fruit juice do you have?"

"Fruit juice?" The cocktail waitress seemed surprised. "This is a bar, sweetheart. We sell beer, wine, and spirits, not fruit juice. How about a scotch like the mayor here?"

Perry looked at the glass and shook his head. "No thanks. But I'll tell you what. Don't they make a drink with vodka and orange juice?"

"Sure. It's called a screwdriver."

"Good," Perry said. "I'll have one of those."

"Attaboy," the waitress said.

"Hold the vodka," Perry added.

The waitress rolled her eyes and walked away.

"I hope I didn't offend her," Perry said.

"She's seen it all," the mayor said. "It would take a lot to offend her."

"She doesn't look old enough to have seen much of anything, Mayor."

126

"Don't let her youth fool you. . .and please call me Anne." She raised the glass to her lips.

"Only if you call me Perry."

"That's easy enough. Thanks for meeting with me."

"It's my pleasure, but I need to say right up front that I'm not answering any questions about the project."

Anne made a face. "My life would be a lot easier if you weren't so stubborn."

Perry laughed. "I was thinking the same thing about you."

The waitress came back and set a glass of watered down orange juice on a cocktail napkin. "There you go, sir. Go easy on that now." She zipped away.

"I think my sarcasm detector just went off," Perry said.

Anne raised her glass. "To stubbornness."

Perry raised his glass and gave a gentlemanly nod. He took a sip. The orange juice was weak and thin. He set the glass down.

"So what is it?" Anne asked. "Recovering alcoholic or health nut?"

"What do you mean?"

"The virgin orange juice. Are you a recovering drunk or a health nut?"

"Neither. There are people who choose not to drink alcohol. I'm one of them."

"I used to be that way," she replied, then raised her glass and took a sip. "Not anymore."

Perry detected a sadness and anger in her words. He wondered whether he was being invited to probe a little deeper, but uncertainty sealed his lips.

"How long have you been mayor?" Perry asked. It seemed an innocent and safe enough question.

"Not long. I've been on the city council for three years. Each year a mayor is selected from the council, not elected like in bigger cities. That's a little too general, I suppose. Some small cities elect their mayor in open elections, but in most towns our size, it just rotates through the council members."

"Do you like it?" Perry chose to pursue the small talk. Maybe they could find some common ground that would move them beyond an adversarial relationship.

"I suppose. I mean I returned to it not long after I moved here from Ridgeline."

"Ridgeline?"

"It's a small town in the San Bernardino Mountains. I served on the council close to ten years there and was mayor for six years."

"But then you moved here, exchanging one mountain community for another."

"Ridgeline is much higher than Tejon. We got a fair amount of snow each year, and the trees were pines, not oaks. There's quite a difference."

"And what brought you to Tejon?" Perry asked, sipping his orange juice and pretending to enjoy it.

"Death."

The reply was blunt and delivered with resignation. Perry was uncertain what to say. "It appears I've stumbled into a sensitive area."

Anne shrugged. "My husband was killed several years ago, and my father died two months after that. Three months later, my mom had a stroke. We lost her too."

"I'm sorry."

"Yeah, me too. We were close. All of us. Mom, Dad, my sister. They say bad news comes in threes. It sure did for me."

"You have a sister?"

"Yes. The jewel in the crown of Ridgeline. A medical doctor. Smart cookie."

She paused and blinked several times then added, "You know, my sister knew a Perry Sachs. You don't know a Gates McClure, do you?"

Perry shook his head. "I've never been to Ridgeline. I imagine there are other men with the same name."

"You're sure? He's an attorney. You didn't used to be a lawyer, did you?"

"No need to be insulting," Perry quipped. "I've never been a lawyer or anything other than an engineer. So your sister is still in Ridgeline?"

"Yes. She's a lot tougher than me. She had her practice to keep her going. I needed a change." Anne took a larger gulp of the Scotch then set the glass down. "How about you? Your family still around?"

Perry nodded. "I come from a small family. Just me and my parents."

"An only child, huh?"

"I was enough for my parents." Perry paused then decided to get on with things. "You said you wanted to give me a heads-up about something."

She ran a finger along the rim of the glass. "I know I've been a pain," Anne said. "And just to keep the record straight, I plan on remaining a nuisance until I find out exactly what you're doing and why. But something has come up that's beyond even me. I thought I'd tell you now, since you're sure to find out tomorrow."

"You called in the national guard?" Perry joked.

"No, but it's an idea. Tomorrow's paper has a front-page article about what you're doing up in the hills."

"What? How?" Perry asked. "No one knows what we're doing up there."

"That doesn't seem to be a problem for David."

"David?"

"David Branson. He's the editor of the local paper. As you might guess, there isn't a lot in our town to fill up more than a few columns of newsprint. Slow news means slow subscriptions and ad sales. David also has a bit of an imagination."

"And just what has he imagined we're doing?" Perry pressed. He was unhappy with what he was hearing.

"I haven't read the article, but he hunted me down this evening while I was having dinner. Have you had dinner? They make a decent sandwich here."

"No, and I'm losing what little appetite I had."

Anne frowned and looked down into her scotch. Perry expected her to hoist it for another belt. She didn't. "Anyway, apparently David's headline is going to read 'Mayor Uncovers Treasure Hunt,' or some nonsense like that. I don't remember exactly, but it's along those lines."

Perry leaned back in the booth and sighed. "Sounds like he's making you look good."

"Like I said, I haven't read it, but I imagine that's what he has on his mind."

"That and increasing circulation."

"Yeah, that too."

"Do you think anyone will believe it?" Perry inquired.

Anne shrugged then raised her eyes from the glass. "I had nothing to do with this. That isn't my way. If I want to know something, I ask the person with the answers."

"So I've noticed."

"Yeah, well, I've never been accused of being shy and retiring."

"There's no way to stop the presses?"

"None that I know of. I only know of one thing that will help: Tell the truth. Let David run a story about what you're really doing up there."

"Is that what all this is about? Some kind of scheme to get me to reveal a secret or two?"

"No, not at all. I told you I had nothing to do with it."

Perry tried to hold back the disgust he was feeling. "I'm sorry, Mayor, but all this seems a little too contrived."

Anne leaned over the table and spoke in hard, hushed tones. "You listen to me, Mr. High-and-Mighty-Engineer. I took the initiative to set up this little meeting. I could have just let everything run its course. Tomorrow you could have awakened to this problem, and it would have been no skin off my nose. I suggest telling David what you're doing to take the mystery out of it. Tell him anything, lie if you want to, but the die has been cast. Everyone in town is going to think you're up at the Trujillo ranch digging up gold doubloons or something."

"Did you tell him about our presence?"

"What's to tell? You drove your convoy right through town. Hundreds of people saw your crew roll by."

"I'm not buying that. How did he know we were at the Trujillo Ranch?"

At first Anne didn't speak. Instead she stared back through angry eyes. "He did his research. He's resourceful, I'll say that." Anne shook her head. "You'll have visitors. At least some, maybe a lot. I don't know. I just thought you should know."

"This isn't fair to the Trujillos. They don't deserve to have people crawling all over their land. I should let them know."

"I imagine David has spoken to them," Anne said, "but he didn't say so specifically."

"They don't need the stress."

"It shouldn't be that bad."

Perry looked at Anne for several moments. "Do you know Hector Trujillo?"

"Can't say that I do."

"He's dying, Mayor. I seriously doubt he would appreciate a line of people coming by to ask questions about something they don't understand."

"Then tell the people so they will know."

"Do you think they will believe anything I say after that article hits? You and your buddy have just told everyone that there's gold in the hills. You have no idea what you've done."

Perry stood, reached for his wallet, and pulled out the first bill he saw. . .a twenty, and dropped it on the table.

"I didn't do anything," Anne protested. "I've told you, I'm as much a victim as you."

"Really? In one day, you've tracked down our location, made two trips to the site, harassed some of my crew, came banging on my motel room door, tried to involve the police, and inadvertently cranked up the media."

"But. . ."

"Do you really think it's going to end here?" Perry asked sharply. "What happens when some local radio show reads about it? Who knows, maybe television stations will be down with their cameras whirring."

Perry turned and marched from the pub and into a night of darkness that matched his mood.

Anne watched as Perry strode toward the door and exited into the night. She felt hollow, devoid of any value. Her intentions had been legitimate. While she wanted to know exactly what Perry was up to, she had no desire to find out through skullduggery. Silently she cursed David Branson.

"Is your friend coming back?" The waitress stood by the table.

"No."

"He didn't finish his orange juice," she said with a smirk. "Ha, big guy like that and all he wants is juice."

"Let it go," Anne snapped.

"Sure thing, Mayor. How about you? You want another scotch?"

Anne studied the tumbler; it was as empty as she felt. *Yes,* she told herself. Yes, she did want another scotch. "No," her voice said. "Excuse me." Anne rose, paid her tab, and walked toward the door.

Joseph Henri sat in the backseat of a car he couldn't describe. He rocked and rocked, stopped, rubbed his arm, then started rocking again. He turned and looked out the window nearest him. Light from buildings and street lamps fluoresced through drops of rain on the window. He turned to look at his mother. Her eyes were raining too. Looking back at the window, he crossed his arms and stared at the glass ornamented with droplets.

He counted the drops. Then he counted them again. With each new raindrop, Joseph recounted. He also counted the cars that passed, the lampposts on the sidewalks, and the windows in each building they passed.

The car began to move faster, and the street grew wider. This road was more interesting. It had evenly spaced white lines that zipped past.

Joseph counted the lines.

CHAPTER 10

D r. Kenneth Curtis sat in the passenger seat of the Ford Explorer with his head back and his eyes closed in sleep.

Perry couldn't blame him. After all, it had been he who had called him in the late evening. It was only dinnertime in California, but Boston was on the other coast and three hours further along in the night. While he had not awakened the archeologist, he had insisted that he pack a few things and make the flight west that evening. Arrangements had been made, and at 6:10 that morning, the weary academic arrived at the small airport in Bakersfield. No sooner was the man's luggage loaded than he was seated in the passenger seat, fast asleep. He didn't move during the forty-mile trip back to Tejon.

Initially, Perry had intended to hire a helicopter to fly Dr. Curtis to the site, but after Anne Fitzgerald's revelation the night before, he thought the extra time spent in the car would draw much less attention than a helicopter swooping into the mountains.

There was a small bump as Perry turned from the paved road onto the dirt path he had traveled several times in the last twenty-four hours. Curtis was jarred awake.

"Enjoy your nap, Professor?" Perry asked.

"Too little, too short." His voice was higher than might be expected of a 250-pound man, especially when that weight was

133

compacted into a five-foot-nine frame.

"I apologize for the rushed trip, but I promise that you'll be amazed."

"I'm fifty-six years old and have dug holes on three continents. I'm beyond being surprised."

"Care to bet a pizza on that?"

"Sure. I want Canadian bacon on mine." He rubbed his eyes and repositioned his bulk in the seat. "I should get a gourmet meal for being made to fly in that puddle jumper I just crossed the country in."

"I tried to get you the corporate jet, but Dad had dibs on it."

"How is your father?"

"Well and very active. I don't think he'll ever retire. Of course, I haven't seen him much over the last six weeks or so. I've been working overseas. Scotland, actually."

"Sounds nice," Curtis said. "Now enough of the small talk. Spill the beans. What is so important that it costs me a night's sleep?"

"I'm not going to say. If I did, you wouldn't believe me. You're going to have to wait five more minutes. You don't have a heart condition, do you?"

"Oh, please," Curtis said. "I can survive whatever trinket you've uncovered."

"Wait until you see this trinket."

The academic huffed. "Let me guess. We're in Southern California, so you've probably come across something Native American. . . maybe even a graveyard. Is that it? You've dug up an Indian grave, and you want me to verify it? Probably Yokut, Chumash, or some other Uto-Aztecans."

"Nothing so simple, Dr. Curtis." Perry steered from the dirt road to the access path. He saw the trucks and equipment parked alongside. "Let's take a walk. I'll have someone run your things to the motel."

"This isn't going to be a lengthy stay, is it? I'm doing some research for your father."

"I'll let you decide." Perry parked and led the chunky scientist up the grade, taking the ascent slower than he would if alone. A few minutes later they stood under the canopy of oak leaves that covered their "office." Jack, Gleason, and Brent were there waiting. Brent looked as if he had been dragged from bed.

"A real paradise," Curtis said between panting breaths. The men exchanged greetings. "Did you guys bring coffee?"

"We brought a thermos of the high octane stuff," Gleason said. "I'll get you a cup."

"Bring some oxygen too," Curtis said. "The air seems a little thin."

"We're about five-thousand feet above sea level, Doctor," Jack said. "That's a little higher than Boston."

"That would explain it," Curtis replied.

Perry looked around. "Everything looks the same as we left it."

"Where's your crew?" Curtis asked, taking the coffee from Gleason.

"We gave them the day off," Perry said. "We wanted to give you some elbow room. I can have some up here in short order if you need them."

"Let them relax. Whatever you found has been in the ground for a long while; another day won't matter."

Jack caught Perry's eye. "You have told him, haven't you?"

"Why ruin the surprise?"

"Okay, boys. Enough of the Indiana Jones melodrama. Show me what you've stumbled across."

Perry motioned with an exaggerated flourish to the open pasture, then started for the hole they had dug the previous evening. A yellow ribbon similar to police crime tape was stretched around four metal stakes driven into the ground near the dig's corners. Covering the opening was a wide panel of brown canvas held in place by several large rocks. Curtis stepped to the east side of the tarp and waited for the great unveiling. He sipped his coffee casually, like a man looking at his garden. Jack and Gleason removed the rocks while Brent videotaped the process. Once the anchors were removed, Perry reached under the tape barricade, took hold of the heavy material in both hands, and took several steps back, pulling the covering from its place. The early morning sun flooded the opening.

Dr. Curtis dropped his cup.

"Whoa!" Brent said and shifted the camera's eye down to the cavity in the earth.

Perry threw the tarpaulin to the side and then caught a look of Jack's expression. Not a man easily shocked, Jack's jaw dropped like an elevator. Gleason paled and became wide-eyed.

Stepping forward, Perry peered down expecting to see the skeleton he had met face-to-face last night. What he saw turned his stomach. The skeleton had company. A man, dressed in jeans and a sweatshirt, lay face down in the pit. A trowel protruded from his back, just left of the spine. Perry could see that it had been turned and directed to pass through the victim's ribs. It didn't take a doctor to realize the pointed blade had reached the heart.

Ignoring his instincts to back away, Perry approached, knelt, and bent over the body. He reached to the side of the man's neck and felt for a pulse. His skin was cold, and there was no pulse.

Perry looked up. Everyone was staring at him. He shook his head.

"I. . ." Curtis swallowed hard. "I take it that this isn't what you wanted me to see."

"Brent," Perry said, ignoring Curtis's uncomfortable quip, "drive into town and tell the sheriff's department what we've found here."

"Got it." Brent was off at a jog.

"Can't you just call them on a cell phone?" Curtis asked.

"Not from here. Cell coverage in the area is spotty at best. We're only two miles out of town. The police can be here soon."

"Any idea who our friend is?" Gleason asked. He looked pale to Perry.

"I've never seen him," Perry said. Jack agreed.

"You know," Gleason said softly. "With all due respect our. . . guest, he's going to cause a lot of trouble."

Perry knew where Gleason was headed. "That crossed my mind too."

"I don't follow," Curtis said.

"There are two bodies in the pit," said Perry. "Just below this poor guy is a skeleton that shouldn't be here." Perry paused as he thought about how to phrase his next words. "Our ground penetrating surveys found a buried object. We cored and found wood and what looked like a piece of bone. We excavated and discovered several planks. I'm sure now that it's a type of coffin. Inside are the remains of a person—a man."

"How do you know it's a man?" Curtis pressed.

"There's a metal shield over a portion of his body; a bowed, rectangular shield. Since I removed only one plank I couldn't see the whole thing, but I saw enough. There is an emblem of an eagle on the shield."

Curtis looked more shocked than when he first looked in the pit and saw the murdered man. "Are you. . .are you telling me that there is a Roman legionnaire in that hole?"

"You're the expert, but I've read a little history here and there, and that's my first, best guess."

"That's not possible," Curtis shot back. "Not possible at all. It's preposterous."

"I saw it too, Doc," Jack said.

"Me too," Gleason added.

"No. You're mistaken. It's impossible, I tell you. It must be some kind of prank."

"That's what you're here to find out," Perry said.

"Guys," Gleason said, "I think we may have a bigger challenge before us."

"Greater than a murder?" Jack asked.

"Maybe," Gleason said. "That trowel is ours. It was the one Perry was using last night."

❖❖❖

The phone by Anne's bed rang with an obnoxious trill. It took three rings to break through the cocoon of sleep encasing her mind. She fumbled for the receiver.

"What?"

Her voice was little more than a gravelly croak. She cleared her throat and tried to ignore the thick film that coated her mouth. The taste was bad, as if she had spent the night dining on day-old carrion. It was the price of drinking scotch. She smacked her lips once and tried again: "Hello."

"Sorry to wake you, Mayor," the caller said. "But I knew you'd want to know."

"Who is this?"

"Sergeant Montulli."

Anne sat up in bed and crossed her legs. She ran a hand through the tangle of her hair. "Sorry, Greg. I was asleep." She looked at the clock. Six-thirty. Greg never called that early. As she thought about it, Greg never called her at home. Something was wrong.

"I figured as much, but I knew you'd have my head if I didn't let you know."

"Let me know what, Greg?" Disquiet percolated in her already sour stomach.

"There's been a murder at the Sachs site. Someone from their crew drove to the substation and spoke to the duty officer. He called me at home."

"Who was killed?" The news had snapped Anne awake.

"I don't know yet. I'm heading up there in a few minutes to secure the site. I'll have the office call the detectives in Bakersfield."

"I'm going with you."

"There's no need for that. I have limited traffic in the area. You'd just be. . ." He trailed off.

"I'd be what? In the way?"

"I was going to say bored."

Anne knew he was lying. "I'm going up there. You want to

pick me up or do I drive myself?"

"You'd better drive yourself," he conceded. "I may be there for quite awhile."

"I'll be there in thirty minutes." Anne hung up without another word. Tossing the covers back, she moved into the bathroom and emerged twenty minutes later scrubbed, groomed, and with a minimum of makeup. Striding to the closet, she wondered what one wore to a murder scene. Remembering the slope she had to scale last time she was there, she chose a pair of stonewashed denims and a striped camp shirt. Donning a pair of sneakers, Anne headed for the door.

Claire sat in a dim and dusty room. A meager amount of light was able to push through the window and around the plywood that covered it. There was just enough light for her to know that the sun had risen, but nothing more. The room was the size of a small bedroom and had clearly been uninhabited for a long while. Dust covered the floor and the single throw rug that rested in the middle. Joseph lay on the rug in a fetal position.

Claire did what she had done every few moments since their capture: She checked his breathing. To her relief, she saw his chest rising and falling in an even rhythm. The woman who had identified herself as Veronica, and who had so deftly injected Joseph, had driven them to this spot. They had changed vehicles once, moving from a sedan to a panel truck. Once in the truck, she and Joseph were blindfolded. Joseph submitted to the indignity without protest. Claire had expected him to pull away, but he allowed his eyes to be shielded. It was as if he understood what was going on.

Nor did Claire fight back. She doubted she could defeat the much younger woman in a struggle, and it would have been counterproductive to try. Poison was coursing through her son's body; he needed the antidote quickly. She had no option other than complete submission.

The remainder of the trip seemed interminably long. Seconds

lasted eons; each mile passed slowly. With each minute that crept by, Claire expected to hear something horrible from Joseph: a moan of pain, a scream of agony, or vomiting. Such terrors never came.

The van stopped sometime later, and the back doors opened. "This way," the woman said. "Leave your blindfolds on."

A rush of salt air poured into the vehicle. Rising, Claire felt for the side of the van with one hand while reaching for Joseph with the other. "Please," Claire pleaded. "Give him the antidote. It's been a long time. Please, before it's too late."

The woman didn't respond. She guided them down from the van with hands Claire found surprisingly strong. Once on the ground, she felt a hand on the back of her neck.

"We're going to take a few steps forward then stop," the woman said. "You'll hear a door open. I'll guide you through. You'll be able to take your blindfolds off then, but wait until I tell you. Understood?"

"The antidote. Please," Claire pleaded. Tears were beginning to run. "Let's hurry before it's too late."

They took the steps, heard the door open, and were guided inside. The air was musty and carried a hint of mildew. The sound of the door closing behind them echoed loudly. Claire's head was pulled back roughly, and the blindfold was stripped away.

Blinking several times, Claire quickly took in her surroundings. She was standing in a cavernous room with a ceiling that hovered twenty feet above her. A single light burned from its lamp in the ceiling, weakly pushing back the darkness. It was a warehouse. Salt air and a warehouse. They were at the docks, the shipping center on Elliot Bay. That much she could deduce, but there were many such buildings in Seattle. One thing was clear; this building had been out of service for a long time.

"To the stairs," the abductor said, pointing to a set of wood stairs against one of the walls. The stairs led to a second floor door that Claire assumed had once been the building's office.

"You promised to give him the antidote. You said if we cooperate you'd—"

"Just get to the stairs," the woman snapped and gave Claire a shove.

Turning to Joseph, Claire removed his blindfold, took his hand, and started for the stairs. The steps squeaked eerily under their weight. Claire was certain that the rickety construction would give way and plunge her and Joseph to certain injury.

"Through the door."

Claire reached the landing, saw a door, and opened it. She also saw a shiny band of metal, a latch, and a large padlock. This room was to become their prison, and Claire could think of nothing to do about it.

Once inside she turned to the door. Veronica, if that was her name, stood there staring at the two. "Now?" Claire asked. "Please. Let's not wait another minute."

The woman shook her head. "Sorry," she said.

"You promised," Claire objected, knowing how stupid the appeal sounded. Expecting someone who had abducted them under threat of death could be trusted in what she said was ludicrous, but pleading was the only tool she had.

"I lied," the woman said and shut the door. Claire heard the latch and lock being set. A dim incandescent bulb in an old floor lamp lighted the room.

The rest of the night had passed in blazing anxiety. Claire sat in the only chair the room offered, a rusty, metal folding chair. Joseph sat on the floor next to her and leaned his head on her thigh. She stroked his hair and waited for the awful moment to arrive.

Demons of despair plied her mind with thoughts of burying the only family she had left. Without Joseph, she saw no reason to continue living. All that she had cared for would be gone. When he died, her spirit would die.

Minutes turned into moments.

A few times she had risen from her seat and tried to open the door, even kicking it repeatedly, but got only pain for her efforts. Still, she had to try. She had tried to pry off the thick plywood that covered the window, but it wouldn't budge. Moving the light closer to the covered opening, she saw that someone had used a dozen drywall screws to fix the wood panel to the wall. There was no way she could remove it without tools.

Claire had reluctantly faced the truth of the matter: She and Joseph were stuck where they were, and there was nothing she could do about it.

Moments turned into hours.

The horrible specter of death hadn't come. Joseph showed no signs of illness. When he had first lain down on the threadbare carpet, Claire had joined him, draping an arm over him as an embrace of love and as a way to monitor his breathing. His breathing slowed, but not like a man dying, like a man sleeping. In the abysmal black of the room, Claire thanked God for every rise and fall of her son's chest, for every inhalation.

Joseph slept.

Claire prayed.

Night turned to day.

Joseph continued to live. It was making sense now. The woman had lied about her intentions and had lied about the poison. It was the cruelest abuse Claire had ever suffered, and for the first time in her life, she found herself hating another human. Her husband's assailant had remained faceless and nameless to her. He'd been tried in court, but Claire didn't attend. Joseph's care was too demanding of her time. This was different. She'd seen face-to-face her son's attacker; she'd felt the woman's strong, cold hands on her body. That made her too real not to hate.

Then the hate was extinguished with the cold of fear. Hate was a foreign emotion for Claire; fear she was familiar with.

Again, Claire did all that was left to her: She prayed. Prayer had been a part of her life since childhood; faith a companion for just as long. Her own death seemed a small thing. Her concern was Joseph.

Why do they want my son?

Brent arrived at the site sucking air in heavy inhalations. He approached Perry and the others, nodded a greeting, leaned over, and placed his hands on his knees.

"What'd ya do, kid?" Jack asked. "Run all the way back from Tejon?"

He shook his head then stood erect. After one more deep breath he said, "We have company."

"Deputies," Perry said. "That's why we sent you."

"No, not the police or sheriffs or whatever they are. They're on the way too. I'm talking about the others."

"I don't like the sound of that," Perry said. His thoughts ran to the newspaper article Anne had warned him about.

"I noticed a couple of cars behind me," Brent said. "I didn't think much about it until they followed me up the dirt road. I know you've been really secretive about this project, so I assumed you didn't want visitors."

"You assumed right, but I was expecting it."

"Really?" Brent said.

"I'm afraid so." Perry explained about the article and his meeting with Anne Fitzgerald.

"So people are going to read that and think we've found a hoard of gold or something," Brent said. He paused. "Have we. . .I mean, have you?"

"Not like you're thinking," Jack inserted.

"How far behind you were they?" Perry inquired. His calm exterior was a shell that held his anger in check.

"Not far. I ran up the hill in hopes that they wouldn't see which direction I went. Not that it matters."

Perry knew what he meant. The equipment parked on the dirt path would be a giveaway, as would the wild grass beaten down by the workers moving up and down the hill.

"I'm new to all this secret construction stuff," Brent said, "but I don't imagine having spectators is a good thing."

"You're right, but we have other concerns. This is now a crime scene. If people start wandering around, they will contaminate the scene. The sheriff's department won't be happy about that."

"Everyone with me," Perry said as he started down the slope. "Except you, Dr. Curtis. Maybe you should wait in the office." He motioned to the oak grove. "Let's see if we can keep our guests off the site."

They hadn't gone far when they saw five people struggling up the grade. Perry quickly sized them up: two couples of retirement age and a bald, thin man dressed too nicely for the terrain. What bothered him even more was what he saw behind them: three other vehicles pulling to a stop. Clearly, the secret was out.

"Can I help you?" Perry asked forcefully. He gave a short smile. The winded visitors stopped and took a moment to catch their breath.

"Who are you?" one man asked. He was round and decked out in work boots, a T-shirt, and jeans that were held up by a pair of wide, multicolored suspenders that made Perry think of a circus clown. The man was missing a front tooth and sported a week's worth of stubble on his chin.

"My name is Perry. May I ask who you are?"

"Sure, I'm Don Tucker. People just call me Tuck. This is my wife, Shirley." Shirley smiled sweetly.

"I'm Dr. Lloyd Stevens," the other man said. Unlike the first, he was clean-shaven and had bright eyes. "I'm the town dentist. This is my wife, Nancy."

Perry nodded in their direction and wondered why Tuck didn't visit Lloyd in his office. He looked at the skinny visitor.

"I'm David Branson. I'm the editor of the. . ."

". . .local paper," Perry said, finishing the sentence. The words seemed sour in his mouth.

"You've heard of me?" Branson smiled.

"The mayor mentioned you," Perry explained.

"All good, I hope." The editor let slip a little chuckle.

Perry frowned and cut his eyes to the others. "How may I help you?"

Tuck looked at Perry and then the others; his eyes widened as he took in Jack's size. "We was having some eggs down at the café and readin' the paper. Came across the article about what you guys are doing up here. I said to Shirley, 'What say we take a run up there and say hi to the folks, maybe see what they're doing.' "

"Same with us," Lloyd said.

"I'm afraid there's not much to see," Perry said. "We've only been here for a day."

"Is it true there's treasure?" Branson blurted. "A treasure right here in town?"

"Actually, we're in the county, not the City of Tejon—"

"Don't matter none," Tuck interjected. "We're all neighbors. So how about it? Can we get a tour?"

"I'm afraid not," Perry said diplomatically. "This is private property and—"

"It ain't *your* private property," Tuck insisted. "It belongs to the Trujillos. That's what the paper said. Ain't that right, Branson?"

"Yes," the editor said. "That's what I wrote in the article."

"We have a contract with the Trujillo family," Perry said.

"What kind of contract?" Branson asked.

"I'm not at liberty to discuss that."

"Maybe I should just drive up and talk to Trujillo myself," Tuck said. "We're friends, after all."

"You're friends with Mr. Trujillo?" Perry asked. "How is he doing?"

Tuck's eyes shot back and forth for a moment, and he licked his lips. "Fine. He's doing great."

"No, he's not," Perry said. "He's sick. A friend would know that."

Stepping forward, Tuck raised a finger and jabbed it against Perry's chest. The scraggly man smelled of aged Old Spice and strong coffee. "You callin' me a liar?"

Jack cleared his throat and moved a step closer to Tucker, who immediately took a quick stride back.

"We have a right to know what goes on in our county," the dentist said.

"That's right," Branson interjected. "It's my responsibility to report what's going on."

"Perhaps," Perry said. "But I'm afraid I can't let you on the site."

"Who's gonna stop—" Tucker began then stopped. Perry turned to see Jack at his shoulder, standing calmly with hands clasped in front of him. His sheer size was threat enough. Perry knew what Tucker couldn't: No man was kinder than Jack. Perry decided to keep that quiet for the moment.

"Well, maybe I'll just come back with the sheriff." Tucker was reduced to bluster.

"It's been tried already," Perry said. "You're welcome to do so too."

"Well. . .well, maybe I just will."

"You won't have to wait long," Gleason added. He nodded down the hill.

At the bottom of the slope a white patrol car parked behind the growing line of vehicles. Approaching the slope came five other citizens of Tejon, all men. Perry felt like he was looking at a football team.

Tucker followed Perry's gaze and saw the deputy exit the car, as well as the approaching group. "Well, I guess we'll see who can and can't take a look around."

The answer to that was already clear in Perry's mind. With a body lying in a pit—two bodies, he corrected himself—the police were not going to allow crowds to roam over the crime scene.

"Hey, Doc," a man in his late teens said as he led the second group forward. He wore a letterman's jacket. "You out here to see the treasure hunt?"

"Hey, Vince," the dentist replied. "That was the plan, but we're not getting far. It appears we're not welcome."

"That a fact?" Vince said. He was a muscled man who obviously spent most of his off hours pushing iron and looking in mirrors. "Who's stopping you?"

146

"These guys," Tucker said with a jerk of his thumb.

"Perhaps I can talk some sense into them," the man called Vince said.

"Well, isn't this fun?" Gleason said quietly, then nervously cleared his throat.

"His pals look pretty big," Brent said shakily. He shuffled his feet.

"How about it, buddy?" Vince said. "You gonna stand in the way of me and my friends?"

Perry smiled but said nothing.

"Pop 'em one," Tucker said.

"Stop it," Tucker's wife demanded. "This is getting out of hand."

"There's no need for a riot," Branson offered.

"Ain't gonna be no riot. Me and my friends are going up there to see what you're doing," Vince growled, "and there's nothing you can do about it." He looked at Jack. "You're a big one. Think you can take five of us?"

Perry raised a hand before Jack could speak. "Go home." Perry's words were just above a whisper.

"I don't think so, buddy," Vince said. "I think I'm going to finish my little walk up the hill." Vince drove his point home pressing his index finger against Perry's chest.

There was a cry of pain.

Vince was on his knees, one hand raised, the other holding his wrist. The raised hand was kept in place by the strong grip of Perry as he bent the man's finger back. Vince's knees had buckled at the pain.

"You're breaking my finger. Let go!"

"Hold still, son," Perry said without emotion. His eyes were fixed on Vince's four friends. They started forward, and Perry applied more pressure to the digit. Vince bellowed. His friends stopped. Jack took a step forward and clinched his fists. The message was sent and received.

"Hey!" The voice traveled up the hill. Perry saw the deputy he had met yesterday, marching up the slope. His voice was strong, and his face appeared chiseled in concrete. He had the look of a man not to be trifled with.

Perry braced himself for the officer's verbal assault, but it never came. Instead, he strode up to Perry then looked down at Vince, whose face was twisted in pain. "Mr. Sachs," the deputy said with the kind of nod one gives an acquaintance met on the street.

"Sergeant Montulli," Perry replied smoothly.

"I was expecting something else when I arrived," Montulli said. "Has Vince been giving you trouble?"

"A little," Perry admitted, "but nothing to worry about. You know this man?"

"Vincent? Oh yeah, we go way back. He's a bit of a celebrity around town. Local high school kid makes college football team. He's a linebacker. Pretty good too. Just not real smart."

"Ah," Perry said.

"Come on, man, he's breaking my finger." Sweat dotted Vince's brow.

"Say, Vince," Montulli said. "How many times have you been in my jail?"

"I don't know. Ow. Two, maybe three times."

"Four times, cowboy. You want to make it five?"

"He attacked me!"

"Nah. I saw you poke him in the chest. That's assault and battery. That's a little more serious than underage drinking and disturbing the peace." He turned to Perry. "You want to press charges?"

"I don't know, Sergeant. I think that all depends on your friend here. I suppose I could overlook things."

Montulli hunkered down to make eye contact. "I know you have a problem with authority figures, Vince, but I'm going to give you some advice. You're a big boy now so you can make up your own mind, but if I was in your situation, I'd take Mr. Sachs's kind offer here and leave quietly—or I can slap on the cuffs. What's it going to be, sport?"

"Okay, okay, just make him let go."

Montulli rose. "Ball's in your court, Mr. Sachs."

Perry let go, and Vince popped to his feet, backing up several steps. He shook his hand vigorously. "I should—"

"Watch it!" Montulli snapped. "You're not out of this yet. Now take off."

Vince scowled, threw Perry a hard look, and then started down the hill without a word, his friends close behind.

"I'm sorry that happened," Perry said. "I try to stay away from confrontations."

"You seem pretty good at it. I've wanted to do something like that to Vince since the first time I met him. His father's the same way. The acorn didn't fall far from the tree on that one. More's the pity." Montulli turned to the others. "What are you folks doing up here?"

"We read about the treasure and wanted to see for ourselves," Tucker said.

"You're not seeing anything up here today. So you can go home."

"Why are you siding with him?" Tucker asked.

"I'm not siding with him or anyone else. This is a crime scene, and you're interfering with an investigation. Now go home."

"Crime scene?" Branson asked. "What kind of crime? I need facts for the story."

"Not now, David," Montulli said. "Now go on."

"But. . ." Branson began.

"I said, not now," Montulli snapped. "I've got my hands full. Now unless you want to spend time in my jail for interfering with an investigation, you best head back down the hill—all of you. "

"I need facts," Branson insisted. "I can't write a story without details and facts."

"It didn't stop you yesterday," Montulli shot back. "Now beat it."

To Perry's relief, they grumbled but left. Branson remained for a moment, stammered, pursed his lips in indignation, and then followed the others back to the road. "You handled that well."

Montulli shrugged. "I've been at it for awhile. Most of the

people out here are good, quiet, and respectful. Some of them, however, wake up stupid each morning."

"We all struggle with sin nature," Perry remarked.

"That sounds like church talk," Montulli said. "You one of them church-goers?"

"That's one way of putting it, but yes, I'm a Christian."

"That's probably a good thing, because you may need all the help you can get. Okay, it's time to get to work."

"How can I help?"

"Tell me where the body is." Perry did, explaining how the body was discovered. "Did you touch anything?"

"Yes," Perry admitted. "I touched the body searching for a pulse, and Jack also touched the tarp." He explained about the pit and how they discovered the body.

Montulli frowned. "How many people were working up here yesterday?"

"Maybe twenty or so," Perry replied.

"Twenty-two," Jack corrected. "That's not counting two visits by the mayor."

"Yeah, the mayor," Montulli said somberly. "I should let you know she's on her way."

"Oh, great," Gleason said.

Montulli continued. "Here is what is going to happen. I need to see the body, but I want to limit the number of people tracking in and out to the crime scene. So I want everyone but Mr. Sachs to stay here. There should be two deputies arriving anytime. They'll cordon off the crime scene area. Sometime this morning a homicide detective from Bakersfield will show up. At that point, he'll take charge of the investigation.

"I will also need to speak to each of you individually. The boys from homicide will want to talk to you and your crew. I assume they will be available."

"They will," Perry said.

"Good. I'm going to walk up the hill to the site. I'm going to do so through the undisturbed grass. Less likely to step on the killer's footprints that way. I want you," he said, pointing to Perry, "to follow directly behind me."

"You're the boss," Perry said.

"You'd think so, wouldn't you?" Montulli said. He was looking down the hill. A car had just parked. "I think the real boss just got here."

Perry watched Anne Fitzgerald exit the car.

CHAPTER 11

You know him?" Montulli asked.

"No," Perry mumbled. He and the deputy sheriff were staring down into the pit. The lifeless body lay prone on the moldering wood planks Perry had uncovered the previous evening, the head twisted awkwardly to one side. Perry could see the face clearly. The senseless taking of a life bothered him

"What's he lying on?" Montulli asked pointing.

"Planks, wood planks."

"Did you put them there?"

"No, we uncovered them last night during our excavation."

"So that's what you've been looking for? That's the treasure?"

Perry said nothing. Things had gone from difficult to impossible in a short time. According to the communications on Sergeant Montulli's handheld radio, the other officers had arrived on scene just in time to turn back another small crowd of curious townspeople. Montulli had put in a call for additional officers so the first group could do the job of taping off the crime scene.

"Mr. Sachs," Montulli said, "I asked you a question."

"The planks are the lid of a coffin."

Montulli screwed his face in disgust. "You mean the victim is lying on someone else's coffin?"

Perry nodded. "And before you ask, yes, the coffin is. . .occupied."

Perry could sense the confusion in Montulli. The deputy gazed at the open grave and blinked several times. He started to speak, but then stopped.

"Did you open the casket?"

"It's not a casket," Perry explained, "at least not as we use the term today. It's a crude coffin and very old."

"This just gets more and more interesting. Of course, it makes your problems even worse."

"How's that?"

"There are laws about desecrating graves."

"That's pushing it a bit, Sergeant," Perry replied with a frown. "This isn't a public cemetery. For that matter it isn't a private one either."

"Do you know, for a fact, that that coffin down there is the only one?"

Perry thought of the survey results and the other five dark objects it revealed. "No."

Montulli opened his mouth to speak but was stopped by the crackle of his radio and the voice of one of the other deputies. "We've got a bit of a situation here," the distant deputy said. "Mayor Fitzgerald is insisting that she should be allowed to come up."

"Oh, brother," Montulli said. Then he keyed his radio. "What's the crowd situation?"

"Clear for the moment. We made them leave. They weren't happy. You may be getting a few phone calls later."

"That's why I get the big bucks," Montulli mumbled loud enough for Perry to hear. "All right. You bring her up and try not to step on anything that might be evidence."

Perry chuckled. "Your mayor is a handful."

"She's a good woman, Sachs, a real good woman. She just has a bit of the bulldog in her, that's all. She takes her work seriously."

"So you don't find her annoying or troublesome?"

"Of course I do. She is insistent to a fault, she pokes her nose in places it doesn't belong, and she makes more work for me.

However, she does it for good reasons."

For a moment, Perry considered telling Montulli about his meeting with Anne the night before but decided against it. The image of the town's mayor knocking back a tumbler of scotch was something he didn't want to be responsible for.

Montulli's radio came to life again but with a woman's voice. The words sounded distant and indistinct. ". . .on, come on, Deputy. Can't you move any faster?"

"It's a crime scene, Mayor," the voice Perry had heard moments earlier said. "We move slowly through crime scenes."

"If you don't speed it up, I'm going to pass you."

"No, ma'am, you're not. I told you the drill. You walk directly behind me. . . ." Then before the radio went dead, Perry heard the deputy mumble, "Hazardous duty pay."

"He keyed his mike," Montulli explained. "Apparently he wanted me to know the mayor's mood."

"And to know what he's going through."

"Yeah, that too." Montulli took a deep breath as if steeling himself for the onslaught of hurricane Anne. "You know that I'm closing the site down."

"I figured you would," Perry said. "I need to ask that you open it again as soon as possible."

"Why?"

"What we're doing here is important," Perry explained. "More important than you know."

"Now you see there, Mr. Sachs. That's part of the problem. I don't know what you're doing here, and you have been less than cooperative in that area."

"I have my reasons."

"I'll just bet you do, but that's coming to an end."

"What do you mean?"

"I mean that you're going to be telling us exactly what you're doing here, and you're going to be telling us today."

"I can't do that," Perry said.

"You seem to think you have a choice in the matter, but you don't. A crime has occurred on your work site, a murder no less. What you're doing here will be deemed as material to the case. You don't want to obstruct justice, do you?"

"Perry!"

Someone shouted his name. Perry turned to see Jack motioning him to come to the grove. Even across the twenty yards of pasture that separated them, he could see that Jack was not happy.

"May I?" Perry asked.

"Yeah, but I'm going with you."

"Don't trust me?"

"The mayor doesn't need to see this," he said, motioning to the body. "And no, I don't trust anyone."

Once in the shade of the oak grove Perry quickly assessed the mood of his friends. Jack's jaw was set tight like a clamp, Gleason looked stunned, and even Brent appeared shell-shocked. Dr. Curtis simply looked bewildered.

"May I have a moment?" Jack asked and started away from Montulli.

"No," Montulli snapped. "Whatever you have to say to Mr. Sachs, you can say in front of me."

Jack made eye contact with Perry, and the communication was clear: Something was wrong. "They're gone."

At first the comment made no sense to Perry, but then meaning hit him like a tsunami. He snapped his head around and looked to the north end of the grove. A plastic worktable was where it had been the night before; a few baseball-sized stones rested on its surface, stones used to hold papers down against the unrelenting breezes that swept through the camp. Under the table was something that should not have been there: a gray, heavy plastic box the size of a footlocker. The lid was open.

"Everything?" Perry asked.

"I'm afraid so."

"It's my fault," Gleason said. "I'm responsible."

"No," Brent chimed in quickly. "I blew it. Mr. Lane told me to lock the stuff in the trailer, but I didn't. I guess I was too caught up in what we found."

"I'm responsible for the documents," Gleason said. He was morose. "I should have double-checked Brent. He's my intern. The responsibility is mine."

"What?" Montulli asked, clearly confused. "What was taken?"

"What about the duplicates?" Perry asked, too taken aback to be angry.

"I have those back at my room," Gleason said.

"Someone had better fill me in," Montulli said. "I've had enough of this cryptic talk."

Perry turned to the deputy. "That gray box over there is our secure document box. It contained the printouts of our surveys, among other things. It's supposed to be locked in the trailer when we leave. We were planning around the clock work, but we sent the crew home early after we did our core samples."

"Didn't want them around while you were digging, eh?" Montulli suggested.

"Our crew is the best, but experience has taught us that a bad apple can get into any group." Perry felt his ire rise. His site had been violated in several ways: trespass, theft, and murder.

"So one of your crew may have stolen the documents."

"Probably the murderer," Perry said.

"How do you know they're not the same person? Maybe one of your crew is the murderer. He, or she, would know exactly where to look for the documents."

"That doesn't explain who the dead man is," Perry said.

"I'm so sorry," Brent moaned. "I'm an idiot. There's no excuse for such a bonehead mistake."

"Was there anything else of value in the box?" Montulli asked.

"Nothing could be more valuable, Sergeant," Perry said. "We have duplicates, but someone out there now knows everything about the site."

"Finally," a woman's voice said. Perry turned to see Anne Fitzgerald tromping through the grass. Walking in front of her was one of Montulli's men. "Did I miss anything?"

"Hello, Madam Mayor," Montulli said. "Yes, I'd say you missed a great deal."

Perry found one of the folding chairs and sat down. The day couldn't get worse.

The room was cleaner than Perry had expected. The walls were white and appeared freshly painted. The floor was covered in cheap, uninspired brown vinyl tile. In the center of the room sat a gray metal table large enough for six people. The chairs were made of the same gray metal. On one wall was a large mirror. It didn't take a genius to know that the mirror was a screen that allowed people in the other room to view interviews and interrogations. He resisted the urge to wave.

Sergeant Montulli sat opposite him and seemed as comfortable as if it were his own dining room table. Next to him was an olive-skinned Hispanic man. A thin mustache decorated his lip. He wore a white shirt and silk tie. He'd also worn a blue suit coat when he entered the room. Once inside, though, he quickly removed the coat and set it on a chair. His shoulder holster dangled menacingly, but Perry recognized it as a cheap theatrical ploy meant to intimidate him. But Perry Sachs didn't scare easily.

"My name is Detective Tony Sanchez," the officer said, with just a hint of an accent. He struck Perry as an intelligent man who was confident in his skills. "I'm with the Homicide Division of the Kern County sheriff's department. I assume you already know Sergeant Montulli."

"Yes," Perry said.

Sanchez pushed a button on a small tape recorder in the middle of the table. "We will be recording our conversation, Mr. Sachs." It was a statement of fact. Sanchez was not seeking permission. He first gave his name as well as the names of Montulli and Perry. He then stated the time and the date.

"Mr. Sachs, you understand that this conversation is being recorded," the detective continued.

"I do."

"Do you also understand that we have asked you here as part of our ongoing investigation into a murder?"

"Yes."

"Although you are here at our request, you understand that you are not under arrest at this time and that our goal is merely to gain information that will help us solve this case. Is that true?"

"It is."

"Although you are not under arrest, we have taken the precaution of reading you your Miranda rights. Have you been advised of your rights?"

"I have."

"And do you understand those rights?"

"I do."

"For the record, please state your name and occupation."

"My name is Perry Sachs." He spelled it. "I reside in Seattle, Washington. I am the vice president of Sachs Engineering and the director of field operations."

"Sachs Engineering is a family operation."

"Partly," Perry said. "It was founded by my father, who still serves as president and CEO."

"How long have you been associated with Sachs Engineering?"

"Since high school. I came on full time after graduating from college."

"And which college is that?"

"I took an architectural degree from MIT and did post-graduate work in civil engineering." Perry saw Sanchez raise an eyebrow.

"I went to Yale, myself," Sanchez said.

"I'm sorry," Perry said with a grin.

"I played baseball. Did you play sports?"

Perry knew he was attempting to establish common ground, make the interviewee feel comfortable. He would be more likely to make a significant slipup. "Lacrosse."

"Ouch," Sanchez said. "Rugby with sticks." He leaned over the table and continued. "You are currently involved in construction work on the property of Hector and Rose Trujillo. Is that correct?"

"No." Perry said and waited a moment for the surprise answer to sink in. "Exploration and excavation. There's a difference."

"Really?" Sanchez probed.

"Construction has to do with building. We are erecting no structures."

"All right then, I sit corrected. You are currently involved in excavation and exploration on the property of Hector and Rose Trujillo. Is that correct?"

"It is."

"Are they aware of the activities you are conducting on their site?"

"They are."

"How are they aware of those activities?"

"We entered into a contract with them that allowed us exclusive rights to undertake our survey and exploration."

"Were they recompensed for the privilege you received?"

This man talks like a lawyer, Perry thought. "We were happy to pay for the privilege."

"How much were they paid?"

Perry shook his head. "Since that's a personal matter, I would feel uncomfortable divulging that without receiving permission from the Trujillos."

"We can subpoena that information," Sanchez shot back.

"I'm sure you can," Perry said evenly. He said nothing more.

Sanchez nodded, seemingly unperturbed by Perry's remark. "This morning you found a body on the site. Is that correct?"

"It is."

"Please explain how you came to find the body."

Perry did, beginning with the early morning visit to the site, the removal of the tarp, and the discovery of the corpse. He also related the events that followed up to the moment he was asked to sit in the interview room.

"The body was found in a pit dug by you and some of your crew. Why did you dig there?"

"Our surveys revealed an object underground. We investigated."

"And what did you find?"

"The same thing you found when the coroner removed the body. I assume the coroner has removed the body?"

"He has. I must admit it gave him quite a jolt. He was expecting only one body. You could have warned us about that."

"I was already down here, Detective. Sergeant Montulli was interviewing us then."

"Did you kill the man found in the pit?"

It was an abrupt question, and Perry knew it was meant to throw him off guard. "No. Neither one of them."

"Do you know who killed the victim? The one not inside the coffin, I mean."

"No."

"There was a trowel in the man's back. Do you know to whom that trowel belongs?"

"It's one of our tools," Perry said. "In fact, I was using it the night before."

"So your fingerprints would be on it?"

"I doubt it. I was wearing work gloves."

"What are you searching for up there?" Sanchez asked bluntly.

"I'd rather not say."

"You don't have that choice, Mr. Sachs," Montulli piped in.

"I have the right to remain silent. You said so yourself."

"Such a tactic might imply guilt on your part," Sanchez said.

"Implied guilt is not the same as guilt, Detective."

"Sergeant Montulli tells me that word around town is that you've found some kind of treasure trove. That could be a powerful motive to kill a man."

"I didn't kill him."

"Where were you last night?"

"After I left the site, I went to my room to do some paperwork."

"And you stayed there the whole night?"

"No. I went out once. About eight, I think it was."

"You went out? Did you meet anyone? Where did you go?"

Three questions all at once. Sanchez was getting eager. "Yes. Yes. A place called O'Tool's."

Sanchez looked at Montulli. "A pub just off the main drag. Pretty nice place."

"So you felt the need for a couple of beers after a hard day of tomb digging?"

Perry sighed and pursed his lips. "Did you learn your sarcasm at Yale or the police academy?"

"Just answer the question, Mr. Sachs."

"I felt no need for beer, Detective. I don't drink. I went there because someone asked me to meet there."

"Who was that?"

The image of Anne Fitzgerald seated in the booth drinking scotch straight up flashed in his mind. For some reason, he felt a need to protect her but couldn't avoid the direct question. It was wasted chivalry, he decided. O'Tool's was a public place, and the mayor drank there by her own choice. "Anne Fitzgerald."

Again, Sanchez looked to Montulli. "She's the mayor and a local real estate broker."

"You met with the mayor? If I asked her about it, would she confirm that meeting?"

"I can't speak for what another person will or will not do. However, I know of no reason why she wouldn't."

"Did anyone else see you there?"

"Everyone in the room, I suppose, but I know none of their names. You could talk to the cocktail waitress. She would remember me. She was amused that I ordered orange juice." Perry described her.

"I'll do that," Sanchez said. "I understand that you had some things stolen from the site."

"Some survey documents."

"Who would want to steal them?"

"I don't know. Maybe someone who read the local paper. It seems everyone thinks we're sitting on a cache of gold."

"Are you?"

Perry shrugged. "I doubt it."

"Then what's so valuable that an engineer from Seattle would bring in thousands of dollars of equipment and men?"

"I can't say."

"Can't or won't."

"Both."

Sanchez leaned back in frustration. Perry could see that he was about to speak again when the door to the room opened. A uniformed deputy stood at the threshold and motioned for Sanchez and Montulli to step outside.

The best he could tell, Perry was alone for the moment, depending on who, if anyone, was standing on the other side of the mirror. Not prone to depression and familiar with setbacks, Perry nonetheless felt an overpowering despair. He had been so close, and now mountains of obstacles stood in his way. But there was more to what he was feeling than depression; there was a sense of foreboding, something he was unfamiliar with. Something was wrong; something evil was at work, and he couldn't identify it.

In many ways Perry felt as if this journey of discovery had been plotted out for him—and as if someone was dedicated to making him fail. Too many coincidences; too many unexplained events. Coming upon the attack on Dr. Henri in the early morning six months ago; meeting his wife, Claire, and her exceptional child, Joseph; the mysterious satchel and the life-changing item it contained; the interference of the mayor; the sensationalist newspaper article; the crowds and a murder. There was darkness surrounding this light, and for a moment, it seemed that the darkness might win.

He closed his eyes and tried to drive the uncertainty away. He was not beaten, not yet at least, and, God willing, he wouldn't be. This work was a mission, and God wouldn't let him down. Not now.

Still, despair tried to ease into his life, pushing through the tiny cracks of doubt that threatened his courage. He took a deep breath and let the image of the room disappear from his memory. Once that evaporated, he pushed away all other thoughts. "Trust God or don't," he told himself. "Make up your mind. Is God in control or not?" Perry reminded himself that God had not given up on him. And he wouldn't give up on God.

A silent prayer floated from his mind.

The door opened with a whoosh and slammed against the wall. Perry jumped at the sound of it.

Sanchez plowed in like a steamship crushing through a wood pier. Montulli was on his heels. "Guess what we found, Mr. Sachs." The detective threw several Polaroid snapshots on the table. "Know what these are?"

Perry pulled the pictures closer. "Binoculars, for one. The other looks like a parabolic dish with a microphone. It's probably a listening device. What does this have to do with anything?"

"They were found at your site."

"My site?"

"Yup. We had deputies searching the area. They found this about a hundred yards from the pit you dug. Someone had you under surveillance."

"You're not suggesting I killed him, are you?"

"It's a good motive. You're working, talking about your treasure or whatever it is you're hunting for, and then learn your secret is out, that someone has found out."

"Let me get this right," Perry said. "I find out that someone has been watching us, I kill him with one of my own tools, carry his body a hundred or so yards across an open pasture, dump it in the very place I'm trying to protect, then forget to go back for his equipment. Is that what you're suggesting?"

Sanchez said nothing, but Perry could see that he got through.

"Then how do you explain it?"

"Have you identified the victim?"

"He had no ID on him, but we will discover who he is—was—soon enough."

Perry stood. "Gentleman, I've been patient, and I've tried to be helpful. I have spent hours waiting on you to do your work. That's fine, but I'm not under arrest; I'm calling it a day."

"Don't go far, Mr. Sachs."

"I'm not leaving the area, Detective. I need this resolved more than you do."

Anne gazed through the two-way mirror and watched Perry Sachs stroll out of the interrogation room. A moment later the door to her observation room opened, and Montulli entered. "Satisfied?" he asked.

"With what? His answers? He's cool under pressure, I'll say that for him."

"I meant with getting your wish to watch the interrogation."

"Being mayor ought to have some perks."

"Just don't let those perks get in the way of this investigation. I like you, Mayor, but I won't sacrifice my career for your curiosity. There is a limit to the latitude I will allow, even if you are the mayor."

"I appreciate that, Greg. Your warning is understood."

"You caused quite a scene up at the site. We were lucky that Sanchez hadn't arrived yet. He's a by-the-book guy. Having you at the crime scene wouldn't have been healthy for my career."

"Did he do it?" Anne asked. "Did Perry Sachs kill that man?"

"I doubt it," Montulli replied. "I don't think he's the type. He's one of those religious people."

"What makes you say that?"

"He as much as admitted it when I arrived on the scene this morning. You know the type."

"Yes, I do. I know the type very well."

CHAPTER 12

"All right," Dr. Curtis said. "Someone needs to fill me in and do it soon."

"This wasn't the trip you had in mind?" Jack jested. He pulled a large slice of pizza from the pan. "Explanations are Perry's domain."

Perry set his soda down and looked at the people around him. They were at Pizza Joe's, indulging in an early dinner. He'd chosen the place because of its proximity to the motel and because he needed a place to be alone with his key crewmembers. The manager had been gracious enough to open the back room for them, so for the moment they had privacy.

Gleason sat to Perry's left, Dr. Curtis to his right. Across the table, Jack was making short work of a Canadian bacon and pineapple pizza. At the edge of the opposite bench, Brent toyed with a slice of pepperoni and sausage pizza before finally letting it sit on a paper plate. They'd been there twenty minutes "decompressing," as Perry put it. Perry had made a point of inviting Brent who, he knew, was feeling lower than dirt.

"Yeah, I suppose you have a right to know," Perry said.

"I'll wait out front," Brent said and rose from the bench.

"No, it's okay," Perry said. "Sit down. Eat your pizza and listen carefully."

"I can't apologize enough," Brent said. "I'm so sorry that I—"

"Forget it, kid," Jack said. "We don't hold grudges here."

"Besides," Gleason added, "I could have, should have, double-checked you. That's what we do. Everyone watches out for each other. I didn't do that."

Perry turned to Brent. "Look at me. What's done is done. Gleason is right. Any one of us could have checked to see if the docs were secure. Truth is, we were all taken aback by the. . .find."

Curtis was becoming impatient. "Now that we're all lovey-dovey, can we please get to the point? I gave up my beauty sleep to jet across the country only to be grilled by the local cops about a murder. All I know so far is that you found the remains of a skeleton, and that if Perry is right—and there is no way he can be right—it's where it doesn't belong."

"Pull in close, guys, because I'm not going to talk very loud, and I'm not going to repeat myself. There are only a handful of people who know what we're attempting to do here. Besides myself, there is Jack and Gleason, my father, and Mrs. Henri; I'll tell you about her in a moment.

"Brent, those people I mentioned are insiders. Dr. Curtis has been advising the firm for many years. What I'm about to say cannot go beyond this group. Not in idle conversation, not spoken of with your family. Not until I say it's okay to do so. You must understand that clearly. The ramifications go beyond imagination. I know that sounds like advertising talk, but I mean it. No one living knows more about this than I do, and I can't begin to guess the impact. Have I been clear so far?"

Brent nodded.

"I need a commitment from you, Brent. I need your word that this stays in the group. Nothing illegal is involved. I've made sure of that. Do I have your word?"

"I swear, Perry. I swear by—"

Perry waved him off. "I don't want you to swear. I don't want an oath. Gleason has told me you're trustworthy, and I'm willing to take his word for it. All I need is your promise."

"I promise. I won't let you down again."

Perry wondered if he had ever before seen a young man so serious.

"Yeah, yeah, I cross my heart too," Curtis said. "Cut to the chase."

"Six months ago I left the office in Seattle late. I rounded a corner and saw what looked like a fender-bender, except no one was around. I looked down the street and saw a man running. He wasn't running well, and I could tell he was an older man. Another guy was walking quickly after him. It didn't seem right, so I parked and followed."

"You poked your nose in," Jack said. He looked at Brent. "He's always poking his nose in things."

Perry ignored him. "The long and short of it is that I got there in time to see a young man about to shoot the old gent. I. . .persuaded him otherwise."

Brent looked puzzled.

"He cleaned his clock," Jack interpreted. "He's just too modest to say anything."

"Anyway, the old man was Dr. Jamison Henri, a professor at North Pacific Seminary. He'd already been shot in the leg once, but to make things worse, he was having a heart attack." Perry told of Henri's agitation over the safety of the leather satchel, then of his cardiac arrest. The minutes flowed by as he recounted the scene at the hospital and his meeting with Claire and Joseph and how Henri had died an hour later.

"I gave my card to Mrs. Henri and offered to help in any way I could. I also gave her the satchel."

"Without looking inside?" Brent said with surprise. "Weren't you dying to know what was in there?"

"It wasn't my satchel. I had no right to look inside."

"Man, you are a straight arrow," Brent said then quickly added, "but I mean that in a good way."

Choosing not to respond, Perry continued. "I walked Mrs. Henri to her car and waited for her to drive off, and then I went home. About a week later, I got a call at the office. It was Claire. She was concerned about the satchel. She told me that after the funeral she'd gone home and discovered her house had been ransacked. The satchel was gone. She thought she'd hidden it well, but whoever did the deed was a professional and knew all the tricks. Claire had hidden the thing in the pantry behind some cereal boxes."

"The whole house was ransacked?" Curtis asked.

"From one end to the other," Perry replied. "It was probably done by a team of two or three. There's no way to tell for certain. The police found no fingerprints."

"How did they get in?" Brent inquired.

"Through the front door. No sign of forced entry. The police think the lock was picked."

"What was in the satchel?" Curtis prodded. Perry had worked with him several times and knew him to be a man of keen insight and little patience.

"A document," Perry said flatly. "A very old document. I went to Claire's home to help straighten things up and to help her deal with the police. After they were gone, she told me how her husband came home from the seminary clutching the satchel to his chest. She said his face was white and vacillated between giddiness and astonishment. Claire pressed him for information, but all he would say was, 'The greatest find ever.' "

"So she never actually saw the document," Curtis intoned.

"Oh, she saw it on several occasions," Perry corrected. "Dr. Henri would work on it at home, sitting at the dining room table taking notes and consulting books."

"Tell me she described it to you," Curtis pleaded.

"She did. It was a brownish paper with what she called 'crude, dark writing.' Dr. Henri told her it was a type of Greek."

"Not paper," Curtis said. "Not if the document was truly ancient and since Henri said 'a type of Greek,' I assume that he's referring to either Classical or Koine depending on the age of the writing."

"What's the difference?" Brent asked.

"Koine was a latter form of the earlier language," Curtis explained. "It was the common language and was used in some literature, the courts, and in business. It's the language of the New Testament. Classical Greek is more formal."

"So the satchel held a bunch of papers written in Greek?" Brent asked.

Curtis spoke before Perry could. "As I said, it can't be paper. At least not paper as we use the term. Paper is made from plant material. Early paper came from the reed-like papyrus plant. In fact, the word 'paper' comes from papyrus. The word 'bible' comes from the name of a town where the papyrus plant was harvested: Byblos, later known as Gebal. Over the years 'Byblos' became 'bible' meaning 'book.' "

"Man," Brent said. "You should go on *Jeopardy.*"

"Don't interrupt the professor, newbie," Gleason admonished.

"Documents were also written on vellum, which is made from animal skin. The ancients would take the skin of a slaughtered animal like a lamb, goat, or calf, clean it, and rub it with a coarse powder or pumice. The younger the animal the finer the vellum."

"Hence," Jack interjected, "the proverbial sheepskin given at graduation."

"I don't suppose you know if it was papyrus or vellum," Curtis asked Perry.

"No. I never saw the documents. Claire said that there were dozens of little pieces and Dr. Henri would work long into the night trying to assemble them at home."

"Wait a minute," Curtis said. "Something isn't right. If I understand you, you're telling me that a scholar who teaches at a seminary somehow came into possession of an ancient document written on vellum or papyrus, took it home, and worked on it in his dining room."

Perry affirmed the summary with a nod. Curtis shook his head. "It can't be," he said. "No true scholar would do that."

"Why not?" Brent asked.

"Because," Curtis explained sharply, "ancient documents are extremely fragile and require specialized care. Too much moisture, too much handling, and you end up with little piles of dust. If Henri truly had an ancient document, then he wouldn't treat it in such a cavalier fashion. He'd have to be crazy or—"

"Terrified," Perry inserted. "And he was. Terrified. Claire said he became almost paranoid. She'd make plans to have people over to the house for dinner, but he canceled them all. In fact, he canceled everything they had planned, including a vacation. He rose early, worked on the documents, went to work, returned, and worked late into the night. Claire was sure he was losing his mind."

"What would terrify a man so much that he would break all scholastic protocol and endanger valuable historical documents?" Curtis asked.

"What would make you behave that way?" Perry asked.

"Nothing. Nothing could be so important that I'd risk losing something irreplaceable."

Perry said nothing, allowing the conversation to settle into silence.

"Well," Curtis said after a moment. "I suppose I might do something like that if I felt the documents were in greater danger among others than with me."

"Bingo," Perry said. "Something or someone had him scared."

"Who or what force could do that?" Curtis asked.

"The force that had Dr. Henri attacked. The same force that put a murdered man on our site."

"That sounds an awful lot like a conspiracy theory," Curtis shot back.

"The thing about conspiracy theories is that some of them are true."

Curtis lowered his head, and Perry let him think. "It would have to be more than that. The content, there must have been something about the content. He deciphered enough to know that some enormous impact would come from the knowledge of the writings."

171

"That's how I figured it," Perry stated.

"Where did Henri get the docs?" Curtis asked.

Perry shrugged. "He never told his wife. We don't know. It's because of those documents that we're here."

Curtis rubbed his eyes. "Okay, wait a minute. You said the documents were stolen and that you never saw them. Yet here we are because of them. And if I understand you, Mrs. Henri is no scholar. She couldn't have told you what was on those fragments."

"She has no idea. Claire is a kind and caring woman, but she has no desire to understand her husband's work. He was an ancient language expert, and such things held little interest for her."

"If the docs were stolen, and Dr. Henri's wife doesn't know what's on them, then how did you know to come to the Tehachapi Mountains?"

"Well," Perry began, "this is where things get weird."

"Good," Dr. Curtis quipped. "I was getting bored."

"Claire has a special son," Perry explained. "Are you familiar with the term 'Savant Syndrome'?"

"I'm not," Brent cut in.

"Savant Syndrome describes individuals who are socially and educationally dysfunctional but who exhibit great skills at art, math, and memory. Usually they cannot express themselves verbally, and although they might be able to mentally calculate the first solar eclipse in the year 2023, they generally have no idea what it is they're doing. Experts say it has something to do with damage to the left hemisphere of the brain. Joseph Henri is just such a savant. He's skilled at calculations, able to do multiplication problems faster than you can enter them in a calculator. He can draw pictures that look near photo quality. He also has a prodigious memory. He reads everything and can replicate everything he reads or sees. He can reproduce every word of a book he's looked at, apparently without understanding any of it."

"You're not telling me. . ."

"Yes, I am," Perry continued. "After the satchel was stolen,

Joseph began to reproduce the document it held, letter for letter, line for line, even the accent marks."

"He rewrote the text?" Curtis asked.

"In a sense, but it's more than that. I've gotten to know Joseph over the months, and he doesn't think as we do. It's almost as if he's a foreign intelligence. So when he reproduced the documents he had seen his father working on, he wasn't just rewriting the Greek works, he was making a piece of art. Clear the table."

Pizza pans, plastic cups, napkins all disappeared quickly as the group made room for Perry. "I stopped by the motel before coming over here. I picked up what Joseph did." Reaching down by his side, he picked up a hard plastic tube that was capped on one end. He removed the cap and pulled out a roll of paper.

"It looks like butcher paper," Curtis said.

"It is," Perry replied. "Joseph goes through an enormous amount of paper. This stuff is cheaper and comes on a large roll. It can keep him occupied for several months." Perry spread out the roll, aided by his friends around the table. "As you can see, Joseph did more than rewrite the letters; he actually drew the fragments and colored them to match what he saw. To Joseph, these are not words, they're images."

Perry gave Curtis time to take in what he was seeing. He watched as the archeologist let his eyes trace the pictures before him. The roll of paper was two feet wide and close to six feet long. Drawn in detail not thought possible in art were dark brown shapes that were unmistakably reproductions of vellum fragments. Dark squiggles were barely visible on the "fragments" but clear enough to be read if studied closely.

"My Greek is rusty," Curtis said. Perry noticed his voice shook. "I. . .I specialize in North American archeology, but I studied some Greek in graduate school. It's the language of the New Testament, you know. . .oh, I think. . .I think I already said that. I read the New Testament a lot. I like to study it in the original language. . . . This can't be." His hands began to shake, and he licked his lips several times. "No, no, this is a joke. You're having fun at my expense, aren't you, Perry? Yeah, that's it. . .this. . .no. . .this can't be right. . .I must be reading this wrong. Have you had this. . .have you had this translated?"

"You okay, Doc?" Jack asked softly, his brow furrowed.

Curtis slapped his hand on the table; the sound of it filled the room. "I asked you a question! Did you or did you not have this translated?"

Perry quickly laid his hand on that of Dr. Curtis. He was trembling. Perry said nothing at first; he just looked in the stunned academic's eyes. "I should have prepared you, Dr. Curtis. I'm sorry."

Curtis took a ragged breath. "Please, Perry. I must know. Am I reading this right?"

"Do you remember my saying that Joseph can recall everything he sees or reads? He translated it. . . Well, he didn't truly translate the text, but he associated each Greek word on the drawing with those he found in his father's books." Perry pulled up the second cylinder and opened it as he had the first. Again he removed a roll of paper and spread it out on the table. "This is what brought us here."

It took only seconds for Curtis to absorb the images before him. The drawing was the same as the first, with one exception: Greek words had been replaced with English.

"He couldn't have done this," Curtis said. "To do this requires years of disciplined study. . .the declensions are right, the parsing; he's even maintained the Greek syntax." His voice faded. "This can't be. Someone is playing a huge joke, a monumental practical joke. No, I refuse to believe it. This would turn the world upside down."

"Brent," Perry said. Brent was trying to read what was before him. "Brent," Perry repeated.

"Huh? Oh, sorry."

"Did you bring the video camera you used last night?"

"Yeah, I have it right here, just like you asked."

"Set it to play back for Dr. Curtis."

Brent pulled the small camera up and opened its digital display panel. "Here you go, Doc. I've got it cued to start when Mr. Sachs pulls the first board out."

Curtis took the camera in trembling hands. Jack reached over and pressed the play button. Perry watched Curtis watch the video. A minute later, Curtis set the camera down, rose without speaking, and left the room.

"What's with him?" Brent said.

"Read the translation," Gleason said to his protégé.

"I was but. . ."

"Just read it," Gleason stated.

Brent did. A few moments later he said, "But that would mean. . .that would mean. . ." Unable to finish his sentence, he whispered, "Oh, everything is going to change."

CHAPTER 13

oncessions had been made, and Perry supposed he should feel grateful, but feelings were spurious things that never quite seemed synchronized with the facts of life.

A person could be depressed on a beautiful day as well as on one covered in gray skies. Depression was knocking on Perry's emotional door. His mood was darkening faster than the sky overhead. The sun was well into its daily plunge toward the horizon. In a few moments it would drop behind the hills west of him and twilight would be in full swing, lending its eerie tone to an already dark situation. The powerful work lights beamed down a wash of illumination, causing anything in their path to cast long, ebony silhouettes on the ground.

The longest shadows were cast by uniformed men who combed the land for clues, and by a detective in a white shirt and dress pants. Perry watched as the last of the crime scene investigators bundled up their equipment and started down the slope to the police van now on the site.

Perry was not one to allow depression to linger. It was an unwanted guest, and while he was as human as the next person—and therefore vulnerable to such invasions—he never surrendered to it. Emotions, he knew, were frail, misleading things, and the best way to deal with them was to choose how he would feel. He had heard his pastor describe emotions as blind things. "Never let them drive." Perry thought the point was well made.

Perry believed the best way to expel negative thoughts was to be involved in positive action, but there was the problem. For the moment he could do nothing but wait. He'd tried everything he knew, pulled all the strings available to him, and had only limited success. His father had placed a call to California's governor, a man with whom Sachs Engineering was acquainted—and to whose campaign they'd made sizable contributions. All that guaranteed was that the governor would pick up the phone. Perry prided himself on his ethics, and the only man he knew who took such matters more seriously than he was his father. Henry Sachs would never ask the governor to interfere with a police investigation, and neither would Perry. Still, there was the hope that a little pressure from Sacramento might gain some latitude.

It had.

Montulli and Sanchez brought in more officers to search the site and promised they would soon release it back to Perry. The Sachs Engineering team offered whatever assistance they desired. So far that had only been the use of the work lights.

After meeting with Jack, Gleason, Curtis, and Brent in the pizza parlor, Perry had returned to the site with Dr. Curtis in tow. The scholar had taken some time to himself, trying to understand all that he had heard and seen on the video. By the time they made the short drive out of town and onto the Trujillo property, the archeologist was back to his old self. In fact, he was manic, asking question upon question, floating suppositions like a child blowing bubbles into the air. "Greatest find in American archeology. . . no, in all archeology. . . stand the world on its ear. . .change everything. . .rewrite the history books." Complete sentences had given way to bullets of thought as Curtis's machine-gun mind went fully automatic.

Now, as Perry sat in a canvas camping chair watching the police do their business, Curtis was at the plastic folding table reviewing copies of the survey documents that had been stolen the night before. He mumbled aloud to himself: "odd," "curious," "of course." Perry had stopped listening; he continued to gaze over the yellow crime scene ribbon.

"You look glum."

Anne Fitzgerald approached, still wearing the jeans and striped camp shirt he had seen her in earlier that day. Perry was mildly surprised that he hadn't noticed her arrival. "Not glum, meditative."

"Is there a difference?"

"I think so." Perry started to ask how she got past the sheriff's deputies, but quickly dropped that thought, noting that this town mayor seemed to go wherever she wanted.

Pulling another camp chair next to Perry, she sat down. "Sergeant Montulli told me you called in the big guns. It's not every day the governor rings our little town."

"Maybe you can use it against him and run for governor yourself."

"Thank you, no," Anne said with a slight chuckle. "I'm not cut out for that kind of politics. The small town stuff is better for me. This is where I can do the most good and have the greatest impact."

"Is that what motivates you? Good?"

"You *are* glum," Anne said, giving him a second, appraising look. "You probably won't believe it, but yes. This is the second small city that I've served. The money is lousy and the headaches many, but there's also satisfaction in it."

Perry gave no response. He continued his vigil.

"I thought you might like to know something. A few things, actually."

"You're not here to pump me for more information? I know you didn't get what you wanted when the police interviewed me."

Anne tried not to look surprised. "Not much gets by you, does it?"

"Or you."

"I know you think I've been a pain, and I have been. That's my nature. I'm curious and meddlesome. I admit it. Actually, I'm proud of it. My husband found it endearing when he was alive."

Perry wanted to ask how sure she was of that, but suppressed the urge. "Well, what can I do for you, Mayor?"

"I came to do something for you," she replied. "I thought you'd like to know that the victim wasn't killed by your trowel. His neck was broken."

"How do you know that?"

"Greg Montulli told me. I pester him as much as I do you. He said the preliminary report by the medical examiner indicated a broken neck."

"Not from falling into the pit," Perry said. "It was only three feet deep, and it was covered when we came back in the morning."

"I imagine that could be far enough," Anne said, "but it wasn't from a fall. The M.E. told Greg that there was no bruising on the head, but there were some bruises along the man's left jaw. He thinks. . ."

"An assassination. Someone came up from behind, grabbed his head, and yanked with a twist."

"Is there anything you don't know?"

"I read a lot. Why the trowel?"

"To implicate you or your crew, I assume. The equipment they showed at the sheriff's station was found over in that clump of trees. The man was probably killed there and then moved to your pit."

"So someone was spying on us at a distance, then is killed and tossed on our work site."

"Right, and they know the victim's name: Edward Dawes. Since he had no identification on him, he had to be traced by fingerprints. He was a private detective out of Bakersfield."

"Private detective?" Perry mulled the news over. "Someone hired him to spy on us, then killed him? Not only that, they placed the body where it was certain to be found. The killer wanted the police to know of the murder."

"That's the way Greg and Detective Sanchez see it. The question is, why?"

"That's obvious: to stop our work. It doesn't take a genius to know that a dead body would turn the site into a crime scene and that would halt our work. . .which it has."

"And implicating you and your crew by burying the trowel in the back of Dawes would really grind things to a halt."

"Why are you telling me this?" Perry asked.

"Because you didn't kill him and you have a right to know."

"But isn't it to your benefit for this plan to work? You share the same goal: stopping our work."

"No, I don't, and that's your problem. You assume that I'm against what you're doing here. I never said that. I just wanted to make sure that what you're doing is on the up-and-up and that it wouldn't adversely affect my town. For all I know, you're burying hazardous materials out here that will contaminate the ground water."

"That's a stretch."

"No, it's not. It's been done before, and if a few more city and county leaders had shown the courage of curiosity, a great many environmental disasters could have been avoided. Just ask the residents of Love Canal, New York. Their children were sickened by chemical dumps that affected the soil and the water."

"Okay, I get the idea. I can assure you that we're not doing anything like that."

"No, but you are digging up bodies."

There was no answer to that. Proof of her words was in a pit just a few yards away.

She didn't press the point. "I thought you might also want to know that the crowds are getting bigger. The motels in town are full, and those in Tehachapi are filling fast. Before I came up here, I had the misfortune of encountering David Branson."

"Your newspaper editor?"

"One and the same," Anne said. "He is a happy camper. He's been on the phone all morning talking to media around the country. It seems the world will soon be on your doorstep."

"They've already begun arriving," Perry said. "I saw a media

180

van with a microwave dish. Fortunately the police have kept them back."

"What happens when they release the crime scene?" Anne asked. "Greg isn't going to be able to keep a crew up here twenty-four hours a day."

"I've thought of that. I've hired a security firm to help with crowd control. And I have a man buying every NO TRESPASSING sign he can find. That'll give the sheriff's department clear reason for arresting anyone who comes on the property without permission. I may fence the place off, but that would take a little time."

"So you've thought of everything," Anne said.

"No one can think of everything," Perry admitted, "but I try."

Anne shifted her gaze to the site. "I must admit," she said, "that you seem less stressed than I thought you'd be. I mean, things like this don't happen on every project, do they?"

"No. I've dealt with my share of setbacks before, but nothing like this. Our firm has been courted by admirals and generals and lambasted by congressmen and senators. I thought I had seen and experienced it all."

"Yet, here you sit, a little somber perhaps, but as cool as an ice cube. How is that?"

Perry turned to her and studied her for a moment. She'd been a problem for him, but she had, at least, been direct. Nothing required that she make the drive to the site and walk up the tiring slope, yet here she was, and this time she came bearing information instead of demanding it. She deserved a straight answer. "Faith."

"Faith?"

"I'm a man of faith, Mayor. It guides everything I do."

"What kind of faith? You mean like faith in humanity or faith in the religious sense."

"Faith in the Christian sense."

"Ah. Greg said you were one of those."

"If by 'one of those' you mean a Christian, then yeah, I'm one of those."

"Is this where the sermon comes?" Anne asked. Her words were tight, strained.

"You asked, I answered. I don't do sermons. My faith has seen me through many things. It'll see me through this."

" 'Faith is the substance of things hoped for, the evidence of things not seen,' " Anne said.

Perry's eyebrows rose. "Hebrews 11:1," he said. "You are full of surprises, aren't you, Mayor?"

"I've heard Bible passages since I was a child. My parents took my sister and me to church every week. Even after we moved to Ridgeline, they found a church and made sure we put ourselves in the pew every Sunday."

"Sounds like you didn't like it."

Anne sounded bitter. "Actually I did. I continued through my teenage years and as an adult. Then I quit."

"May I ask why?"

Anne paused and scowled, as if remembering. "My husband was killed by a street thug. He traveled a lot for his business. He did commercial real estate. He was good, the best I have ever seen. Like you, he was a Christian. Taught Sunday School, was a deacon, all that stuff. One Tuesday night he was in San Bernardino inspecting a set of concrete tilt-up buildings in the industrial area. A guy robbed him, then shot him in the face."

Perry closed his eyes for a moment, driving the image from his thoughts. "I'm sorry," he said.

"Yeah, well, everyone was sorry. Everyone but God. The police called. I drove down the mountain to the hospital. He lived long enough for me to get there. He was a mess, his head swollen to twice its size. I couldn't even recognize him. The nurses told me that the disfigured person on the bed was my husband, and all I could do was believe them. I held his hand and told him everything would be all right. My sister arrived. The pastor was with her, so were my parents. They joined hands and prayed around us. Ten minutes later my husband died. Apparently God had taken

His phone off the hook.

"Over the next few months, I lost both parents," Anne continued. "All three were gone in less than six months. I prayed for them too. God wasn't listening to me, so I decided that two could play that game. I stopped listening to Him."

"What about your sister?" Perry asked. "What did she do?"

"What's that got to do with anything?"

"You said she went to church with you and the family. Did she give up on God too?"

"No, she still believes. I don't know why, but she does."

Perry took in a deep breath and let the story settle. He could hear the bitterness festering in Anne. She hadn't turned her back on faith; she made herself its enemy, hating every mention of it.

"I don't tell the story much anymore," Anne added. "Don't know why I'm telling it to you now. Maybe I feel guilty about my pestering you." Like Perry she took a deep breath, then blew it out noisily. There was derision in the way she did it. "Well, go ahead. I'm ready."

"Ready for what?" Perry asked.

"The few times I've told the story to a Christian, they immediately tried to explain things away. They say they're sorry, then try to explain why it's not God's fault. So go ahead. Who knows; maybe you'll say something new."

"You don't want to hear what I have to say."

"What, no pity? No pat answers to deliver from the Word of God? No 'You'll get to see them all in Heaven'? You disappoint me. Go on, regale me with your Christian wisdom. I want to hear it."

"You're an idiot."

"What. . .what?" she sputtered.

"I said you're an idiot. You blame God because you've faced a tragedy. You want fairness in an unfair world. You want sinless behavior from sinners. Come on, Anne, you're smarter than that."

"That's uncalled for!"

Perry shrugged. "You asked what I thought. Well, now you

have it. You've been through a horrible ordeal and feel cheated by it. You've been in a pity party for years now, using the death of your loved ones to avoid the responsibility you have before God."

"How dare you speak to me this way?"

Perry continued, his voice even but as firm as granite. "Do you prefer the easy platitudes? You said you didn't. How dare you speak about God like He's some frivolous clown? Do you think you're the only one who has suffered in this world? In Sudan, Christians are abused, and women sold into slavery. Every apostle but one died a martyr's death. By the time of Nero, the streets of Rome were lined with Christians hanging on crosses. Emperors would wrap them in wax and light them on fire, using their burning bodies as torches. Even God's own Son was nailed to a cross. What makes you think you should be spared pain and difficulty?"

Anne started to speak, but nothing came out, so Perry continued. "I'm grieved at your loss, but I won't waste time joining you in your pity party. Every one faces hardship, disappointment, and, sooner or later, tragedy. It's called life. If you want to talk about how unfair God is, you'll need to find a different audience, because I'm not going to listen to it."

Perry watched Anne's jaw tighten and her eyes narrow as if to hold back the hurricane of fury swirling within her. "You owe me an apology," she said through tight lips.

"You owe God an apology," Perry countered in the same steel voice.

Anne sprang from the chair and stepped toward Perry, raised her open hand, and swung. It stopped a half-second later, her wrist in the firm grip of Perry.

"No, ma'am, you are not going to slap me and then walk away. This isn't an old movie. It's real life. Think about what I said." He released her wrist. She stood there for a moment, and he saw a glint from the work lights in the tears that brimmed in her eyes.

She turned and walked away.

"That was pretty harsh," a voice said behind him.

Without turning, he spoke to Dr. Curtis, who still sat at the table. "You've been in the faith longer than I have; would you have handled it differently?"

There was silence, then, "Probably, but you handled it better than I would have. She needed someone to be honest with her for once."

"I just hope I didn't overdo it."

"Time will tell. Time will tell."

Rutherford's head bobbed as he tried to focus on the stretch of butcher paper that dominated the conference room table in front of him. "You say Henri's boy drew this?"

"Yes," Julia said. "He was working on it when I gained entrance to the house."

"It looks too real to be a drawing."

"I saw him doing it," Julia added. "The paper was draped over the dining room table, and he was drawing this with crayons."

"Remarkable."

"Eerie is more like it," Alex said. "That's the place to a tee."

"And that is the man you hired?" Rutherford asked.

"That's how I left him, face down in the pit."

"Why the. . ." Rutherford began. "Is that a trowel?"

"Yes, sir," Alex said. "My goal was to disrupt the dig until we could formulate a plan to gain the prize."

"And the trowel was used to implicate Sachs?"

"Exactly."

"How is it a retarded man can know what you've done hundreds of miles away?" Julia asked.

Alex shrugged. "I have no idea."

"Move the drawing and let me see the survey images," Rutherford demanded. Alex stepped to the table and rearranged the documents so his boss could see them. "I see six objects laid in two lines of three."

"This one," Alex said, pointing at the most southwesterly object, "is the grave they opened; the one with the Roman soldier in it."

"And you saw that with your own eyes?"

"I did. The remains are not fully visible. Only one plank has been removed. They probably stopped at that point to protect the find."

"The larger object to the north," Rutherford asked, "that's what we're looking for?"

"Yes."

"It's ill-defined," he blurted.

"They may have reached the limits of the ground penetrating radar," Alex said.

"Perhaps, but we can still determine that it's man-made and not a natural formation. I see no reason to doubt the find. What remains is getting the contents out and back here."

"That may be difficult," Alex said. "It's become a media circus there. Newspapers are picking up the story, as is the electronic media."

"It's too bad word got out," Rutherford said. "Had Sachs been able to work unmolested and in secrecy, our job would be easier. We could've let him do all the work."

"The newspapers changed the situation," Alex admitted. "That's why I felt the need to slow things down. Beside, Dawes knew too much. I doubt he could've traced things back since I was meticulous about concealing my connection with you, but I wanted to be certain. He won't be talking now."

"We still have a big problem," Julia added. "Whenever they pull the contents out, the media is going to be there."

"We have to play our ace in the hole," Alex suggested.

"Yes," Rutherford agreed. "I want our two guests brought here. I want to see this prodigy for myself."

"Is that wise?" Julia asked.

"Of course it is," Rutherford snapped. "I wouldn't have suggested it if it weren't. They can't know where they are, so keep them confused. Julia, your job is to bring them here. Alex, I want you to set up a room where they can be comfortable. I want full video access. Understood?"

"Yes," Alex and Julia said simultaneously.

"And, Alex, make sure there are plenty of art supplies for young Mr. Henri. I want to see what else is going on in his mind. He bears some research."

Anne marched into O'Tool's Pub and took a seat in her usual booth. She'd been driving around for fifteen minutes pushing back tears and venting anger into the empty car like a geyser. No matter how many times she drove up and down the streets of Tejon, she couldn't quiet her wounded spirit.

She stopped at her office, retrieved a few business messages, and chose to return none of them. Five minutes after she entered her office, she left again. With little forethought she drove to the pub, parked, and strode into the dark lounge, longing to be alone with her overheated thoughts.

Fury crashed in her like storm waves on an empty beach. Conflicting thoughts ricocheted in her mind. One moment she wanted to drive back to the site and pin Mr. Perry Sachs's ears to one of the oak trees. She was angry enough to toss his body into the same pit in which Dawes had been found. Yet another part of her hungered to go home, collapse on the bed, and cry herself to sleep. *That isn't going to happen,* she determined. That would mean he won, that he had succeeded in hurting her, and she couldn't tolerate that. Instead, she decided it was time for a drink.

As she plopped down, the cocktail waitress walked over with a scotch in her hand. "You're early, Mayor."

"I hadn't noticed."

The waitress set the glass in front of Anne. "That friend of yours is causing quite a stir. Everyone who walks in is talking about it. He's become something of a celebrity."

"He's something, all right; I just hesitate to say what." Anne pulled the glass closer.

"So what's he digging for up there? Besides bodies, I mean."

"I don't know. I'm not in his confidence."

"You must know something. I mean, you are the mayor, aren't you?"

"I don't come in here to be quizzed by a cocktail waitress. Don't you have drinks to serve and flirtations to make?"

There was a weighty, enduring pause. "You don't have to take my head off, Mayor. Drink up. Enjoy. Have fun by yourself." The waitress disappeared as quickly as she had arrived.

The last comment burned Anne like a brand. She *was* alone. She'd been alone for years. She liked it that way. Less trouble. Less conflict. Less everything. Loneliness was the preferred choice.

She lifted the glass and stared at the amber fluid. Light from a candle flickered through the drink, glitter fairies dancing to unheard music. The pungent fragrance of oak-aged alcohol rose in her nostrils. Normally the smell enticed her, comforted her, made her eager to consume it in search of the salve for the still oozing wound in her soul. Bringing the glass to her lips, she cursed Perry for his mean words. *Pity party,* she thought. *Pity party indeed. What does he know of it?*

Anne paused. For a moment she could see herself sitting in the booth of the dark pub, glass of liquor held to her lips, as if she were having an out of body experience. She felt pity for the woman she saw in her mind's eye, felt remorse that she'd come to the point of sitting in a dark place drinking scotch in hope of lessening a deeper, more abiding darkness in her heart.

Slowly Anne set the drink down and stared at it. The heat of anger flickered like the candle then slowly went out. Fury was replaced with melancholy. The man that killed her husband had killed her too; she just hadn't realized it. He'd killed her hope, her confidence, her self-esteem, and her ability to trust anyone, including herself.

That was a sharp, piercing realization. The pain remained. She'd chosen to flee her home, where she felt miserable, to move to a town where she now felt even more wretched. No matter the amount of success, no matter the number of lies she told herself, she was still in agony and was self-medicating her pain nightly with a substance that only made things worse.

Anne pushed the glass away, opened her purse, and removed a twenty-dollar bill from her billfold. She laid it on the table. Then, taking a pen from her open purse, she wrote a note on the cocktail napkin: "Having a bad day. Sorry for what I said. Anne F."

Slipping from the booth, Anne walked from the bar wondering if she really did owe God an apology.

CHAPTER 14

The ever-present breeze had evolved into a stiff wind that ran invisible fingers through Perry's dark hair. He stood in the middle of the site as unmovable as the oaks that surrounded him. The sun had tucked itself away behind the hills, and darkness flooded the perimeter of the work area, kept at bay by the powerful work lamps. Around the site was abysmal blackness, but the work was awash in gold-tinted light.

Perry took in the activities around him. Thirty minutes earlier, just an hour after sunset, the crime scene was released and once again became a worksite. Montulli had given the word, and Perry wasted precious few minutes in mustering his crew. The downtime had not been wasted. Perry had thought about his next set of actions, weighing each decision carefully, like a jeweler measuring a diamond.

Things had changed, and Perry had to adapt his plan. It had been his intention to move quickly, but still one step at a time. "B" would follow "A." Then, and only then, would "C" come into play. That was before—before the media reports, before the gathering crowds, before the murder, before the theft of the documents he had hoped to keep secret for awhile longer at least.

Just yesterday he'd arrived on scene as the captain of his ship, a vessel that was plowing forward under full sail and across even seas. Now his ship was stuck in the midst of a storm, a squall that threatened to break the keel and send everything sinking to the bottom.

What had to be done now had to be done fast. It galled him to have to change his timing, but too much was at stake, too much of the unknown. Someone was working against him. He didn't know who, but he did know that whoever it was, that person was capable of bringing death.

The serene hillside was a churning mass of activity. Over a score of men worked carefully but with urgency they had drawn from their boss. Chatter and banter were nearly nonexistent. The only real sounds were those of shovels hitting dirt and the slow process of a backhoe moving up the site.

Perry was committed to finishing the task before anything else could go wrong. Despite having had only a few hours of sleep spread over the last few days, he wouldn't return to his motel room. He was on-site and on-site he'd stay until the work was done. Despite the faster pace, it was not done in a frenzy. Every man had a job to do, and he did it quickly, but not carelessly.

"I must admit, I'm impressed," Sergeant Montulli said.

After releasing Perry to do his work, he'd asked to stay and observe. Perry felt he owed the man that much. It had been Montulli that had ordered additional men for crowd control. Perry knew that he could send them home at any minute. Instead, he agreed to keep them on-site until the private security guards could arrive. A fence would be set up in the morning. It would take several days to complete the chain link perimeter, and with luck, Perry's major work would be done by then, but he was unwilling to take chances. If things took longer, he wanted to be ready. The price of the fence was small compared to the peace of mind it brought.

"Impressed with what?" Perry asked.

"Your crew. You spoke, and they went to work. No grumbling, no questions."

"They're the best, and we treat them well. A good employee is more valuable than gold."

"Can you fill me in?" Montulli asked. "I mean, what are they doing?"

"I'll tell you what I can," Perry said. "You already know about the coffin and skeleton, right?"

"Right. I saw it when the coroner removed the murder victim's body. Gave me the creeps."

"You should have been face-to-face with it," Perry replied. "We found it because our surveys showed something beneath the surface." Perry turned to face the pit. Men were digging away the edges of the grave. "They're widening the opening. If all goes well, they'll dig back the side walls of the pit to form a slope on two sides. Then we'll push canvas straps beneath the coffin. When Dr. Curtis gives the okay, the coffin will be lifted out of the hole by those straps and set to the side. This one was fairly close to the surface, so the team should be able to lift it by hand."

"That one? There are more?"

"Yes, five more." Perry turned again and pointed with his finger, indicating five other groups of men. "Each team is responsible for a coffin. At least we assume they're coffins. They gave the same readings as the first one, except each one is deeper than its counterpart farther up the slope. The deeper ones will take longer to extract."

"Kinda like pulling a bad tooth, eh?" Montulli said.

"Something like that. Dr. Curtis will oversee each extraction and make sure that the contents are prepped for travel. Everything needs to be preserved. Even the dirt that is being removed is being bagged, marked, and shipped off for study."

"Where are you sending all this?"

"Dr. Curtis has connections with several universities. He's well respected in his field. He has arranged to have the coffins and their. . .inhabitants studied in the best environments and by the best people. I imagine the studies will go on for years."

"So that's it? You pull up a few old bodies, and then you're done. There's no treasure?"

"That's just the beginning, Deputy. Once the burial material is removed. . .and by that I mean the corpses, coffins, and surrounding soil. . .then we plan to dig a ditch—a long ditch."

"Why?"

"To get what we came for," Perry said. "And don't ask. That's as far as I can go."

"Perry!"

Perry turned to see Curtis motioning for Perry to join him. After several strides up the grade, Perry and Montulli stood next to Curtis, who was giving orders to six workers, each of whom held a flat canvas strap in his hand. The straps descended into the now widened pit, ran under the coffin and out the other side, up that slope, and into the hands of another worker. The three straps formed a cradle for the coffin.

"I thought you might like to see this," Curtis said. "After all, you're going to be the one blamed for ruining all the history books."

"I'm honored. . .I think," Perry said.

"There's a fine line between being famous and being infamous," Montulli said. "It's all a matter of interpretation."

"Why don't I feel comforted?" Perry asked.

"I'm just a cop," Montulli said. "I leave those questions for your shrink."

"Ready?" Curtis asked the men. Several grunted their affirmation. "Okay, then, let's do this. Pull evenly. We want the coffin to stay level. I don't think it can take very much jiggling. Perry?"

Taking his cue, Perry said, "Haul away, boys. Slow and steady."

Instead of pulling the straps hand-over-hand as a man might pull a bucket up from a well, the men each took a step back, then another one, like a drill team marching backward. Each step followed a cadence called out by Perry. "Step. . .step. . .easy now. . . step. . .step." One tediously long minute later, the top of the coffin rose above the surrounding grade. Two backward steps more, and the bottom of the ancient casket cleared the hole.

"To my right," Perry ordered. "Step. . .step. . .step." Each small stride moved the dark, fragile box away from the open maw that had been its home for so many centuries. Once over solid ground, Perry gave the order to ease the straps. Inch by inch the workers lowered it to the ground until it rested in the tall grass.

Perry approached, as did the others, staring at the unbelievable sight. A wood box, close to seven feet long and three feet wide, rested on the ground. The coffin was made of flat boards, now bent, warped, and moldering. A single plank was missing, the one Perry had removed when he first found it.

Staring back at them was the grinning skull of a man long dead. The space where the board had been allowed a limited view of the coffin's occupant, but it was enough to see a helmet on his head and the shield that covered his body.

Stooping, Perry took hold of one of the remaining boards and gave a tug. It came loose easily, leaving behind square iron nails. One of the other workers did the same with the last board that formed the lid. They stood and took a step back to allow the light to fall upon their macabre find.

"If it weren't for that bony face," Montulli said, "I'd think I was looking at a robot."

"You cops have a weird sense of humor," Perry said.

"Can we join the party?" Jack, Gleason, and Brent joined the group. Brent carried his video camera.

Too many bodies, Perry thought and dismissed the other workers, thanking them and then assigning them to the other groups. "Sure," Perry said. "I think Dr. Curtis was about to give us a history lesson."

"I don't know what to say," Curtis replied. "What we are seeing is impossible. Flat impossible. No one is going to believe it. I'm looking at it, and I don't believe it."

"Facts is facts, Doc," Jack said. "No matter how you spin this, we're looking at a dead soldier. I took my share of history classes in college, and even I know that's a Roman helmet."

"That period of history is not my bailiwick, but I know enough to believe you're right."

"Could it be some kind of prank?" Montulli asked.

Curtis answered first. "No. If it were, it would be the most elaborate and best executed prank in history. Look at the cassis—the helmet. The rust indicates that it's made of iron, typical for a Roman soldier. Some helmets from the period were made of copper or even bronze, but iron was more common. It has everything you'd expect on a Roman military helmet: cheek-shields to protect the face, a brow-guard, and judging by the awkward position of the head, I bet we'll find a protruding neck guard on the back of the helmet."

"Look," Brent said, "even his sandals are intact. A little worse for wear, but still in one piece."

"Boots," Curtis corrected. "I know they look like sandals, but they were called boots. In grad school, I had a professor say that the design of Roman boots showed some of the same design factors of the modern sports shoe." He bent down and pushed the foot of the dead man forward. "Iron hobnails. The boots were cut from a single piece of leather. It's pretty fancy work."

"The shield is badly warped," Gleason noted.

Curtis agreed. "That's to be expected. Shields were made of layered wood with a copper alloy binding."

"Should we remove the shield and see what else our friend has on?" Gleason asked.

"No," Curtis replied instantly. "We've gone far enough. It's possible that whoever buried this man put his arm through the shield straps. Moving the shield might do some damage to the remains. That kind of work should be done in the lab."

Perry looked at Curtis for a moment but said nothing. He knew the archeologist was being careful, at least as careful as the circumstances allowed. Still, Perry's curiosity was in high gear. "This is your decision, Doc, but I have to admit that I want a little peek at the rest of our friend."

"I suppose," Curtis sighed after a moment, "we could see how easily the shield separates from the body. We might get lucky. But I want everything taped."

"I'm on it, Doc," Brent enthused, raising the camera to his eye. "Quiet on the set. . .roll 'em."

Curtis studied the shield and the occupant upon which it rested like a chess master planning his next ten moves. "Perry, you take the corner opposite me; Gleason, you take the lower left; Jack can have the lower right. We're going to lift gently and evenly. I will set the pace; the rest of you will lift as I do—no more, no less. Everyone got that?" They all agreed and took their positions.

Curtis reached forward and slid two fingers under one corner of the shield. Perry did the same and waited for the others to follow suit. "Here we go," Curtis said, and he gently pulled up.

Perry fixed his eyes on Dr. Curtis's hand. He was determined to keep the shield flat and level. For a moment the shield felt stuck, and Perry was afraid that Curtis would back off in the name of caution, but he didn't. Letting his eyes rise from Curtis's hand for a moment, he looked at the professor and saw that he was biting his lip. Perry expected to see blood any moment.

The shield rose with a gentle crackle. Perry had visions of the ancient soldier's arm dangling beneath, but his fear was unfounded. The four men removed the shield from its centuries-old resting spot.

"Okay, this is good," Curtis said, sounding like a man who had just run a mile uphill. Perry realized that he too had been holding his breath. "I think two of us can handle it now."

Perry slid his other hand down the shield to the opposite corner. Curtis did the same. It felt remarkably light. As soon as Gleason and Jack were out of the way, Perry and Curtis took several side steps and then gently set the shield down on the grassy ground.

"This guy was buried in full military dress," Jack said.

Perry returned to the coffin and took in the sight of a skeleton dressed in deteriorated and crumbling armor.

"Brass greaves on the legs," Curtis said. "Segmental armor

strips probably held in place by leather ties." He hunkered down again. "He's got it all: long double-edged sword called a 'Spanish sword' on his right side, leather belt, iron ring mail, and a dagger."

"That's quite a sheath," Perry said, looking at the dagger's inlaid enamel and silver scabbard.

"He's wearing a baldric," Curtis commented. "That could be significant."

"A what?" Gleason asked.

"A baldric," Curtis replied. "It's the leather sash running from his shoulder to his hip. It was used to provide additional support for the sword."

"Oh, silly me," Gleason quipped. "Why would it be significant?"

"It may help date the soldier. If memory serves me, baldrics came into use around the first century."

"It looks like there are shreds of red material," Jack said. "Is that his uniform?"

"Tunic," Curtis answered. "This is amazing," he admitted. "If the other objects in the survey are like this, then archeologists are going to have a field day."

"And historians are going to have migraines."

"So this is why you wanted to keep things quiet," Montulli said. "Trying to keep all this undercover until the research is done. I can understand that."

That's only one reason, Sergeant, and a small reason at that, Perry thought to himself. He turned to Jack. "How is the other digging going?"

"Good. The ground is firm but easy enough to handle. The two digs farthest from us may need to use the backhoe. The objects are too deep to reach with shovels."

"What's your plan?"

"Use the backhoe to get within three feet of the objects. Shore the sides of the pit and put men down there to do the sensitive digging."

"Just make sure the backhoe doesn't dig too deeply and upend our precious find," Curtis said.

"I've got our best man on the job," Jack said. "He has a gentle touch. He can scratch an itch on your back with a bucket, if you want."

"No thanks," Curtis shot back. "I'll just take your word for it."

"As soon as any team hits their target, I want Dr. Curtis standing there, directing the extraction. We'll open each coffin for a brief look, then wrap it in ten mill plastic sheeting. We'll crate them after that."

"That part is easy," Jack said. "The real challenge is getting the coffins through the crowds and into the trucks."

"Can you help us with that, Sergeant?" Perry asked. "I know that I'm not on your good list, but a few deputies helping the private security would be appreciated."

"I don't have a problem with you, Mr. Sachs," Montulli replied. "Sure, you've turned my town upside down and put the mayor on the war path, but I can't say you've done anything more criminal than annoy me."

"Does Detective Sanchez feel that way?" Perry asked with a wry grin.

"No. Him you ticked off quite nicely," Montulli answered. "Getting a call from the governor's office didn't put him in a good mood. Sanchez is a good cop, but he doesn't like to have his work meddled with."

"It couldn't be helped," Perry said. "I had to do what I did. Can I count on you for a little more help?"

"Yeah, I'll pitch in again, but I want to stay on scene. This stuff fascinates me. I love surprises."

"Then you are going to be one happy man, Sergeant. One happy man indeed."

Claire's heart began to slow from its hour-long frenetic pounding. Her breathing came easier now. The woman said she could take off the blindfold five minutes after she heard the door close. Claire had no idea how much time had passed.

The woman had come to the old warehouse office, opened the door, and strolled in as if paying a visit to an old friend. Claire bolted to her feet; Joseph remained seated on the floor, rocking back and forth. "You're moving," she announced without emotion. "I'm going to blindfold you. Sit down and tilt your head back."

"My head?"

"Just do it," she demanded. "Tilt your head back and close your eyes."

Claire did. Thoughts of escape ran through her mind. Maybe she could overpower the woman, or at the very least, push her aside and escape through the open door. But the thoughts never became action. The woman was less than half Claire's age and looked to be twice as strong. Claire had rarely been athletic and never confrontational. Violence sickened her.

With her head back and eyes closed, Claire felt the soft touch of material. It had a slight but familiar odor to it. Gauze. The woman was putting medical gauze on over Claire's closed lids. "Can't you just let us go? We don't have anything you want."

"No, I can't let you go, and yes, you do have something we want."

"We?"

"Shut up and hold still."

Something else was laid against Claire's eyes, something hard and round; small disks about the size of a half-dollar. It occurred to her a moment later that that was what the objects were: coins. A second later there was a ripping sound followed by a tearing noise. Something sticky was placed over the coins and gauze. It stuck to her forehead and cheek. Tape, she realized. Her abductor had taped the large coin and gauze to Claire's face. She did the same to the other eye.

"Okay, tilt your head forward."

Claire complied, and she felt a band of cloth placed around her eyes.

"That ought to do it," the woman said. "One down, one to go."

"You don't need to do that," Claire objected. "Joseph can't talk. He's harmless and no threat to you."

"Uhh. . .uhh. . .Perry. . .uhh. . .uhh."

"That sounds like talking to me," the woman snapped.

"That's all he can say. That and just a few other words."

"Too many words for my comfort. Okay, buddy, head back." A second later: "I said, head back."

"He doesn't understand you," Claire said. "Let me sit by him."

Another pause, then, "He's right in front of you, in the same place he was when I came in. And make him stop rocking."

Claire scooted forward on her seat, extended her right hand, and reached for her son. She found him, touching him on his shoulder. He rocked twice more then stopped. Easing forward, Claire reached out with her other hand then slipped from the chair to the floor. With only touch to go on, she quickly determined Joseph's position and sat on the floor next to him. Slipping her arm around his shoulders, she pulled him close. He responded by laying his head on her shoulder. Moving her hand from his shoulder, she felt along his body until she found his hair, then his forehead. Gently she pulled back. Joseph offered no resistance.

"Be gentle with him," Claire pleaded.

The woman gave no reply. Through the subtle motions of Joseph's head, Claire could sense the work her captor was doing: the gauze, the coins, the tape. Joseph took it all with no resistance or sound.

Events moved quickly after that. The woman demanded that they rise and Claire did, helping Joseph to his feet. "We're going for a little ride," she said. "I'll lead you down the stairs and to the van. You will do exactly as I say. The stairs are treacherous, and a fall could be. . .painful." Claire understood the threat.

The trek down the stairs went without incident, something Claire was thankful for. Once on the first floor of the warehouse, the woman took Claire by the arm and started walking, towing Claire after her. Joseph followed closely as he always did, with his head pressed against Claire's shoulder. Time passed, but Claire had no means to measure it. Blindfolded and in a strange environment, minutes seemed like hours. She had few sensations. They were placed in the back of a vehicle that seemed to be the same as the panel truck that had brought them to the warehouse. The drive was punctuated with stop-and-go driving. After what seemed like an hour, the vehicle stopped and the back doors opened.

"Everybody out."

Claire prayed that someone would see them exiting the van, that someone would notice the blindfolds and call the police. It was a prayer that Claire began in detail but that quickly became a mantra, "Please, please, please, please. . ."

In her lifetime, Claire had felt helpless on several occasions. First, when the doctors first told her that Joseph would never be like other boys. That moment had sent her reeling, emotions tumbling like a skydiver who has lost control of his descent. The worst had been the moment the hospital called to give her news of Jamison's injury and heart attack. Uncertainty descended like rain in a hurricane. The reality of his death had made the past precious and the future a place to fear. In each of those cases, she'd survived the shock and pain. She could do it again, she told herself. If she were careful, if she were smart, if she made no stupid moves, then she and Joseph might make it through all of this. God willing, they would survive.

The rest of the journey was on foot over a hard surface that Claire guessed was concrete. Her footsteps echoed harshly, and she assumed they were in a parking structure. There was a slight smell of oil. Moments later the unforgiving concrete gave way to a softer, but still firm, floor. She could feel a low pile carpet under her feet. A bell also sounded, and the purring of a quiet motor floated in the air. They were familiar sounds. Claire and Joseph were led three more steps and they heard the moving of metal doors. The floor lurched to the accompanying sounds of rattling nearby, as if behind the wall. The sensation of motion was proof enough for Claire to know they were in an elevator.

Moments later, another ding preceded the sound of the doors opening. The woman, who was both captor and guide, took Claire's elbow again and moved her forward. The floor felt softer underfoot, a sign that they were walking on a thicker, plusher carpet. She heard no other sounds. The pace picked up.

"Not too fast," Claire said. "It's hard for Joseph to keep up."

"No talking," the woman snapped. There was anger in her voice, but she slowed her pace.

At first, Claire tried to count her steps, making a mental map like she had seen people do on television movies, but it was impossible. Without her sight she soon became disoriented and fearful of tripping or bumping into something. She felt more helpless with each step.

"In here," the woman said and pulled Claire at a right angle to the course they had been walking. The constant pressure of Joseph's head on her shoulder suddenly disappeared. Unable to see, he had no way of noting the change in direction.

"Joseph," Claire cried and pulled loose of the woman's grasp. Claire turned and extended her hands, reaching for her son.

"He's right here." Claire felt the woman's grip again and a pulling motion. She bumped into Joseph. "Here, take his hand."

Joseph's hand made contact with hers, and Claire took a firm hold. Next, she felt herself being tugged along. Her shoulder hit something solid, sending a scorching pain down her arm. She let slip a small cry of pain. The woman pulled harder, and Claire stumbled forward.

"Stand here for five minutes," the woman said. "After that, you may take your blindfolds off."

Claire stood frozen in place listening, straining her ears to hear anything. A few seconds later, the thud of door meeting jamb filled the room. So did the sound of a lock being set. Claire waited, Joseph's hand held firmly in hers. Seconds jerked by like the halting steps of pallbearers.

"Stand still," Claire said as she released Joseph's hand. Reaching to her face, she removed the cloth band that circled her head and dropped it to the floor, then she gently removed the tape on her face. The glue pulled at her skin and took whatever hairs had been unfortunate enough to be under the tape. The coins and the gauze came off as well, and Claire blinked several times before being able to take in her surroundings.

She was in a room much larger and cleaner than the one they'd left behind in the warehouse. The walls were smooth and white; the floor was also white and covered in industrial-looking vinyl tile. There were no windows, and the only sound was the gentle breathing of the air conditioner. Overhead were recessed fluorescent lights, only half of which were on. Turning, she saw several metal cabinets against one wall, their doors open revealing empty shelves. Next to the cabinets were two plastic folding chairs. A large counter dominated the center of the room, with a small sink to one side. The counter was covered in black Formica. It reminded her of the lab stations in her high school chemistry class. In the back wall was an open door. A small light burned inside, just enough for Claire to know that she was looking into a bathroom. She was thankful for that.

"Let's get this nasty stuff off you," she said to Joseph. It took several minutes for Claire to gingerly remove the tape from her son's face. Seeing Joseph's face taped had filled her with churning pity and boiling anger. She could do something about the tape, but she could do nothing about the emotion she felt or the situation they were in. It frustrated her to know she had no more influence over the events that surrounded her than a cork had in the ocean. If help were to come, it would have to be from the outside.

"Uhh. . .uhh," Joseph said and pushed past Claire. She turned, uncertain where he could go. He didn't go far. Shuffling as he went, Joseph stepped to the side of the center counter and pointed. Claire walked to his side. At his feet lay something she'd not seen in her hurried examination of the room: a thick roll of butcher paper like they kept at the house. On the counter were a dozen boxes of crayons, colored chalks, and even watercolors.

Joseph bounced on his toes and continued pointing.

"Okay," Claire said. "At least you'll have something to do."

The roll of paper was too heavy for Claire to lift; it would have to remain where it was. Reaching down, she took hold of the edge of the two-foot-wide paper and took several steps back. With a practiced pull and twist, she ripped off a length of paper about four feet long and draped it across the counter. She opened one of the boxes of crayons and stepped to the side. Joseph immediately began to draw, his face hovering over the paper by mere inches. Claire made use of the bathroom and then insisted that Joseph do the same. No sooner was he out than he returned to his project.

Claire sat in one of the chairs. And waited.

"Interesting," Rutherford said and tapped a key on his keyboard. The image on the video monitor zoomed in slightly. "Only mildly vocal, but he seems aware of things around him."

Julia looked over her brother's shoulder. "He shows no sign of fear and has offered no resistance. He's the most passive person I've seen."

"He doesn't seem all that intelligent," Alex said.

"He's not," Rutherford said. "He's a savant, brilliant in a few things he cannot himself understand. Beyond that, he's dysfunctional in every way. I did a little research while Julia was gone. Extraordinary material. Seems it all centers on damage to the left hemisphere. There are several cases on record in which adults, even the elderly, become savants after injury or disease. Our boy here may be a 'prodigious savant.' Not many of them around, maybe fifty in the world."

"Prodigious savants?" Julia said.

"People with skill levels beyond any expectation. They'd be remarkable even if they were normal in other ways."

"What's his fascination with drawing?" Alex asked.

"It's one of the few communication outlets he has. I doubt his brain processes information as ours do. Our brains work by retention and relation. We see things or events happen, and we store them away. The brain then processes that information through relation to other events and expresses it in the form of emotion or thought. I'd bet the way his brain relates to its stored information is nothing like that. He might as well be a creature from another world, evolved in a way we can't imagine. And here he is, stuck among five billion people who are nothing like him at all."

"He's also stuck in one of our unused labs," Julia said. "And I'm not comfortable having them here for long. After all, I did kidnap them. I believe that's still a felony."

"The lab is in a secured wing. We are in no danger, and we can observe them at our leisure. Here."

Rutherford punched another few keys with his one still-obedient hand. The color printer on the side desk came to life. It spat out several color images from the monitor.

"Take those, Alex. It's time for another trip to California."

CHAPTER 15

The late hour getting to you, Doc?"

Perry found Curtis sitting in the oak grove office, his arms crossed over his chest. His face was pallid under the artificial light, his shoulders slumped as if holding bags of wet cement. "Maybe you should try to get a couple hours of sleep."

"Couldn't sleep if I tried, Perry. Not tonight. I may not sleep for a week."

"That's understandable," Perry answered. "You're walking on the greatest archeological find ever. I imagine you're pretty excited."

"So you'd think," Curtis replied morosely.

Perry pulled up a camp chair and joined the doctor. "Something eating at you?"

"This is *not* the way to run a dig, Perry," Curtis blurted. "We're moving too fast, taking too many risks. Things are going to be overlooked. Archeology is built upon bits not just blocks. Secrets are hidden in the small things. We should be sifting the dirt from the pits; we should have a team of archeologists here and graduate students too. At the very least we should have an expert in Roman archeology." He sighed, and his shoulders dropped another notch. "I'm going to be vilified in the literature, Perry. I'm about to become the poster boy for bad archeology."

"You know why we're doing this, Professor," Perry soothed.

"The speed isn't a choice; it's a requirement that was foisted upon us. I agree we should be moving slowly, but there are forces against us. If there were any other way, we'd do it, but we've been compromised, and a man has been killed. When the whole story is known, you won't be vilified, you'll be honored."

"It still gets under my skin."

"Why do I think there's something else percolating in your brain?" Perry asked.

"Am I that transparent?"

"Not really, but I am good at guessing games. For example, I bet what's really eating at you is that you've seen five ancient Roman soldiers where no such soldier should be. Am I right?"

Curtis uncrossed his arms and leaned forward, gazing at the ground. "How can it be, Perry? It's been known for decades that Columbus wasn't the first man to cross the oceans. There's some evidence that Vikings landed on the east coast nearly a thousand years ago. There is even slight evidence that Asians may have made it to the California coast long before Columbus was around. It's all speculative and hotly debated. It's certainly not mainstream science, but it's nonetheless there, hovering at the fringes."

"And now. . ."

"And now I have five fool-proof, undeniable evidences that the new world was visited by first-century Romans, and a sixth one being unearthed as we speak."

Perry looked across the pasture. Five gaping holes punctuated the terrain, marked off by yellow plastic construction tape, their gaping mouths covered with sheets of plywood. At each dig, two men shoveled the remaining mounds of dirt into heavy plastic bags, each marked with a large number painted on the side. A paper tag containing the same number and additional information was wired to the twisted top of each bag. The sixth coffin was being excavated and was due to be extracted in the next few minutes.

Curtis had overseen each removal, supervised the opening of each coffin, made prodigious notes, and then supervised the resealing. Each coffin was wrapped in thick plastic sheeting, and finally a crate was built around it. Once the last excavation was finished, the six ancient caskets would be carted under guard to a waiting truck and driven to the airport. Perry had leased a large private plane to fly the bodies to the various universities Curtis designated.

Curtis had been on the job since his arrival, with the hours filled by unexpected stressful events. He'd been pulled from his home by Perry's call, flown across country, witnessed the uncovering of a murder victim, been grilled by the police, learned of Perry's remarkable find, and confronted the archeologically impossible. *All in all*, Perry thought, *he's holding up quite well*.

"Every moment brings new questions," Curtis said. "At first all I could ask was, 'What's a nice Roman like you doing in a place like this?' Silly way to put it, I know, but it sums up the problem. . . I should say, problems. It's just one problem layered upon another."

"I think I know what you're getting at," Perry said. "How did they get here? I don't think the Romans of that period sailed the open ocean. They weren't true deep-water sailors."

"They didn't have to be," Curtis said. "Their army owned the land, and their navy had only the Mediterranean to contend with. They extended their influence all the way to Spain, but the Atlantic was too big a barrier to cross. Besides, as far as they knew there was nothing beyond, so why bother?"

"That's one thing that bothers me," Perry said. "If my geography is right, even if a Roman ship sailed out of the Mediterranean, they would be in the Atlantic. That's the wrong ocean. Could they sail from one ocean to another?"

"Long-distance sailing could be done in ancient cultures. The technology of sailing wasn't that different from that available to fifteenth-century explorers. The later sailors had larger ships, multiple sails, and navigation skills the Romans lacked. All in all that's significant, but there's nothing to say that a Roman cargo ship or warship couldn't have endured a transatlantic trip, even by accident.

"The Norwegian anthropologist Thor Heyerdahl sailed a balsa-log raft he called Kon-Tiki from Peru to the Tutamotu Islands, east of Tahiti. He crossed 4,300 miles of open seas in just over one hundred days. On board were only five men, and the raft was basically a log and lashing construction. The boat endured harsh conditions, but it survived. He also crossed the Atlantic from North Africa to Barbados in less than sixty days. So it's possible for a small boat to cross the oceans.

"The ancient Romans had some pretty sophisticated ships," Curtis continued. "Most people think of their warships like a penteconter, a vessel with a square sail and room for fifty oarsmen, but there were also large merchant ships with two or three masts sporting square sails and measuring five hunderd tons. Some historians are convinced that there were ships twice that size to move grain from Egypt throughout the Empire."

"So it's not impossible for a Roman ship to sail across the ocean," Perry said.

"Not impossible, but highly unlikely. Why would they bother? Unlike the Vikings, Romans were not known for being great explorers."

Perry thought for a moment then said, "People do the unusual out of need or fear. Maybe they were fleeing."

"Because of what you expect to find below the ground?" Curtis said.

"Yes. I think they might have been driven to protect their precious cargo. Many questions remain. As you said, we're on the wrong side of the continent. If a Roman vessel left the Mediterranean, it would be afloat in the Atlantic, not the Pacific."

"I've been thinking about that, Perry." Curtis leaned back in his chair and gazed skyward. The work lights washed out any chance to see stars, but Perry knew the archeologist was not looking skyward; he was looking inward. "Ancient sailors usually stayed within sight of shore. Coming past the Pillars of Hercules, they could have

209

followed the African coast south and rounded what we now call the Cape of Good Hope, then sailed up the coast in the Indian Ocean. From there they would follow the trade route to Asia."

"A long and rough journey," Perry said. "The seas around the southern tip of Africa are notoriously bad."

"They would have needed a lot of luck and all the breaks they could get."

"They needed more than luck; they needed Providence," Perry added. "Still, they would have to cross the Pacific or follow the coastline north into the cold and treacherous waters around the Bering Strait and down the western edge of Alaska. Not a trip I'd want to take."

"That's just one possibility," Curtis said. "It's also possible that they were blown out to sea and forced to cross the Pacific. The truth is we just don't know, and we may never know."

"And that's just part of the mystery," Perry added. "Why come all the way to the Tehachapi Mountains? We know they made it this far regardless of the path they may have taken, but why settle here? The coast is eighty miles away by air. These guys would have to have walked that distance. Why go through that much trouble?"

"Perhaps they didn't know where they were. If they were blown to sea by a storm then continued east, they would encounter land, but not a land they would recognize. Maybe they were confused. Maybe they weren't welcomed by the coastal Indians. Maybe they lost their minds. I don't know."

"Or maybe they wanted to make sure their treasure was as safe as they could make it," Perry said.

"Perhaps, perhaps. I don't think anyone will ever know."

Perry shifted his gaze across the field. Jack was standing at the last grave, Site Six as it had been dubbed, and he was motioning for them. "It looks like they have our last friend out of the ground, Doc. It's time for you to make your inspection."

Curtis rose and started across the field. Perry stepped to his side. "You know, Doc, once we make the needed extractions, you will be free to scour the site for years to come. The agreement we have with the property owners allows us access for quite some time."

"That's good to know. It may take years to piece the whole story together. We've only scratched the surface. For every one thing I see, fifteen new questions arise. For example, did the people take up residence here? If so, where is the evidence of their habitation? There should be rubbish pits, evidence of homes, and more. And the planks, where did they come from? Did they hew them from the surrounding trees? Somehow I don't think so."

"I'll bet you a breakfast that the coffins are made from the wood of their ship," Perry said. "I know, I know, that opens even more questions. Why tear up the boat and then cart it a hundred miles or so away from the shore?"

"It would be an insane act, but nothing would surprise me now," Curtis said.

When they arrived at the open grave, Jack, Gleason, and Brent hovered over the dark wood box. Two other workers stood nearby. Brent stood ready to fire up the video camera. "Last one," Jack said as he unhooked the straps that had been used to secure the casket. The moment he finished, he gave the backhoe operator the signal to move the rig back from the site.

"Let's pop it," Perry said. "Then we can bring the backhoe around to start on the primary dig."

Jack took a small crowbar and slipped its thin edge between the center top board and the coffin's vertical front surface. The square iron nails protested the intrusion but gave way easily. Jack passed the tool to Perry, who adroitly worked the other side. Together they lifted the board and gently set it to the side.

The men gazed into the coffin expecting to see what they had seen in the other five. They didn't. There was no shield, no helmet, no cloak of iron mail, and no sword.

"Well," said Curtis softly. "It appears I was wrong, Perry. I am still capable of surprise."

"It's. . ." Brent began, then realized he wasn't taping. He raised the camera and activated the tiny halogen light. "It's a woman."

Perry was staring down at the small, skeletal frame that seemed far too small for the coffin. A cloth, darkened by centuries, lay across the bones. The skull was tilted to one side, resting on a thin pillow of long brown hair. He said nothing. He had expected the unusual. The whole idea, the whole project was beyond the scope of the expected, but this sight rattled him.

"I'm right. . .right?" Brent said. "I mean the hair, the skeleton is smaller, and the hands are tiny by comparison."

"Let's take the rest of the lid off," Perry said eagerly. The flat metal pry bar did its work efficiently, and the planks that made up the remaining lid were placed on the ground in the order they were removed. Perry dropped to his knees and peered into the long box.

Curtis squatted by Perry. "What do you think, Doc?" Perry asked.

"I think the young man is right. The hair itself isn't proof, but it's a good indicator. The proof will be in the shape of the pelvis and in the DNA. Still, my first guess is that this is a woman of. . ." he trailed off as he examined the skull more closely. "Teeth are all mature and show wear. She had reached her middle years. I'd guess that she was in her mid-thirties."

"Not very tall," Gleason said.

"Neither were the soldiers," Perry said. "I'd be surprised. . . more surprised if their height was comparable to ours."

Something caught Perry's eye: scratch marks just above the head of the corpse. "What's this?" He leaned forward and strained his eyes, but the marks were too faint to make out. "Chalk," Perry said. "I need some chalk."

"We have the chalk powder we used to mark the survey grid," Gleason said. "I'll grab a handful." He was gone before the sentence was finished. Two minutes later he held the white powder in a paper cup.

Perry reached into the cup and pinched the substance between his fingers. He sprinkled the powder over the scratch marks.

"Perry, we shouldn't be contaminating. . ." Curtis began, but Perry waved him off.

Slowly, as if he could will each flake of chalk into the right place, Perry sprinkled the dust, then he leaned over, his head just an inch from the head of the dead woman, and gently blew the excess away.

"You getting this, Brent?" Perry questioned, his voice bouncing off the coffin.

"I'm on it, boss. Move your head so I can zoom in a little."

Perry did, but his eyes remained fixed on the image before him. The white chalk had settled into the grooves contrasting with the age-darkened wood.

M R AE AGD ENAE

"Is that a sentence or something?" Gleason asked. "It looks like three, maybe four words. I don't know Latin, but it doesn't look like any Latin sentence I've seen."

"Some of the letters are still unclear," Perry said. "Let me see that cup of chalk." Perry took the cup from Gleason and sprinkled more of the fine powder on the area. This time he rubbed gently before blowing away the excess. It achieved little.

M R AE AGDA ENAE

"One additional letter, that's not much help. I'm sorry, Doc," Perry said, his eyes still fixed on the enigmatic sentence. "I'm afraid I contaminated the artifact for nothing. Have you got any ideas as to what we're looking at?"

There was no answer.

"Dr. Curtis?"

Nothing.

Perry turned and saw Dr. Curtis sitting on the ground, his knees up and his head resting on his crossed arms. It looked like he was taking a siesta.

"You okay, Doc?" Jack asked.

Curtis lifted his head, and Perry saw that his skin was as white as the chalk he held in the cup. Perry rose from his place by the coffin, stepped to where Curtis sat, and joined him on the ground. "You know what it says, don't you?"

Curtis nodded. "I know everything you've told me should have prepared me for this, but my mind wouldn't accept it. How can any of this be? It can't, it's impossible. The treasure you seek is just too remarkable to believe. No scientist would accept it. I've been telling myself that it's all a hoax, or a colossal misinterpretation of the facts. But this. . .this. . ."

"What's it say, Dr. Curtis?" Perry prodded gently. "We need to know."

"It's Latin, and it's not a sentence; it's a name—MARIAE MAGDALENAE—Mary Magdalene."

CHAPTER 16

Perry had been face-to-face with one of the most famous people to walk the earth, and the significance wasn't wasted on him.

The shock of the find fired through the gathered group like multiple lightning strikes. The light banter had evaporated under the heat of witnessing the impossible. The men stood huddled around the coffin, the group immersed in silence, each man lost in the forest of his own thoughts. Only Dr. Curtis was distant. He remained seated on the grass, staring across the distance like a blind man might stare into his darkness.

The site had taken on a surrealistic feel: Yellow light rained down from the work lights high on their aluminum stands, the sound of the backhoe's diesel engine idling nearby, the oak-scented breeze wafting through, and the lifeless remains of one of history's best known people lying in a fragile box.

"I hate to be the stupid one of the group," Brent said, his voice a single level above a whisper, "but I need to ask. Exactly who is Mary Magdalene? She's mentioned in the Bible, right?"

"Yes," Perry said. "Mary Magdalene is a key personality in the ministry of Jesus. Everything about her is unique, and she has been the source of inspiration for many; she's also been the subject of the wildest speculation."

"Such as?" Brent prompted.

"Such as Jesus didn't die on the cross but lived to an old age with Mary as His wife, such as she is the author of the Gospel of John, such as she presented a threat to the pride and position of the disciples, and other nonsense."

"If she was none of that, then what was she?" Brent asked.

"Her name is Mary, which is the Greek form of the Hebrew Miriam. The Bible refers to her as Mary Magdalene. Most likely the Magdalene refers to a town in Galilee called Magdala. The first time she's mentioned in the Bible two things are noted: One, she was possessed of evil spirits which Jesus cast out of her; two, she provided support for Jesus' ministry from. . .I think the passage says personal means."

"Private means," Curtis said. "She and the other women supported Jesus and the disciples through their private financial resources."

"Thanks, Doc," Perry said, glad that Curtis was still with them in mind as well as body. "Jesus was an itinerant preacher going from town to town with His message. Some of the monetary support for the ministry came from people like Mary."

"Wait a minute," Brent interrupted. "Evil spirits? Demons? That was just a convenient way for the ancients to describe illness they couldn't explain. . .right?"

"No," Perry explained. "The Bible uses other words for diseases. It distinguishes between demonic activity and human disease."

"So you really believe that Mary was inhabited by non-human, intelligent forces?" He laughed and looked for support from the others. No one else was laughing. He shuffled his feet then said, "Sorry. You were saying. . ."

"Mary and other women traveled with Jesus and the disciples. They heard what the men heard, saw much of what they saw. They were there from the early days of Jesus' ministry, and they were there when Jesus was nailed to the cross. In fact, Mary watched Him die.

"The following Sunday morning, she went to the tomb and

found it open. The sight crushed her already injured heart. As she wept, an angel told her that Jesus had risen from the dead and that she should go tell the disciples, which she did. Later she came back to the tomb and Jesus—back from the dead—appeared to her. As would be expected, she was overcome with emotion and began clinging to His feet. He had to tell her to let go. Her place in history is unique because she is the first person to see Jesus after his resurrection."

"What's she doing *here?*" Brent asked. "California is a long way from the biblical lands."

Perry looked down at the body, amazed and humbled at what he was seeing. "I don't know, Brent. I'm as surprised as you."

"Man, you weren't kidding when you said this project would change everything," Brent said.

"We have to treat this differently," Curtis said. Perry looked over his shoulder and saw the scientist rising from his place on the ground and walking toward him. "I can't send this to just anybody. I want to handle it myself."

"I was hoping you'd say that," Perry said. "I'll have it moved out of the way and let you examine it. . .er, her. . .for as long as you like. In the meantime, we have some more digging to do." Perry's words were strange and even, the words of a natural leader with a mission to complete. On the outside he was rock solid; on the inside he felt like Jell-O.

After leaving O'Tool's, Anne had driven around town for an hour. Perry's words reverberated in her mind and heart.

"You owe God an apology."

At first the comment galled her, eating at her insides as if she had downed acid. Anger had raged in her like waves in a stormy sea crashing against the hull of her fragile emotions. But there was another emotion flowing in her, and unlike her anger and bitterness, this emotion was cool and promised a refreshing release.

It's a trick of the imagination, she told herself. She was tired, upset, hurt, angry, and in need of emotional freedom, but there was no freedom. Sorrow and hatred were two coals that refused to go out, two embers that burned hotter with the passage of time, and they burned right in the center of Anne's heart.

She drove up and down the streets of Tejon, her adopted town, and tried to regain her fury. She wanted to stay mad, wanted to feel the blaze of anger in her. It made her feel alive and, ironically, in control. When she was angry, she was not heartbroken. It was an odd, illogical fact, but one she had learned to live with. Anger drove away other emotions, those emotions that hurt too much to ignore.

The anger wouldn't hold this evening. Perry's words about owing God an apology were pervasive, wheedling out of her thoughts she didn't want to have.

Once she considered herself a friend of God, His child, His servant, but after her husband's brutal murder, she could no longer see herself that way. She had tried going back to church, but it seemed a hollow gesture. People looked at her through eyes of pity; some even avoided her, perhaps to avoid having to face the fact that bad things happen to good people. The pastor had been kind and supportive, but there were no words in his vocabulary, no techniques in his training that could sponge away the black veil of sorrow from her mind.

Her faith collapsed like stacked dominoes clattering around her feet. Her family had rocks of faith, wounded by the searing heat of the event, but still unshaken. Of course, they had only lost an "in-law," where she had lost the one true love of her life and not by disease or accident or anything that might be considered "normal." No, John had been shot in the face, his life of lesser value to the murderer than the money carried in her husband's wallet.

God let it happen, Anne had reasoned. If He was God, if He is omnipotent, then He could have—should have—done something.

But He didn't, and that meant He was either a powerless pretender or criminally apathetic. Either way, He was not the God she had believed in since childhood, and not a God she wanted to associate with.

The old emotions rose to the surface like magma up a volcano's flue, pushing, pressing, expanding until something had to give and the inevitable eruption would take place. Most eruptions came in silent tears as she sat in her dark home; sometimes the anger won, and those closest to her became the victims of catastrophe. It was why she left Ridgeline. It was why she had not spoken to her sister more than a handful of times over the last half-decade.

"An apology!" Anne said. She had uttered the phrase a score and more times. The words were spoken hotly, awash in the bile of long pent-up animosity aimed at the Divine. But each time she spoke the word, the indefinable emotion made itself known. The anger was cooling, the magma receding, and she felt puzzled.

Something rattled in the back of her mind, like an indistinguishable sound heard in the dead of night that awakens one from deep slumber. Instead of fear, the thing, the emotion, the presence was making itself welcome. Anne tried repeatedly to push it from her thoughts, preferring to wallow in the misery that had been her constant companion for five years. The feeling wouldn't be evicted. Instead, it quietly pushed forward, expelling the bitter darkness with the glow of its own life.

It was an impossible task, Anne had decided as she steered her car home. It would be easier to empty the ocean with a teaspoon than expunge the sorrow she carried with her, but with each mile that passed under the tires of her car, more blackness dissolved. By the time she returned home, parked the car, and entered the house, she was dangerously close to feeling good.

She turned on no lights, fixed no refreshment for herself; instead she dropped her purse on the floor by the door as she shut it and turned the latch and walked through the dark room which was lit only by the front porch light as it pressed into the room though the glass panes of the front door. A few steps later she sat upon her sofa, eyes closed and mind confused. The anger was ebbing like a tide.

"Apology!" she said to the darkness. "Not as long as I live."

The warmth had spread now, filling each brain cell and trickling down to her heart.

"I refuse to apologize to a God who let my husband. . .let someone kill. . ." She couldn't finish the sentence; the words choked in her throat. "What does Perry know about it. . .Mr. Righteous Man. . . He can't understand. . .doesn't care. . ." She knew the thoughts were lies, each one, every one a fabrication meant to shield her from the truth.

Tears welled and brimmed, hands shook, emptiness filled with a wash of golden comfort—comfort she had avoided every day of the last five years. And with the comfort came peace. Still Anne fought back. It made no sense. Comfort and peace were what she needed, but it came with a price: To accept the offer, she had to admit she had been wrong, that God was not responsible for her husband's death and that she was responsible for living in a purgatory of her own creation.

She had kept the room dark to avoid the light, but an illumination grew inside of her, and there was no denying it, no extinguishing it. The light wouldn't be ignored, wouldn't be sent away. Anne wanted to hate God, to withhold every positive emotion from Him. It was His fault, He was to blame. No, she wouldn't apologize, she wouldn't bend, she would feed the vicious animal of hatred and never let it weaken, never let it die.

The dam cracked.

The tears poured out.

The truth flooded in.

The fortress of lies had been breached, not by an invading army but by the constant, pervasive, unyielding love of God. Anne had always been aware of its presence; had always known that no matter how bitter she had become, no matter how abusive of God's good name, she was still loved. She had resisted so fervently because to accept the peace God offered meant accepting the fact that John was dead and had died in a horrible way. To let peace reign, she had to leave behind the shield of anger.

Now there were no more shields. The hiding was over. She had been wrong, and she knew it.

Praying was hard. The only words Anne had directed heavenward had been curses, but new words needed to be uttered. No sentences formed in her mind, no formal phrases. Only two words: "I'm. . .I'm sorry."

The business jet cut through the night sky, its lone passenger sitting in a darkened cabin, in a plush seat, staring out the window at the glistening drops of light below.

He recognized it from his previous flight south. This was his second flight over the central valley of California in as many days—third if he counted the return trip. Below him was one of the richest areas of farmland in the country. The soil below, when combined with the sweat of the farmer and migrant worker, yielded everything from grapes to almonds. The overfed stomachs of Americans were touched by the work that went on below. The high-pressure sodium lights on the ground looked hued with gold. The city below was Fresno, and the next stop was Bakersfield. His plane would land there as it had the day before.

And as before, he would do what he needed to do in an effective, efficient, untraceable way. That's the way Rutherford Straight wanted it; it was the way Alex Olek would do it.

The metal bucket of the backhoe hovered in the air, its shaped metal teeth securely welded to steel gums. Perry nodded and the operator pushed a lever. The bucket dropped in an even motion and took a bite of the topsoil, a bite measured in hundreds of pounds. Smoothly the articulated arm of the big tool curled the bucket under, holding the dirt in place until it had completed a ninety-degree swing to the left where it deposited the dirt in a pile. The bucket returned and inhaled another load, then another, and another. Perry had to admire the work of the operator. He'd been hand-selected by Jack with the promise that he was the best heavy equipment operator on the West Coast. Watching the ease and confidence with which he did his work made Perry believe it.

"I'm back."

Perry turned to see Sergeant Montulli standing next to him. "I thought you called it a night."

"Nope. I said I was staying, and stay I will. One of my deputies told me that Detective Sanchez wanted me to call. Since we don't have cell service tucked away as we are in these hills, I took a quick trip back to Tejon. Did I miss anything exciting?"

Perry laughed, partly from the irony of the question and partly because weariness was catching up with him. "You might say that." He explained about the Site Six excavation and the discovery of the woman's remains. He also mentioned the name they found etched inside the coffin.

"No way!" Montulli said. "I don't believe it."

"That's your prerogative, Sergeant. I saw it with my own eyes, and I'm having trouble believing it too. Unless it can be shown to be a hoax, we have unearthed one of history's most important people."

"Can it be a hoax?"

"I suppose it's possible, but I doubt it. Right now I'd have more trouble believing that it was a setup than in believing that the body of Mary Magdalene is resting up by the trailer."

"Is that where your Dr. Curtis is?"

"Yes. He's doing a cursory examination and taking still photos."

"I imagine he has his work cut out for him," Montulli said.

"And more is on the way," Perry said, nodding at the hole being dug by the backhoe.

"So you gonna tell me what you expect to find?"

"Let's not go there now, Sergeant. If I'm right, you'll know soon. And remember that you've agreed not to say anything to anyone."

"Unless it involves a crime. I'm not setting aside the law for you or anyone else."

"I'm not asking you to. I'm just calling on your honor and discretion."

Montulli nodded.

The two fell silent for a moment as each watched the graceful ballet of man and machine. "Sanchez had some news," Montulli said finally. "The murdered man you found was a private detective named Dawes."

Perry nodded. Anne had told him that much earlier, but he saw no sense in mentioning the conversation. He was uncertain if Anne should have been revealing such information since he was, technically, still a suspect. "News of his murder was aired on the eleven o'clock news in Bakersfield. A guy by the name of Willis called the sheriff's department and said he had seen the man the day he died."

"Really? When and where?" Perry asked.

"This Willis guy owns an aerial survey business with his brother. He told Sanchez that Dawes breezed in demanding an immediate survey and wanted pictures right away. Want to guess where he was surveying?"

"Here?" Perry remembered gazing at the sky when he first arrived at the site and seeing a small plane flying overhead. He wondered if he had been watching someone watching him.

"That's right. Sanchez asked for copies of the photos, which they sent him over the Internet. He forwarded some of them to me." He reached into his back pocket and pulled out several folded pieces of paper. "These were printed on plain paper so the quality is a little iffy, but they're clear enough to make the point."

Perry took the paper and glanced at it. He didn't need to study it; he knew exactly what he was looking at. He had seen it from the air when he flew in the morning before. "That's the site, all right. So we have one more piece of information indicating that he had us under surveillance."

"But now we know he was working for someone else," Montulli added. "We suspected that since he was a P.I., but Mr. Willis said the man mentioned his boss. That's the word he used, 'boss.' "

"Any idea who that might be?"

"No, but we think he's from out of town. Willis offered to deliver the pictures in digital format. That seemed to please Dawes. Digital photos can be sent over the Internet. Sanchez is searching the man's office even as we speak."

"This late?"

"Like you, Mr. Sachs, some of us are dedicated to what we do."

"I never thought otherwise, Sergeant. Is your detective going to trace Dawes's E-mail?"

"He has people working on it. He said the photos were sent to a dummy account. It's untraceable. You know what that means, don't you?"

"It means that you can't use the E-mail to track down Dawes' contact."

"It means more than that," Montulli said seriously. "It means you're not dealing with an amateur. I think you should be careful, Mr. Sachs."

"That thought had already occurred to me. That's why we've stepped everything up. Time only serves those who are against us." Perry returned his attention to the backhoe. It moved like a graceful dinosaur, chewing up the ground one giant bucketful at a time.

"How deep does he need to go?" Montulli asked.

"The top of our target is fifteen meters down. It goes deeper than that, but we're not certain how deep. We'll have to bring in a larger excavator because the backhoe has depth limits."

"So you just keep digging. It looks like you're off to a good start."

Perry studied the hole. The operator had opened a four-by-five-meter trench. Perry judged the hole to be two meters deep. The operator was making good progress. At this rate. . .

Suddenly the backhoe shuddered ominously.

"What was that?" Montulli said with alarm.

A rumble rolled through the ground, the backhoe convulsed, and then Perry saw something that froze the marrow in his bones.

"Jump!" he shouted to the operator. "Jump, jump!"

He saw the crewman grab the metal uprights that supported the metal roof above the cab and pull himself up. It was an act of desperation that came too late.

The ground opened up, and the multi-ton machine dropped like an elevator car suddenly detached from its cables. The backhoe fell awkwardly, pitching to the side. The worker fell with his machine. A cloud of dust and smoke rose from the opening as if hell itself had surfaced. Perry sprinted forward, stopping at the edge of a hole that now had to be considered a crater. Dust obliterated his view. "Hang on, partner," Perry shouted. He was ashamed that he didn't even know the worker's name. He had left crew selection to Jack.

Montulli was immediately by his side, radio to his mouth. Perry heard something about the fire department, but he had no intention of waiting for them. Against every urge and desire, he held back for the smoke and dust to clear. He heard the diesel engine cut out and was thankful for that.

"What happened?" Jack asked. He and Gleason had been aiding Dr. Curtis. Now the three had joined him. A moment later Brent came running up, camera in hand.

"Ground gave way like a sinkhole," Perry said. "I want rope, and I want it now!"

"Got it," Jack said and disappeared.

"Gleason, get one of the Explorers over here." Gleason didn't waste time with words; he was off in a sprint to the closest four-wheel drive.

"The sides are still caving in," Brent said. "How can that be?"

"The poor soul is going to be buried alive," Curtis moaned.

Perry heard a cough and a deep moan. He took in the situation. Brent was right, the sides of the sinkhole were expanding, and as it did, it dumped more dirt in the direction of the downed man.

"Give me that," Perry snapped, grabbing the camera from Brent. He studied it for a moment. "Light. How do you turn the light on?"

Brent reached over and pushed a button. The small halogen light blazed to life.

"What are you doing?" Montulli asked suspiciously. "I want you to wait for the fire department. They have the equipment to. . ."

Perry didn't wait for the rest of the sentence. Instead, he stepped forward with a hop and disappeared down the hole.

The house proved too confining for Anne. Something had happened to her the hour before. Something inside her that needed breaking had finally broken. The shattered pieces dissolved at her feet like cotton candy in the rain. She was worn out; the grief, the anger, the release, the submission to truth had been more grueling than any physical work she had ever done. While her energy level was close to empty, she felt full for the first time in half a decade.

The epiphany had been cleansing, cathartic. It had begun with a firm word from a man she barely knew, but the pointed admonition had punctured a hole in the darkness she had draped her mind and heart with. In that moment, a small amount of light had made its way in, and once in, it wouldn't be denied.

Perry Sachs hadn't brought about the change. Someone far more insightful and powerful had invaded her and dispelled the artificial wall of protection that kept nothing out, but that kept her in like a prisoner. God deserved her apology, and despite initial and hard-fought refusal, He had gotten it. She had uttered the words "I'm sorry" a hundred times, and with each utterance a layer of self-pity filth was washed away.

Her grief had been real and appropriate, but she'd nursed it into something that sorrow was never meant to be. In a moment, the years of conflict with God melted; in a second, the self-loathing and hatred evaporated under the loving light of God. She had left Him years before, but she now knew He had never left her.

In a dark living room, on a dark night, a woman scarred by pain and regret and poisoned by hatred and anger was healed from the inside. It didn't come with a refrain from the "Hallelujah Chorus"; it arrived without sermon or Bible study. It came without a preacher. One woman, one God, one healing.

How long the moment lasted, Anne couldn't tell. Perhaps it had been an hour, maybe two, but it happened. Her prayer was simple, uncluttered, and devoid of pretension. The prayer flew heavenward on wings of honesty. The answer came like a fresh, cleansing brook, bubbling through the deepest areas of her soul.

She drank in the forgiveness, gulped the understanding, and absorbed the unmeasured, indescribable love. Sleep was impossible. Weary as she was, spent as she was, she had to move outside to find a space big enough to contain the release that radiated from her.

Anne left her home and drove. At first she traveled with no destination in mind, but then found herself heading from town, toward the place she had last spoken to Perry. The hour was late, but he might still be there. He was a man consumed with a cause, and she suspected that sleep was a secondary thought to him now.

Behind her, red lights flashed, and the wail of a siren wafted through the closed windows of the car. Dutifully, she pulled over, and the Tejon fire department drove by in a pumper, ambulance, and chief's car. Anne followed, and her apprehension rose with each minute.

They were headed out of the city.

The fire department, like the police, was handled by county departments. When she saw them turn onto the dirt road that led to Perry's site, her heart began to race. A new fear inundated her mind.

CHAPTER 17

Perry slid down a slope of loose soil, descending into a cloud of dust and diesel smoke. He tried to slow his descent by digging the heels of his work boots into the dirt. It helped some, but not much. What he had done was foolish. It was also necessary. One of his men was in danger, perhaps injured, and Perry wanted to waste no time in getting to him.

Perry stopped suddenly when his feet hit something hard. Light from above filtered through the dust, creating an eerie, fog-like scene. Pausing for a moment to be certain he was no longer moving, Perry rose slowly, the video camera in hand. He used the camera's light like a flashlight. Most of the light reflected back, diffused by floating particles of dust and smoke. A dark shape loomed before him. Waving his hand in front of his face, Perry tried to clear the air. It was a futile gesture. The dirt would settle in its own time, and Perry could do nothing about that.

He coughed then gagged. Perry pulled the collar of his shirt over his mouth and used it as a breathing filter.

The shape in front of him was tinted yellow through the haze. He reached forward and laid a bare hand on the metal. It was the underside of the rig. The backhoe was on its side.

"Perry! Perry!"

Jack's voice pierced the dark distance. Perry had no idea how deep he was, but he knew that some sinkholes were large enough to bury a ten-story building. "Yeah," Perry shouted back. "I'm okay."

"I'm coming down," Jack said.

"No, not yet. I may need you up there."

There was no response, but Perry could imagine Jack gritting his teeth. He was not one to sit on the sidelines. Perry took a step forward and noticed that his feet were buried in the loose soil. Walking was difficult, as if he were slogging through shin-high snow. The smell of diesel fuel and oil permeated the already choking atmosphere. Perry felt like he was on another planet.

The backhoe was small compared to some, and Perry was glad since he was now faced with scaling what had been the underside of the powerful piece of equipment. Small or not, it was heavy, and his biggest fear was that the machine had fallen on his worker.

"Talk to me, Perry," Jack said. It was more an urgent order than a request. "Can you see Lenny?"

Lenny. At least now he knew the worker's name. "Not yet, the backhoe is on its right side. I'm at the undercarriage." Perry set the camera on the rear tire, its light directed toward the overturned cab. The dust was starting to settle, and Perry could see the outrigger used to stabilize the tractor reaching skyward like a man's outstretched hand grasping for help. He placed both hands on the edge of the foot rail and pulled himself up, kicking his feet to gain the extra inch or two needed to throw his leg over the side. If the backhoe were in its normal upright position, the handhold that Perry used would be the rig's footstep.

It was a struggle but Perry soon positioned himself so that he could see into the open cab. It had no windows, just a metal roof supported by corner posts. The supports were bent at an odd angle. Perry saw Lenny lying on his back, unmoving.

"Lenny," Perry said. "You with me, buddy?"

There was no answer, and Perry feared the worst. "I found him," Perry shouted to his friends. "He's not moving. I'm going to try to get to him."

Using the cab supports, Perry lowered himself to the injured man, straddling his prone body. He felt for a pulse and found one. He strained his eyes to peer through the darkness. Standing again he reached up and took hold of the video camera, aiming its light at the injured man. Blood trickled from his forehead and left ear. *Not good,* Perry decided.

In the distance, the squeal of sirens grew louder. "We're going to need a backboard to get him out safely."

"There's no need to yell," Jack said. The voice came from a foot behind him, and Perry jumped. "I'm right here."

"I thought I told you to stay topside," Perry said.

"Did you? Must've missed it."

"You're impetuous, you know that?"

"Look who's talking," Jack retorted. He was standing awkwardly on the side of the cab. "How is he?"

"Head injury of some sort. There's blood from his ears. We need an air ambulance. The best hospital is going to be in Bakersfield."

"Agreed."

"How big is the hole?" Perry asked.

"I'm guessing we're down forty or fifty feet from grade," Jack said. "I didn't take time to measure the opening, but I'm betting that this thing is as wide as it is deep."

"That's big. Why didn't we see it coming?"

"No idea, Perry. You'd think the surveys would have given some clue."

"We'll deal with that later. We're going to have to cut away the cab," Perry said, patting the steel uprights. "We can't fit a backboard in here, put Lenny on it, and pull him up without moving him in ways that would make his condition worse."

"The firemen should have an extrication saw or something. If not, we have a plasma torch on-site. That should do the trick."

A voice from above: "The fire department is on scene." It was Gleason. "I sent Brent down to the road to guide them up."

"Good," Perry shouted. "Good. Lower some lights to Jack."

He returned his attention to the unconscious man at his feet and felt helpless. He removed his shirt and laid it over Lenny to help keep him warm. There was nothing to do now but pray. And Perry did.

Perry was the last one out of the sinkhole, insisting that Lenny and the paramedics go first. The injured worker had not regained consciousness, and Perry could read the concern on the faces of the emergency personnel. They'd bravely lowered themselves into the hole, which still rumbled occasionally. If the situation and noises frightened them, they didn't show it. That made them heroes in Perry's eyes.

He watched as they placed a padded cervical collar around Lenny's neck and checked his vitals. Deciding that the hole was still dangerous, they opted to move him as quickly as possible. Perry helped them gently slide a rigid backboard beneath Lenny's back and strap his body and head to it, immobilizing him to avoid additional injury. An aluminum litter was lowered, and the patient, still strapped to the backboard, was placed in it. The firemen above pulled the stretcher up, guided by the paramedics.

Moments later, the medics and Jack were assisted out, then Perry started up the side, holding tight to a rope that was anchored around Jack's massive body. He found a sense of security in that. Once out of the hole, Perry ordered everyone back from the sinkhole's rim.

Perry struggled to breathe. The dust and smoke had filled his lungs and now his chest hurt with each inhalation. His clothing—and his face—were covered in dirt several layers thick. He coughed again, clearing his throat. Jack joined him.

"Here," he said, "take some of this." He held out a clear plastic medical mask with a plastic tube running from it. It was an oxygen mask. Perry took it gladly. "The paramedics said we could return it tomorrow."

"Lenny in the ambulance?"

"Yeah," Jack said. "They're taking him to the same place our helicopter landed yesterday. An air ambulance is on the way." Even as Jack spoke, the solid thumping of rotors filled the hills.

After a few deep inhalations of oxygen, Perry turned to the wide hole in the middle of the pasture. "How did this happen, Jack? Why didn't the GPR and other surveys show the kind of geological weakness that would cause this?"

"The weakness may have been too deep," Jack replied. "Or. . ." he trailed off.

"Or what?"

"Maybe it wasn't a function of nature. Maybe it was intentional."

Perry studied his friend for a moment trying to determine if he was making a joke. "Intentional? Like a booby trap?" He began to dust himself off. "That would have to be the world's biggest animal trap, Jack."

"I know but take a look at it."

Perry stepped back to the edge of the depression. Below he could see the backhoe lying on its side like a sick elephant, a full quarter of it buried in loose soil. He let his eyes trace the rugged edge of the pit. It hit him. "It's rectangular."

"I was under the impression that sinkholes generally collapsed in a circular or oval shape, not a rectangular one. At least I don't ever recall seeing a rectangular sinkhole."

"Me neither. How long before we can get a geologist out here?" Perry asked.

"I bet we could have one by noon tomorrow."

"Let's do it," Perry said then examined the site again. "I suppose it could be done, although I don't know how. That would have been a lot of work."

"So were the pyramids," Jack rebutted. "Given enough time and enough people, almost anything is possible."

"What triggered it? The weight of the backhoe? I doubt an ancient people could have imagined a device like a backhoe."

"Not weight," Jack said. "Something else."

Perry thought for a moment. "The digging."

"Right," Jack said. "Digging is digging, no matter how it's done. Dirt is moved. We're just a few meters from the leading edge of our target. If we were digging by hand the ground would have given away at some point."

"But the size, Jack. It's enormous."

"A lot of years have passed since then; who knows what has happened below grades. Centuries of water percolation could have enlarged the underlying cavity."

"It's something to look into," Perry said. "In the meantime. . ."

"I should arrest you," a familiar voice said. Perry turned slightly and saw Montulli walking up the grade.

"I wondered where you went," Perry said. "Arrest me? Why? Did I double-park?"

"You know why. I told you stay put. You could have been killed down there."

"If it's any comfort, Sergeant, I told Jack to stay out of the pit too, and he came in anyway."

"You two deserve each other," Montulli snapped. A moment later he asked, "You okay?"

Perry said he was.

"Okay, I guess I'll let your total disregard for my authority in a disaster area go this time," he said, nodding at the downed back-hoe. "How are you going to get that out?"

"We'll have to tow it out with the dozer," Perry said, "but not until after a geologist looks at things."

"So you're shut down for awhile," Montulli said. "Again. That'll disappoint the crowd."

"They're still there?" Perry said. "At this hour?"

"They've thinned some," Montulli explained, "but they'll be back tomorrow. With all the excitement, there may be even more of them. You're the best entertainment in the county."

"Great," Perry said as he pondered what to do next. "The last thing we need to be is someone's entertainment."

In truth, the crowd bothered him less than the decision he needed to make next. In any other circumstance, he would halt the project until a complete investigation had been performed. But this was not a typical project. So far his secrecy had been compromised, confidential documents had been stolen, crowds were gathered just out of sight, a man had been killed and another injured. Add to all those things that history had just been turned on its ear by the finds already made, and Perry realized that the situation was not going to get any better. Stopping work might actually make things worse.

"Jack," Perry said, "I want to meet with you, Gleason, and Dr. Curtis. Send as many of the crew you can spare back to the motel for the night. I want everyone here tomorrow, but let them sleep in a little."

"Will do," Jack said. "You still want the geologist?"

"Absolutely, and the sooner the better; however, our primary goal has to be reached soon. Additional work can carry on after that." He paused then said, "Let's meet in the trailer. Where is Gleason?"

"He and Brent went down to the ambulance with Lenny," Jack explained. "He said he'd follow them to the landing spot and come back once the air ambulance was on its way. They should be back soon."

"Good," Perry said. He lowered his head, something he did when his mind kicked into high gear. "Brent can wait out here. I want it to be just the four of us."

"I understand." Jack motioned to the oak grove office. "I think someone else wants to meet with you."

Perry raised his head and directed his weary eyes in the direction Jack indicated. Anne was standing in the penumbra created by the work lights. Her hands were folded in front of her, and even at this distance she looked tense.

"I found her in the crowd when I was coming back up from the ambulance," Montulli explained. "She wasn't able to get past my deputies. She said she wanted to talk to you."

"Demanded, don't you mean?" Perry said.

"Not at all. In fact, she seemed. . .different. Reserved. I thought she'd be livid about having been kept away from the accident site, but she wasn't. Emotionally up one moment, down the next. They have a word for that. Mercury-something-or-the-other."

"Mercurial," Perry corrected. "Like mercury in a thermometer."

"Yeah, that's it," Montulli said.

"Give me a few minutes with her," Perry said.

"Sure, but if you need help, just scream," Jack said. "I'll send the sergeant in with guns blazing."

"You're trying to get me killed," Montulli said. "He's on his own. As for me, I'm going to call it a night. There are enough deputies to handle what's left of the crowd until your rent-a-cops get here."

Perry turned to the officer; he held out his hand. "Thanks for your help and concern," Perry said. "I know we have been. . .something of a problem."

"You got that right," Montulli shot back. He paused then said with a slight nod, "I'm glad you weren't hurt."

Perry returned the nod and started toward Anne, steeling himself for another onslaught.

Anne took a deep breath as she watched Perry approach. She was relieved to see him walking. From what Montulli had told her when he escorted her up the slope, Perry was lucky to be alive.

"Um, hi," she said with a slight smile.

"Hello," Perry said. "I didn't expect to see you again, especially at this hour."

"I couldn't sleep," she offered. "Greg. . .Sergeant Montulli told me what happened. I'm glad you weren't hurt."

Perry laughed lightly. "Me too. Unfortunately, my worker wasn't so fortunate."

"Will he be okay?"

"I don't know. He had a head injury, and it looked serious." Perry motioned to one of the camp chairs. Anne took it, and Perry pulled another chair close to her. On the ground behind them rested six crates in two rows. An uncomfortable silence grew between them. Anne shifted in her chair. "May I ask what happened?"

Perry explained what little he knew, leaving out Jack's idea about an ancient booby trap.

"And you just jumped in?" she asked with amazement.

"Well, it seemed like a good idea at the time."

"You're a brave man, Perry Sachs. I don't know anyone else who would have done that." She shifted in her chair again. Her stomach turned; her breathing went shallow.

"It has nothing to do with bravery," Perry said. "You seem nervous."

"What does it have to do with?"

She watched Perry look off in the distance, staring at the big hole in the ground. "Faith, I suppose. Faith and responsibility. He worked for me. I felt responsible."

Anne inhaled deeply. "You were right," she blurted. She felt her throat tighten.

"About what?"

"About my owing God an apology." She bit her lower lip then continued. "Something happened to me tonight, something good. . .wonderful. I didn't expect it, but it happened anyway. I don't know how to explain it."

"You faced God," Perry said flatly.

"I suppose you could say that. What you said got to me."

"No, it wasn't what I said. I just brought up what you already knew, at least subconsciously. The Holy Spirit did the rest. Care to share what happened?"

Anne did, recounting her trip to O'Tool's, her anger with him, her frustration with herself, and the spiritual catharsis that followed. She left nothing out, and when she finished, she felt new, fresh. "The pain of my husband's loss is still there. I suppose it always will be."

"Did you love him?"

The question surprised her. "Yes, I did. I loved him very much."

"Grief is a function of love," he said. "Much love means much grief in loss. Hard as it is to live with, it's a. . .tribute."

"I suppose. I've never thought of hurt as honorable."

"Our society does everything it can to avoid discomfort. We are pleasure driven these days, not purpose driven."

"Is that what you are? Purpose driven?"

Perry ran a hand across his face and then through his hair. Dust flew skyward; dirt fell earthward. "I guess so. I'm happiest when I'm working at something that matters."

"Like your secret mission here?"

"It won't be secret forever," Perry said. "Hopefully not for much longer."

"So you're pressing on?" Anne asked.

"I have to. I'm meeting with my key people in a few minutes. We'll make decisions then."

"Looks like that's them," she said, nodding toward the bottom of the slope. A yellow Ford explorer was pulling up the slope.

"Jack went to the road to wait for Gleason and Brent." He stood. "I'm going to have to cut this short."

Anne understood. She rose. "I'll leave you to your planning. I just wanted to apologize for trying to slap you."

He smiled. "I was pretty direct. Maybe we can start over."

"Agreed," she said and held out her hand. He took it in both of his. His touch was warm and strong. "No more jumping in pits."

"I'll do my best."

The small trailer was crowded with somber men. A narrow work-table served as desk and equipment catchall. Several metal folding chairs were stacked against the opposite partition. Perry moved coffee cups, handheld radios, and a few other items to make room for survey drawings made the previous day. Finding a red marker pen, he drew a loose shape on one of the drawings. It represented the cavity that had swallowed the backhoe and its operator in one gulp.

"We were blindsided, guys," Perry said. "Somehow this got past us all."

"There was no indication from the GPR or any other survey we did," Gleason offered. "We did it right, and we did it multiple times, except. . ."

"Except we didn't do a deep search," Jack said. "Our initial survey found what we were looking for in general. We used shallow survey devices. Once we got returns on that, we were able to map out the site and plan our coring and digging. I should have called for a deep radar search. That would have shown the sinkhole."

Perry turned to his men. Jack stood straight and met his eyes, but Perry knew he felt responsible. It had been he who oversaw the project until Perry's arrival. Gleason looked as if the world had been dropped on his shoulders. He leaned against the wall, head down. Dr. Curtis stood silently in the corner, hands dangling at his side. These were men with unique qualifications for the work they did, but they were also men with feelings and pride. Something had gone terribly wrong, and with the exception of Curtis, they felt responsible.

"Hindsight is always 20/20, guys. You know that." Perry spoke directly and firmly. His men, his friends, didn't need to be soothed; they needed to know that they were not to blame. "You did things exactly as I would have. If we knew of every possible problem ahead of time, then we could test for it, plan for it, even avoid it. That's not an option available to us. We do the best we can and take what comes our way. I could have asked for a deep GPR survey, but I didn't. Why? Because I knew, as you did, that what we were looking for would be shallow. We weren't looking for geological faults; we were looking for something man-made. And we found it." Perry turned to Curtis. "When do we ship out the crates, Doc?"

"I've made all the contacts with researchers that I trust, and they're ready to receive the finds. I didn't tell them what they would be receiving. I thought they might enjoy receiving the shock of their lives. Just a little academic humor on my part. I'd pay money to see their faces."

"You're an animal," Jack said. "We can't take you anywhere."

"Is that true for. . ." Perry was having trouble saying it. Like the others, he was having trouble believing his own eyes. ". . .Site Six?"

"No," Curtis said. "She will be sent to my university. I have a couple of aides to receive the shipment and put her under lock and key. I've also notified the president of the college. He said he'd make sure security was provided."

"So you told him what we found. . .who we found?" Perry inquired.

"No. Just that the college was about to be put on the map."

"Will he open the crate?" Gleason asked.

"I asked him not to. He's a man of science himself so he understands protocol."

"Good," Perry said. "I need advice, men, and I'm turning to you. I want to press on toward the mark. Am I crazy?"

The silence only lasted a moment. "Of course you are, Perry," Jack answered. "You've always been crazy. That's what we like about you. Normal people are boring. I say we push on without interruption."

"Even though you think we might have our own Oak Island here?"

"It would explain a few things," Jack said.

"Oak Island?" Gleason asked.

"It's an island off the coast of Nova Scotia," Jack explained. "In 1795 two young men went exploring on the island. They found an oak tree with unusual marks on it, like rope marks. Long story short, they found a treasure pit, and a deviously clever one at that. To this day, despite many repeated attempts, the pirate treasure has eluded recovery. Six people have died trying to get it out."

"What makes it so hard to excavate?" Curtis asked.

"It appears that whoever buried the treasure—and ideas ranging from Captain Kidd to Francis Bacon have been suggested—booby-trapped the site. In a nutshell, there is a thirteen-foot-wide shaft that descends to about two hundred feet. Coring has brought up bits of oak board, charcoal, putty, spruce, bits of gold coin, cement, iron chain, and more. The booby traps were as ingenious as they were deadly. Sloping shafts ran from the vertical shaft to the ocean. When the digging got deep enough, the shaft opened and flooded the site. Over the years other would-be treasure hunters found another such shaft."

"But there's evidence of treasure there?" Gleason asked.

"Oh, yes. One group bored a hole about ninety meters from the money pit and found several artificial cavities. They lowered a remote camera down the borehole and they saw three chests, a severed hand, and a body."

"So you're suggesting that the sinkhole was a cleverly devised trap?" Curtis said.

"I'm suggesting that we consider the possibility. A lot of time has passed since our Roman friends set up camp here. Maybe they planned a trap, and the passing years made it more dangerous. Or maybe this was exactly what they meant to happen. We don't know, and we won't know until geologists have had time to do a proper examination."

"Jack's point is well taken," Perry said. "The Oak Island pit was probably dug centuries after this site, but it does show that such traps can be devised and implemented by people with nothing more than hand tools."

"Considering everything else that has happened," Gleason said, "I think it would be wise to assume that there may be other dangers."

"You advocate pulling back?" Perry asked.

"No, just the contrary. I'm saying that we move forward, but we assume that something else is going to happen and take precautions. If you're right, we're after more than mere gold."

"I agree," Perry said. "We may or may not be facing dangers from the past, but we know that we have present-day problems to deal with, not the least of which is a murderer. We push on. Agreed?"

The men agreed.

"All right then. I want to limit the crew's access to the site. The fewer bodies, the less chance of injury. Now, we have one other thing we need to do."

Perry turned his back on the table with its papers and reached for one of the folding chairs. He passed one to each man, who opened it and took a seat, each facing the other. Perry sat leaning his arms on his knees, his head bowed forward. He closed his eyes and shut out the room, the trailer, the site, and the rest of the world. Silence settled in the cramped trailer. A moment later, Perry spoke. "Our Father in heaven, we praise You for this day and this opportunity. . . ."

The prayer lasted fifteen minutes as each man intoned praise and lifted a request for wisdom and safety. They prayed for their fallen worker, Lenny, and asked for healing. When each man had prayed, Perry made one last intercession, a heartfelt prayer for Anne Fitzgerald.

CHAPTER 18

Joseph set the crayon down, folded his hands in his lap, and started rocking. "Perry. . .uhh. . .uhh."

Claire rose from the chair she'd been sitting in for the last few hours. Emotions churned wildly within her, alternating anger with depression, despair with determination. The place they were held in now was a better room, cleaner, larger, and not so oppressive, but it was still a locked room, a cell in which she and her son were held captive. More than once she'd tried the door, but it remained locked from the outside.

The fact that the door could be locked from the outside told her that her captors had thought things through. Prior to Joseph's birth, Claire had taught elementary school, and she knew that fire codes prohibited rooms in which people could be accidentally locked inside. Someone had changed this lock just to keep them from leaving, and that worried her.

For the first time since Joseph's birth, Claire felt glad for his condition. They'd not eaten since the previous day, and she was feeling the effects, but Joseph showed no indication of discomfort. He was oblivious to the danger, to the fact that they were not home. She was grateful for that.

Walking to Joseph, she placed a hand on his shoulder. He immediately ceased his rocking. Yes, she was glad that he was unaware of the danger, but she still wished he could turn to her and say, "It's going to be all right, Mom. You'll see. Everything is going to be fine." It was a senseless, useless wish. Such a thing could never happen. In most ways, she was totally alone.

Allowing her eyes to drift, she let her gaze fall on the picture Joseph had been drawing. At first she thought he'd just colored the page black, but when she looked closer she could see a faint outline.

"This is different." She leaned over the picture. Instead of putting down lines on the paper as he had always done in the past, Joseph covered the drawing area with the thick, waxy crayon—black. Then he carefully etched a line in the soft material, allowing the off-white paper to bleed through. It was an image drawn in reverse; etched instead of drawn.

"Let me see your hands," Claire said, reaching down to Joseph's lap and pulling his palms up. She turned his hands to look at his fingernails. As expected, his nails were caked with black crayon. She released his hands, and he slowly lowered them back to his lap.

Peering even more closely at the artwork, Claire made out a silhouette image against the black backdrop, outlined by a thin line carved out by Joseph. It took a few moments for her to grasp that it was the outline of a man. The man appeared to be on his knees, body hunched over his legs, his hands covering his face.

"What does this mean?" she asked, resigned in the knowledge that no answer would be forthcoming. She studied the image and decided that the man was shocked or overcome with sorrow. She couldn't be sure since his hands covered his face, but the body position seemed to indicate sadness. Or fear.

Claire sighed and set the picture down. All these years Joseph had been drawing animals and such. Now this. The darkness of the picture troubled her. Maybe Joseph did sense some danger, and this was his way of expressing it.

"I love you," she said softly. She kissed him on top of the head, then walked back to her chair, sat down, and waited for the next indignity from her captors.

"I can't make it out," Rutherford said to Julia. She approached his desk and peered at the monitor.

"Can you zoom in more?" she asked.

"I tried that, but it didn't help." He tapped a key on his keyboard. The video image tightened on the drawing the Henri boy had drawn.

"It's just a big black blob," Julia remarked.

"No, it's more than that. There's an image; it's just too faint for the camera to pick up." He closed his mouth, focused his attention, and then successfully swallowed the saliva buildup. One more victory. "I want to see that drawing."

"You want me to go down and get it?"

"Yes. You are to be their only contact. The more people they see, the greater the danger to us." Julia started to walk away. "Wait. I want you to take this to young Mr. Henri." He keyed a few buttons, and the printer came to life, spitting out a white piece of paper with a series of dark smudges on it.

"What's this?"

"My DNA profile."

"What? Why do you want me to give this to him?" Julia said, furrowing her brow.

"Just do it."

She started to leave when Rutherford's private line rang. Only two people had access to that number: Julia and Alex. A keystroke later the phone came to life.

"Yes," was all Rutherford said.

"I've arrived back in Tejon," Alex said. That pleased Rutherford.

"Very well. Enjoy your stay."

"I will," Alex replied.

Rutherford hung up.

"I'm hoping you're right," Perry said to Jack as the two looked down the sinkhole. The harsh shadows cast by the work lights gave Perry the impression he was standing on the moon, except this moon had grass and a stiff breeze. "If this is an unnatural event, then there must be a bottom to it. Who knows how deep a natural sinkhole would have gone?"

"I've seen pictures of some that are huge," Jack replied.

Perry studied the fallen backhoe, which lay on its right side like a weary dinosaur. "You sent the men?"

"Yes," Jack said. "Two of them. They're on their way to Bakersfield to pick up the trackhoe. They'll truck it here within the next two hours. It's a good thing I staged more equipment there."

Perry recalled Jack telling him he had done that when they were on the helicopter. "Great. We need the bigger machine. When they get back, let's off-load the truck as quickly as we can. Gleason and Curtis are overseeing the transportation of the coffins. Curtis wants to ride with them all the way to the Bakersfield airport. Gleason will drive. I'm sending a follow-up vehicle with them. I want you to choose three men you can trust. Dr. Curtis has arranged for two of the Romans to go to one university, two more to another on the East Coast. He's decided that Roman number five and Site Six will go to his university."

"Will do. I assume he has people taking possession as soon as they land?"

"Yes. They'll begin work as soon as possible." Perry turned, faced the oak grove, and spent a moment watching Gleason and Curtis supervising two workmen and Brent as they checked and reinforced the crating.

"I don't think we should try and load the crates onto the flatbed up here. It's a sturdy truck, but I think it might have a problem with the slope. Maybe we should run a round-robin with the Explorers. Their four-wheel drive is better suited for the terrain. We can run two Explorers in tandem and have the whole thing done in short order."

"Good idea. Go with that." Perry looked back at the downed

backhoe. "Do you think we can bring it up?"

"Setting it upright is going to be the hard part," Jack said after a moment's thought. "Once it's back on its wheels, we can tow it back to the top of grade. We could call for a heavy-duty tow truck, the kind used to haul big rigs and motor homes. Or. . ."

"Or use the dozer," Perry said.

"That's what I was thinking. We bring the dozer up here, connect it to the backhoe with chains, set it on its wheels, then tow it out of the hole."

"Think you can still drive one of those beasts?" Perry asked with a knowing smile.

"I was driving dozers before I could ride a bike."

Perry laughed. "Well, that would explain the damage to your neighborhood. Let's wait to bring the dozer up until Dr. Curtis is well off-site. Seeing a bulldozer driving over an archeological dig just might make his heart seize, and he's had enough shocks already."

"Agreed," Jack said then asked, "Do you think he believes what his eyes see?"

"I don't believe what my eyes see," Perry answered. "It's beyond belief. Everything we've found goes against all that we've been taught, but then we expected that, didn't we?"

"That we did. Mystery makes life interesting."

"Let's make the most of our time. Since we have to wait for the other backhoe, let's use the time to weld a few tow loops to the backhoe. It will make it easier to make connections. I also think we need to finish cutting off the rest of the canopy. Since we cut two of the four supports away to get Lenny out, the canopy is going to flap around, and those cuts I made with the plasma torch are a little on the sharp side."

"I'll get the equipment then head down the hole. You can hold the rope."

"Nothing doing, partner. This job is mine. Get a couple of guys up here to help, and you can join me."

"You're getting greedy in your old age," Jack said, "but I guess

I can live with it."

"I hope we both can live with it."

The sight was unexpected and surprising enough to make Alex stop mid-step. He last saw the work site the night he broke Dawes's neck and dropped him in the hole. Now there were more holes, several like the first and one that looked as if it had been hollowed out by a bomb blast. *They've been busy,* Alex thought.

He stood near the same set of trees that Dawes had used for cover while spying on the dig. Getting to that point had been more difficult than the last time. Since sheriff's deputies cordoned off access to the site, he had to go out of his way to avoid them. That meant driving his rented car—a car he obtained under a false name and with a bogus credit card—several miles past the site, parking, then spending the next hour walking across the pasture land of the adjoining property. Hiking through the tall grass on uneven terrain slowed his progress, as did the delicate act of slipping between strands of barbed wire. An ivory gibbous moon aided him, though.

The sound of a straining diesel engine punctuated the otherwise quiet night. Before him lay the grassy slope that so interested his employer. *More specifically,* he thought, *what lay beneath the serene ground.*

Alex stood a football field's distance away and watched as a bulldozer slowly pulled back from the craterous hole. It was towing something. He watched with interest as a yellow backhoe slowly materialized out of the depths, rolling up the depression's steep side on its wheels. It crested the rim then moved freely away.

He watched patiently. Of the four men he could see on the site, two left a few minutes later, walking down the slope. Alex assumed they'd been sent to retrieve something, or maybe they'd been given the rest of the evening off. In any case, only Perry Sachs and a large black man were left. Those were good odds, he decided.

Alex would've loved to hear how a backhoe got to the bottom

of that huge hole, but he had other things to do at present. It was time for a conversation with Mr. Sachs.

Alex started forward.

"That worked better than I thought it would," Jack said as he stepped down from the large bulldozer.

"We could use a few things to go our way," Perry replied as he walked around the digging machine. "Tires are still inflated. Good. I was afraid they would have pushed off the rim when it tipped. I guess the soft soil helped us on that one."

Jack began fiddling with the engine. "Everything looks in place. Fuel lines are still connected. Just a little dirt here and there, and some oil and fuel that leaked from the tank. Shouldn't take long to clean up. I'll bet your next paycheck that it'll kick over first time."

"My paycheck? Bet your own money, pal."

"Where's the wisdom in that? I could lose money. It's safer to risk your assets."

"I wouldn't be so sure about that. . ." Perry trailed off.

A man was approaching, apparently coming from out of nowhere. He wore slacks and a polo shirt. *A little too dapper for this area,* Perry decided. The man walked with confidence, as if he were expected. "We have company." He motioned toward the approaching man.

"I wondered when that would happen," Jack said. "Sooner or later someone would find a way past the security. Think he's a reporter?"

"Could be," Perry said. "He has that city look."

The two waited for the unexpected guest to make his way to them.

"Perry Sachs?" the man asked. It was the kind of question a man asked when he already knew the answer.

"That's me," Perry said. "I don't wish to be rude, but you're trespassing on private property. I'm going to have to ask you to leave."

The man laughed lightly. "I leave when I'm ready, Sachs."

"Is that a fact?" Jack asked and took one step forward.

"Yes, it is, big man, and I wouldn't take another step if I were you." There was menace in his voice. "While I would enjoy a little tussle with you, this isn't the time, nor is it the reason why I'm here." Clearly, he didn't intimidate easily.

"Are you a reporter?" Perry asked.

"No need to be insulting, Sachs. And don't bother asking for a name. You don't need it, and I won't give it."

"I think it's time for you to talk to one of the deputies," Jack said. He stepped forward and seized the man's left arm in his right hand. It took a second for Perry to realize what he had seen. In a blurred motion, the trespasser brought his open right hand up, impacting Jack on the tip of his chin. Jack's head snapped back from the force of it. Perry could hear his friend's teeth clash. Then Perry saw something he never believed possible. Jack crumpled like a blanket and dropped to the ground.

Instinctively, Perry charged but made only one step before finding himself staggering backwards, doubled over, his hands clutching his stomach where he'd just been kicked by a foot he never saw coming. The air rushed from his lungs, and his solar plexus went into spasms. He dropped to his knees and struggled for breath. For a moment, he thought he would never breathe again. Pain circled his body. Lights flashed in his eyes.

Perry forced himself to look up while willing himself to breathe. The breath would come in time, but time seemed to have stopped. He stared into the emotionless face of his attacker. He watched as the attacker pulled a folded piece of paper from his pocket, opened it, leaned over, and displayed it with the pride a father might show toward a child's drawing. "Look familiar? Know these people?"

The paper held the image of Claire and Joseph. Joseph was situated at what looked like a laboratory workbench. Claire was standing next to him. "Claire. . ." Perry whispered. A whisper was all he could muster. "Joseph. . ."

"Very good, Mr. Sachs. You're absolutely right." The intruder straightened himself. "They have the privilege of being our guests. For the moment they are in good health." Picking up the paper, the visitor folded it neatly and slipped it into his front pants pocket.

"What do you want?" Perry finally managed.

"Here's the drill, Sachs. Listen carefully because this is no game. You're out of your league; I can promise you that. Despite the fact that you've interfered with our work, we've decided not to view you as an enemy, but as a fellow worker. We know what you're after, and we want it. You're going to get it for us."

"No."

"Oh, yes, you are," the man barked. "You're going to do everything I say, and you are not going to deviate from it in the slightest. If you do, your friends will die in. . .oh, let's call it a creative way."

Perry started to get up, but was forced to his knees again by a swift kick to the ribs. He doubled over.

"I am not in this work alone. You might have surmised that, Sachs. The operation I'm engaged in is well planned and tightly constructed. The lives of your friends rest squarely in my hands. Do you hear that? My hands, not your hands, not even God's hands.

"I must report back to my employer at specific times. If I call too early, your friends die. If I call too late, they die. What that means is this: If I'm detained in any way, either by some stupid exercise of heroics or by police intervention, I will miss my call-in time. Your friends will die ten minutes later.

"So if I so much as get stopped for a speeding ticket, it will be the same as if you pulled the trigger yourself, or flipped the switch, or injected the poison. . .whatever way my employer has decided to kill the woman and her son. Do you understand me so far?"

"I understand," Perry croaked.

"Smart man. You have twenty-four hours to finish your work. You will crate it and place it in a truck that I will provide. You will not interfere in any way. You will be responsible to make sure the police remain uninvolved."

"How do I do that?"

"I don't know, and I don't care. You will not follow me. Once I deliver the prize, I will arrange for your friends' release. Let me ask again: Do you understand?"

Perry didn't answer. The man was asking two impossible things. Perry couldn't turn over the very thing he and the others had worked so hard to find; but he couldn't allow Claire to be executed. "You'll kill them anyway," Perry said. The pain in his ribs had diminished to barely endurable.

"Maybe. Maybe not. You have no other choice. Deviate from my directions by an inch, and you can bury your friends in that big hole over there. Still listening? There are a couple more details you need to know. Do exactly as I say."

Perry pushed the pain from his mind and focused on the orders being given by his attacker. Fury raged inside him, but he bottled it like a roughneck capped a spurting oil well. The image of Claire and Joseph as prisoners in some unknown place forced him into compliance. At least for now.

Jack groaned and rolled to his side. Perry looked at his friend and knew that he was still out. The attacker was incredibly strong, Perry reasoned. He had the personal pain to prove it.

"Twenty-four hours, Mr. Sachs. I suggest you get busy." The intruder took a step closer then threw a vicious punch, his knuckles striking Perry on the right cheekbone. Perry grunted and dropped forward. He felt blood fill his mouth.

The man strolled back the way he came.

Perry was still in too much pain to stand. Instead he leaned forward and rested his head on the ground.

Perry began to pray.

(CHAPTER) 19

Perry pulled a lever and the steel bucket of the backhoe bit the earth with thick metal teeth. A second later the bucket swung around and dropped its load a few meters away, then spun back to chew another bite. The device moved with the furious urgency of its operator.

Fire still burned in Perry's side where the intruder had kicked him. His ribs, while unbroken, had been separated and moved in an unnatural way. Every breath was the same as being stabbed, every cough, piercing agony, but Perry moved anyway, pushing himself until the darkness of unconsciousness threatened from the edges of his vision. Then and only then would he slow, force himself to inhale as deeply as his injuries would allow, and then begin work again.

The backhoe he operated was the one liberated from the sinkhole. Jack worked the recently arrived, larger Komatsu trackhoe from Bakersfield. The trackhoe looked like a long-necked yellow Jurassic beast that moved on metal, twenty-eight-inch wide, tank-like tracks. Unlike the backhoe, which was a hybrid of a loader and a digging device, the trackhoe was designed to dig holes in short order.

Jack mirrored Perry's urgency, digging the trackhoe's thirty-inch bucket into the soft soil the moment Perry's left with his load. They dug in tandem as men pressed by danger. All caution was evicted. Before, they had bent every rule of archeology; now those rules were shattered by need.

As Perry swung the bucket for another gouging movement, he looked at his longtime friend. Their eyes met and a communication was exchanged that was only possible between two who had trusted each other with their lives. Jack's eyes were narrowed, and his swollen jaw was set tight. He'd revived a few minutes after the brutal visitor left, groaning, sitting up, shaking his head, then suddenly springing to his feet, looking for the assailant but finding only Perry doubled over and leaning against the backhoe. After the painful act of straightening himself, Perry relayed everything Jack had missed while unconscious.

Discussion was minimal. Both men immediately applied themselves to restoring the backhoe. When it was cleaned up and ready to go, they started it and moved it into position to unearth the final treasure under the earth. Jack served as observer, standing a few steps from the ever-widening hole Perry made. The minute the second excavator showed up, Jack was in the seat.

Gleason, Curtis, and Brent had returned thirty minutes later. Dr. Curtis was furious at the sight of the damage being done by the equipment and the dozer parked to one side, but his anger quickly subsided once the tale had been told. He and Brent stood to the side as Gleason directed Perry and Jack.

The five men worked with a single purpose. The rest of the crew they sent back to the motel with instructions not to return until further notice. There were questions, but none were answered.

The buckets dug, raised, swiveled, emptied, and returned. It was a dance that repeated itself with a determined precision. The hole deepened and widened. Not even the fear of another sinkhole could assuage their determination. What was being done was what had to be done. They were no longer in control of their circumstances—an undefined evil was.

Another pain swept and swirled in Perry. It wasn't physical, not associated with assault; it was harsher. Perry was unfamiliar with helplessness. Reared in a healthy family, he had never known what was common to many: need, rejection, hopelessness. Now he was faced with all those emotions in large measure. Two people he cared about were in the hands of others who could—and apparently would—harm them at a moment's notice. Perry didn't know where they were being held or how long they had been there. Had they been hurt already? Had the vicious visitor done to Claire and Joseph what he had so effectively done to Jack and him? Perry couldn't even be sure they were still alive. A photo was proof of the past only, but never of the present.

Perry pushed the thoughts away. Those were questions he couldn't answer. For the moment all he could do was follow the instructions he'd been given, and that ate at his insides.

The hole in the ground widened with remarkable speed, yielding a gaping opening. The excavators worked with choreographed precision. Initially they worked on the same area, but under the direction of Perry, Jack shifted his approach, turning the hole into a deep trench. The plan was simple: Lay bare the deep rectangular object revealed by the GPR survey. Penetration by the radar had been less than they had hoped for, but it had been enough to locate the right site and reveal the basic size and shape. Jack dug on the forward edge of the object, Perry directly overhead.

The fever of desperation pushed the men forward. There was no conversation; no unnecessary emotion, just the work, the pulling and pushing of levers and pedals. Buckets rising, dipping, digging, dumping, only to start the process again. Minutes passed with mule-like resistance, but Perry's focus remained steady and unshaken.

Finally, with a rapid waving of arms, Gleason called Perry off. Gleason trotted closer to the hole than to Perry, leaping onto the steel step. "You're at your fifteen-foot depth limit," Gleason announced. "Jack is still going but he's going to max out at twenty-two feet. That's less than half the depth we need."

Perry knew this would happen. He knew the top of the chamber was fifteen meters below grade. That was over forty-five feet, the equivalent of a four-story building. Initially he'd planned to grade out a ramp as the first builders had, but he no longer had the time. "Tell Jack to keep going until he maxes out the reach of the trackhoe, then tell him to get it ready to bring to my side of the dig."

"He won't get any more depth on this side than where he is," Gleason objected.

"He will when I'm done," Perry said.

"What are you planning?" Gleason asked with suspicion.

"If I can't extend the trackhoe's reach, then I'll just have to lower the trackhoe. Hang on." Perry pulled the bucket in and secured it. He then raised the outriggers that kept the machine from tipping. Dropping the machine in gear, he backed it away from the large hole in the ground. Gleason stood on the steel step hanging on to the metal stubs left from where Perry had cut the canopy off.

"I'm going to doze away some ground from the side of the target. If I do it right, Jack will be able to drive the Komatsu down the new grade and clear more dirt. At some point we're going to have to use shovels. I want you and Brent to bring up shovels, crow bars, and anything else you think we might need to get into the chamber."

"Jack packed some of the pneumatic tools. Actually he packed everything."

"That's our Jack, and you gotta love 'im for it," Perry said as he hopped down from the cab. "Fill Jack in. I don't want to waste a minute."

"To do that, you're going to have to get close to the sinkhole edge. That makes me nervous."

"Good, I didn't want to be the only one with butterflies in my stomach."

Perry jogged to the Case 1150 bulldozer and fired up its 108 hp diesel engine. Black smoke belched into the night sky, and its throaty idle rumbled through the hills. Had he the time, he could bring in major earthmoving equipment, but he had chosen to use smaller equipment to preserve as much of the property as possible and lessen the risk of damaging valuable artifacts. It was a wise decision when time was abundant; now it hamstrung him. There were earth-moving machines that could have made short work of the project, but they lacked the finesse he initially needed. Now he would have given a year's salary to have a Komatsu PC1000 whose massive bucket could have plowed up the fifteen meters of depth in minutes. But wishing was a waste of time and mental energy. This was the hand he had been dealt, and he planned to play it for all it was worth.

Pressing his skills beyond anything he ever thought possible, Perry powered forward until he lined up with the east side of the hole, lowered the bright yellow blade, and started forward. Earth came up like water before the prow of a ship. Perry dug a wide swath, pushing the excavated dirt down the side of the sinkhole. Jack's excavator would need more room than the dozer could provide in a single pass, so Perry repositioned the dozer and dug in deep again. Back and forth, side to side, a wide and long slope appeared. Perry knew that he would have to lower the grade by at least twenty feet for the excavator to have a chance of reaching the buried chamber.

The night wore on as Perry finished grading a level area for Jack's trackhoe. He finally backed his machine out and watched Jack work his way down the all-too-steep slope, settle on the dirt pad Perry had created, and begin digging again, scooping dirt and piling it to the side. Perry could do nothing but wait, wishing it were he down there at the controls. He had tried to commandeer the excavator from Jack, citing the danger of taking such a large machine into a wide pit that hadn't been properly shored. Jack had just smiled and said, "Get your own ride, buddy," and started down the precipitous path before Perry could object.

Jack moved the bucket with precision and determination, and Perry knew that each scoop of dirt moved them closer to their goal. Gleason stood waiting with Perry. Each man was eager to add his labor to the task, but nothing more could be done until Jack had dug to within a few feet of the buried cavity.

"It has to be close now," Gleason said. "I think we should start shoveling."

"I think you're right," Perry said. "If we're on target, then we should be right over it." Perry picked up a shovel and started down the incline toward Jack's position. He noticed that Gleason was following with another shovel in his hand. "I can't ask you to do this, Gleason. I don't know how secure the walls of the pit are. They could cave in."

"You and Jack have put a nice angle on the walls. I don't think it'll collapse on us."

"The base can give way, and dirt can slide in faster than we can run," Perry said. "As I understand it, being buried alive isn't much fun."

"That's why I plan on avoiding it. You'd be surprised how fast I can run when death is behind me. Now be quiet. Two shovels will work faster than one, and you know it."

"Three shovels," a voice said. Brent approached from behind. "I didn't come out here to watch. You made me part of the team when you told me what you suspect is in the chamber. I'm not going to sit in the stands."

Perry started to object, but Brent cut him off. "Save your breath, Mr. Sachs. I'm in for the duration."

Brent's courage was remarkable, and Perry found himself filled with admiration. "Okay, kid," Perry said, "but anyone who risks their life with me gets to call me Perry."

"Will do," Brent said as he approached. "You know that when all this is over, the pizza is on you. Tell me where to put the business end of this shovel."

The three men walked to the excavator, and Perry told Jack what they were planning. "Once we've discovered the lid to this thing, we'll try to find its edges. When we do, you can rip all the ground on two sides of the perimeter."

"Did you bring me a shovel?" Jack asked. "It's getting a little cramped in here."

258

"You can use Brent's. He's young and won't mind trotting back up to get another."

Digging continued, but muscles provided the power this time. Perry stood on the uneven ground over the chamber and dipped his blade in the dirt. He did it again and again, until, thirty inches down, the dense ground turned hard and the shovel hit something unforgiving. The others joined him in clearing a three-foot square hole revealing a hard, dark stone.

"Bingo," Jack said. "I don't think I've ever been so glad to see rock."

"Let's expand the hole and make sure that we haven't found just a rock."

"It's pretty flat, Perry," Gleason said. "I'd be surprised if it isn't what that GPR showed."

Perry agreed, but he continued to dig. Fifteen minutes later the four men had doubled the size of the hole, and the rock remained consistent. "This has to be it," Perry concluded. "Back to your office, Jack, and see if you can't get rid of the last meter of dirt. I'll guide you from out here. Let's give him some room."

Gleason and Brent moved up the access incline that Perry had created with the dozer and watched. Jack moved the excavator's bucket smoothly, following Perry's hand signals with unwavering attention. Perry's goal was to have Jack scrape another two feet off the chamber without damaging the stone lid beneath his feet. Formerly he would have been concerned about maintaining the integrity and appearance of the stone, but now his greatest fear was causing the ancient construction to fall in on itself and damage the treasure inside. If things had been different, if lives weren't hinged on his success, he would've been more cautious. But patience now was too expensive a luxury.

Jack was a maestro at the controls, making the beast of a machine behave and do what it was not designed to do, dig by the inch instead of the yard. Perry directed Jack to scrape from the hand-dug test hole to where he knew the front of the chamber must be. Once done, Perry picked up his shovel and started digging away the last foot of rocky soil. He had barely finished his second strike with the shovel when the others joined him.

With a gently sloping, nearly fifty-foot wall of dirt just a few steps away, the men worked in concentrated intensity. Sweat oozed from every pore, breathing became labored, hands blistered, but no one complained.

They pushed on toward the edge until they found it, then began digging at right angles. The edge remained.

"That's it," Perry said. "Jack, dig in front of this edge, and let's see if there's a welcome mat and front door."

"I figure I can scoop out another eight feet of depth," Jack said. "I can make the trench four or five feet wide."

"That'd be perfect," Perry said.

"I'm worried about the stability of the trench," Jack admitted. "We'll have to finish the digging by hand, and the trench could collapse on us."

Gleason spoke up. "Brent and I could bring up some plywood and two-by-fours. We could make a down-and-dirty shoring system."

Perry agreed. "Good idea, but let's do it quickly."

As the men scrambled off, Perry felt a strong sense of thankfulness that God had given him friends of such courage and sacrifice. He prayed that he wouldn't make a mistake that would cost them their lives. As dangerous as standing four stories below ground was, he knew a greater danger lay ahead.

Rutherford's body was in bed, but his mind was elsewhere. He paid little attention to the predawn morning and even less attention to the nurse who washed his emaciated form with a damp sponge. It was a daily routine he'd successfully blocked from the forward part of his brain. Displacement. That's what he called it, the ability to project his mind to another place, a place where he didn't have to endure the indignity of having someone else do for him what nearly everyone in the world could do for themselves.

The nurse—a likeable brunette whose name he should've known but that he had refused to learn—ran the wet sponge along a withered arm. He thought of the day. It was, at long last, here. By sundown, the items would be securely in place, manipulated by the skillful hands of Dr. Benton Carmack and under the vigilant eye of Rutherford himself. The work ahead would take weeks, maybe even months, but it would progress. All he had to do was live to see it, to benefit from it. And live he would, if mental strength and determination had anything to do with it.

It was a thin hope, true, but slim hope was better than none. A drowning man would clutch at a thread if a rope were not available. This was his thread, his flimsy, last-ditch effort to beat the gods of disease that had afflicted him with this cruel disorder.

It had to work. He would make it work. There were no other options.

The nurse rolled him on his side and applied the soap and sponge to his back.

CHAPTER 20

Anne Fitzgerald awoke fresh and with a sense of vitality she had long missed. For the first time in years, her drive to get up was found in something other than work.

Although it was still early, she slipped from bed, trod across the hardwood floor, and looked out the window. The black of the night sky was dissolving into a pale blue. Just outside her windowpane, several sparrows bickered over a few seeds from the surrounding plants. It amazed her that she took notice of the little creatures. She wasn't one to pay attention to such things, at least not recently.

Although she had yet to shower, she felt cleaner than usual and she knew why. A half-decade of bitterness had been washed away with unexpected efficiency. Today would be different. She had no idea how long the cathartic euphoria would last, but she planned to enjoy each moment of it. For now, she planned a quick wash and a brief breakfast at the Table and Grille. That would be nice: a casual breakfast, a cup of coffee, and the newspaper. Then she'd slip into her real estate office early and catch up on all the work that she had let slip over the last two days.

Yes, she thought, *this is going to be a great day.*

Joseph had not slept, and other than occasionally nodding off in the chair, Claire had remained awake as well. Joseph now sat motionless at the work counter, staring at the paper the dark-haired woman had brought him the previous evening. The moment she'd set it on the counter, Joseph had leaned over it until his nose hovered an inch from the paper. He rocked gently, then stopped. He moved his head side to side as he studied the paper, then up and down. After the woman had left, Claire had stepped to her son's side and peered over his shoulder. The image on the paper puzzled her. All she could see were bands of black and gray laid out in neat columns.

"What is this?" she asked Joseph, knowing no reply would come. Joseph continued to study the paper. She was sure he'd never seen anything like it. He had been known to stare at pictures of animals for hours until he had memorized every detail of their appearance, but he had never seen anything so abstract.

She was also puzzled as to why they would bring such a picture to Joseph. What could they hope to achieve by that? Most likely he'd reject the document or, at best, copy it with the crayons they'd provided, just as he had with Henri's precious fragments.

Nothing made sense. Not their abduction, not their imprisonment, not this picture. She had nothing to offer. The document they wanted had been stolen months before, and she was certainly no expert in ancient languages.

Claire returned to the chair and watched Joseph. He had been still, too still. His rhythmic rocking was absent. Instead, he stared and stared, and it frightened her. What did he see that she couldn't?

Joseph sat suddenly erect and tilted his head. A second later he picked up a black crayon, pushed the strange paper to the side, and began drawing.

Anne found her usual booth occupied by four burly men. One was telling a story, and the others listened with pre-laughter smiles pasted to their faces, anticipating the punch line.

She surveyed the Tejon Table and Grille and found it unusually full. She took a seat at the counter. There were eight stools, and men occupied four of them. Each took notice of her and nodded. She returned the gesture then spied Sara coming out of the kitchen with three plates of food balanced on one arm and another in her free hand. The waitress looked frazzled.

"Hi, Mayor. Be with you in a sec."

"Okay," Anne said, uncertain how to respond.

Moments later Sara slipped behind the counter, poured a cup of coffee, and brought it to Anne. "You're here early."

"I wanted to get a jump on the day," Anne said, then leaned over and spoke softly. "Sara, what's going on?"

"You mean all the people," Sara replied. "They're with that construction group working up in the hills."

"Sachs Engineering?"

"Yeah, that's the one. You want some eggs?"

"Um, sure. The usual," Anne said. "What are they all doing here?"

"Eating, of course. How should I know any more than that? You want rye toast?"

Anne was getting frustrated. "Rye is fine. Why are they all here *right now?*"

A shrug was all the response the waitress offered. "Okay. I'll have your food up in a moment. I have to run to the kitchen. Poor Tony is overwhelmed back there." Sara turned and slipped away.

"Day off," a voice said to her right. She turned to see a man in his twenties taking a long draw from his coffee cup.

"Excuse me?" Anne said.

The young man swiveled his stool to better face Anne. He offered a smile of teeth as straight and white as piano keys. His skin was deeply tanned but still held the smoothness of youth. "We've been given the day off," he said.

"Then why are you here so early?" Anne inquired.

"It's one of the drawbacks of working construction. We're used to getting up early."

"Why would you have the day off? I mean, isn't that strange?"

The man shrugged one shoulder. "Sachs knows what he's doing. I've worked with him on several projects. He's no dummy. If he wants us off-site, then he's got a reason for it. None of us are going to complain about a day off with pay. So, is there anything fun to do in this town?"

"Is Perry. . .Mr. Sachs here?" She looked around the room but didn't see him.

"Don't waste your time, ma'am. I doubt he came down from the hills. He's probably still up there."

"He stayed all night?"

"I guess. A couple of us knocked on his motel room door and didn't get a response. We thought he might like to have breakfast with us, but since he didn't come to the door and a couple of the SUVs are missing, we assumed he stayed on-site. That's the kind of guy he is. He'd give a bulldog a bad name."

Something wasn't right. It was a feeling, illogical, nearly groundless, but Anne was certain that something was out of place. Rising from the stool, she turned toward the door.

Sara called after her, "Hey, Mayor." Anne didn't turn around. "You don't want your coffee? What about your breakfast?"

Anne left the restaurant without looking back.

There wasn't an inch of Perry's body that didn't ache. His side hurt from the beating he'd taken; his back hurt from the hours spent in the backhoe and with a shovel; his hands felt bruised to the bone from constant use of the shovel and hammer. The last tool was used to help Gleason and Brent build makeshift shoring out of plywood and two-by-fours, as Jack had continued to put the excavator through its paces. He worked with remarkable speed and accuracy. Together the weary team had uncovered the roof and the chamber and dug a ditch along one side—the side they assumed would be best to open.

The top of the chamber had been fifteen meters below grade—forty-five feet. The trench in which they stood was another seven feet below that. Perry looked up past the fifty-plus feet of sharply sloped walls. Only the six-foot-wide trench was shored. The rest of the hole was bare ground, an OSHA inspector's nightmare. Perry wasn't feeling very good about it either. This was the second time in less than twenty-four hours he found himself at the bottom of a hole.

A framed wall made of wood studs covered with plywood stood behind him. Double two-by-four braces that ran from the top of the wall to similar braces on the ground held the wall in place. The connections formed a triangle, nature's strongest geometric shape.

In front of Perry rose the stone wall of the chamber. He studied it intensely, as did Jack, Gleason, Brent, and Dr. Curtis. No one wanted to miss the next few moments, despite the great risks.

When Perry was a teenager, his father had tried to tame his son with the aphorism: "The difference between a fool and a brave man is motivation. The man who loses his life and leaves a grieving family because he was seeking a thrill gets what he deserves, but a man who dies while attempting something great is a hero." Perry got the message. He knew his dad would understand, even if this expedition left him without a son.

"Piled stone construction," Curtis said. "Just one stone on top of another. It's a wonder it remained standing."

"It's more than that, Doc," Perry corrected. "Do you see how the surface is at an angle? The wall is thicker at the bottom than the top. It's an ancient construction technique. The roof and static dirt loads are transferred to the walls which in turn transfer the load to the ground."

"But there's no grout or anything," Brent said. "It's just. . .a pile of rocks."

"Look closer, kid," Jack said. "Notice how the stones are fitted.

You're right, there's no binder like mortar, but each stone is arranged to fit tightly with its neighbor. That took long, hard work."

"The roof is the same way," Perry added. "It's fitted stone, but there has to be something beneath to hold it up. It doesn't matter how tightly you fit stone to stone on a horizontal surface, gravity is going to win. There's no place to quarry stone, so this was the only way to do it. Gather large stones, organize them, then piece them together like a puzzle."

"What now?" Gleason asked.

"I wish we had time to excavate properly," Curtis said.

"We all do, Doc. It would be safer too." Perry thought for a moment and approached the wall, laying his hand on it: This wall formed a room that hadn't been seen for two millennia.

He had longed to do just what he was doing, touching the physical evidence of what could only be considered a miracle. And here it was, just as he'd imagined. Perry had wondered how he would respond, what words he'd say, what careful steps he would take. All of it was now overshadowed by the threat to Claire and Joseph.

The fire in Perry's belly grew hotter. He couldn't recall being this angry before, but anger was a luxury for others. It was time to make his next move. He looked skyward as if hoping God had written something on the blue dome overhead. The sun was rising quickly, dispelling the blackness of the night, but unable to touch the darkness within Perry.

"We open her up," Perry said.

"How do we do that?" Brent asked.

"Carefully and one stone at a time." Perry pointed to an area near where roof met wall. "There are two stones larger than the rest. They look like they've been set as cantilevered headers over an opening. They would've filled in the opening last. I think we can start there and work down."

"I sure wish I knew what was holding the roof up," Jack said. "I hate going in blind."

"I can only think of one way to find out," Perry replied. "We have to open the wall and take a look."

"I have an idea," Brent said. "Let's just move one or two stones then use the camcorder. You open a spot, and I'll stick the camera in with the light on and pan it around some. Then we can play it back on the built-in monitor."

"I like it," Perry said. "You just won a burger from Jack."

"What? Why me?" Jack protested.

"Because you're Brent's hero," Perry said. The light moment lasted only a second, then the driving need returned to the forefront of Perry's mind. "I'm limiting the crew to two people at a time. If the wall gives, then we'll need someone to clean up our mess. Jack and I'll stay down below. I may need his muscle. The rest of you go topside."

"Isn't there anything we can do?" Gleason asked.

"Prayer would be nice," Perry said, "and lots of it."

Anne drove directly to the site, weaving her Camry along the winding dirt roads that led into the hills. The sun was now high enough to have sponged away the last of the lingering darkness. Things seemed uncomfortably still. Even the relentless breeze had ceased, leaving the air as placid as glass.

At the place where the road met the slope to the site were several of the vehicles she had seen on earlier trips. Missing was the bulldozer that had rested on a large trailer. The bus was gone too, but that was to be expected. Not having a four-wheel-drive vehicle that could negotiate the sloping terrain, Anne parked along the roadside, then started the tiring ascent, glad she'd worn tennis shoes instead of business pumps.

Halfway up, she encountered three uniformed men. Each wore blue pants and a white shirt with patches on the sleeves. *Private security,* Anne reasoned. She knew Perry had hired guards to replace the deputy sheriffs that had kept the crowds away yesterday. Apparently the shift change had happened sometime during the night. The three men sat on the ground. The crowds that had been there the day before were gone, but Anne had no doubt that many would be back soon.

The guards stood when they saw her approach. One walked toward her. "I'm sorry, ma'am," he said, "but this area is private property. I'm going to have to ask you to leave."

Anne smiled. The young man looked fresh out of high school. "Where are you from?" Anne asked.

"Tehachapi," he answered. He looked askance at her. "Why?"

"I'm from Tejon," she said. "In fact, I'm the mayor of Tejon."

"I wouldn't know about that, ma'am, but I do know that my job is to keep people out."

She sighed, then said, "I'm here to see Mr. Sachs. . .the man who hired you."

"How do I know you're mayor?" he asked. The others joined him.

She had left her purse in the car and had no desire to retrieve it and hike back up the hill. "My name is Anne Fitzgerald, and I really am the major of Tejon."

"Mr. Sachs didn't tell me he was expecting you."

"Have you spoken to him?" Anne said.

"Well. . .no. We just got here an hour ago and the deputies told us not to let anyone up there. Our boss told us the same thing."

"What do you plan to tell Mr. Sachs when he comes down here and finds you've turned me away?"

"That I did my job."

Anne frowned. She was getting nowhere. "How about this: You escort me to see Mr. Sachs."

"I don't know if that's wise," the young guard said.

Anne didn't miss a beat. She turned to one of the other guards. He was taller, thinner, and looked several years older. "How about you, sport? You're not afraid to take me up there, are you?"

"Hey, I'm not afraid," the first man said. "I didn't say anything about being afraid."

"Good," Anne stated as she started up the hill. "Let's get going."

"Ma'am. . .ma'am. . ."

Anne ignored him and continued her ascent of the incline. She hoped that if the man refused to join her he would at least be hesitant to lay a hand on a woman. . .especially fifteen or more years his senior. By her fifth step, she had company.

"Okay, but I had better not get in trouble for this. And you had better be the mayor."

The incline eased as she and the security officer neared the work site. Anne paused to catch her breath. Jays sang in the oak trees, the sweet smell of grass perfumed the air, and the gold of the sun mingled with the blue of the cloudless sky. It should have felt idyllic; standing there, she should have felt a sense of peace in the Eden-like borough, but she didn't. It was too quiet.

She could see the bulldozer sitting in the distance as if fossilized. A large backhoe rested a few feet away. Another piece of equipment, similar to the backhoe but much larger and without the skip loader on the front, was farther away but just as lifeless. Three men in hardhats stood with heads down. Mounds of dirt surrounded them. Anne approached, and as she did, she saw a large hole in the ground. The men were staring down into the pit. After another dozen steps she saw the sinkhole. It was uneven in shape, and its sides were unstable.

"Wow," the guard said. "What happened here?"

"You wouldn't believe me if I told you." As she approached, the three men among the mounds noticed her. She recognized them, and apparently they recognized her.

Now within earshot, she heard the man who had been introduced to her as Gleason shout into the hole. "Perry, we have company. . . the mayor."

"Told you," she said to the guard.

"That you did," he replied.

Anne led the way and approached the Sachs men. "Madam Mayor," Gleason said with a gentlemanly nod. She returned the gesture and looked down. Her stomach dropped. Deep in the ground Perry and Jack stood next to a stone wall of some kind.

"Are you Mr. Sachs?" the guard shouted down.

"I am," came the reply. "Who are you?"

"Larry Duncan. I'm with Enterprise Security. We're the replacements for the deputies."

"I don't mean to be rude, but what are you doing here?"

"This lady says she knows you." Duncan's bluster was dissolving.

"That lady is the town mayor, and yes, she does know me."

"So I can leave her here?"

Perry didn't answer right away, and Anne steeled herself for the rejection she knew was coming. "She can stay," Perry finally said, but they were words without confidence. Clearly he was conflicted by the decision.

"Okay. I'll be returning to the post," the guard said as he left.

Anne looked down at Perry, and he returned her gaze. He looked weary, his shoulders slightly stooped, his gloved hands hanging limply at his side. The connection lasted only a moment, then Perry turned back to the stone wall. He removed a stone, then handed it to Jack, who used a piece of construction chalk to mark it. Anne could see that twenty or thirty stones had already been removed, chalked, and placed to one side.

Anne walked over to Gleason and the others. "What's going on?"

"It's a long story, Mayor. And complicated."

"It doesn't look safe down there," Anne said.

"It's not," Gleason admitted.

Anne turned and read the concern on Gleason's face. "Then why. . ."

"Don't ask," Gleason said. "Just don't ask."

The stones fascinated and frightened Perry. Each time he laid a gloved hand on one of the rocks, he wondered about the men who had so skillfully placed them there eons ago. He wondered what brought them this far from home, how they had made an impossible journey across the oceans and then traveled so far inland from the sea. He thought of their sacrifices, the families left at home, the illnesses and pains they endured, the fears they conquered. He also wondered about the jigsaw arrangement of the stones. With each stone he removed he prepared himself to flee the collapsing wall. So far he had been able to stay in place.

Perry pulled the stones from top to bottom and left to right along the courses. All of this was done as a concession to Dr. Curtis. It took no more time and would allow the archeologist to rebuild the wall if necessary.

Despite the unrelenting concern of structural failure from the wall and dirt slides from the pit walls, Perry worked at a steady, driven pace. A part of him wanted to tear into the wall, throwing stones to the side. Time was working against him, but he also knew that he couldn't help Claire and Joseph if he were trapped under a crushing pile of rubble. So he worked just beyond what caution demanded and just under what desperation pleaded for.

One minute turned to ten; ten morphed into thirty; thirty became sixty, and as it did, Perry had removed all but two courses of stone. Those could easily be stepped over. Jack moved to his side. "God is good."

"No matter what happens," Perry agreed, "God is good. Shall we see what's inside?" They already had an idea of what lay beyond the wall. Brent's creative idea of opening a small hole just large enough for the video camera and the hand that held it had revealed a bare chamber, a space with the dimensions of a good-size bedroom.

Perry had felt sick. Empty. Nothing. Just four stone walls dimly lit by the video camera's built-in light. The despair spread in a suffocating wave through the others: All the work, all the frustration, all the danger for nothing?

Then an odd sensation had tickled the back of Perry's brain. He pushed the camera through the opening again, panning it back and forth, but to a lesser degree. Removing his arm from the opening, he had brought the camera out, rewound it, and played it back through the small color view screen.

"What are you thinking?" Jack had asked.

"I'm thinking that the room the camera shows is smaller than the returns we got on the GPR survey. I'm thinking that we're seeing an anteroom, a lobby, and not the real treasure." He passed the camera around, and each man agreed. Then Perry did as he said he would: He banished everyone from the pit except Jack. As soon as they were clear, Perry removed another stone.

Now an opening the size of a bathroom door stood before them. Perry called for two large flashlights, and Brent brought them down, exiting under Perry's orders as quickly as he came.

"This is what we came for," Perry said. "No sense in putting it off."

"Yea, though I walk through the chamber of death, I shall fear no evil. . . ," Jack said in Shakespearean tones.

"You have a sick sense of humor, buddy," Perry quipped.

"I prefer my danger served up with a dash of smile."

Perry activated a flashlight and pointed it into the opening. Centuries of darkness gave way to the bright beam. Before crossing the threshold Perry poked his head in and surveyed the room. It smelled of long-settled dust, and the air was surprisingly moist. The other three walls looked identical to the one they had just opened. Pointing the light up, he saw round timbers set side by side.

"There's your explanation," Perry said. "They stacked timbers log-cabin style to hold up the roof. They are a foot or more in diameter." Perry pulled back to let Jack have a look.

"Impressive. That much lumber could hold fifty times the stones they have on there. There are no gaps between the logs. Even after all these years and the weight of all that dirt, it held. If engineers got medals, these guys would deserve a case of them."

Perry turned and gave a little wave to his friends above. "Here goes," he said softly and stepped into the room, placing his right foot just over the threshold marked off by the remaining two courses of rock. Slowly he brought his left foot in.

Perry stood in a room that had not seen the light of day for twenty centuries. The ceiling hovered just a foot above Perry's head. He raised a hand and touched the thick timbers. They were still covered in bark.

"If you like the place," Jack said, "we can make an offer and drop a down payment on it."

"I'm afraid it doesn't have much of a view." Now that he was inside, Perry could see that the opposite wall was much too close to the still buried back wall of the chamber. There were two chambers; he was standing in the anteroom. What he was after was behind another stone wall eight feet away. He took a step forward.

"Room in there for one more?" Jack asked. "I promise not to break anything."

Perry took another step toward the center of the room. "That'll be the day—"

There was a faint grating noise, and Perry froze in place. He turned to face Jack. "Did you hear that?"

"No, I didn't hear anything."

There was a crack.

Perry's heart began to race. "I know you heard that—"

The stone floor gave way beneath Perry, the sound of it crashing off the hard walls.

Things went dark.

Anne watched as Perry waved her direction. She waved back. Then she held her breath as he cautiously stepped through the opening in the stone wall. She also watched as Jack stepped forward and poked his head in. All she could see of him was his back and legs. A moment passed, then another, and Anne allowed herself to breathe.

She saw it before she heard it. Brown dust suddenly poured out of the opening, billowing into the still morning air. Anne blinked, waiting for her mind to believe what she was seeing. The trench in front of the stone wall disappeared into the fog of airborne dirt.

A slight rumble coursed under her feet.

"What. . .what happened?" She turned to Gleason, but he wasn't there. Neither were the others. She spotted them a second later running down the compounded ramps that led to the wide trench. Gleason was in the lead followed by Brent and Dr. Curtis, who struggled to keep up.

The dust settled quickly, and Anne could see the opening once again. Projecting from it like two logs were Jack's legs. They weren't moving.

"Perry!" Anne shouted. "Oh, Lord no. Perry. Perry!" Anne found herself running after the men, oblivious to any danger that might await her.

Perry shook his head and tried to focus his thoughts. It seemed like minutes had passed, but only seconds had. He came fully conscious in a moment. He was suspended in air, his feet kicking, probing for some purchase but finding none. Fiery pain pierced his side, his head throbbed, and his left wrist felt like it was being crushed in a vise.

"Stop wiggling," a voice above him said. Jack? Jack!

"What. . .where. . .?"

"Stop moving, Perry. You're killing me."

Perry looked up and saw the face of his friend less than six feet away. His entire mind began to work, and events came back to him in instant replay. He had heard a grinding sound followed by a crack, then a rumble. The next sensation was one of falling. As the floor gave way he had jumped toward the opening, but with little to push off from he fell short. He hit something head first, and things went dark.

"I've got you, buddy," Jack said. "But. . .stop. . .moving."

That explained the crushing sensation on his wrist. The big man was holding him in both of his spade-sized hands. Perry looked down into the stygian abyss and saw nothing. He could, however, hear something: water—running water.

"Um," Perry said, forcing himself to be calm, belying the freezing terror he felt. "I'm not real comfortable with this situation."

"Ya think?" Jack's voice was strained. "Okay, now. Can you find a foothold?"

Perry spread his legs out hoping to touch something. His right foot found a vertical surface directly beneath the opening, but nothing that he could put his weight on. "No. I'm afraid not."

"Hold on, Jack," a new voice said. Perry recognized it as Gleason's. "Don't let him slip in."

"How?" It was Brent.

"Sit on him," Gleason ordered. "Doc, you grab Jack's legs."

Perry looked back into the opening and saw Gleason's face appear. He could see his eyes darting back and forth as he took in the situation. The face disappeared. "Doc, you take one of Jack's legs and hold it. Brent, you do the same. Hang on, Jack, I'm going to have to get a little close and personal."

All conversation stopped: The only sound to be heard was that of the water running far below Perry's feet. His shoulder felt as if it was coming out of the socket, and his hand was deprived of circulation by Jack's adrenaline-laced grip. Forcing himself to think instead of feel, he willed himself to be as still as possible. His life was literally in the hands of his friend.

"Perry," Gleason said loudly, "here's what's going to happen. My arms aren't as long as Jack's, and there's not enough room for both of us in the opening. I'm going to lie down on top of Jack and reach over him with my arm. I have my belt in a loop and wrapped about my wrist. If Jack can pull you up a few inches and if you can stretch out your free hand, you should be able to reach. Got it?"

"Yeah."

A second later the light in the chamber dimmed as another head came through the opening. In the dim illumination, Perry saw Gleason's face, then his arm, then the belt. He felt himself being pulled up. His vertical distance changed by only a few inches, but it was enough for Perry to grab the looped belt and twist it around his wrist.

"Got it!" Perry shouted. Immediately he felt a pull on the belt. "Now what?"

"Now the. . .hard part," Gleason said, grunting each word. "Jack is lying over the last two rows of stones. . .he won't have leverage to lift you. I'm straddling him. He. . .needs to reposition, which means. . ."

"He has to let go of me," Perry said, completing Gleason's sentence. "Swell." He thought for a moment. "Do it."

Gleason gave more orders. "Brent, Curtis. Take Jack by the legs and when. . .I say. . .pull him away from the opening. Jack. . ."

"I got it, buddy. As soon as I'm clear of your legs, I'll be back."

"Don't take too long," Gleason pleaded. "I don't know how long my back will hold out. Perry weighs more than I do. I could get pulled in."

"Lovely," Perry remarked.

"Okay, let's do this," Gleason said. "Three. . .two. . .one. . . now."

Perry felt two things. First he felt the release of the one thing that kept him from falling to his death: Jack's grip. Second, he felt himself inching lower. Gleason couldn't hold him. He was about to release the belt rather than drag his friend in when he noticed that he was no longer slipping down. The large black hand of Jack came back in view. The angle was different, and Perry knew why. Jack was no longer prone; he had repositioned himself to better reach him. The hand came down, and Perry reached for it, grabbing it at the wrist.

There was a loud grunt, a powerful scream, and Perry felt himself traveling up as if he were seated on a rocket. Before he could do anything else, Jack and Gleason dragged him across the rough rock threshold. The dark of the chamber had been replaced with the blue of the morning sky. It was the most beautiful blue he had ever seen.

He lay on the ground, as did Jack. Neither man moved at first.

Perry was filled with pain as if someone had released a bag of hornets inside his body. Everything hurt, and he was thankful for it. If he hurt, it meant he was alive.

"You know," Jack said, finally pushing himself into a seated position on the ground, "I'm never going to let you forget this."

"I didn't think you would," Perry said with a weak laugh. "I suppose that now I owe *you* a burger."

"I was thinking a new car," Jack said.

Perry sat up and moved his arms, trying to work out the pain. "Thanks, guys. You're the best."

"We know that," Gleason said, "but you need to thank someone else. The mayor helped save your bacon."

"Anne?"

"Oh, yeah," Gleason said. "I was losing you. I knew I was going to be following you down that hole before Jack could move into position. I slipped forward, and Anne grabbed me by the collar. She held me until Jack and I pulled you out."

Perry looked at Anne, who seemed embarrassed by the whole thing. "Thank you, Madam Mayor."

She smiled and looked at her hands. "I think I broke a nail."

CHAPTER 21

"Is it just me, or does anyone else get the idea that these people didn't want this place disturbed?" Brent asked.

"I don't know how they did it," Gleason added, "but someone had a devious mind."

They were standing in the pit. Perry was now using Jack's flashlight to study the inside of the floorless chamber. Perry's light had taken the trip to the bottom of the pit.

"I can't give you the details," Perry said, "but I can see wood along the sides of the pit. It must have been what they used to support the stone floor. Unlike the timbers in the ceiling, these look small. More like branches. They strung these dowel-sized branches from wall to wall, covered in thin stone, then dirt. I thought I was walking on something solid before it gave way."

"And the water?" Brent asked. "Why do I hear running water?"

"Aquifer," Perry said.

"Aqua...what?" Brent asked.

"Water-bearing rock," Perry explained. "Ground water that runs in underground streams. Many rural towns get their water from aquifers. If memory serves, the Edwards Aquifer meets the water needs of about two million people."

"So the builders placed this over an aquifer," Gleason said. "How would they know where an underground stream was?"

Perry turned to the others. "There's no way to know. Maybe they didn't plan it that way."

"There was some planning going on," Curtis said. "Whether they built here because of the aquifer or they stumbled upon it by accident doesn't matter. They made good use of it."

"I'm the last guy on the planet to argue that point," Perry said. "The presence of underground water would explain the sinkhole. Sinkholes are often associated with underground springs."

Perry took a deep breath. "Well, if everyone is rested, it's time to get back to work."

"I'm calling the union," Jack said. "These working conditions are brutal."

"You don't belong to a union," Perry shot back.

"In that case, I guess I'd better hustle." Jack rose from his seat on the ground. Perry saw him grimace and knew that the big man was feeling soreness all over. He wanted to order him away but knew Jack would never obey. He was in for the duration, and Perry was glad for it.

"We need a bridge," Gleason said. "Unfortunately, we didn't think to bring one of those along."

"Then we'll have to make one," Perry said. "There's a small ledge at the base of the far wall. I imagine it's made from foundation stones used to support the partition. The span is about eight feet. We need something to cross that distance, something a man could stand on."

"A ladder," Brent suggested.

"We don't know if that little edge will hold the other side of the ladder," Gleason said.

"We could rig it to work as a cantilevered support," Jack said. "We would have to weight this side, though. Rule of thumb is, for every foot of cantilever there should be two feet this side of the fulcrum point. Otherwise the moment arm becomes too high, and that's just inviting disaster."

"Can someone translate what the big guy is saying?" Brent

asked. "He's hurting my brain."

Perry smiled. "A cantilever is any projection that is supported on one end while the other end hangs unsupported. Think of a diving board. It's fixed on one end but projects over the pool. Jack's rule of thumb is correct. An architect would like to see a two-to-one ratio as well as having the supported end anchored. Since we have to bridge about eight feet, we would need about sixteen feet on this side of the opening, or a very strong way of tying the end down. Otherwise our cantilever bridge becomes a seesaw."

"Oh, well, why didn't he just say so?"

"I'd be worried about deflection," Gleason said. "Once we're on the far end and the ledge doesn't hold, the ladder might bend and even fold—especially an aluminum ladder, and that's all we brought with us."

"But we have two of them," Perry said. "We can defeat the deflection problem easy enough. We just set the ladders on their sides, tie the right rungs together so the extensions don't slip, set them thirty or so inches apart, and span the distance with the left-over two-by-fours from the shoring you built."

"Trusses," Jack said. "You're thinking of turning the ladders into the equivalent of floor trusses."

"Exactly," Perry said. "I think it'll work."

"I agree," Jack said, "but I don't think we should trust that little ledge. For all we know our weight might bring the whole wall down. Nothing would surprise me now."

"Then let's get to work," Perry said with a clap of his hands. "Just to be safe, let's build our truss bridge someplace other than this trench. I'm getting claustrophobic."

The work went smoothly and intensely. Every setback increased the danger to the captive Claire and Joseph. While Jack cut two-by-fours into thirty-inch lengths, Gleason retrieved a box of carriage bolts from the supply truck. In the time it took them to make their way to the surface, the plan had been refined even more. Engineering minds began to percolate with ideas.

They decided that wood planks should be bolted together, sandwiching the ladders together. This would provide a rigid deck as well as keep the ladders securely apart but still part of the structural whole. When done, they would have a narrow, wood-and-aluminum bridge similar to a ship's boarding ramp. It would be fourteen feet long. The ladders set on edge would provide the strength to hold a man's weight; the planking would provide a deck upon which to stand.

While the others worked, Perry took Anne aside. "I want to thank you for helping Gleason save my bacon," he said. "You shouldn't be here, but I'm glad you are."

"Turnabout is fair play," she said. "In some ways, your words saved my life."

"Why are you here?" Perry asked. "It's a little early for most people."

She told him about her conversation in the restaurant with one of his workers. "I became concerned," she said. "I don't know why, but I just felt that something wasn't right."

"Several things aren't right," Perry said.

"You seem rushed," Anne said. "I didn't get that impression last time I was here. You were working swiftly but carefully. Now your crew is told not to show up, and you almost lose your life. What's happened?"

Perry started to dismiss her question. The fewer people who knew of the problem the better, but somehow that decision seemed wrong. She was in the right place at the right time to help save his life and that was because of. . .of what? Instinct? Was her arrival coincidence? Perry doubted that. Coincidence was seldom what it seemed. Anne had shown up because she'd followed a leading in her heart. She'd become God's instrument to save Perry's life.

Some would scoff at that idea. The rationalist might appeal to luck or twist of fate, but Perry found nothing rational in that philosophy. He was a man who tried to remain open to the leading of God. What better time than this to trust that leading?

"Anne, I'm going to tell you a story. You may or may not believe it, but I assure you it's true. And I may need your help to save two lives. But you must keep everything in the strictest confidence. Do you understand?"

"I do" was all she said. Perry found her decisiveness endearing.

Perry took her back to the early morning hours when he intervened in the attack on Dr. Henri. Over the next hour, while Jack and the others built the jury-rigged bridge, Perry laid out the unbelievable account up to the point where he crashed through the floor. She occasionally asked questions but spent most of the time listening to each word.

"Pretty wild story, isn't it?" Perry finally said.

"Wild is right. Sounds like something from a movie script."

"Well, I have the bruises to prove it isn't."

"And this mysterious visitor is supposed to be back tonight?"

Perry nodded. "Two lives rest on my ability to retrieve what's in that chamber."

"Can you really release the treasure?" Anne asked. "I believe life is sacred, but. . ."

"I'm not sacrificing Claire and Joseph," Perry declared. "I'll just have to find a way to make things work." Moments of silence flowed, and the two walked through the field. The sun was higher, and its warmth was being pushed through the trees and tall grass by a new breeze. "The God who made those trees is still in control," Perry said. "I must trust in Him."

"You're going to need His help," Anne said. "You can also count on me. I'll help in any way I can."

"Thank you," Perry said. "I may need your help with Sergeant Montulli. If he gets wind of this, he'll want to intervene. I understand that; I even admire it, but we're dealing with the worst kind of man. He seems to have power, intelligence, and no conscience. For now, I have to play his game. If Montulli interferes, my friends will be killed."

"I understand," Anne said. "But at some point the police are going to have to get involved."

"At the right time, Anne, at the right time."

Jack shouted across the field. "We're set, Perry. Let's rock and roll on this."

"Rock and roll?" Anne said with a raised eyebrow.

"Don't let him fool you. He only listens to polka music."

Perry led Anne back to the work area and prayed that he had done the right thing in telling her all that he had.

It took all four men to carry the awkward contraption down to the chamber; each one fell at least once on the way. The sun continued its climb in the sky, shortening shadows and bathing the work area in more light. Very little of that light would make it into the chamber, so two additional flashlights were brought along. Anne had volunteered to carry them. More light would be made available by portable work lights run from the generator. Perry had run the electric line himself while his friends finished cobbling together the ladder-bridge.

Working like a well-drilled team, the men angled, twisted, and turned the long, ridged bridge through the opening Perry and Jack had made in the stone wall. It was stressful work and sweat poured freely, especially from Dr. Curtis. No one complained; each focused on what needed to be done.

Once in place, the makeshift bridge worked better than hoped. More than half of it was in the floorless chamber. To keep it from tipping and falling down the shaft, the crew had to weigh down the exposed end with their bodies. Perry called out directions and, after fifteen minutes of effort, managed to rest the far end on the small ledge at the base of the opposite and inner stone wall. Slowly the men released their end. The bridge stayed in place.

"It's almost level," Jack said. "The guy who dug the trench deserves a medal. Oh, that would be me."

"I'll see that you get everything you have coming to you,"

Perry quipped. "The question is: Will the other side hold once weight is put on?"

"We can't chance it," Jack said. "We have to weigh this end down with at least twice what's going to be on the other side."

"Agreed," Perry answered. "Let's start with the stones we removed from the wall. We can pile them on. There's at least five hundred pounds of rock there, maybe more. That should provide enough counterbalance for one person. We can retrieve a couple of shovels and cover the stones in a mound of dirt. That should add weight too."

"Good idea," Jack said.

Dr. Curtis groaned.

"I'm sorry, Doc," Perry said. "But we don't have the privilege of doing things slowly. Your stones have survived centuries under the dirt. They'll survive a few more hours."

"I know, I know," Curtis said with a resigned wave of a hand. "Do what you must."

The work began. Brent went to retrieve the shovels while Perry, Jack, and Gleason loaded on the stones from the wall. It took another thirty minutes to return a portion of the dirt dug by the excavator to the trench and bury the stones on the near end of the bridge.

When done, Perry stepped over one of the ladders and examined the work. "I think that's it. If the ledge on the other side gives way, our bridge will be fully cantilevered. It *should* hold."

Perry turned. "Now for the real test. Hand me a flashlight, Anne." She passed over the light, exchanging a meaningful glance with Perry as she did.

"Hang on a second," Jack said.

Perry stopped and turned to see Jack step on the ladder-bridge, back up to the dirt mound, and sit on it. "Just contributing another 280 pounds to the safety process. If this things tips and your end goes down, I'll come sliding after you, so be careful. Mama Dyson would miss her little boy."

"Well, we can't have that, can we?" Perry said. "Gleason, since

Jack has decided to sit down on the job, you'll have to set up the work light after I get in there."

"Will do," Gleason said.

Perry turned to Dr. Curtis. "Doc, I'm going to be removing some of the stones. . . ."

"And you can't keep walking them back here, nor can you set them on the bridge without turning this into a seesaw," Curtis sighed. "Just drop them down the shaft."

The words went against every fiber of Curtis's archeology sensibility, and Perry knew it. He also knew that Curtis understood that life was more important than artifacts.

" 'For You light my lamp; the Lord my God illumines my darkness,' " Perry quoted. "I could use some illumination, Lord."

Perry walked through the opening, leaving behind the bright light of morning for tomb-like darkness.

The hurriedly constructed bridge felt solid under Perry's feet. The slim ledge seemed to hold. He'd hoped that by counter balancing the device with the rocks and dirt—and Jack's added bulk—the downward force on the shelf would be minimal. His theory held, so far.

The chamber was cool, damp, and dark. The flashlight in his hand helped push away some of the black, but it couldn't exhaust it. Perry wanted to look down toward the sound of water that ran through the aquifer, but chose not to. Curiosity was a powerful force in his life, but today he had a more pressing job before him.

"I'm at the wall," he said loudly, his voice echoing off the stones.

Dirt trickled down from the ceiling like soot from a forest fire. A new concern entered his mind. He had no idea how secure the ceiling was now. It had spent hundreds of years under the compression of nearly fifty feet of soil. The compression was now gone. How would the timbers and the stones above them react? Moisture that had been kept from the supporting timbers by the treacherous stone floor now had free access. Would that weaken an already precarious structure? If the ceiling collapsed, it would mean the end of Perry and the bridge.

Suddenly the chamber was awash in brightness. Gleason had activated the work light. Its powerful beam was blinding at first, and it cast a shadow of Perry's body against the wall. The light was set low, so Perry's shadow reached from ceiling to bridge. After his eyes adjusted, the work light was a big help, but Perry still had use for the flashlight in his hand. Running its beam along the surface of the wall, he studied each stone within reach, hoping to find an indication of a previous opening.

He was not disappointed.

Just as with the first wall, this one had a pair of large stones that seemed to be placed as lintels. Once Perry felt he had discovered all there was to be discovered about the stone partition, he clipped the flashlight to his belt, raised his gloved hand, and set it on the first stone to be removed. It was positioned right below the large stone header. Unlike the other opening, Perry had planned to make this one as small as possible but still allow the free passage of a man.

"We're dying of suspense out here," Gleason called in. "How about some play-by-play before we have coronaries?"

Perry chuckled, as much from nerves as from Gleason's request. "The wall is identical in construction to the first, including a couple of cantilevered lintels. The stones are fitted tightly together. It looks like mud or something was used to fill the joints. It's a masterpiece. I'm getting ready to pull the first stone. Stand by."

"We're not going anywhere without you," Gleason said.

"Good," Perry retorted. "You know how I hate to be alone."

He took a deep breath and wondered if the builders were devious enough to create a wall that would cave in on itself if tampered with. Tightening his grip on the first stone, he pulled. Nothing. He pulled again, attempting to wiggle the stone from side to side; bits of compacted dirt fell from the joints. *Hermetically sealed*, Perry thought. *A good sign.* He pulled gently but firmly. Still nothing. He was considering trying another rock when it finally budged. Gently he pulled, and the stone came free.

Perry waited for something to happen: for the ceiling to crash down or the wall before him to fall forward in a single mass, squashing him like a bug under a boot. Neither happened. The only result he could detect was a dank, sour smell rushing out of the small opening. The chamber was breathing for the first time in two millennia.

"First stone is out," Perry announced. He held it up and examined it for a moment. It looked like all the others. He dropped it over the side. It took a full second before he heard it crash into the water below. There was no doubt now; the pit was deep.

"Tell me that was the stone," Gleason said with apprehension.

"It was the stone. I'm removing the next one." The next stone came free easily, as did the next. One by one, Perry gently removed stone after stone, dropping each into the pit and forcing himself to ignore the cracking, splashing sound. In what seemed like hours, Perry had successfully removed enough stones to leave an opening of three feet wide by four feet high. It was enough for now.

"I have a decent-sized opening now," Perry announced. "It's time to take a peek."

He pulled the flashlight from his belt, took a deep breath, and tried to calm his anxious nerves. It was a monumental task. Leaning forward, he clicked on the light and shone it in the room.

The beam pushed through the ebony darkness and reflected off dust that floated in the air. The dust, Perry assumed, had been set to flight by his removal of the stones. The light shone on the distant wall. "I see another stone wall about ten feet back. I assume that it's the back wall of the chamber." He aimed the light up. "The ceiling is identical to the one in this room." Perry let the light track down the wall.

His heart thundered in anticipation. His mouth was dry; his stomach became a tight knot. Slowly, he let the light fall until it fell on something different than a stone wall. There was a protrusion, a bench made of stones identical to the chamber. Perry let the light trace the bench. It rose from the floor by three feet, and he estimated it to be seven feet in length. From his location he couldn't judge its depth.

He was breathing harder now, taking in air in ragged inhalations. "Perry," Gleason called.

He didn't answer.

There was something on the bench. His light shook as he traced its form in the white beam.

"You okay, Perry? Talk to me, buddy."

"Uh. . .yeah. . .I'm fine."

There was a noise. . .a crunch. . .a grinding. . .a pop.

The wall collapsed with a roar. Dust billowed everywhere, filling the compartment with a choking cloud.

Perry dropped to his knees and covered his face.

Joseph stopped rocking.

He sat straight up and stared at the distant wall.

"Joseph?" Claire said. "Are you okay, sweetheart?"

"Uhh. . .Perry. . .uhh. . .uhh." Joseph bolted to his feet and stepped back from the workbench. "Perry. . .uhh. . .uhh." He put his hands to his face, dropped to his knees, and bent forward until his forehead touched the tile floor.

"Joseph, what is it?" Claire kneeled next to her son. "Joseph? Sweetheart?"

Joseph began to weep in giant, explosive sobs that belched out like smoke and ash from a volcano. The sound of it terrified Claire.

"What's going on down there?" Rutherford asked Julia. His eyes were affixed to one of the monitors on his desk. "What's wrong with him?"

Julia stepped to her brother and looked over his shoulder. "He looks sick."

"Not sick," Rutherford corrected. "He's paralyzed with fear. Why?"

"I don't know. I'll go check."

"No. Stay here. Let's see what happens."

Rutherford zoomed the video camera in on Joseph.

Anne's heart seized as she heard the sound and saw dust fly from the opening like heat from a blast furnace. "Oh, dear Lord, no," she gasped.

"Perry!" Gleason shouted and hopped on the bridge. He lowered his head, clearly intending to charge through the mouth of the chamber.

"Gleason, no!" Jack bellowed. The sound of his voice rattled Anne to her core. "Stand fast." The sheer force of the words made everyone freeze in place.

"I've got to get to Perry," Gleason objected just as loudly.

"I said no. Back off. Now!"

Anne watched as Gleason's gentle faced hardened into a mask of dark anger. "Why?"

"Because you may kill him if you go in there," Jack said with words sharp enough to cut stone.

"What?" Gleason's hands turned to fists as he stood on the fabricated bridge.

"Think, man. Think," Jack said. "If he's fallen, then there's nothing we can do. If he's injured and you rush it, then you may overstress the bridge and we lose both of you. You'd be killing him."

Gleason started to speak but then stopped, his mouth open, poised to deliver a scathing comment, but no words came. His expression changed. He understood, and now so did Anne.

"Everyone listen to me. We're going to do this, and we're going to do it right." Jack had seized full control in a moment. "Gleason, come back here with me. You too, Doc. I want your weight back here." The men did as they were told.

"What about me?" Brent asked.

Jack's face softened. "I have no right to ask this, pal, but you're the lightest one. Do you think you're up to going in and seeing what happened?"

Brent looked at the opening that glowed ominously as the work light lit up the dust that hung in the air. "Yeah, man. I'll. . . I'll do it."

"No," Anne said. "I'm the lightest one here. I'll go."

"I can't let you do that, Mayor," Jack said. "It's bad enough I'm asking an intern to do it."

Anne had been in too many negotiation situations to know that she would never win this debate, and precious seconds were ticking by. She looked at Jack and the others who had joined him as human counterweights. "My mother used to say that it's easier to get forgiveness than permission." She crossed the distance from her position to the bridge, and with no further comment, walked into the dusty void.

"Mayor!" Jack bellowed. "Anne, get back. . ."

Anne had stopped listening.

The room was thick with dust that filled Anne's nose and mouth. She coughed several times and felt a suffocating fear. But a greater fear drove her forward. She *had* to know what had happened to Perry.

She waved at the dust to clear her vision, an effort that was both futile and silly. One tentative step followed another, and the terror of falling grew within her. Her mind registered the facts: she stood on two-by-four decking strung between the rails of two aluminum ladders. There was no rail to hold onto, just the twenty-four-inch vertical wall created by the width of the ladders set on end.

A pressure grew inside her, an impulse to turn and run for the opening. For a moment she felt like a dam about to give in to the unrelenting force of an engorged reservoir. She was foolish to have done this. Who was she kidding? Death was eighteen inches to her right or left. One misstep and she'd plummet to the aquifer below. It was a certain, horrifying death.

Voices of despair rang in her head: "Flee. . .run. . .escape. . .it's too late."

Anne took another step forward. Fear or no fear, voices or no voices, blackness or light, she was going to push ahead. If that meant careening to her death in abysmal blackness, then so be it.

Another step.

"Perry?" The dust began to settle, and the work light began to do its job. Anne's body cast a long shadow, and in the shadow she could see a form—a human form on its knees, bent over, face down. "Perry!" She turned to the opening. "He's still on the bridge."

Kneeling on the coarse boards, Anne laid a hand on Perry's back. It rose and fell. He was alive. "Perry? Perry, can you hear me?" There was no response.

She moved her hand forward and touched his head. His hard hat was gone. She felt moisture in his hair. Raising her hand so the light behind her could shine on it, she saw a dark crimson. Perry's head was bleeding.

"Talk to us," Jack shouted. His voice weighed heavy with concern.

"He's unconscious. There's some blood from the back of his head, but he's breathing." She wondered what to do next. The first thought was to drag him out to safety, but his position, size, and dead weight was more than she would be able to manage. Although it was only eight feet or so, it might as well have been a mile. She'd have to think of something else.

She looked ahead, to the place where the wall had once been. A pile of stones littered a floor—a floor that was only two feet away. If she couldn't go back, then she had to go forward. That was the safest thing to do. . .maybe.

Rising, Anne steadied herself and stepped over Perry's body. Unconscious and in the position of a penitent saint, his body filled the narrow space between the ladders, leaving her to make one big step, the most important step of her life. To totter, to tip, to fall would be the end. Anne chose not to think about the matter any longer. Instead she raised her left leg and gently placed it on the other side of Perry's bowed body. "Don't wake up yet,

Perry," she whispered. A vision of his coming to and suddenly sitting up played on her mind.

Once her left foot found purchase on the wood deck, she raised her right leg, completed the step, and breathed a sigh of relief. Another stride and she was standing on the other side of the stone rubble, feet planted on the ancient floor that had, only moments before, been hidden by the now defunct wall.

Quickly she began to pick up some of the detritus and toss it to the side. With the area in front of the leading edge of the bridge clear, she reached forward with both hands and grabbed Perry's collar. Clutching the material in her hands, she pulled with all her strength.

The man's body moved forward barely a foot. She tugged again, and his limp form stretched out on the bridge. Several more back-aching pulls and his whole body finally rested on the room's rugged floor.

"He's off the bridge," Anne shouted. She looked back to the opening, blinded by the brilliant work light.

"What?" Jack said. "Off the bridge?"

"I've moved him into the new chamber."

There was silence. She expected a cheer, but heard nothing at first, then the sound of footsteps on the bridge. The work light dimmed as a body stepped in front of it. Gleason appeared. "Don't move," he said.

"Why?" she asked.

"The last floor collapsed. Remember?"

Anne suddenly felt sick. She hadn't thought of that. "I'm an idiot."

"Not necessarily. How is he?"

"Still breathing. He took at least one blow to the head. I don't know how serious it is, but he's out cold."

Gingerly, Gleason stepped from the bridge to the floor. "Get back on the bridge," he said.

"I'm not leaving."

"No one is asking you to," Gleason said quickly. "Until we know the floor is safe, we should limit the weight on it."

"Oh," Anne said and moved to where Gleason had been a moment before. She watched as he bent over Perry and rolled him onto his back. "This is a lousy place to practice first aid," he said.

He felt for a pulse in Perry's neck. "Heartbeat seems steady." Seeing Perry's flashlight clipped to his belt, Gleason removed it and, bending over Perry, continued his examination. "Is this where you felt the blood?" he asked as he ran his hand along his friend's scalp.

"Yes."

"The cut feels small, and the bone seems intact. That's good. . ."

"Ow." Perry moved, batting away Gleason's hand.

"Take it easy, buddy," Gleason said. "You took a knock on the noggin. I'm just checking to see if any marbles are missing." Perry remained still as Gleason finished his field exam. "Anything else hurt?"

"My pride," Perry said. "When did you become a medic?"

"You know me, I read a lot. Let me ask you some stupid questions. Do you hear any ringing in your ears?"

"No."

"Blurred or double vision?"

"I'm fine," Perry said sitting up, then swayed. "Whoa. . .a little dizzy."

"You got smacked on the head, remember?"

"That explains the headache." Perry looked around. "How did I get here?"

"Anne dragged you off the bridge while you were napping."

"Anne? You shouldn't be in here."

"It seemed like a good idea at the time," Anne said, quoting Perry's earlier words to her. "What happened?"

He moved his head in a circle and grimaced. "I was looking through the opening when I heard something, and then the wall started down. I dropped and covered. One of the rocks must have beaned me behind the ear. Next thing I know, Dr. Kildare is poking the lump with his bony finger."

"Wait until you get my bill."

Anne watched Gleason help Perry to his feet. He wobbled for a moment then found his legs. He drew a deep breath, coughed from the dust, then Perry's expression changed as if the fog had finally cleared from his mind. He looked at the empty bridge, then his feet.

"We're in the chamber!" He spun and gasped.

Anne had been too frightened and too preoccupied to look past Perry. Now she followed his eyes. "What is that?"

The sharp pain in Perry's head was extinguished by the onslaught of raw emotion within him. Before him were the objects of his search—the treasure that had driven him the last six months. Here, right in front of his eyes, were the objects of such value that dollar amounts meant nothing. No monetary value could be applied to them. The diffused light from the doorway filled the area with an eerie twilight. He took a step closer.

"Careful, Perry. We should check the floor." Gleason sounded apprehensive.

"No need, buddy. This is what they were protecting. The people that buried all this did so to protect it, not destroy it."

"Yeah, well, they've already surprised us three times; I think we should avoid a fourth."

Gleason was right, but Perry was confident in his assessment. He walked across the floor. It felt rigid, and his footfalls returned a solid sound, not a hollow one that would indicate a cavity beneath.

"What is it?" Anne repeated. She moved close to Perry, standing by his side looking at the unusual sight.

"A chrysalis," Perry said.

"A what?" Anne said, clearly confused.

"A chrysalis. . .a cocoon." Perry kept his eyes riveted to the object. "How's the bridge, Gleason?"

"I'll. . .I'll check." His voice was soft and held the waver of amazement. A moment later he said, "It looks sound. This end is resting firmly on the ledge. It should be okay, as long as nothing pulls it back, or we don't bounce too much."

"Invite the rest over," Perry said. "Tell them to come one at a time. You follow last and bring the work light with you."

"Got it." Gleason disappeared down the bridge.

"A cocoon?" Anne said. "Of what? It looks like. . .mummy wrappings."

"A good description," Perry said. "The chrysalis is what's left of the burial."

"This is what you were telling me about? This is from the tomb of Christ?"

"Yes," Perry whispered. "We're looking at what no one has seen since the first century."

A gasp came from behind them. Perry turned to see Dr. Curtis with a hand to his mouth. His hand shook. "It's here. . .it's really here. I couldn't make myself believe it. Even after you told me about the document, even after I saw what was in the coffins, I still couldn't believe."

"I'm behind you, guys," Brent said. "Man, this place is eerie. Glad to hear you're okay, Mr. Sachs. . . ." He stopped short, the sight of the object stunning him to silence.

"I bet you thought I was pulling your leg back at the pizza parlor," Perry said.

"I. . .I. . ." Brent laughed. "I can't even talk. This is really it?"

"It has to be," Perry replied.

"Give the anchor man some room," Jack said. The group parted and moved to the sides of the room. Jack moved easily from the bridge to the floor, but he froze in his tracks. He said nothing, his big frame casting a shadow the size of a bed sheet. After a moment, he stepped two feet to the side to let the light land on the thing before him. The beam wiggled and danced. Gleason had picked up its stand and was moving it across the bridge. He now set it in the center of the room and took a step back.

Perry looked at Jack. "Well, big guy, what do you think?"

Jack didn't budge. He did, however, begin to weep.

It seemed appropriate.

Silence permeated the space more deeply than had the previous darkness. The only sounds were the running water in the aquifer and the sniffing of men as they fought back tears.

"I suppose we should do something," Jack finally said.

"Yeah, we should," Perry answered. He bowed his head and began, "Our Father in heaven, we are unworthy to behold this. . . ." As he prayed, tears ran from his eyes.

CHAPTER 22

D r. Curtis was childlike in his enthusiasm. He moved through the room pointing and talking nonstop. Perry had given him thirty minutes to evaluate the items while Brent, who had retrieved his camera, shot video.

"The amazing thing is that the chrysalis has maintained its shape," Curtis enthused. "It was too much to hope for. The ancient Jews often wrapped the deceased in strips of cloth that ran from the feet to under the arms. That's why all we see is the shape of a man from the chest down. The hands of the deceased would be tied in front with a linen strip." He paused and looked around the linen cocoon. "Here," he said with excitement. "Right here on the pedestal, a cloth strip."

Brent moved in for a close-up. "Just don't touch it, lad," Curtis said to him and then continued his impromptu lesson. "Spices meant to honor the dead as well. . .as well as. . .well, just say it, to mask odor, would be poured over the body. As much as a hundred pounds of spices might be used. Another band of linen would be wrapped around the head to keep the mouth shut."

"If it's cloth," Anne asked, "why did it keep its shape? Shouldn't it just collapse on itself?"

"There's a passage in the New Testament, John chapter twenty, that has puzzled scholars for many years," Perry said. "The disciples

Peter and John hear of the empty tomb and race to the grave to see for themselves. It says that they saw the linen wrappings lying there. After examining the empty tomb, it's said that John saw and believed. The question is: What did he see that made him believe in the resurrection? Some have suggested that he saw what we see now, the linen in the shape of the body of Christ."

"Doesn't it mention a facecloth too?" Jack asked.

"Yes," Curtis affirmed. "In fact, it says the cloth was off by itself, not with the linen wrappings but rolled up and placed by itself. The word that is translated from the original Greek as 'rolled' means 'to be wrapped.' Some think that what the disciples saw was the face napkin still in the position it would have been if wrapped around Jesus' head. The simpler explanation would be that it had been folded up and set aside. The truth is, we don't know."

"Would it be here?" Gleason asked.

Curtis acted as if he had been shocked. "That hadn't occurred to me." Curtis started looking around. Perry and the others joined.

"Here," Perry said.

"You found it?" Curtis asked.

"No, but I found something else. There is a small rock ledge and something is resting on it." Perry turned to Brent. "I need more direct light. Bring the camera over." Brent did and shone the high-intensity light where Perry indicated. "They look like medallions. Take a look, Doc." Perry stepped aside, and Curtis hurried over.

"I can't be sure, but. . ." He took a deep breath. "This is almost too much to believe. I think these are clay seals. They bear an impression." He leaned over the objects and then straightened. "Pontius Pilate," he said in a whisper. "These are the remains of the seal that was on Christ's tomb."

"Seal?" Brent said. "You mean like a wax seal? Remember I'm new at all this."

"A clay seal," Curtis said. "To break the seal was punishable by death. The tomb was cut out of rock, and a large, round stone had been rolled in front of the opening. A seal would have been set by stretching a cord around the stone door and setting it with clay medallions. A signet ring bearing Pilate's name would have been pressed into the clay, and the ring returned to the procurator."

"I found it," Anne said. She was kneeling down at the head of the stone pedestal. "There's a cubby hole here and what looks like a folded dish towel."

Curtis scampered over. "Please, don't touch it. It's very old and might turn to dust if moved." Anne moved so the archeologist could kneel down and see for himself. "Yes, yes, this very well could be it. It must be it. It's the only thing that makes sense."

"What about those?" Jack said, pointing to two jars that were tucked away in a corner. "Should we open them?"

"No, not here," Curtis said sharply. "This must be done in a laboratory, not in the field." He stopped, realizing the foolishness of his statement.

"We all agree with you, Dr. Curtis, but you know the problem," Perry said softly. "We're going to have to move these, no matter what."

"But they're invaluable," Curtis moaned. "They're more valuable than anything on earth. They're more valuable than my life or. . ."

No one corrected him. Perry understood the man well enough to know of his faith and the goodness of his heart. Curtis plunked down on the floor, pulling his legs up into a fetal position. "You're right, of course," he whispered.

Perry walked to the scholar and crouched down next to him. He placed a hand on his shoulder. "You know if there was any other way, I'd seize it, but for now, someone else calls the shots."

"I know," the heartbroken archaeologist said. Perry felt the same emotion and had, for the briefest of moments, wondered if he shouldn't just call the police and hope for the best.

"Jesus died for the many, Doc," Perry offered. "He also died for the one. We have to do what is right."

Perry rose, approached the stone bier, and looked at the wrappings that had once touched his Savior. Hot feelings churned in a roiling, emotional stew.

Brent stepped to his side, shooting more video of the unusual object that had endured more than Perry could imagine. As he did so, the camera's lights illuminated the chrysalis. For the first time, Perry saw a dark spot on the left side: an ancient bloodstain. He immediately thought of the spear thrust between Jesus' ribs, and a profound sadness poured in to form a void in Perry where confidence had once been.

In front of him rested objects that had touched the Christ, the Son of God. Once, the chrysalis had embraced the lifeless form of the Savior, then somehow, in some miraculous way, had retained its shape during the resurrection. Few doubted the reality of the historical Jesus, but many debated His words, His life, His miracles, and His resurrection. Here was proof. Doubters would work hard to find fault, but they would be left on shifting, shaky ground. Those who did not want to believe never would, but certainly many would recognize the truth when they saw it.

Whoever moved the artifacts, whoever built the replica tomb endured the worst kinds of hardship and danger. It wasn't something that one would do for a prank or a hoax.

Chrysalis. Face napkin. Pilate's seal. Even Perry was having trouble believing it. Here was corroboration for those who had eyes to see. Everything in the stone room was mentioned in the Gospels. Matthew, Mark, Luke, and John all gave details of the event, and here was evidence of their accuracy—each item attested to the truth recorded in those Bible books. If they were accurate about the burial of Christ, certainly they were truthful about all He had said and done. They showed him to be the Christ, the Messiah, the very Son of God, and before Perry lay artifacts that gave silent but soul-shaking testimony to the truth.

And he had to let it all go.

An image came to his mind: An older man lying in a rain-soaked alley of Seattle; a man who clutched a battered leather satchel and said, "I've failed. I've failed the world. I've failed God."

Perry now knew what Dr. Henri had meant. He too felt he had failed the world and, worse, failed God.

Under Curtis's precise direction, Brent shot what seemed to Perry to be miles of video footage. Curtis provided running commentary on everything, recording his observations for future study. It was a wise course of action, Perry decided. The odds were great that the world would never see the precious treasure again. The thought sickened him.

While the video record was being made, Jack and Gleason worked outside the chamber to build wood crates for the artifacts. Perry did nothing visible. He stood stoically to the side, watching Curtis and Brent work. His mind was anything but stoic; it was racing, plotting, conceiving, analyzing, and rejecting one idea after another. Anne stood quietly by his side.

"So this is the treasure you were after," Anne whispered so her voice wouldn't interfere with Curtis's dialog with the video camera. "I thought you were after personal gain."

"How do you know I wasn't?" Perry asked. "We're looking at items more valuable than anything in the world. On the underground antiquities market, just one artifact would bring millions of dollars."

"Treasure hunters and tomb robbers don't pause for prayer," Anne said quickly. "Nor do they give over spectacular, history-changing finds to crooks to save the lives of others. I misjudged you, Perry, and I'm sorry."

"You're not the first," he replied. "Now you understand why I had to keep things secret, not that it matters now."

"I understand. You were right to do so." She chuckled. "My whole town thinks you've found gold or pirate treasure up here."

"That would be a lot easier to surrender," Perry said. "All the planning, all the security, and I still lose it all; the world loses it all."

"You sound like you're giving up. You don't strike me as a man who just rolls over when things go south."

"I haven't given up," Perry said resolutely. "God didn't bring us this far and protect us through all of this just to let go now."

"God helps those who help themselves," Anne said. "Doesn't the Bible say that somewhere?"

"No, but Ben Franklin did, and in this instance, I think he's right."

"So what do we do now?" Anne asked.

"We hand over the artifacts," Perry said, then strode across the bridge and into the bright afternoon sun.

The crating had gone smoothly but also under a somber veil darker than the pit over which their makeshift bridge was suspended. Curtis maintained a steady dialog of why everything was wrong.

"We should be guarding against moisture. . .dehumidifiers are what we need. We must double crate and prevent jarring. Everything could turn to dust, the pots could break open if mishandled. . . ."

Since Perry had known from the manuscript what treasure would be found, he'd made plans for shipping the objects. The crates built by Jack and Gleason were to serve as outer shells for a combination of plastic bags, inert packing material, and commercial packets of silica gel to remove moisture from the air.

The ancient, dust-covered stone floor in the anteroom and the airtight stone wall separating the two chambers had kept moisture from the artifacts, but that had all changed when the floor had given way beneath Perry's feet and when he breached the tightly fitted stone partition. Speed and care were essential now. Every moment the artifacts were exposed to the air endangered their existence. There were also several large plastic containers that Jack had called "Tupperware for giants."

With the reverence of a monk and the gentleness of a surgeon, the team placed the items in plastic bubble wrap bags, then in the large plastic containers with packing material. Those in turn were loaded into the wood crates.

The process was slow and tedious. Perry and the others moved deliberately, knowing that any mistake could irreparably damage the precious find. The chrysalis and face-napkin were tenderly packed in one crate, the two earthenware jars in another. The stamped clay medallions were bagged, enclosed in bubble wrap, and placed in a small mailing box and set in the crate with the pots.

After the delicate packing was done, while the crew was still in the chamber, Perry pulled Gleason and Jack aside. The conversation was carried out in hushed tones. Perry did the talking; the two men listened intently, nodded, shook hands, and returned their attention to the artifacts.

Perry and Jack carried each crate across the bridge and into the light of day. With careful steps and awkward lifting, the two crates were finally carried out of the pit and set on the grass-carpeted ground.

"It's time to clear the area," Perry said. "Gleason, you take Brent, Dr. Curtis, and Anne back to town. Jack is going to stay with me. It will take more than one man to carry the crates, and I doubt our friend will be hoisting anything heavier than a gun."

"I'd rather stay," Anne said.

"I can't allow it," Perry said. "I've already endangered your life enough."

"You've done no such thing," Anne shot back. "I'm here of my own free will."

"It's out of the question," Perry said. "This guy already has two of my friends. I don't want him to have a third."

"At least let me stay a little longer," Anne pleaded. "You said the guy gave you twenty-four hours. That means he's not going to show up for awhile. I'll leave before he gets here. I drove my own car here, so I don't need a ride home."

Perry looked to Jack, who just shrugged. "I'm sorry, Anne, but the answer is still no. You're going to have to go."

Anne's face clouded with the same expression of anger Perry

had seen before, but then it softened. "Take care," she offered. "I would like to see you again. Alive."

"We agree on that," Perry said with a big smile. "I owe you a great deal, Madam Mayor."

"Yes, you do, and I expect a fancy dinner as payment, Mr. Sachs."

Anne bounded forward, threw her arms around Perry, and pulled him close. The embrace lasted only a moment, but it said many things. Releasing him, she quickly turned and started down the slope, Gleason, Brent, and Dr. Curtis following a few steps behind.

"So now we wait," Jack said.

"Now we wait," Perry agreed.

The sun moved behind the hills, casting long shadows over the empty site. Overhead, the sky darkened into twilight. Perry and Jack had passed the time resting from the night's labors and eating various snack foods that were kept on the work site. They ate for energy and not hunger. The tension of the previous hours and the anxiety of what was to come had eroded any hunger they should have felt.

They were men in waiting, and waiting was agonizingly difficult work. They didn't speak of what was to come. They made no speculations about what the visitor would do. Perry paused to pray awhile for Claire and Joseph. He was a weary man. He'd had far too little sleep over the past few days, and he doubted any meaningful sleep was in his near future.

As the sun dropped out of sight, a new stillness settled over the land. Where once there had been the constant murmur of men working, of motors humming and engines cranking, there now was almost no sound. The breeze was gone too, as if it had abandoned the area for fear of what was to happen.

Staring over the site, Perry saw the sinkhole that almost took his employee's life. He also saw the scarred ground he and Jack had so quickly dug up to uncover the chamber.

In the distance a sound interrupted the stillness.

"You hear that?" he asked Jack.

"Yeah. Sounds like a helicopter."

"Agreed, but it can't be ours," Jack said.

"Sounds low."

The distant thumping turned into a roar as a white Robinson R44 Raven helicopter flew over, its skids less than a couple of meters above the trees. The power of its engine and the beat of its blades vibrated the ground beneath Perry's feet. The copter shot overhead, then spun 180 degrees and returned.

"He's landing," Jack shouted above the noise. "The idiot is going to land right in front of us, right on the sloping ground. He must be crazy."

Helicopters were versatile machines capable of full three-dimensional motion, but landing one on sloping ground was madness. If the tail hit the ground the rear rotor would shatter and, without the counterforce of the blade, the craft would spin out of control. Takeoff would be even more treacherous.

The pilot circled the area once and then, remarkably, set the craft down without incident. Immediately the engine powered down to an idle. The pilot's door swung open, and the villain exited. He was dressed in a suit.

"Load it up," he ordered.

"A crook and a pilot. Impressive. You're early," Jack said nonchalantly.

"Always keep your opponents guessing. Now shut up and load the crates."

"You don't want to inspect them?" Perry asked. He made direct eye contact. The fires of fury burned hot in Perry's belly.

"No need," Alex said. "You're too smart to play those kinds of games. You could only lose your friends. Now load up the crates, boys. I have to call my boss in five minutes, or your friends eat a few bullets."

Perry stepped to the first crate and lifted one end. Jack did the same and they moved in tandem to the helicopter. The slowly moving blades swung threateningly overhead. Behind the pilot's seat was a cabin designed to hold seats for two passengers. The seats had been removed. This man, Perry realized, had thought of everything.

It took only two minutes to load the back compartment.

"Now, back off," Alex said. "I've got less than three minutes to make the call. I don't think you want me to spend it talking to you."

Perry doubted the thief's words, but he couldn't risk challenging him on it. The man's plan was smart. Fly in, limit the amount of time available to Perry, then fly off.

One thing was certain: He was as smart as he was devious. He was getting his way without outside help and without guns. Perry could do nothing but watch as the suited man entered the craft and expertly lifted it from the ground, mindful of the helicopter's altitude. A moment later he disappeared over the hills.

"I don't care how good a pilot I was," Jack said, "I'd never try that."

"He's showing off," Perry said. "His kind aren't happy without making some display. You ready?"

"Absolutely. I hope Gleason made all the necessary contacts."

"Me too." Perry raced to his Ford Explorer. "Call Gleason on the radio. Tell him things are in motion." Perry started the car and slammed down the accelerator.

Jack picked up the microphone and keyed it as Perry directed the big SUV toward the dirt road then up the hill to the place he had first set foot on the site, the place his helicopter had set down a few days before.

Stopping at the landing area, he and Jack sprang from the front seat. "We should hear. . .there it is."

More thumping of a rotor, then another helicopter appeared. This time it was the Augusta A109 that had brought Perry from Lindberg field in San Diego to the Tehachapi Mountains. Perry watched as the pilot landed on the flat ground at the top of the hill. Before the pilot could slow the engine, Perry and Jack were in the passenger compartment snapping their seat belts.

Perry slipped on the headset. "Hit it," he ordered.

The engine whined and the craft took off fifteen seconds later with enough vertical acceleration to press Perry into his seat and make his stomach drop to his feet. "North-by-northwest. A white Robinson R44."

"I saw it on the way in," the pilot said.

"Did he see you?"

"I doubt it. I took a very wide approach from the Tejon community airfield. He looked like he was headed toward Bakersfield."

"See if you can find him, but stay out of his line of sight." Perry said.

"Gleason said this was an emergency," the pilot said. "Is that true?"

"Absolutely."

"Good," the pilot replied. "I hate to think I was breaking all these rules for nothing." He banked the helicopter. "I'm supposed to tell you that Gleason made the contact you asked for. General somebody-or-the-other."

"Hitchcock," Perry said. "General Hitchcock. We did some work for him at Edwards Air Force base in the Mojave Desert. He liked what we did and said I could call on him if I needed anything. He probably meant if I needed a personal reference or something. I doubt he expected this. Can I contact him?"

"On the seat next to you is a cell phone. See it? Just push 'send' and it will dial his number."

"It won't mess up your instruments if I use it now?" Perry asked.

"Not enough to bother me. Make your call."

Perry did and heard exactly what he hoped to hear: General Hitchcock was tracking the helicopter through several military and civilian sites. "I had to call in a lot of favors," the general said. "You can't tell me what's going on?"

"Not now, but I promise to give you a blow-by-blow account later."

"You'd better. I could lose my stars over this."

"We can always use a good man at Sachs Engineering."

"That's good to know. . .hang on. . .your man is landing at the Bakersfield airport."

"I bet he'll be leaving from there too, and soon."

Perry asked the pilot to slow. "We have Sachs Engineering painted all over the side. I don't want our man to see us."

The pilot did as instructed and slowed the craft.

"Now the cat and mouse game begins," Perry said to Jack.

"I just hope we're the cat."

CHAPTER 23

The Sachs Engineering helicopter slid sideways in the stiff wind, but Perry's eyes remained fixed upon the small form of the other copter half a mile in front of them.

The distance between the two helicopters grew steadily. That was fine with Perry. His pilot was doing an admirable job of staying behind and above the other one, thereby staying securely in the blind spot.

"He's not in a big rush," the pilot said. Since Perry and Jack were in the passenger compartment behind the pilot, he had to take his word for it. Perry could only catch glimpses of the aircraft they were pursuing.

"He doesn't want to draw attention to himself," Perry said. His mind was working at high speed. Despite little sleep, despite long hours of physical labor, despite the crushing weight of concern, his thinking processed like a Swiss watch. He could be weary later. Now he had to use his mind, his heart, and his faith to achieve two things: the rescue of Claire and Joseph and the recovery of the world's most precious objects.

The fact that Alex was landing at the airport in Bakersfield failed to surprise Perry. The R44 had a limited range. He could have flown several hundred miles, but not much more. That might have been enough if his destination was in Southern California, but Perry doubted that it was. Even if true, he knew that Perry and Jack had seen the helicopter and could identify it later. Like an experienced bank robber, a change in getaway vehicles would be needed.

The question was, what kind of vehicle?

The thief could land at the airport, offload his stolen cargo into a van, a rental truck, or another aircraft. Since he was headed to an airport instead of some secluded landing area, Perry assumed the latter.

A part of Perry wanted to let the man go. After all, he had what he came for. Maybe he would simply release Claire and Joseph, but the logic was clearly flawed. This crook and his cronies stood to lose too much if Claire could identify the location of her captivity or the people who abducted her. He was certain they would kill his friends—if they hadn't done so already.

The last thought made Perry's heart quake. Claire was a simple woman who loved her special son. Neither deserved the treatment they had received. Perry had to see this through, even though he had little idea of what he would do next.

"Airplane?" Jack asked. "It's what I'd do."

"I think so," Perry said, "but what kind? Not that it matters. We're going to have trouble keeping up with a fixed-wing craft."

"The guy has money," Jack said. "The suit he wears comes at a price. He may have a private jet waiting for him. If he does, we'll be left in his exhaust."

"General Hitchcock can track him, but not on the ground. Once he touches down, we lose him. We're going to have to change horses."

"To what?" Jack asked. "The company jet is back in Seattle. I suppose we could charter one, but that may take time."

Perry frowned. Jack was right on both counts. Perry hit "send" on the cell phone, and Hitchcock picked up immediately. "General, I have another favor to ask."

"Why do I feel nervous?" the general asked.

"I'm going to owe you big time, General."

"You've got that right. When this is all said and done, I want all the details. Got it?"

"That's fair."

"What else do you need?"

Perry told him, listened, then rang off. He pulled the headset's microphone to his lips and spoke to the pilot. "We think he's going to switch aircraft. Once we're sure of that, I want you to pull off and head east."

"To where?"

"Edwards Air Force Base."

"I can't fly there, Mr. Sachs. That's restricted airspace. They take that seriously."

"I've made arrangements."

"They better be good ones," the pilot said.

Edwards Air Force Base was a sprawling affair laid out on the flat, near featureless land of the Mojave Desert—home to not only the Air Force but also Dryden Flight Research Center, an arm of NASA. While certain areas were open to the public and school children were often led on tours, much of what went on in the beige buildings was secret. It was here that test pilots risked their lives to fly the newest aircraft. It had also been home to many historical aircraft including the X-1, X-15, and others. And it was the alternate landing site for the space shuttle. Private aircraft were not welcome unless invited. Fortunately, General Hitchcock had opened the door.

He had done something else. Throwing the weight of his stars around, he'd been able to get the municipal airport in Bakersfield to cough up much-needed information that meant that Perry's copter was relieved of following the thief's all the way to landing—something that would be hard to miss. Once the thief was on the ground, it would be impossible to follow his actions without being observed themselves.

Perry's pilot set the A109 down gently on a concrete helicopter pad. Perry and Jack were out the door one second later. Hitchcock was there to greet them.

"You boys been playing in the dirt?" the general asked, tracing their soiled work clothes with his eyes. He was a stout man with gray temples whose brusque manner made him seem taller than this five-foot-eight-inch frame.

"We had a little time on our hands," Perry said, shaking the general's hand. "This is our lead project manager, Jack Dyson." The men exchanged nods.

"This way," Hitchcock said. "Your chariot awaits. We can talk as we walk. According to the tower people at Bakersfield airport, there was only one business jet on the ground, a Citation X. They were able to give me the registration number. I called back fifteen minutes later and was informed that the craft had departed two minutes before."

"The timing fits," Jack said. "The cargo was small and fairly light, even crated. A strong man could move it himself, if need be. Throw in a hand-truck, and it would be a piece of cake."

"Well, we know he's a strong man," Perry said, remembering the beating he and Jack had taken at the hands of the man they were now tracking. "You said you have the registration number?"

"I did," Hitchcock replied. "I even called a couple of folks I know in the FAA. The jet belongs to a pharmaceutical firm: RS BioDynamics. Get this: They're headquartered in your stomping grounds."

"Seattle?"

"That's right. How's that for irony?" The general led the men from the helicopter to an aircraft parked on the tarmac. "Here's your ride. My fanny is on the line for this, so I want it back in better shape than it leaves in."

Before Perry stood a sleek white Lear Jet. Blue letters on the tail fin read NASA. "The space boys made this available?"

"We exchange favors now and again," Hitchcock replied.

"There was a fee. I asked. They said yes. You will be billed for the air time and the fuel."

"What, no stewardesses?" Jack said.

Hitchcock gave an icy stare. "Two pilots have been provided. They know that we're tracking another aircraft and will take directions from the ground. I'll stay on the project until your man touches down. After that, you're on your own."

"Thank you, General," Perry said. "If this weren't life and death, I wouldn't have asked."

"Glad to help. Just keep it to yourself and give your father my best."

"I will."

Once inside, Perry took his seat, snapped on his seat belt, and activated his cell phone.

"Who you calling now?" Jack asked as he settled in.

"Karen Brant."

"Your administrative assistant? The office is closed, you know."

"That's why I'm calling her at home." Karen Brant had been Perry's assistant for twelve years, and her organizational skills and freethinking intellect made her invaluable.

"I've been trying to get her to move to my office. I know it's unethical to steal employees from the boss, but a man's gotta do what a man's gotta do."

"You stay away from Karen. She makes me look good."

Perry waited for an answer. When one came, he asked for several things in quick succession. "Can you do that?" he asked. A moment later he said, "You're the best," and rang off.

Five minutes after, the Lear Jet lifted off.

Hitchcock's people tracked the RS BioDynamics craft all the way to the SEATAC airport in Seattle. The Lear Jet touched down thirty minutes later. After thanking the pilots, Perry and Jack stepped from the craft and walked quickly to the terminal.

A gray-haired woman with bright blue eyes and a wide smile met them. She held a long roll of papers in her hand. Karen Brant gave them a once over then said, "You guys give up bathing?"

"It's overrated," Jack said. "Beside, they have a water shortage in Southern California."

"They can have some of ours," she replied. "It's been raining for the last three days."

Perry motioned to the roll of papers. "You got them."

"Of course I got them," she said. "I also talked a SEATAC customer aide into letting us borrow a meeting room. This way." She strode off without another word. Perry and Jack followed.

The room was an empty office off one of the wide corridors that ran like arteries through the terminal. A metal desk was situated in the middle and Karen unrolled the papers on it. Perry found himself looking at a set of blueprints.

"Here they are, the blueprints to the RS BioDynamics building. Since the building department was closed," Karen said, "I got hold of Tim in Information Systems and told him what you needed. He was able to access our firm's computers from home. He's a smart one, that Tim. Anyway, since he keeps track of all major construction jobs around the world, he was able to learn who the architects and engineers were. The electrical engineer for the project was Ron Mion. We lucked out on that."

"We've subcontracted some work to him," Perry said. "So he had a set of plans from his work on the building?"

"Right. I tracked him down, found him at home, and he agreed to meet me at his office. Then *voila!* You have the plans you requested."

Perry and Jack both nodded appreciatively.

"As far as the other info you requested," Karen continued, "I can tell you this: The 'RS' in RS BioDynamics stands for Rutherford Straight, the company's founder. He's a *wunderkind* in the field and has made tons of money with innovative pharmaceuticals. He leads the world in selective cloning—that is, where they clone only parts of animals or people. Working from stem cells, they can force a growth process that creates heart cells, muscle cells, skin, and so on.

"I couldn't get as detailed as I'd like—just not enough time—but I learned that his company has more patents on biological material than any other. He's been the cover boy for *Fortune, Time, Newsweek, Forbes, Money,* and at least a dozen other high-end periodicals. They love showing him in his wheelchair."

"Wheelchair?" Perry asked.

"He has ALS. Apparently he has this gigantic intellect trapped in an ever-weakening body. Like that physicist guy."

"Stephen Hawking?" Jack said.

"That's the guy. He's like him. It's kinda sad." Karen drew herself up and looked Perry in the eye. "Now, may I ask what all this is about?"

"Sorry," Perry said. "For the moment I need to leave you in the dark. I'll fill you in later."

"Sure, cast me off like a dirty shirt," she quipped. "Anything else you boys need?"

"A car," Perry said. "Could you head over to the rental counter and arrange a car for us? Jack and I'll stay here and go over the plans."

"No need," she said. "Here are my keys. I also put the tool boxes you requested in the trunk."

"How will you get home?"

"Taxi, of course. I plan on billing the company for it. What would you do without me?" she asked.

"The same things; I just wouldn't do them nearly as well," Perry said.

"Coercion through compliments," Nancy said. "It's devious behavior, but it works. I'll be back soon."

"Pharmaceuticals is a competitive and secretive business," Jack said after Karen left the small office. "I'm betting they have the best security possible."

"That makes things more difficult," Perry said.

"Difficult? How about impossible?"

"I don't believe in the impossible, Jack. Think about what we pulled out of the ground over the last two days: Roman soldiers in California, a woman's remains with the name Mary Magdalene etched in her coffin, and artifacts from the tomb of Christ. None of that is possible, but you've seen and touched it."

"Point well taken," Jack said. "So how do we get Claire and Joseph out—and recover the artifacts?"

Perry studied the plans: blue lines on white paper laid out in a complex fashion. It was a substantial building of nineteen floors. The top held offices and conference rooms, the next four floors held laboratories of some kind, and below that were more offices and open space. Most likely, Straight leased the lower floors to pay for the building. It was a common practice. By leasing lower floors to other businesses, the building would pay for itself. Perry studied the first floor and saw what he was looking for.

"Here," he said, pointing to the lobby on the first floor. "The ground floor was designed to accommodate a restaurant. You can see the kitchen area. Ron calculated higher loads for the equipment. It also shows several other exits. Building codes would require that. Of course," he added, "it's a business office. The lobby should be open for employees on the swing shift."

"Okay, so we can get into the building through the restaurant or lobby, then what?"

"Then, we play it by ear. Let's go page by page through this. Memorize what you can. We'll improvise once we are there."

"Shouldn't we notify the police?" Jack asked. "They're better equipped for this than we are."

"In any other situation I would," Perry agreed, "but we have some special circumstances here. The police are going to have as much trouble getting in as we are. They would also need enough proof to get a warrant. We have no proof. I've seen a picture of Claire and Joseph in an empty lab, but that's it. Calling the police would take too much time. We're on our own for the moment. You up for this?"

"You have to ask?"

Perry smiled at his friend and hoped he wasn't leading the man to his death.

Karen's Mercury Cougar sped easily along the dark streets of downtown Seattle. Perry was at the wheel, Jack in the passenger seat. A gentle drizzle peppered the windshield.

Perry found it ironic that it was here that he interrupted the attack on Dr. Henri that had changed his life. Perry didn't believe in coincidence. He had come upon Dr. Henri after leaving a very late meeting. Had he not called for that meeting, had he left fifteen minutes earlier or later, everything would have been different. But that didn't happen. He left at just the right time, made just the right turn, saw just the right thing. There was no doubt in Perry's mind that Providence was at work. He comforted himself with the thought that God was still on the job.

"The stairs," Perry blurted as he parked the car a block from the RS BioDynamics building.

"What about the stairs?" Jack asked.

"We can take the stairs up," Perry said. "Fire codes require sealed exit stairways."

"No good, buddy," Jack said. "True, there will be at least two stairways, but I doubt that the doors will open into the upper offices. They're exit doors and have to open in, but they're allowed to be locked on the stair side. That way, panicked people don't exit on the wrong floor. Only those doors that lead outside will open."

"And the one to the roof," Perry said. "I'm not suggesting that we can get access to the offices on the upper floors from the stairway. I'm suggesting we go to the roof. Exit stairways must exit to the roof as well as the ground floor."

"What do we do once we get there?"

"You'll come up with something," Perry said. He exited the car, popped the trunk, and removed two plastic toolboxes, handed one to Jack, and then started down the street toward their destination.

The stairway door was open as expected. Perry and Jack had entered the lobby separately. To the right of the lobby was the restaurant they'd seen on the plans. Since it was well after nine in the evening, the place was nearly empty. To his left was a smaller office that was home to a travel agency.

Perry was sure that video cameras were trained on the lobby. He had no way of knowing if anyone was paying attention to them as they entered. When he first approached the building, he noticed lights burning on almost every floor. People moving in and out of the structure would be normal. Dressed in work clothes and carrying toolboxes, he hoped they'd look as if they belonged.

The air in the stairway was stale, lacking the ventilation the rest of the building enjoyed. Perry started up. According to the architectural plans, the steel frame building consisted of nineteen habitable floors and one additional floor for equipment. Above that was the roof and Perry's destination.

He didn't run. Exhausting himself on the stairs could only be counterproductive. His mind and body had already been strained beyond anything he'd experienced, so he took his time despite the constant nagging of fear in the back of his mind. He kept his head down, partly in thought but also to keep any cameras that might be trained on him from seeing his face. His hope, his prayer, was that he and Jack would be taken for maintenance workers. They were certainly dressed for it.

They came to the twentieth floor and found a steel door with a plastic sign attached: "EQUIPMENT ROOM—AUTHORIZED PERSONNEL ONLY." Perry tried the door. It was locked. No surprise there.

One flight later Perry stood in front of a metal fire door. This one had a panic bar across it as was required of all exit doors. He paused.

"Do you suppose it's alarmed?" Jack asked.

"I don't see any obvious sign of it, but it would make sense. If we open this, we may be inviting company."

"Maybe. Let's do it."

Perry pushed the bar, and the door opened freely. He steeled himself for the piercing shriek of an alarm but heard nothing. Of course, an alarm could be ringing in some security office on the premises or at a remote site. It didn't matter now. The deed was done.

Damp air greeted the two as they left the stairwell. Before them was a wide expanse of treated concrete that, with the metal decking below, formed the roof of the building. The stainless steel boxes that housed HVAC fans, cooling coils, and more were scattered along the open surface. Several satellite dishes were anchored near one edge. The still night air was filled with the droning of equipment that breathed air into the building. Near the center was a ten-foot-high structure that looked like a wide shed.

"Elevator overrun," Jack said.

Perry agreed, setting his toolbox down and opening it. He removed a flashlight and closed the box. In buildings this tall, elevators were moved by cable. Smaller buildings could get by with hydraulic elevators, but such devices were too slow and too difficult to make work in mid- and high-rise buildings. Cable elevators required a room above the shaft to house the drive equipment and pulleys.

Suddenly Perry had an idea. He moved swiftly to the elevator structure and found the door. He tried the doorknob but found it as he expected, locked.

"We need a way in," Perry said.

"That's not going to be easy," Jack said. "The door is designed for security. It's steel-cased. It swings inward. That means the hinges are on the inside and out of our reach."

"There's machinery in there, it has to be vented somewhere. Look for a vent." Jack did and found it moments later. Perry rounded the corner to find his friend chuckling. "What's so funny?"

"I just caught myself praying for God's help to illegally break into a building. Seemed like an unusual prayer."

"It's one for the theologians. What did you find?"

Jack pointed with his light. "It's a typical louvered vent with a wire mesh insect screen. It looks to be about eighteen inches wide and four feet long. We can fit through that, although it'll be a tight squeeze for me."

"It's our best option," Perry said with determination. "Let's open her up."

Perry rifled through his tool case. He had told Karen to fill the boxes with an assortment of hand tools, and she had taken the request to heart. Between the two boxes was a range of tools including a hammer, chisels, screw drivers, wrenches, and more. The vent cover was painted aluminum and attached to the wall with large lag bolts.

"I've got it," Jack said, pulling a ratchet and socket set from the box. "That gal thought of everything."

"Her father was a mechanic. She once told me she cut her teeth on a Craftsman box wrench."

"Yuck," Jack said as he set about removing the bolts. There were eight bolts in total and some were welded by years of exposure to sun and rain. Jack brought his great strength and weight to the task. Perry was sure that he would strip the heads off a couple of them. His fear was unfounded. The vent came free.

As Jack set the metal vent to the side, Perry poked his head in the opening and saw a room filled with large motors. He crawled through the opening. The room smelled of heavy oil and electronics. Mounted to one wall was an electrical panel. Just to his right sat a large-gear drive drum and cables. The cables were called ropes even though they were made of woven metal strands. The ropes disappeared down the shaft. Perry moved the light around the room, playing its beam on the floor.

"Cozy," Jack said as he squeezed his bulk through the opening.

"We're in luck," Perry said. "Each shaft has an access panel. We'll be able move through the shaft."

"And you call that lucky?"

"Come on, big guy. Adventure is your middle name."

"Oh, that's right," Jack said. "I almost forgot."

"Sarcasm is ugly on one so educated as you." Perry stepped to the access panel in the floor, found the recessed ring-shaped handle, and gave a twist and pull. The panel opened easily. Despite the easy banter between the two men, Perry knew that Jack was as tense as he. But he couldn't allow that to matter. What had to be done would be done.

He shone the light down the shaft, found the safety ladder that ran along the back wall, stuffed his flashlight in his pocket, and began his descent.

Elevator engineers were a cautious bunch, and elevators were fantastic inventions. A metal ladder ran the length of the shaft to allow workers to conduct maintenance and repairs. Unlike the movies, there was little chance of Perry getting squashed like a bug by the moving car, should it begin to ascend—at least in principle. That knowledge gave him little comfort. A fall, however, could be deadly.

The ladder was located near the front of the shaft, the door to the various floors were to Perry's right. As he descended, he could hear the heavy, booted footsteps of Jack on the ladder.

That reminded Perry of another problem: He didn't know where Claire and Joseph were confined.

He tried to picture in his mind the photo he'd been shown back at the site. Claire and Joseph were in a small, windowless room. Windowless meant the room most likely didn't adjoin an exterior wall. Perhaps there were a series of such rooms off a corridor with larger labs around the perimeter of the building? That was likely but not a certainty. The room was devoid of equipment, so it must not be presently in use.

There was also the problem of which floor. Generally, executive offices were on the highest floor. The plans he had committed to memory bore that out. There were four floors of laboratories and small offices. Most of the laboratories were larger than what he'd seen in the photo. What was it Karen had said about magazine covers? "They love to show him in his wheelchair."

Thoughts began to percolate in Perry's mind. Wheelchair. . . ALS. . .empty lab. Could the lab be a private one associated with Straight's office? Since his condition hindered his mobility, he would no longer be able to work in a lab made for a person who could stand and walk. Perhaps he abandoned it? It made sense and was a place to start.

After descending a few more feet into the darkness, Perry stopped, removed his flashlight, and directed the beam toward the front wall. He was at a set of doors. Since he had only taken a few steps down the ladder he knew that he was looking at the doors that opened to the machine room. He extinguished the light and returned it to his pocket. In the dark, he had to feel for each rung below him in a slow, methodical process.

He estimated that he had traveled another twelve feet. *That should put me near the next set of doors,* he thought. Once again he reached for and switched on his light. He had estimated correctly. Another pair of stainless steel doors reflected his light.

"We're going in here, Jack," Perry whispered. "Shine your light down here. See the doors?"

A light beam from over Perry's head pierced the black. "Yeah, I see them."

"I'm going to pull them open. As soon as I do, I'm going in. Feel free to follow."

"I was hoping you'd invite me."

Perry secured his light, tightened his grip on the ladder with his left hand, and stretched his right arm to the side, feeling along the cool, smooth metal. He found the juncture of the two doors and pressed his fingers in there, slowly parting them. Elevators were designed to allow forced opening in case of prolonged power outages.

Just as he started to pull, the shaft was filled with a clanking and whirring noise. Perry snapped his hand back. The elevator was moving. He waited, his lungs holding in breath as tightly as his fingers gripped the rungs of the service ladder. He could hear the metal cables rattling and the heavy counter balance sliding in its track.

Then it stopped.

"I can't tell you how much I'm enjoying this, Perry," Jack said in a barely audible voice.

"Only the best for you, friend," Perry retorted.

"You always did know how to make people feel special," Jack said.

"I'm going to try this again."

Once more, Perry reached to his side, found the joint caused by the edge of the sliding doors, pushed and pressed until his fingers found enough surface to grip, and pulled. Nothing. His ribs protested hotly. He pulled again and the door budged an inch. Mustering as much strength as he could, he pulled and leaned away, pulling the door with him. The opposite door, connected by the gears and motor device above them, moved as well.

Perry wasted no time. With his hand still clutching the door, he extended his right leg until it touched the metal sill, then pulled himself through the opening and dropped to a crouch. He was in the elevator lobby of the nineteenth floor, and he was alone—for the moment. Glancing at the ceiling, he saw what he feared: video cameras.

Perry stood and took a step to the side. Jack lumbered through the doors a moment later. Perry pointed at the ceiling-mounted cameras. Jack looked straight at them, smiled, and waved.

CHAPTER 24

A re you certain, Dr. Carmack?" Rutherford Straight asked. "I want to move along as quickly as possible."

Dr. Benton Carmack shook his head vigorously. "No assistants. They get in the way. There are too many distractions already. You should all leave."

Rutherford looked at Julia, then Alex. Alex started to say something to the researcher, but Rutherford called him off. "It's the price of genius," he said.

Rutherford, Alex, and Julia sat in a side room adjacent to the laboratory. A glass partition separated them from Carmack, who moved around the lab in a sterile, white body suit. A loose-fitting non-permeable material and faceplate formed a hood over Carmack's head. He looked something like an astronaut.

Rutherford spoke to him through an intercom system. "Your desire to work alone is legendary, Doctor, but I stay. Alex and Julia are necessary because of my special needs. You understand that, don't you?"

"Of course, of course," Carmack said. He was looking at an unusually shaped set of linens that rested on one of the large work-tables. His eighteenth-floor lab was directly below Rutherford's office and was the largest facility in the building. "I didn't mean you had to leave. Of course you can stay. It's your place. Of course you can stay. Now, where did you get this?"

"That doesn't matter now. I want to know if you think it will work."

"Maybe. . .possibly. . .it should. Maybe." He lowered his face and squinted. "This dark spot—is that blood?"

"I assume it to be so. It's old. . .very old," Rutherford said.

Carmack walked around and stared into the cavity of the chrysalis, studied it for a moment, then pulled a magnifying glass from a drawer in the worktable. He began to scrutinize the inside of the body-shaped shell. "Hair. There is hair here. Body hair stuck between some of the layers of the wrappings."

Rutherford's heart quickened. Blood and hair was a good sign. What he hoped to achieve would require the DNA, and those were two good sources.

"Extraction will need to be done delicately," Carmack said more to himself than to the others. He was known to carry on long conversations while sitting alone. Rutherford worked with some of the finest and most innovative scientific minds in the bio-industry; many had quirks. He had learned to live with them.

"Sample the bloody linen," Rutherford said. "I want to determine the extent of degradation. We should be able to type the blood and do some genetic profiling."

"I will start with the hair," Carmack said flatly.

"Dr. Carmack, I would prefer—"

"The hair! I will start with the hair!"

"All right, Doctor."

A ringing filled the observation room. Alex snapped his cell phone to his ear. "Olek," he said. He paused, and his face tightened. "When. . .where?" Another pause. "No, I'll take care of it." He hung up.

"We have visitors," Alex announced. "Nineteenth floor. Security picked them up on surveillance cameras."

"Who are they, and how did they get in?" Rutherford snapped.

"They came through an elevator shaft. As to who it is, I won't know until I find them, but the description I just received makes me think of Perry Sachs and Jack Dyson."

"Go," Rutherford asked. "Take care of them. Better yet, bring them to me. Take Julia with you."

"I can handle this."

"Take her with you. We're too close to my dream to take any chances."

"Very well," Alex said. He exited the room in long strides. Julia followed.

Claire watched Joseph with a mixture of fear and amazement that made her ache with worry. He sat at the bench, paper stretched before him, crayons scattered in an arch around his drawing. He was sketching so fast that Claire could hear the crayon scraping the paper. Joseph always drew slowly, never in the manic fashion she was witnessing.

"Joseph? Honey?"

He ignored her. The crayon broke in his hand, but Joseph seemed not to notice. He kept moving, kept drawing with the stub of crayon.

He stopped suddenly, sitting up straight. Then he slipped from his stool, walked to the locked door, stood before it, then leaned forward, resting his forehead on its wood surface.

"Uhh. . .uhh. . ."

Claire moved to the bench and gazed at what her son had been drawing. Again he had constructed an image far out of character for him. This one included people—and it included an amazing likeness of himself standing at the door just as he was now.

Stranger still, he'd drawn the scene in section showing not only the room they were in and the door, but a hallway outside. A man stood in the hallway, just on the other side of the doorway. He was looking down at the floor. Claire recognized the man. It was Perry Sachs.

"I don't understand," she whispered. "Perry is in California, not here. Why would he be standing at the door looking down. . . ?"

Realization hit Claire like a flash of lighting. Seizing the picture, she ripped it from the table and raced to the door. She had to move Joseph to the side to make room for herself. Kneeling, she offered a prayer as she pushed the picture under the door and into the hall.

She stood and took a step back, wondering if she had just done a wise or foolish thing.

Joseph moved to the door and once again leaned his forehead on its smooth surface.

"Which door?" Jack asked. "I can see half a dozen doors down this hall."

Perry and Jack moved away from the elevator opening. "I don't know," Perry admitted. "I'm just guessing that they're on this floor. Maybe we should try each door, just turning the knob. If the knob turns, we move on. I don't think they would be kept in an unlocked room."

"Makes sense," Jack said.

They came to the first door and Perry turned the handle. It moved freely. Slowly, he let it return to its resting position and moved on. Jack did the same on the other side of the corridor. As Perry was about to try his third door, he saw a piece of paper slip out from beneath the door a few feet from where he was standing. He walked to it and saw an image drawn in crayon: a picture of him standing in front of a door and Joseph on the other side. Perry softly called for Jack and showed him the drawing.

"Bingo," Jack said. He reached forward and turned the doorknob. It didn't budge. "Tight as a drum."

"We should have started here," Perry said as he pointed to an electronic keypad. It was set low so that someone in a wheel chair could reach it.

"Hindsight is always clearer."

Perry studied the keypad. "It's high-end tech," he said. "Not only do you need to know the code, but it reads your fingerprint. We're not going to crack that."

"Step aside for a second," Jack said. He examined the door, the doorknob, and the frame. He then looked at the picture he still held in his hand. "Joseph would recognize your voice, wouldn't he?"

"He should, and Claire's with him," Perry answered.

"Tell her to move Joseph away from the door. I'm going to provide a low-tech solution to a high-tech problem."

"Claire? It's Perry, can you hear me?"

"Yes, I can, Perry," came an excited but muffled reply.

"Move Joseph away from the door," he said. He placed his ear to the door and heard Claire talking to her son.

He heard her say, "Okay."

Perry turned to Jack. "Are you going to do what I think you're going to do?"

"It's a wood door, solid core no doubt, but I should be able to persuade it to open." Jack took a step back, raised his right foot, and let fly a brutal kick. The force of the kick against the solidly hung door forced Jack back a step. "Give me a little support here."

Perry took a position behind his big friend and placed his shoulder into Jack's back. "What you do, do quickly. We're making enough noise to wake the dead."

Jack kicked again. . .then again. . .and again. Perry could feel the force of each blow as the door resisted Jack's attempts. "It's giving," Jack said. "A couple more ought to do it."

"How come it always works the first time in the movies?"

Jack answered with another kick, and this time the wood splintered. Perry came to the door and saw that it gave way at the lock. Shards of wood lay in the carpeted hall. Perry charged in and was greeted by Claire, who threw her arms around his neck and began to weep. Joseph stepped forward and laid his head on Perry's shoulder. Perry threw one arm around Joseph and the other around Claire.

The embrace lasted only seconds. "We have to get you out of here, quickly."

"Perry, we have company," Jack said. "Get them moving."

Perry turned, but Jack was gone. "Follow me." Perry entered the corridor and saw Jack marching toward two people. One he recognized as the intruder at his site, dressed in yet another suit. The other was a mahogany-haired woman, dressed in a beige pantsuit and carrying a small purse.

"To the stairs," Perry commanded, pointing away from the approaching duo. He guided Claire out of the room and down the hall. Alex was coming from the direction of the elevators.

"We meet again." The words came from behind Perry. It was Jack. "We never finished our little chat." There was a thud. Perry turned and saw the well-dressed man bounce off one of the corridor walls. "I'm not napping this time, partner," Jack said. "You only get to sucker punch me once."

Perry could barely believe what he saw next. The thief had hit the wall hard enough to drop several men, but he didn't go down. He straightened himself, unbuttoned his suit coat, and started for Jack. Perry's friend remained in the middle of the hall like a giant defending his horde against thieves. His attacker was shorter by half a foot, but he seemed unfazed by the mismatch. He threw a brutal punch, but Jack deflected it, as he did the next punch. The fists came faster and faster, and to Perry, the man's hands seemed to blur.

Jack was backing up now, having more difficulty fending off the blows that came at him so quickly that he could mount no offensive of his own. A punch landed hard enough that the sound of it echoed down the hall. Jack staggered back and threw a fist of his own, something Perry knew he wouldn't do unless he felt his life was in danger. The attempt was not even close. The well-dressed man moved to the side just enough to avoid being hit and threw a right hand of his own. It caught Jack in the side. Another punch followed, connecting with the big man's jaw. He spun around and stumbled.

Perry froze for a moment and then started for his friend.

"No," Jack shouted but only managed a hoarse whisper. "Get them out."

The man stepped forward and threw a blow into Jack's back. A kidney shot. Jack dropped to his knees. "Run. . ." Perry watched helplessly as the impossibly strong man brought a sweeping backhand to the side of Jack's head. Jack crashed forward, landing face down on the carpet.

The man stepped over him and started quickly toward Perry.

"Get in the stairway and run," Perry commanded. "It will lead to the first floor. Go. . .go."

Perry was not going to wait for the man, nor was he going try and exchange blows. After seeing how easily he felled Jack, Perry knew he stood little chance of surviving a toe-to-toe encounter. The man he faced was stronger and clearly a trained fighter, but physics was physics.

Perry charged, lowering his head as if to make an open field tackle on the football field. He saw the man set himself. At the last instant he changed his course, aiming not for the assailant's middle but for his head. Perry dipped his shoulder and launched himself.

It worked. Perry's right shoulder landed squarely on the head of the other man. The force of Perry's forward motion sent both men toppling and twisting to the floor, Perry on his back, the other man face down.

Perry scrambled, not to his feet, but to his hands and knees. Before the well-dressed fighter could move, Perry was on top of him, putting his full weight on the man's chest. It was a struggle, but Perry got one leg on each side of the other man's torso and grabbed at his head. Knowing that where the head went so went the body, Perry placed both hands on the attacker's skull and leaned forward with all his weight, pinning it to the floor. Since he was on his stomach, the thief could throw no punches. For the moment he was incapacitated. If Perry could hold him long enough, Claire and Joseph might escape. He heard the door at the end of the hall open. Claire had made it to the stairs. He heard something else.

There was a loud pop, and Perry jerked reflexively. A startled scream rolled down the hall, then Perry felt something hot and hard touch the back of his ear—a gun barrel.

"Come on back, Mrs. Henri, and bring your son with you. I won't miss next time." The barrel was pushed into Perry's neck. "As for you, I suggest you get off Alex."

"This is the way you're supposed to use the elevator," Alex said.

"It's cleaner," Perry replied.

They rode in the elevator car with Jack, who now walked with a limp and was having trouble straightening up. Claire and Joseph stood in one corner, the dark-haired woman standing next to them, gun pointed at Joseph's side.

"Mind if I ask where the gun came from?"

The pistol was small, just a little larger than the hand that held it. Perry thought it might be a .25 caliber, one of those dangerous-hide-almost-anywhere weapons.

The woman patted the small purse she had hung over one shoulder. "Got everything I need right here: lipstick, mace, handgun."

"Where are you taking us?" Claire asked, her voice shaking with fear.

"Someone wants to meet your friends."

"Rutherford Straight," Perry said.

"You know of my brother?"

"Brother?" Jack said. He was still struggling to get his full breath. "Well, that explains what a nice girl like you is doing in a place like this."

"It's his building," Perry explained. "And it was his company's jet that flew from Bakersfield to Seattle."

The elevator doors parted after descending only one floor. Alex grabbed Perry and shoved him through. He did the same with Jack. The woman led the other two out. A few moments later they passed through a door that led to a room with one glass wall.

Near the window sat a frail-looking man in a wheelchair. He leaned precipitously to one side, kept from falling by a strap around his chest. Hearing the door open, he pushed a lever on the arm of the chair, and it turned in place. His hair was a mixture of gray and black, and his head bobbed continually.

"You must be Perry Sachs," the man said. His voice was thready. A small trickle of drool lined his chin.

"I am," Perry said. "You are Rutherford Straight."

"Guilty as charged. I see you've met my sister and my right-hand man."

"He's a pretty good left-hand man too," Jack said, rubbing his ribs.

Perry turned his attention to the room beyond the glass and the sight made him sick. A man in a baggy white suit and hood with a face shield moved around a bench. On the bench was the chrysalis. The man was reaching inside the cocoon-like shape with a pair of tweezers.

"Interesting, isn't it, Mr. Sachs?" Rutherford said. "That is quite a find you made. It may change the world." The man offered a weak smile that looked more like a grimace. "Change the world in a way you never imagined."

"Do you know what that is?" Perry asked. He made no attempt to conceal his anger.

"Of course I do," Rutherford said. "I read the same document as you—"

"The one you stole," Perry interjected.

"Yes, that would be the one." Rutherford seemed unbothered by the accusation. "We're looking at the linen wrappings of Christ. Extremely valuable in its own right; more valuable to me in other ways."

"What are you doing?" Perry asked, as he watched the strangely suited man take what looked like a long Q-Tip, dip it in a small bottle of solution, then rub it on the linen shell. He focused on the dark blood-stained area.

"Sampling DNA," Rutherford said. "We would prefer tissue samples of course, but we take what we can get.

"You want DNA from Jesus?" Perry was astonished. "You can't be serious."

"Why not?" Rutherford asked pointedly.

"It's two thousand years old," Perry said. "Surely it's not viable."

"You'd be surprised, Mr. Sachs. DNA has been harvested from mummies around the world, and many of them are far older than two millennia. DNA has been taken from ancient insects, reptiles, humans, and other mammals. This is no different. In fact, it's not even much of a challenge. Did you know that DNA testing was done on two mummies to evaluate whether King Tut was truly of royal blood? That was DNA over 3,300 years old. That work was conducted back in 2000."

"But what can you hope to accomplish?"

"Think, Mr. Sachs, think. What is the one primary difference between Christianity and other world faiths?"

"Many things."

"Pick the one you think is most significant," Rutherford urged.

"The resurrection. The fact that Jesus rose from the dead."

"Very good, Mr. Sachs. For an architect, you're pretty smart."

"You believe in the resurrection?" Perry asked, puzzled. "How do you reconcile that with, with. . .?"

"My business practices?" Rutherford suggested. A gurgle poured from his mouth. It took a moment for Perry to realize the man was laughing. "There's nothing spiritual in all this, Mr. Sachs. I have no time for the mumbo jumbo of faith. I just happen to believe that an unusual and unexplained event happened, that's all."

"And you want to explain it."

"I want to capitalize on it, first personally, then financially."

"But why?"

"Look at me, Sachs. Take a good look." Rutherford's words were as sharp as his emaciated body would allow. "I'm a dying man. I die faster than most. I'm also the most brilliant biologist in the world, and the second most gifted is in that other room doing what I can no longer do. I want my life back, Sachs. I want to live and to do my research. I want to walk again. If I can find out what happened to Jesus, then maybe I can find a way to defeat this disease."

"That seems impossible," Perry said.

"When you have no hope, the impossible looks pretty good." Straight turned back to the viewing window. "We will sample, we will analyze. I've developed some techniques that may allow some DNA replications and transfer. We do things here other scientists can only dream of. Bio-engineering is the current wave, Mr. Sachs.

"Industry has had its day, as has the Information Age. The present and the future belong to those who can manipulate life. Here we make artificial skin for burn victims; we are close to finishing the development of a technique to grow a new pancreas.

"Do you know anyone with diabetes, Mr. Sachs? If you do, then I may be that person's best friend. We've made crops safer, food last longer, grain grow larger heads, pigs that produce low-fat meat, and more. Oh, we can also improve the functionality of humans. You may have noticed that Mr. Olek is stronger than anyone you've ever met?" He turned his wheelchair and looked at Perry and Jack.

Jack answered. "It seems he may have done a little working out."

The choking laugh returned. "He has no need to work out, at least not to get stronger. I've fixed that. My good friend is genetically improved. Like some doctors do gene therapy to treat certain diseases, I created a way to improve the human reaction time, energy usage by muscles, and overall strength. It has caused quite a stir among the military types. My sister, Julia, is his only competition."

That explained Alex's ability to beat a man taller, younger, and physically superior—except Jack wasn't physically superior. It was a wonder he wasn't dead.

"Do you know what chimeraplasty is, Mr. Sachs?"

"Can't say that I do."

"I suppose I shouldn't be surprised. Gene therapy is generally done through an altered vector such as a virus. A virus is altered so that it cannot hurt its intended host or replicate. Some of the patient's cells are removed, injected with this altered virus, and then the cells are replaced. If things work right, the cells replicate, and a cure is achieved. That's the simple version, but you get the idea.

"The problem is the technique is cumbersome and slow. That's where chimeraplasty comes in. A Chimera is a mythical creature made up of parts of different animals. By taking short segments of DNA known as oligomers, defective genes in a cell can be identified, causing the cell to undertake its own repairs.

"That's what I want, Mr. Sachs. I want my body to heal itself, but I need the right catalyst to do that. Soon we will be able to genetically treat hemophilia and cystic fibrosis. Closer to my heart, of course, is ALS."

"And you think you might find it in scraps of DNA taken from Jesus' burial linens." Perry was aghast.

"That's the idea. If anyone can make it work, I can."

Perry looked at the chrysalis and felt a heavy ache of sadness. No wonder Dr. Henri had been so frightened about the material falling into the wrong hands. Perry could understand the emaciated man's desire to live, to be healed of the horrible disease, but so far he was responsible for two deaths, two kidnappings, assaults, and probably more than Perry could know. And Perry felt sure the number of murders was going to increase by four in the near future. There seemed little he could do about it.

"That's a remarkable boy you have there, madam," Rutherford said. "Idiot-savant is the term, I believe."

"Just savant. Thinking people don't use the outdated term."

"Danger has made you grow feisty, I see. He's perplexed me some, I must confess. I've been a proponent of genetic treatment. I still am for the most part. Had you gone through the process, you might have been able to spare yourself the burden of his life."

"He's no burden. And if genetic testing told your parents that you would have ALS, they might have aborted you."

There was a loud slap, and Perry spun to see Claire holding a hand to her face. Julia had backhanded her.

"Still," Rutherford continued as if the assault had not occurred. "He is an enigma. Do you remember that piece of paper Julia brought to you earlier today?"

"Yes." Claire sputtered softly. "She gave it to Joseph."

"Correct, and he drew a picture based on it. Most people would have missed the subtle change, but I didn't. That paper I sent down was a detailed print of my DNA. Your son not only copied it, he *corrected* it. That's right, he corrected it. How does he do that?"

"I don't know. No one knows. He just does things like that from time to time."

Rutherford's head moved, but Perry couldn't tell if he was nodding in agreement or had just lost control. "He is worth studying. The secret is locked in him somewhere."

"No," Claire said. "I'd rather die first."

"We agree on that," Rutherford said coldly. "At least you won't be alone."

"We are people of faith; death is not frightening to us."

"No? We'll see. Since you're a person of faith, you can do me a favor. When you see Jesus in heaven, ask, 'What was Your secret to success?'"

It had all played out so badly, Perry realized. It started with an assault and death and now more were to die, including himself. And when all was said and done, the madman Straight would still possess the artifacts.

Perry shook his head slightly, and although it was barely perceptible, when he turned to Jack, he knew he had seen it. Jack shrugged then nodded, moving his head less than an inch. Perry wished there was more he could do, or a wiser course of action to take, but there was none. Maybe, just maybe, if he and Jack could restrain Alex and Julia long enough, Claire and Joseph could escape. The odds were nearly nonexistent, but a slim chance was still better than none.

Perry took a couple of quick steps toward Rutherford. Immediately he heard a woman's voice. "Hold it right there." He turned and saw the gun that had been pointed at Claire now pointed at his head. He also saw Jack's big hand shoot forward and grab the woman's wrist. Jack jerked her arm, redirecting the gun's muzzle away from Perry.

There was a curse, a bang, a pop, a crash, and a scream. Instinctively, Perry ducked and covered his head. The tempered glass exploded behind him, falling in a sheet of tiny cubes. Lifting his head, Perry saw Jack raise his other hand to Julia's wrist. She was screaming obscenities. Alex, who had been only a step away, threw a vicious right fist into Jack's rib cage. Perry heard the air forced from his friend's lungs. Despite the power of the blow, Jack continued to clutch Julia's wrist.

"No. . .no. . .no. . ." Rutherford bawled, but his weak voice was barely heard over Julia's screeching.

"You're breaking my wrist," she bellowed. Another shot escaped the gun. Perry flinched and charged toward the struggle.

"Let her go," Alex said. He threw another punch, this time at Jack's head, but the blow glanced off his shoulder.

Another shot followed by a hissing sound. A second later the room was filled with a loud blast, like an electronic horn. It repeated the same note over and over and over.

Perry lowered his head, aiming it at Alex's middle. He knew he couldn't overpower the genetically strengthened thug, but even the strongest man couldn't fight if he couldn't breathe. With his head down, he couldn't see all of Alex, but he did see enough to know the man had turned toward him at the last second.

Perry found his mark, his head plowing into Alex's torso, just below the sternum. Perry continued to drive forward until his momentum carried both men into the back wall.

The impact jarred every inch of Perry. His teeth clashed together, and it felt as if every disk in his spine compressed. He had hit Alex with every bit of his strength.

"Carmack. . .Carmack. . .get up," Rutherford ordered. "You're ruining everything."

Perry staggered back, surprised to find himself still on his feet. Alex was doubled over, but Perry knew that in seconds the man would be angrier and more motivated than ever to take Perry apart.

"Get out!" Perry ordered Claire. "Take the stairs. Go." Claire grabbed Joseph by the arm and dragged him through the doorway.

He turned his attention back to Alex just in time to see him slowly straightening, his face covered with a demonic scowl. Perry clenched his jaw and kicked for all he was worth.

He had hoped to catch Alex in the gut again, preventing him from taking another breath and regaining his strength. With a speed Perry thought impossible, Alex caught Perry's foot by the ankle. In a fluid motion, Alex pulled up, and Perry was on his way down to the floor. It was the last place he wanted to be.

Another motion caught Perry's eye. Julia was backpedaling for all she was worth. Jack, his viselike grip still clamped on her wrist, was spinning her around toward Alex, using her as a human battering ram. It worked—her unbalanced frame impacted Alex with a discernable thump.

Alex released a chilling scream of rage and pushed Julia away with such force that it loosened Jack's footing. Still holding her wrist, he kept the gun pointed away from himself and Perry.

Another bang as the gun went off for a fourth time.

Perry scrambled to his feet readying himself for the next onslaught. Alex started forward and launched himself, hands outstretched, fingers reaching for Perry's throat.

A heartbeat later, Perry's feet were off the ground, his legs kicking wildly.

Perry couldn't breathe.

He gulped for air that wouldn't come.

He could feel Alex's thumbs pressing his trachea shut. Perry tried everything. He batted at Alex's arms, reached for his face, kicked at the man, but nothing prevailed. His abnormal strength was now fueled by uncontrolled fury.

The lights dimmed, or so Perry thought. His lungs burned, and his head felt as if it might explode. Then he dropped to the ground. Air. . .sweet air. . .rushed into his lungs.

Why had Alex released him?

Righting himself, Perry tried to steel himself for what would come next, comforting himself that Claire and Joseph were gone, on their way to the safety of the streets below.

Nothing happened.

Alex stood, his head lowered, his hands raised in front of him. Moist, dark red blood spread out in an ever-growing disk. He had been shot, and the amount of blood made Perry realize that the wound was serious. An artery or maybe the heart itself had been punctured.

Alex looked up at Perry, tilted his head to the side quizzically, dropped to his knees, then to his side. His eyes remained open but saw nothing.

"Rutherford! Rutherford!"

Perry turned to see Julia. She no longer fought with Jack. Her eyes were glued on some sight behind Perry. She went limp and the gun fell from her hand. Racing forward, Perry picked up the gun, took two steps back, turned, and saw what had subdued the woman.

Rutherford Straight sat in his chair, unmoving. His head no longer bobbed. A trickle of blood ran from a hole behind his left ear.

Julia collapsed in a heap. The shock of what had happened floored her. In the struggle, she had killed Alex with a wayward bullet.

And her own brother.

She had shot something else too. Perry now knew what the electronic horn was. It was the fire alarm, sounding because one of the undirected rounds had struck a fire sprinkler head in Carmack's lab.

Carmack was gone, and so was the chrysalis.

"Oh, no," Perry said.

He charged from the observation room, through the space

340

where the glass partition had been and into the cascading shower from the sprinkler head. Water flooded the room and immediately soaked Perry. He took no notice.

Rounding the work counter that dominated the room, Perry saw the nightmare he expected but prayed wouldn't be. Dr. Carmack lay on his back, staring at the ceiling through sightless eyes. Water rained down from above, washing the blood from the bullet hole in his forehead. On his chest lay a white mass of ancient, dissolving linen.

Perry didn't have to be a homicide detective to know what happened. Julia's gun had gone off several times. One bullet had broken the window. Another had struck Carmack in the head. It was a small caliber gun without enough power to knock the man from his feet, but with more than enough deadly force to end his life. He must have fallen forward, Perry reasoned, landing on the chrysalis and dragging it to the floor with him.

Over the last two days, Perry had been beaten, kicked, hit on the head with a stone from the falling wall, and been in battle with a man more powerful than God ever intended a man to be, but all he could feel was the deep ache of sorrow in his soul.

The chrysalis was gone, reduced to a useless, meaningless paste, dissolved by the unrelenting spray. The world's most valuable treasure was being washed down the drain of the floor, its two-thousand-year-old fiber unable to withstand the onslaught of the moisture from a sprinkler.

"You okay, buddy?" Perry looked up to see a battered Jack.

"The woman?"

"After you picked up the gun, I lost my grip. She ran, and I'm afraid I don't have it in me to chase her."

"It doesn't matter."

"I'm sure the alarm is electronically monitored," Jack said. "The fire department will be here soon."

"What happened here?" a voice said. Perry turned to the laboratory door and saw two uniformed men: building security.

A TREASURE DEEP

"You had better call the police," Perry said softly. Then he set the gun on the counter, lowered himself to the floor, raised his hands to his face, bent over, and wept.

EPILOGUE

Perry Sachs stood in the inner chamber of the room he and Jack had uncovered two weeks before.

A bank of work lights shone down from metal stands and lit the underground area. Crowded into the space with him were Jack, Anne, Gleason, Brent, Dr. Curtis, Sergeant Montulli, Claire, and Joseph. Also present were the owners, Hector Trujillo—in a wheelchair—and his wife, Rose. Joseph stood, as he always did, with his head resting on Claire's shoulder.

The crowded chamber was still off-limits to the rest of the world, but it had been made safer. Modern shoring kept the ground outside from crashing in; a new semi-permanent bridge had been built to replace the makeshift one they'd made before.

"Thank you all for coming," Perry said. "I wanted to thank you each for your great contribution. I also wanted to make sure everyone had the latest word on things. Dr. Curtis has some information for us."

Curtis cleared his throat. "As we guessed, the archeological community is still very skeptical about our preliminary findings. It's only been two weeks, but we have received Carbon-14 data that puts the uncovered remains to the first century. Specialists in Roman history have verified that the shields, swords, and other items we found associated with the soldiers are genuine. There remains a great deal of testing to be done, but for now we can rule out a hoax. Of course we already knew that."

"Will the scientific community ever come around?" Jack asked.

Curtis shrugged. "Some will. The evidence is strong, but we must remember we're asking them to believe the impossible. Having Romans in the New World upsets everything. However, there is enough evidence to suggest that other ancient people made it to our shores. The Vikings on the east and oriental influence in the west indicate that others had crossed the oceans; whether they came intentionally or not is another matter. Things like the Los

Lunas inscription in New Mexico may or may not be hoaxes."

"Los Lunas?" Anne said.

"The Ten Commandments written in ancient Hebrew," Curtis explained. "Found a few decades ago in New Mexico."

"Ancient Hebrew in North America," Gleason said. "Is it real?"

"That's debatable on several counts. We simply don't know. It used to be easy for me to dismiss such things. For example, a sculpted terracotta Roman head was found in Mexico. Some date it to about 200 A.D. In 1963 a construction worker found a small hoard of Roman coins near the Ohio River. A similar thing happened in Kentucky. Did the coins come from Romans, or were they part of someone's collection that was lost decades before? Who knows? But we have much more here."

"But how did they get here?" Montulli asked. "We're a long way from the Roman Empire."

"That leads us to the second manuscript," Perry said. "After we sorted things out with the Seattle police—a grueling task, I might add, but with Sergeant Montulli's help as well as the distinguished mayor's, we recovered those items that didn't interest Rutherford Straight. We were able to take custody of Pilate's seal and the two earthenware jars. The face napkin remains missing. The police continue to look for it. Dr. Curtis opened the jars."

"Under controlled conditions, I might add," Curtis said. "One jar held the residue of spices. It appears that when these people took the artifacts from Christ's tomb after His resurrection, they took everything, including the spices used to treat Jesus' body. The other jar contained a manuscript."

"The manuscript was in the jar?" Claire asked.

"That's right," Curtis replied. "Just like the Dead Sea Scrolls that were found in 1947. The jar provided a great deal of protection. Still, the document is delicate and takes expert care just to open it. Move too fast or in the wrong environment, and it will crumble to dust. I've brought in the best manuscript experts I can find. We've succeeded in opening it. Age has damaged it greatly, but I was able to get snippets of information. It was written in Aramaic, the language of first-century Jews. We think Mary wrote it. It's a brief account of some of her experiences."

Curtis took a deep breath and stated: "The short version is this. As you know, Roman guards were posted at the grave of Christ. The Gospel of Matthew tells the story in chapter 28. It says that some of the guards returned to the city to report what they had seen and what they had seen had frightened them to the point of unconsciousness. 'They became as dead men' is the way the Scripture puts it. I've always wondered why the Bible says that some of the guards returned to the city and reported to the Jewish elders. Why just some? Why not all? What happened to those who didn't go back to report?"

"I always assumed that, of the twelve or so guards who would have been present, only a couple would be needed to make a report," Perry said.

"That's a reasonable interpretation," Curtis said. "But the manuscript tells a different story. After the 'some' went back to report, Mary—who came to the tomb twice—saw the risen Christ. It appears that the remaining guards witnessed that encounter. You can imagine the shock to the Roman mind. After Mary encountered Jesus, she ran to tell the disciples what had happened. We find that information in the Gospel of John.

"The manuscript is unclear at this point, mostly because of damage," Curtis continued, "but a few of the guards took it upon themselves to clear out the tomb. You have to remember that you're not dealing with religious Jews or disciples of Jesus. Instead we have men brought up in a polytheistic world. Their religious training taught them that there were many gods. I imagine they believed that Jesus was one such god. Therefore, anything associated with Him would be valuable, even holy."

"So they took the linens and other things, but how did they get here and how did Mary hook up with them?"

"That's one of the many parts that is unclear," Curtis said. "It appears they had some reason to fear reprisal from their superiors, maybe for failing to guard the tomb or maybe because they removed the artifacts.

"In any case, they fled Palestine on a Roman cargo ship. Romans had a variety of ships that plied the waters of the Great Sea, what we call the Mediterranean Sea. The manuscript has sections of text that have faded over the years, so we're left to guess about many things. The manuscript experts think that with time they can restore portions of the lost text. Maybe we'll have more information then. We can hope.

"Anyway, I sent photos of the scroll to experts in ancient Semitic languages. They've found references to the boat and to the crewmen, who numbered twenty. How the guards booked passage is unknown, but since we found them buried in their armor they may have used their military influence to get on board. Maybe one of them was related to the captain. We just don't know. The linguist found references to what we now call China. There's ample evidence to say that the Roman Empire had some trade connection with China."

"That would explain how they got to the Pacific," Perry said, "but sailing around Africa had to be tough."

"Agreed," Curtis said. "It's not a trip that any one of us would want to make. From there they continued east. There's a passage that mentions a storm. It wouldn't be the first time that a cargo ship was blown out to sea. Currents and wind drove the boat east. As I said, there's evidence that Chinese explorers made the west coast of America; these men, soldiers and the boat's crew, apparently did the same, unintentionally."

"And Mary Magdalene was with them," Anne said.

"Probably," Curtis said. "That has yet to be demonstrated. All we have is a woman's skeleton in what remains of simple clothing and the etched letters inside her coffin."

"That seems pretty conclusive, Doc," Jack interjected.

"Agreed, but that's not proof, at least not in scientific terms."

"Why this?" Gleason asked, motioning to the chamber.

Perry spoke first. "It's their way of paying homage. They built two chambers: an anteroom and a sepulcher. Some ancient Jewish tombs have been found that are similar in design. Here they used rocks they could find and timber from the surrounding trees to, at least in a symbolic way, return what they took. Mary must have had a powerful influence on them."

"Let me add to that," Curtis said. "I've had the wood coffins analyzed and learned that they were made of the same kind of wood as ancient ships. They brought some of the wood from their vessel with them. That would explain how they came to have flat wood like planks. I imagine that their tools were limited to whatever was on the ship."

"Now there's another puzzle," Gleason said. "Why here in these low-lying mountains? We're more than seventy miles from the coast as the crow flies."

"More like eighty miles," Curtis said. "And you're right. A journey on foot would be much longer, still not beyond reason. Migratory people have been known to travel much further. Time wouldn't be a factor. If it took them a year to make the journey, so what? Maybe the area reminded them of home.

"I suspect as we continue to excavate the surrounding area that we'll find other signs of habitation and other graves. Five soldiers and a woman didn't sail here by themselves. And whoever buried them did so with respect and honor. The soldiers were buried in military gear. Whoever they were, they still felt a sense of pride in who they had been. Somewhere between here and wherever they stepped ashore is evidence of their existence. I'm ready to devote my life to finding it."

"There are a lot of unanswered questions, Doc," Jack complained.

"There always are," Curtis said. "And for every question you can raise, I can raise five more. I don't have all the answers."

"The real shame is that the linen chrysalis was lost," Anne said softly. "What a loss for all mankind."

"That was my first thought," Perry said. "I'm not so sure now. I was devastated as I watched it dissolve right in front of me. It was the greatest treasure ever found, and I let it slip through my fingers. I felt that I let slip the greatest proof of Christianity the world would ever know."

"But you think differently now?" Anne asked.

"Yes. I've had time to think and pray about it. Most people read their Bibles without knowing that we do not have a single original manuscript," Perry explained. "That's not to say the Bible is a fabrication or filled with errors. It's not. There are thousands of ancient manuscripts, many of them extremely old. Is that right, Doc?"

Curtis replied, "It is."

"I think there's a reason for that. I don't think God wants us to have objects that can be turned into idols. Humankind has a tendency to worship things instead of God. In Numbers 21 is the story of the brass serpent. Moses was leading the children of Israel through a difficult area. They became bitter and accused God of mistreating them. Judgment came in the form of snakes. People were bitten and died. They pleaded for relief and God gave it, but not as you would expect."

"He told Moses to make a brass serpent," Jack said. "If people looked at it after being bitten, they would be healed."

"Exactly," Perry said. "It seems an odd solution. Why not just send the snakes away? Well, it has to do with faith and trust and looking to God's provision. Fourteen hundred years later, Jesus would use it as an example of His work on the cross. However, it was what happened in between those events that's provocative.

"The Bible records that seven hundred years after Moses made the serpent, King Hezekiah had it destroyed. Why would he destroy such an important object? Because his people had made an icon of worship out of it. They were burning incense to it as they did to other false gods."

"So you're saying that if the chrysalis had remained intact, then it would've become a cultic icon?" Gleason asked.

"Well, that's what I think." Perry said. "God may have done us a favor."

"Do you think people will ever come to believe all of this?" Brent asked. "After all, we do have the videotapes I made."

Perry smiled. "Those who are willing to believe will; those who don't want to believe won't. There has always been plenty of evidence for Christ and His work; still people ignore it."

"I can't speak for the world," Brent said, "but it has changed me."

"That goes for all of us," Anne said. "But I do have another question, Perry. From what you told me, Joseph predicted the woman who came to his house and abducted him and Claire, and that he knew you would be outside the door where Rutherford Straight was holding them hostage. How did he know what was going to happen before it did?"

Perry looked at Joseph and smiled. Joseph didn't respond. "I don't know, Anne. I don't know how he knew those things or could so accurately reproduce the work site and the other things he drew. His mind works in a way we can't understand. Perhaps he sees more than we can. Perhaps like Daniel and other Old Testament prophets, he communicates with God better than we are able."

"He's never done it before," Claire added. "And now he seems back to normal. The pictures he draws are like those he did before all this happened."

"It's a mystery," Jack said. "But I'm glad he was on our side."

"Ironic, isn't it?" Perry mused. "By the world's standards, Joseph is severely handicapped. The truth is, we may be the handicapped ones. Since I first met him, I've wondered what he sees that we can't."

"We will never know," Claire said.

"Not in this life," Perry added.

"So the work goes on?" Brent asked.

Perry nodded. "Dr. Curtis will be leading the excavation here. He tells me there will be years of work. The Trujillos' have generously donated this whole area for as long as it takes."

"You have taken good care of us," Hector said from his wheelchair. "We are happy to help our Lord."

Perry laid a hand on the ill man's shoulder. "One thing remains. I can think of no better church in which to pray."

There was a corporate "Amen."

After Perry led them in prayer, a second, belated "Amen" rang out across the room. Everyone turned to the one who said it.

"Amen," Joseph Henri repeated. "Amen."

AUTHOR'S NOTE

A novel, by definition, is a work of fiction. The characters spring into being from the author's mind and come alive on the page, fleshed out in words and phrases instead of skin and bones. Those characters work before an equally fictional backdrop. To undertake the writing of a novel is to undertake a juggling act, for novels are seldom completely fictional. Elements of truth are introduced to "what-if" questions. The author then follows that "what-if" to see where it goes. Sometimes it leads to strange and wonderful places.

In this book I have created a situation meant to stretch our wonder. The town of Tejon is fictional, but the beautiful Tehachapi Mountains are real. Each character presented here is a work of my imagination. Many of the things mentioned in the book regarding seagoing people making transatlantic or transpacific crossings are based on evidence that is still debated by those who study such things. It's not the intent of this book to say that Romans visited the North American continent two thousand years ago. It's the purpose of the book to ask, "Well, what if they had? And what if they brought something truly special with them?"

Some of you may wonder why this book seems to ignore the presence of other artifacts popularly associated with the burial of Christ, like the Shroud of Turin or the Veil of Veronica. Truth is, I purposely avoided including these artifacts here because their authenticity is still hotly debated and their inclusion would detract from the flow and message of Perry's story.

Still, one set of facts is certain. The greatest chain of events in history is that linking of the death, burial, resurrection, and ascension of Christ. Of this there should be no doubt. Perry Sachs is right in reminding us that what really matters is the spiritual. Biblical artifacts are fascinating and instructive, but supremacy belongs to the one to whom those artifacts point. Jesus was hung upon a cross constructed for Barabbas.

It was not the cross that was special, but He who hung on it.

The burial linens, face napkin, spices, and other items associated with the burial of Christ would, if found, surely be the most valuable objects known. Yet, they are merely accoutrements to that which is really important: the person and work of Christ.

To Him belongs the glory forever and ever. And in any world, real or fictional, He remains the focal point.

For more information about Alton Gansky or to contact the author, visit the web site at: www.altongansky.com

Would you like to offer feedback on this novel?

Interested in starting a book discussion group?

Check out www.promisepress.com for
a *Reader Survey* and *Book Club Questions.*